FOOZLER RUNS

STEPHEN POLESKIE

ONAGER EDITIONS
Ithaca, New York

Onager Editions
PO Box 849
Ithaca, New York 14851-0849

Foozler Runs
by Stephen Poleskie

Copyright © 2013 Stephen Poleskie
ALL RIGHTS RESERVED

First Printing – December 2013
ISBN: 978-1-60047-929-8
Library of Congress Control Number: 2013921308

This book is a work of fiction. Any references to historical events, or to real people or real locales, names, characters, descriptions, places, and incidents are either the product if the author's imagination or are used fictitiously. Any resemblance to actual events or locales or persons, living or dead, is unintended and entirely coincidental.

No part of this book may be reproduced in any form, by photocopying or any electronic or mechanical means, including information storage or retrieval systems, without permission in writing from the copyright owner, except in the case of brief quotations embodied in critical articles and reviews.

Cover photo copyright © 2013 by Stephen Poleskie
Printed and bound in the United States of America
First Edition

1 2 3 4 5 6

Other books by Stephen Poleskie

<u>Novels</u>

The Balloonist: The Story of T. S. C. Lowe (2007)

The Third Candidate (2008)

Vigilia's Tempest (2009)

Grater Life (2010)

Acorn's Card (2011)

Sconto Walaa (2012)

<u>Poetry</u>

Blue Sky (1989)

For my wife, Jeanne Mackin

Acknowledgments

I WOULD LIKE TO THANK the following people, writers and friends, who have read and encouraged my work in many different ways over the past years: Diane Ackerman, Barbara Adams, Cher Bibler, David Borden, Marvin and Pat Carlson, Magda and Larry Day, Patrice and Steven Demory, Antonio Di Renzo, Michael Foldes, Rebecca Godin, Jack Goldman, Sidney Grayling, Rhea Gulin, John Guzlowski, Glynis Hart, Lamar and Amparo Herrin, Nancy Holzner, Tim Keane, Nino Lama, Alison Lurie, Lise Lemeland, James McConkey, Pearson Oldmitz, Tish Pearlman, James Michael Robbins, Thaddeus Rutkowski, Nick Sagan, Wylie Schwartz, Sasha Thurmond, Paul West, and Janusz Zalewski

SP

One can live for years sometimes without living at all, and then life comes crowding in to one single hour.

Oscar Wilde

FOOZLER RUNS

ONE

THREE ANXIOUS WEEKS have passed since Johnny Foozler's return to Eastlake. During this time he has been working hard at running the golf driving range left to him by his late father, while still attending to his elderly mother, and seeing to the mundane details associated with settling, with his wife and grown son, back into a town he once thought he had left forever. It is that sleepy time of summer when the sun hangs high in the sky for hours, and when it does hide itself at night it is only for a brief sultry, humid period, not long enough to cool the land it has heated all day. Out over the lake, the airless sky and the dry parched horizon seem to have melded into a hazy grayness. Shimmering heat rises off the highway out front, and off the tin roof of the driving range's one building, a small wooden shack that has only a single un-glazed window.

In the dim interior Johnny sits surrounded by dozens of empty wire baskets, neatly stacked according to their three sizes. He is using a metal scoop to fill the buckets with golf balls from a large metal barrel. These balls are lined with red bands which mark their inferior status in the golf ball hierarchy; they will eternally be range balls. A large sign on the side of the shack reads: TAKING RANGE BALLS FROM THE RANGE TO PLAY IS ILLEGAL. This dispels the notion that any range ball may have of ever rising above its station and sometime getting to frolic around on a real golf course.

Outside in the blazing sun the temperature is at least 100 degrees. Nevertheless, the line of wannabe golfers is still diligently hitting balls. Dump trucks rumble by shaking the ground. The town of Old Estlake, spelled without an "a" and three miles north of Eastlake, is doing some work on a bridge farther up the road. The trucks shift gears for the little grade just by Johnny's shack, spewing black exhaust smoke all over the hackers, who do not desist in the punishment of themselves and their little round white and red missiles.

Foozler checks his supply of range balls, all lined up on the counter in their wire buckets, vibrating together from the passing trucks. The construction has been going on all summer. Johnny had thought it would slow down his business, but it has not, in fact things have picked up. Route 39 used to be a quiet road when he lived here years ago. No one ever came to Old Estlake. But now there is a new airport, and a prison, all out this way, so everyone uses the road.

The range ball buckets come in three, five, and seven dollar sizes. The jumbo is for those who can't get enough. Some people come here and hit two, or sometimes three, jumbo buckets a day—every day of the week.

"Ya know Parc Park, the Korean guy who owns a Chinese restaurant here in town," Johnny says to one of the hangers-on, beginning a story he has told many times before. "I asked him how come a Korean guy doesn't have a Korean restaurant. Park says: 'Nobody in this town knows what Korean food is. Now Chinese food, everyone knows what that is; it comes in those little cardboard boxes.'"

Johnny laughs, then continues, "Any way . . . Park comes in every morning, like clockwork first thing, and hits three jumbo buckets. Then he comes back in the afternoon and hits three more. So one day I ask him what he does in between. He tells me his restaurant doesn't open until five, so he plays golf all day. I ask him what he normally shoots and he tells me 96."

Johnny smacks himself on the side of his head in disbelief.

"Would you believe that the first time I ever played golf on a real course I shot a 96, and I was only six years old, with cut-down clubs, and after only three lessons?

"My father, who was the pro at the country club at the time, was so excited over my 96 he kept bragging to everyone about it. Normally he wasn't a very happy guy, but this was the happiest I had ever seen him be. He kept saying I was a 'natural' golfer and that I was going to follow in his footsteps and become a pro.

"He was more than a little disappointed when I dropped out of high school to play in a rock band. But heck, I made a good living at it . . . for a while anyway. I'd say I went further in the pop music business than he ever went in the golf business. Although I guess you'd say that with me back here running the range now it means that we have both ended up about the same."

"Oh, I wouldn't say that," the hanger-on adds trying to put a bright face on things, hoping Johnny will hand him a free bucket.

"See that young guy down there, the third from the end," Johnny says, changing the subject. "He thinks he's a real bad-ass, going to try out for the PGA tour or something. He hits nine jumbos a day, only stopping for a drink of water after every third bucket. Now that's 900 balls. Well, more like 850." Johnny backs off. "The sign says the big buckets hold 100, ya know, but I short them a little, especially on busy days like today."

"Like, who's going to count a hundred golf balls?" hanger-on ventures.

"No? You won't believe this. Had an old guy come in here once, a wrinkled, liver-spotted raisin, wearing a shoestring tie with a silver golf ball in the center. He actually counted his balls. Now all the old guys in Florida and Arizona wear ties like that, but up here in the Northeast, I mean, where the hell can you even find one to buy? Anyway, the old fart took a jumbo bucket, hit those, took him a long time, and then came back and demanded four more balls. Said he had counted them as he hit them and there were only 96 in the bucket. Cripes! Can you imagine the old guy actually counting every ball as he hit it?

"I told him: 'Look buddy, I was watching you . . . you kept sitting down for a rest. You probably lost count or something.' I didn't want to tell him I thought he was so damn old that his mind was probably gone long ago. 'Besides,' I told him, 'I saw you go out past the rope to get two balls that you topped. Can't you read the sign? It clearly says: NO PLAYERS PAST THE ROPE. It's required by my liability insurance, ya know. Now suppose you got hit by a ball when you went out there . . . in the eye, or something worse. No doubt you would hire a shyster lawyer and sue my ass off.'

"Not intimidated by my harangue, the old man kept insisting I owed him four more balls. He grabbed one of the jumbos off the counter and started counting them into an empty basket. One, plunk, two, plunk, three, plunk. . . .

"Okay! Okay! I screamed. I didn't want to have a brawl with the geezer. Taking a full jumbo from the counter I shoved it in his face saying: 'Look, you say I owe you four more balls, well here's a fucking hundred, or 96, or whatever . . . anyway there are certainly more than four. So go hit 'em, they're free . . . on me! Now get off my back.' He asked could he come back tomorrow and hit them. 'No!' I shouted at him, 'you can't come back tomorrow . . . hit 'em now or forget about it. That's the deal, period.'

"I guess I musta frightened the old guy. He took his bucket to the line and began hitting his driver. People who don't know how to play always hit their driver; it's as if the game is to see who can hit it the ball the farthest. I've see guys hit their driver about 125 yards, which as you know is not very far, and look over at the guy next to him who has just hit a sand wedge maybe 100 yards, which is about right, with that 'boy did I hit it past you' look. But that's the way the world is today, everyone's too competitive about things they know nothing about. . . .

"Now the old guy started pounding the balls I had given him more like a penance than a reward. Sweat was draining down the back of his pink golf shirt and collecting in the butt of his green plaid polyester pants. The old fart kept looking over his shoulder to see if I was watching, like maybe he was going to try to sell some of his balls to the guy next to him. Well I made sure he hit everyone of those damn balls, ya know.

"When he was done he didn't even bother to wash his clubs off in the water bucket. He just threw then in the trunk of his big old Cadillac, then got in front, started the engine and turned on the air conditioner. He sat there for about half an hour or more, apparently trying to get up the energy to drive home.

"He worried me though, just sitting there with the motor running, his eyes dilated, while sweat poured down his brown-spotted face. I though maybe he was dead, had had a heart attack or something. But then he finally put the car in gear and drove away. I haven't seen him since then; he used to come in quite regularly."

"I think I know who you mean," injects the hanger-on, a dismal fellow who Johnny sometimes employed washing balls, and who has been know to sit outside the shack for most of a day watching nothing happen.

"Well I gotta get the tractor and sweep up balls," Johnny says adding, "before someone I'm waiting for comes. I'm kinda' running short, or will be by this afternoon at the rate they're hitting 'em. Jeez, it sure is hot. . . ."

At least it will be a little cooler on the tractor, Johnny thinks to himself, if I go fast. You gotta' go fast, I mean I got a cage over the top to protect me, but the sides are open so I can get in. The damn assholes all think it's a shooting gallery, and I'm the target. I should hang a sign on the side: HIT ME AND GET A FREE BUCKET OF BALLS, then no one would ever hit me.

Johnny has a five gallon pail as a target out by the 100 yard sign, and has seen guys spend fifteen, maybe twenty bucks trying to get a ball in that pail to win a free three dollar bucket. Maybe once a month someone will win one.

One might think from his attitude that Johnny Foozler has a very deep and weary disdain for all mankind, especially those unfortunates who have to work for a living, but who would rather play golf and aren't very good at it. Yes, John has an aversion to effort, especially productive labor, and was very good at golf once, which he didn't want to play. Everything in his present seems frivolous and trivial to him when viewed from his past, which had come closer to his original dreams. Apparently all Johnny is doing now is waiting impatiently for what he does not know, parading his future that goes forward though he doesn't go anywhere, and his time that advances even though he stays put. Nevertheless, one must not think Johnny is bitter. The only thing that alleviates his present monotony is his love for everyone—especially attractive older women.

TWO

OUTSIDE IT IS as hot as the equator, one of those dog days of summer that go growling and snapping across the landscape, leaving everything covered with a thin layer of dust. Inside Johnny's golf shack it is even hotter, and dustier. There is no air. Foozler has got the place closed up, the plywood window pulled down, shut tight. The shelf out front is lined with buckets of balls, and the: PUT MONEY HERE, sign hung up over the slot. The shack has no electricity, so Johnny doesn't even have a fan. In the darkness we can barely make out two naked forms rolling around on the raw wood floor in the not very much room between the rental clubs and the ball washer.

"Don't make so much noise," Johnny whispers. He reasons that if he can hear his customers hitting balls out there, he's sure they can hear him and his lady friend balling in here—ever though the constant parade of trucks on the highway is creating quite a rack, shaking the building. The sweat is pouring off both their bodies, and they are just getting started.

The woman is the Joanie that Johnny has known all his life, or at least since he was six, when his parents moved back in with his grandparents here in Eastlake so they could stop having to travel around. Johnny's grandfather, a doctor, was on the board of the country club where his father had just gotten a job as the head professional. Johnny's father had been an assistant pro at a good number of places all over the country, but had not lasted too long anywhere. The rumor going around Eastlake was that John Foozler II had lost his various golfing jobs because he drank too much, and fooled around with the clubs married women.

Joanie was the first girl Johnny had actually done it with, well sort of. Years later the drummer for The Artful Foozler would be quoted in *Rolling Stone* magazine as saying, "After a while sex all gets kinda blurred." But being the first Joanie was very special, something he remembered.

They had done it in the bushes, behind the cabana next to the pool, during one of the county club dances. Well, they didn't actually do it. Joanie had let Johnny stick it in, but he didn't have a condom, so pulled it right out, and came all over himself. He supposed that this brief sally had counted as the *first* time.

* * *

The band was playing waltzes so the old folks could dance. Although they weren't too fond of slow tunes, Johnny and Joanie had been dancing together all night. Then Jack, the bandleader, who knew Johnny was pretty good on the drums, asked him if he wanted to sit in for a set. Now the band, Jack and the Beanstalks, didn't exactly play up to what Foozler considered as being his level, so he decided to show their drummer a thing or two. Johnny was really pounding those skins, with everybody getting into it, when a classmate, Randall Benson, who Johnny had thought was gay, came over and asked Joanie to dance.

There was Johnny, the winner of the tournament and the hottest junior golfer in the whole state, banging out his drum solo, showing the crowd the other side of his talents, having his big moment, the biggest moment of his life up until then, and probably since, and Randall Benson gets up and starts dancing with his girl. Well Joanie wasn't really his *girlfriend.* Johnny hadn't given her his letter sweater or anything like that, but it was sort of public knowledge that they were going out together.

When the set ended, Johnny put down the drumsticks, and everyone applauded. But all Foozler could see was Randall hustling Joanie off to get a soda. He took his bows, then started walking over to where Joanie had sat down with Benson, planning to give her a piece of his mind, when Johnny's father spotted him.

Now the elder Foozler, rather a Philistine who had never had any musical aspirations himself, was not too pleased about his son's fondness for music. In Johnny's younger days, when the family had rambled from one golf tournament to another in a beat up convertible, they hadn't even owned a radio.

Backed into a corner, Johnny listened while his father told him: "Your drum playing is an embarrassment . . . a waste of your talents. You should spend more time working on your golf game, and eventually try out for the PGA tour, like I did. You shouldn't have played the drums tonight because it gives folks the wrong impression . . . that you're not serious about your golf game. There are a lot of important people here who can help you get a head start as a pro."

Discarding any respect he may still have harbored for his father, Johnny sassed back: "I'd rather be playing the drums and dancing than schmoozing with some old farts just because they happen to be big shots in the golf scene."

Over his shoulder Johnny could see Joanie and Randall sitting head to head under the flickering globe, sipping soda out of the same glass with two straws. They were staring into each others eyes, which made Johnny angry. This party was supposed to be for him, and now it was ruined. His girl was gone and his father was here ragging on him about the same old crap. Johnny just let go:

"Look," he yelled at his father. "Like I don't want to be a washed up golf bum like you when I get old! You wasted the first six years of my life dragging me and Mom all over the country to tournaments where you never even made the cut, sleeping in dumpy motels and eating in greasy-spoon restaurants. In between seasons you worked as an assistant pro, which meant all you did was wash the members clubs, while Mom had to work in Wal-Mart and places like that. I don't want to end up like you. A golf pro? Like, you're nothing but a boozer who kisses the member's asses . . . and fucks their wives behind their backs. No thanks, Dad, I have better plans for my life. . . ."

Johnny's father didn't say anything. He just looked around to see who had overheard their exchange. But when he turned back there were tears in his eyes. He brushed past his son and headed for the front door.

Not the least bit concerned about his dad, in fact feeling rather freed, Johnny rushed over to Joanie and grabbed her by the hand.

"We have got to talk," he said, pulling her out the side door, in the direction of the cabana. "I love you."

Randall just sat there too stunned, or maybe too much of a wimp, to do anything. It was a good thing too, because Johnny had talked the bartender into slipping a little whiskey into his sodas—after all it was his party wasn't it, the moment that was supposed to mark the beginning of his adult life. If Randall had tried anything Johnny was ready to give him a punch in the mouth.

That was when they went in the bushes behind the cabana and they did it for the first time. Joanie's father was the president of the country club, so Foozler figured Joanie's gift of herself must have been his reward for winning at golf, but losing her to Randall Benson. Johnny had been somewhat taken aback by the fact that Joanie seemed to know a bit more about the activity he thought that he was supposedly initiating her into than he did.

* * *

Joanie's husband Randall is a lawyer in Eastlake now, and they have two children, both teenagers. She still has The Artful Foozler's first two record albums, which she listens to from time to time. The group made a third album, but Joanie never even heard of it. Apparently not many other people did either, which was one of the reasons why Johnny was back here running the driving range after his father died, which was how they got together again after all these years.

Joanie was delighted when she heard Johnny had moved back to town. Randall had been nagging her to improve her golf game. They were moving up in the social order, playing with better people, even going to Florida for two weeks every winter to play. Her husband was happy she was taking a greater interest in his favorite game—or so it appeared from all the time she was putting in at the driving range.

Thinking about the old days has taken Johnny's mind off what he and Joanie are going at here on the floor, so it is taking him a while longer to come, which has got Joanie going really wild, besides which Johnny has a whole bag of tricks that he picked up from groupies while touring with "The Foozlers" as the band was fondly called. Joanie has just reached her third climax, three more than she has had with Randall in the past three years, and is holding on for more.

Foozler Runs

    Finally exhausted they roll off one another. Joanie makes a low moaning sound, the purring of a cat that is not used to being petted.
    "Was it good for you?" she says.
    "Yes. Was it good for you?" he says.
    "It's always good for me with you. . . ." she says.
    "It's always good for me with you too. . . ." he says.
    "I'm glad it was good for you. . . ." she says.
    "I'm glad that you're glad it was good for me. . . ." he says.
    There is a shuffling sound overhead, and seven one dollar bills come fluttering down on their nakedness from the PUT MONEY HERE slot. Someone must have taken a jumbo bucket.
    Alone now, John presses his eye to the money slot and watches as Joanie drives away. He sits back down on his folding chair in the darkened shack and stares at the wall. Solitude devastates Foozler, yet the presence of other people always oppresses him. He finds that they derail his thoughts. To understand himself, Johnny feels the need to lose himself, and he knows of no better way to forget than making love without loving. Richer by one more disappointment, Johnny throws open the plywood window; he is ready for business again. A wren streaks from its nest under the eve. Despite the blazing sun, the outside air seems cool after the heat inside.

THREE

LIKE A GENERAL inspecting his column of troops, Johnny counts the buckets of balls lining the shelf. Three are gone; the jumbo he got paid for and two mediums. Someone hasn't paid. He is about to accost the new players when he spies two fives under a rock next to the window. He wonders if perhaps whoever put the money there didn't see his sign; or perhaps they couldn't read; or perhaps they were discreet and didn't want to disturb him, and whoever else it was making noises inside the shack.

Foozler walks up and down the line, picking up empty buckets, commenting disdainfully to himself about his customers habits: Goddamn too lazy to bring the fuckin' baskets back. Figure they paid five bucks to hit the damn balls so I should pick up after them.

He is even more disdainful of how his clients are hitting. His eyes study the row of wanna-be-better golfers swinging their clubs, evaluating their performance, each in their way dealing with their own private failings.

Goddamn hackers . . . what pleasure could they be getting standing out there in the boiling sun? Johnny thinks to himself. Those two ladies should be home baking pies, or maybe sitting by their swimming pool. Joe College in the middle there thinks he shits ice cream. I can tell by the way he swings that he can't even break 100. His damn clubs probably cost him more than my car is worth. Now that old guy on the end, he's not too bad though. He has a kind of homemade swing—must have started playing later in life and never took a lesson.

Foozler goes back in the shed and returns to filling buckets. His golf bag leans in the corner, tattered, worn. Joanie's damp, red bikini panties hang off his driver like a victory flag. She ran out of there so fast to pick up one of her kids from soccer practice that she probably doesn't even know that she's not wearing them. Rolling the scanties into a ball Johnny pitches them into a box beneath the counter, almost out of sight. He ponders his wife sitting alone at home waiting for him, and of his latest encounter with Joanie. Despite the assurances they had given each other he finds the affair basically empty. Johnny is a man who never accepts anything until he is sure it is what he really wants—the trouble is he has never found anything he really wants.

The golf clubs in the corner, which he still uses, are the same ones his father gave him for his birthday when he was a sophomore in high school. He doesn't use them on a golf course though, as he hasn't played fairway golf in over twenty years. The clubs are "blades" a type of club no one plays with anymore, most golfers having gone for the new technology using "perimeter weighted" and "oversized" clubs. Johnny's clubs are the same ones he used when he shot one under par at the Eastlake Country Club to win the State Junior Championship. That was the summer before his senior year in high school.

His brain a muddle, Johnny tries to remember that final round. All he can recall is that he started the day two shots off the lead. His father had given him a big pep talk about what a great honor it was to have the state championship played at the local country club, and how he had the home advantage and couldn't let the club down. He searches his mind, but cannot recreate the round at all. He must have played well, he thinks, to have shot one under and win by one—or the other players played poorly. His most vivid memory of the day was the softness of Joanie's pink silk underpanties as he pulled them over her knees, and the pungent smell of a place where he had never put his tongue before.

He had gone away the next day, packed his bags and left, while his mother was out shopping and his father was at the country club. He even stole the money he knew his mother kept hidden behind the washer for emergencies, and so that his father wouldn't spend it on booze. He had decided to go to New York City and become a drummer in a rock band. He felt that he was no longer the product of his parents, but would become what he himself had decided to become.

Johnny slides his 8-iron from the mildewed golf bag. This is his favorite club. He could do everything with his eight, approach shots, pitches chips, even using it to putt sometimes. He calls it his "infinity club" the figure eight lying sideways. When he was on the high school team he often played a whole practice round using just this club, and still shot in the low eighties, often beating some of his teammates who were using a full set of clubs.

Taking the eight and six balls from the barrel, Johnny walks out to the line. The sun continues to beat down, yet the line is still crowded with golfers stroking balls. All day long they go at it. Pop, pop, pop. Will they ever stop? Johnny thinks. The more they practice their bad swings the worse they get—if they only had taken a lesson or two sometime in their past.

Johnny, to the unknowing a newcomer, arrives on the line. The hackers will all try to hit a perfect shot now, sure the new arrival is checking them out, trying to establish his place in the pecking order. The line is almost full. Taking a place in the middle Foozler drops his six balls to the ground. They roll toward "Joe College" who looks over his shoulder like don't crowd me. Johnny gives him a look back that says: This is my damn range, and I'll hit fucking balls wherever I like. I could close down and tell you all to go the hell home if I felt like. Then what would you do? Have withdrawals? Go to that other place? You don't even have hit off grass there, just mats. Only I have grass—grass that my father planted. Go away. See if I give a shit. Screw yourself. Real players don't hit off goddamn artificial-turf mats.

The sky to the west has turned from a bright blue to an evil-looking black, contrasting vividly with the white wings of the gulls that circle restlessly overhead, fleeing the constant volley of small, round projectiles hurtling down on what, until the range opens at ten o'clock, has been their space. On closer observation, the huge, dark mass that threatens rain appears as if it is moving south, its brisk winds flittering golden waves through the surrounding hay fields the driving range has been carved from. The storm will probably pass by. The range could use the watering, and Johnny would be more than happy to close up and go home, well maybe not home, but at least someplace else.

Though Foozler doesn't play fairway golf anymore, he does come out to hit balls now and then, after all they're free. So what's he doing out here in this heat. He would rather be back in his shack reading a book, only he hasn't found a book he has wanted to read in a long time. "Too much trash getting published nowadays," he complains to whoever will listen, "everyone's writing books about vampires and zombies that they hope will be made into blockbuster movies."

Johnny's favorite writer is Gabriele D'Annunzio, a writer, he has come to realize, that most people think is just a fictional character from a movie. If D'Annunzio is known for anything at all outside of Italy, it is for what he did rather than what he wrote. The worst fate that can befall a writer is that they become a gossip-star, a favorite of the fashion magazines. D'Annunzio is the political adventurer, the scandalous lover, the friend of Mussolini—forgotten is the fact that such writers as Joyce and Malraux considered him one of the great creative figures of the twentieth century. Johnny has only one of D'Annunzio's books, a battered copy of "The Flame of Life" that he got in a used book store in New York, and that he reads over and over. When he was young, Johnny thought that he might study writing, or maybe even art, when he went to college. As it was he ran away from home, so never even finished high school.

Looking down the line, Johnny takes three rather loose practice swings, and then kicks a ball in place. His posturing with his foot as he rolls the ball in position tells us: Look, I've been here before. I've done this a good few times. Joe College is pretending to take a break, wiping his hands on his towel while keeping his eyes on his neighbor. He wonders: Isn't that the guy from the shack?

Choking down on his eight iron, Johnny hits a 1/2 swing knock-down shot right down the center. The ball takes flight in a low arc, then bounces and rolls up to the 100 yard line. Joe C. is not impressed; anyone can hit an 8-iron knock-down 100 yards.

Johnny re-grips, moving his hands up the handle. Using a 3/4 swing now, he brings the ball in from right to left, lands it in front, and it bounces up, almost hitting the 125 sign. The duffer standing next to him has observed that John's swing is effortless, classical—the kind of swing they use to illustrate how-to golf books. Joe C. is straining to see what kind of club his neighbor is using. He can't believe it's a blade; fairly new to the game, he's never seen anyone hit a blade before.

"Eight iron . . . full swing . . . right to left . . . right at the 150 sign." Johnny is squinting into the sunshine at the target, talking out of the side of his mouth to the young man as if he weren't there. John strokes the ball, again with his fluid swing, a swing that is the confident stroking of the known. It is the unknown that has always given Foozler problems. Like his father, Johnny can stroke the ball perfectly on the range, he can put the ball where he wants it, turn it around corners, almost at will. And like his father, the fairway is a different matter. There the ball seems to have a mind of its own.

Out of frustration Johnny had tried playing golf again when he was living in Florida after his band had broken up. He thought perhaps he might make a living at it in some way, after all except for golf and drumming he had no other skills. However, he never told his father. He did not want the old man to think that perhaps he had been right. But golf, like his rock band, had not worked out.

John had always moved on the periphery of things in his life, and so it was on the golf course. He related to the landscape, the long fairways, the tall trees, the dug bunkers, but he always lagged behind it. A golf match was a confrontation: not just a confrontation with the course, and with the other players, but a confrontation with himself. In high school Johnny had an earnest and serious air; it was not that he was earnest and serious—it was just that he hated confrontation.

Here it is different. This range is Johnny's domain, here he is king and can do anything. His shot starts out right, but does not come back enough; it lands, rolling past the 150 sign on the left. Johnny looks around, sniffs the air which appears to be dead still.

"The wind must have shifted," Johnny says to no one. "Right to left . . . hit the sign," he announces confidently. This is his range, his balls—he cannot be denied.

Johnny re-grips again, then closes his stance and performs another textbook swing. The ball flies out right, and at its apogee begins to draw back to the left. He feels his toes expand in his shoes. So confident in his shot that he does not bother to watch it land, Johnny turns and begins to walk away. Over his shoulder he hears a loud clank as the ball smacks dead into the center of the 150 yard sign.

"Here, Joe College," Johnny scoffs, offhandedly tossing his two remaining balls at the feet of the incredulous youth. "Hit these, they're fucking magic balls . . . they go where you tell them to." Then he adds sarcastically, "And turn your baseball hat around the right way. How the hell do you expect to hit the ball with the damn sun in your eyes?"

Foozler fills up the outside shelf with baskets, and then closes his plywood window. He locks up the shack, even though there is nothing of value inside. All his money is in his pocket. Unlike LA, this town is not a dangerous place, and he is only going a short way up the road for lunch.

FOUR

IT IS ALREADY two o'clock. John's retreat for lunch occurs daily at this later hour. During everyone else's noontime his range is especially crowded with customers who prefer hitting golf balls to eating. Rather than take his car, which is old and not too reliable anyway, John walks the level, half mile up the highway to the Donbar Diner. He considers this walk, and the half mile back, his exercise for the day. Sometimes he even takes dinner at the Donbar; when his wife is in a bad mood and doesn't want to cook, or when he visits his mother who lives in a nursing home a little farther up the road.

Foozler has known Barbara, the "bar" half of Donbar all of his Eastlake life. They had been neighbors, and even played together when he was a little boy. He knew her husband Don, the first half of Donbar, in high school. They were on the golf team together. He remembered that Don had been an excellent putter, but had not hit the ball very long, so was usually only an alternate. Johnny was surprised when he heard Don had joined the Marines as he had always been opposed to war and the military. Then he learned that Don had been a medic, and been killed in Iraq when he had stayed in a house with a pregnant woman who was giving birth. The building was hit by "friendly" mortar fire and collapsed on him. A spaced-out drummer in an acid rock band in New York City at the time, Johnny took the news of Don's death very hard. The rather frail, honey-haired young man he remembered had been the first person he knew of his age to die.

Barbara places a tuna salad sandwich, on toasted rye, and an unsweetened iced tea, down on the counter in front of Johnny. She saw him walking up the road, and has the sandwich ready for him when he sits down. She knows he takes the same thing for lunch every day. She also knows he has not eaten meat, or done drugs, nor had a drink of alcohol since he got out of a rehabilitation center more than three years ago.

"How are things going at the range?" Barb asks. She wipes a sour sponge over the sticky Formica at Johnny's elbows.

"Not too bad . . . could be slower," John answers. "Did ya play in the ladies league last night?" he asks between bites.

"Yeah. . . ."

"How'd ya do?"

"Pretty good! I shot a 96. . . ."

John smiles. He wants to tell her about the 96 he shot the first time he ever played golf, using his little, cut down clubs, but he thinks he must have told her that story before, perhaps many times before.

Barb clears Johnny's plate and glass, and places them in the dirty-dish rack.

"Hey! I still had a few sips of tea left in that glass," Foozler protests with a wink.

"It was just melted ice," Barb comes back. "I'm going on break now! Just for a little while," she yells to the cook.

Johnny gets up and they leave together.

The restrooms are out in the pale green, plasterboard, hallway that separates Donbar from the video game parlor next door. It used to be one big restaurant, but after Don got killed, and a fast-food chain opened up at the intersection just up the road, the business fell off. Barb had to divide her space and rent out half. There is a men's room, a women's room, and an additional large door with the handicapped/unisex symbol.

They close the large door behind them, sliding the lock. Johnny turns off the light, which also shuts off the fan. In the sudden darkness he is aware of the strong scent of pine solvent, an artificial golf course smell.

Barbara is already out of her turquoise polyester waitress uniform, and pink underwear. The only light, that coming in from under the door, sparkles on the whiteness of her nakedness, and on the white shoes and ankle socks she has chosen not to remove. Barb knows how dirty the floor is—she is the one who has to clean it up after the help goes home.

"Hurry up!" she says.

"I am. . . ." he says.

Fumbling with a stuck zipper, Johnny can see that Barbara has seated herself on the large, low, handicapped sink. Her legs spread wide she is fondling herself. The scene seems strange and alien to John, yet it has happened before—yesterday and the day before that. It has all become as regular as the tuna salad sandwich she places in front of him every day.

Johnny kicks off his pants. They slide across the floor, ending up by the bottom of the door, cutting their light source by half.

Barbara looks disappointingly at Johnny's limp member, hanging there at half-staff. "What's the matter, are you tired, or something? Then use your tongue," she urges.

"I'm okay, maybe you can give me a hand," Johnny jokes, his voice buried in his partner's muff.

Barbara bends over, her breasts rubbing on Johnny's head, her hand groping for his sleeping sea serpent. "There . . . the little man is growing up . . . that's more like it. I was beginning to get the feeling that you didn't like me anymore."

The actual sex act is finished rather quickly, and without embellishment, John having worn himself out with Joanie only three hours before. Barbara is washing herself off, one of the obvious advantages of having sex on top of a handicapped sink, when they hear a faint tapping on the door, the sound barely audible above the running water.

The knocking comes again, a little louder, then the frail voice of what sounds like an elderly woman: "Hello . . . is someone in there?"

"Cripes," Barb whispers, trying to pull on her dress without making too much noise. "I had to have this toilet put in six years ago to comply with the building code . . . and there hasn't been a damn handicapped person in the restaurant yet. What the hell is she doing here now?"

"Hello, is anybody in there?" the voice repeats, sounding somewhat more desperate than before.

"Here, put these on. . . ." Johnny whispers, taking his sun glasses from his shirt pocket and sliding them over Barbs eyes. "Now grab hold of my arm," he says, affecting a conspiratorial tone.

"What? Have you gone crazy?" is all that Barbara can think to say.

Although Foozler is a contumacious man, who has turned his back on most of the social order, he still appreciates the delicacy of manners.

"We're so sorry," he says, opening the door, leading Barb by the arm. "The bathroom is all yours now. You have to excuse us. My poor wife has only recently lost her sight . . . and has such difficulty getting around."

A tiny old woman, pushing an even older man in a wheel chair, nods and smiles knowingly. The man, who is wearing a shoe-string tie with a silver golf ball in the center, just stares straight ahead, his eyes empty pools.

"Oh, I'm so sorry for you, it must be such a tragedy; your wife is so young. But that's the way it is . . . God gives us our cross to bear. My husband recently had a stroke. . . ."

Johnny glances down at the man in the wheelchair, and then quickly turns his head away: "A stroke . . . that's too bad."

"Yes, it's such a shame, he isn't that old," the woman continues, not wanting to miss an opportunity to tell her tale. Whoever it is who needs to use the toilet could wait. "He was feeling fine. He went out to that driving range down the road to hit balls. It was a hot day. I told him he shouldn't go out in the sun."

"Yes, I've been by that range. The owner is a real bastard. Well, we've got to go," Johnny says patting his 'blind wife' on the hand.

The woman nudges her wheelchair a little farther into the double wide door, which is not wide enough, however, to allow John and Barb to pass. "When he came back he was just exhausted. He went upstairs to lie down. When he didn't come back down after a long while, I went up and found him just lying there like he was dead. . . ."

"You can't be too careful on these hot days," Johnny says, stepping over the man's legs, and hustling Barb back toward the Donbar.

Johnny's presence brings a sudden flash of recognition to the old man, a dulled sound connects to a blurred image, some frayed wires reattach in a soggy brain. His eyes blink open.

"Hhhhaaaaayyyyyymmmmmmm. . . ." Spit forces a sound from the man's mouth. He tries to point a withered finger at John Foozler.

"Him? Hymn? Why . . . he's saying hymn." The old woman says incredulously. "These are the first words he's spoken since his stroke. Do you want to sing a hymn dear? That's amazing, he never liked singing. . . ."

"HHHHHHAAAAyyyyyyyymmmmmmmmmmmm. . . ." The old man tries again, struggling to raise his hand, attempting to point a finger at the man who owns the driving range that brought him to the edge of his grave; but nothing will work. What little voice the old man still has fails him—his jaw begins to shake. Saliva dribbles from the corners of his mouth.

"Oh my heavens!" The old woman exclaims. She appears to be near fainting. "I've never seen him like this before. Maybe I had better get him into the bathroom. Thank you . . . and you take good care of your poor wife. But I know you will; you're such a kind man."

"I will," Johnny replies. "And you take care of your husband. It's a shame what happened. I guess he won't be playing golf for awhile. . . ."

"HHyyyaaamm, hhyyyyaamm, hhyyyaammm. . . ." the poor man keeps muttering as his wife wheels her husband through the door."

"That was strange," Barb says as they part at the entrance to the diner. "Have you ever seen that man before?"

"No, never, I swear. . . ." Johnny lies, feeling bad about it. He gives Barb a peck on the forehead, and a pat on her behind.

She stands at the door, watching John Foozler walk down the highway.

As Johnny heads back toward the driving range, his steps betray a person carrying a well of guilt in his soul that hasn't yet even been plumbed; not just about the man with the stroke, but about everything. John Foozler lives his life cloaked in his own, habitual, twilight of truth, acting as if his entire existence is mere motion in the shadows. He has the feeling of never being in accord with who he is—or what he thinks he should have become.

Johnny regrets, and yet does not regret, that dubious moment when he decided to run away from home. What he does regret is that having returned, he has not found his way back, but is still wandering from mistake to mistake, only adding to the list of thousands of others that he already has acknowledged.

Looking down the road, Foozler slows his pace—he is in no hurry to arrive back at the range, and the tedium of its activity.

FIVE

WALK ON LEFT FACING TRAFFIC was the legend on a poster Johnny had designed in junior high school for an art competition. It was green and black, colors he didn't like, but that his teacher did. He recalls that the paint was too runny when he tried to brush it on. John did not win but he always remembers to walk on the left. Now he faces the trucks that come roaring at him head on, his mind considering that moment when all he has to do is make one small, incorrect move and he could end it all.

    Johnny felt his life had never been much in terms of finding out, or putting things together. The choreography of power never meant much to him. Foozler prefers that overlooked space which is open to those who live a silent life. Despite being a drummer he aspires to live life as a whisper.

    He watches the size of the truck grow as it moves toward him. Passing his range now the massive vehicle appears small, insignificant, the size of his fingernail, of no consequence, no threat. Its power increases as it moves nearer to him. His blood quickens with the approaching danger. He is master of his fate, protected by the rules. There is a thin white line that defines the shoulder. John will stay on his side, the truck on the other. They will pass without chaos. Johnny likes to believe that there is still order in the universe.

    Down the road he can see a red Mustang convertible turning into the parking lot of the New Old Eastlake Driving Range. Johnny knows who it is; someone he doesn't want to see. He slows his gait. Maybe when the Mustang driver finds he is not there she will go away.

    Johnny clings to the left side of the road, accepting the dust and stones thrown up by the passing trucks. He had made his poster for the Automobile Association competition in eight grade;

the year he decided that he wanted to be an artist. John's best efforts notwithstanding, the prize went to WEAR WHITE AFTER DARK, entered by a boy in the ninth grade who had gone on to become an art teacher in the Southlake Grade School.

Foozler did get an honorable mention though, and had his picture in the paper with the other winners, and the mayor and some local politicians, all of whom were members of the country club. Several people remarked to his dad that he should be proud of his son Johnny, "who was going to be a famous artist someday." That was the summer his father bought him a new set of clubs and packed him off to golf camp.

"You know what most artists are, Johnny?" his father had said. "They're queers. You don't want to become a fag when you grow up do you? You want to be a real man, don't you?"

Johnny had called on his former artistic ability to make the new "New" Eastlake sign that now hangs awkwardly on his shack. The Old Eastlake sign had been up since his father started the range when he lost his job at he country club. The club president hadn't minded him carrying on with the married women among the membership, despite the rumors and complaints, until he had caught the elder Foozler in bed with his wife, Joanie's mother.

Johnny looks up at his sign and tells himself he will have to do something about it. But he has told himself that many times before. His father, not being too creative, had named the range for the town. However, Johnny, remembering his youth here with less than fondness, had decided to change the name. A check with the local sign shop revealed that the lavish GOLFING GODS SMILED DRIVING RANGE board he had designed was far more than he could afford. So he abandoned his grand scheme for a more practical solution.

Johnny carefully lettered the word NEW on a sheet of plywood he had hacked to the proper size, and fastened it over the top of the word OLD. Henceforth, it would be THE NEW EASTLAKE DRIVING RANGE, named after no place, or at least not after anyplace around here. Out of laziness perhaps, Johnny had only fastened his sign with two screws on the top. Unfortunately, the wood of the existing sign was rotted from age. After the first strong storm the upper right screw had pulled out, causing the plywood sign to swing down, partially uncovering the word OLD, but not falling to the ground. Foozler decided he would not climb up on a ladder to fix it, but wait until it fell all the way down before making repairs. So the sign hung that way, the NEW on a 45 degree slant, and the place had come to be known as The New Old Eastlake Driving Range.

"Hi, Johnny. . . ." a pretty, young girl seated in the Mustang convertible says, here voice rising at the end, doing her best to sound all sophisticated and grown up. Her mini-skirt is hiked up to the barely decent level.

"Hi, Pigeon. . . ." Johnny answers flatly, trying not to seem too annoyed.

Pigeon wasn't her given name, that was Joan, or Joanie like her mother. But her father had called her Pigeon when she was little. When she turned sixteen he bought her this first car, a red Mustang convertible. He had gone down to the motor vehicle bureau, more probably he sent his legal secretary, and gotten her a vanity plate with PIGEON on it. Now it was the name everyone called her. She hated the name at first, but had adapted to it, almost taking on the persona of the bird, flighty, skittish, prone to showing up when she was least expected, strutting around showing off a good bit of her trim young body, and always looking for a free handout.

Released from her position as a lifeguard at the local pool after she had pulled her bathing suit top down—she said that in France all the beaches are topless—she has nothing to do for the rest of the summer but ride around in her convertible with its top down, and stop by to pester Johnny. She is sitting there with her knees apart, her skirt riding up, revealing the faintest hint of pink underpanties.

Sliding out of the seat, Pigeon opens up her long, brown legs even wider, confirming to John's eye that she is indeed wearing pink undies, with a white polka dot pattern.

Ignoring her show to the best of his abilities, John goes inside and opens up the window of his shack. He counts the money that has been stuffed through the slot. It doesn't add up. There are only three buckets left on the shelf outside. He looks around the floor, and then back out to the line. He has been shorted three dollars. The fucker probably felt that he hadn't done anything wrong, Johnny tells himself. After all he didn't steal the balls. He only took them from one place and put them in another. It was kind of like picking up a candy bar in a grocery store and eating it before you checked out. You didn't have to pay for it did you?

Foozler runs his eyes down the line looking for a suspect. No matter that the actual culprit is probably long gone—Johnny needs someone to vent his anger on, someone to hate. It is hatred, not friendships that keeps Johnny going. He is a man who rarely makes friends, and then only with great difficulty. He is a man who has known only two or three people well all his life, and they have all turned out somehow to be the enemy.

It was the college student, Johnny is sure of it. "Damn college kids! Their old man gives them all kinds of fucking money, and they go around stealing, just for a joke," he mutters to himself.

"I'll take a three dollar bucket, please. . . ." It's Pigeon. She always comes around to the side door. One of her legs is up on the overly high step, the arc of her short skirt carrying higher and higher as her knee describes a nervous parabola in and out of the shadow of the shed.

"Three bucks," John says holding out a small bucket.

"Like, I haven't got three dollars, ya know. But, I'll let you feel my breasts instead."

"I don't want to squeeze you little titties." John says, putting the bucket back on the table. "I had a hand full last week. Now, pay me three bucks, or go away. . . ."

"Like you did not squeeze my titties last week. . . ."

"Okay. Maybe it was two weeks ago. . . ."

"Gimme a three dollar bucket and I'll . . . let you put your hand underneath my tank top . . . and I'm not wearing a bra. . . ."

"I don't want to put my hand under your tank top. And I can see you're not wearing a bra . . . you don't need one, your titties are too small."

"Hummpf. . . ."

The college kid has finished hitting. He walks by the open window, says "thank you," and puts his empty bucket on the counter.

"Thank yooou. . . ." John mimics. Very few players ever return their buckets to the shed, let alone say thanks. The kid is probably being facetious. Foozler watches the boy load his clubs into the trunk of his car, eying him suspiciously. He is sure now that the kid is the one who has not paid.

"Look! Like, they're not too small. . . ."

Johnny turns around, startled. Pigeon is standing in the back of the shed, naked to the waist, twirling her tank top in her hand. The pink nipples on her modest breasts stand out hard, proud to be on display.

"Cripes! Put your goddamn shirt back on!"

"No I won't. Here's three dollars. I'm going out to hit balls with my shirt off. Like if my titties are so small, you can tell everyone that I'm a boy."

"Well your hair is pretty short," John says, sliding the bucket of balls out of Pigeon's reach.

An elderly woman, her clubs in a pull cart, is bumping her way across the rough gravel. Maybe he should get the lot paved, if he ever gets enough money together, Johnny tells himself. The woman looks like a three dollar bucket customer. Out of the corner of his eye Foozler can see Pigeon standing in the shadows, still topless.

"Uh, huummm." Johnny clears his throat, positioning himself between the woman and Pigeon.

"A three dollar bucket, please. . . ." The please goes up a few notes at the end. She is a polite old biddy.

Snatching at the three one dollar bills, Foozler thrusts the balls out into the sunlight. "Thank you. Hit 'em good," he smiles.

Scrunching up her face, the woman adjusts her sunglasses and peers over Johnny's shoulder. "Oh! How nice. I see you have your son working with you now," she says, then turns and walks to the line.

"My son! My son!" Johnny laughs hysterically. "Wait until I tell my son. I hope the lady doesn't work for the unemployment office. Ha, ha, hah. They might stop the kid's checks. . . ."

"Don't you dare tell Junior!" Pigeon shrieks, struggling to get her tank top back over her head.

When saying "Junior" Pigeon means John Foozler IV, the unemployed theatre arts graduate who shares the trailer with his mother and father, John Foozler III, former drummer with the rock band The Artful Foozler, son of the late John Foozler II.

There are not many opportunities in Wilbender County for a drama major. The area does consider itself rather "arty" because of the two colleges, and the fact that Eastlake has a woman Socialist mayor. And there is a semi-professional theater in an old boathouse down by the lake, where Junior sometimes works painting sets. He has tried out for parts with the local amateur groups, just for the experience, which he got little of as he rarely was cast in a role, and even then usually only as a walk-on. The rest of the time he does odd jobs, like gardening, or house painting.

Johnny had suggested to his son that he might try New York or LA, and even offered him some money to go there and get started. But Johnny IV had rejected his offer, saying that "he didn't want to go commercial." The father took this to mean that his son would rather sprawl on a couch in the trailer watching the classic movie channel, supposedly studying famous actor's techniques, while collecting unemployment checks when he could.

Father, mother, and son lived together in unequal harmony. Johnny and his wife were constantly arguing, which was one of the reasons Foozler stayed away from home every day as long as he could. Johnny hated watching TV, which was always turned on in their small, cramped habitat. Moreover, he can't stand the smell of cigarettes, which the trailer reeked of after his wife and son had spent the whole day puffing away in front of their respective tubes; soaps on one, and perhaps The Three Stooges on the other. Johnny often threatened to throw his kid out, but the mother would always intercede saying: "You don't want him to run off to New York . . . and become a drug addict like you did, do you?"

"No, I won't tell Junior what that old lady said," Johnny confides to Pigeon. He leans out of the window and stretches his arms on the front counter, into the blazing sun, the scarred veins facing upwards. The line of hackers in front of him blurs, and then spins away. For a moment he returns to a former time. He wants to be floating now, floating on a raft of heroine. The sun's rays are a needle, filling his body full. A cloud sails by, a gray form, taking the needle, turning its back on him, walking away. He pulls a loose thread from his shirt and puts it in his mouth like food. He has worshipped a false god, a mirage, the *fata morgana*. The hackers are back hitting their balls—forever swinging their swings that will never improve; as if it made any difference to anyone but them. A door slams behind him.

"Like, promise you won't tell Johnny. . . ."

Johnny, the father, looks at Pigeon. She has put her top back on, what there is of it; her navel exposed, her skirt barely hanging on her hips. He has the sudden urge to put his tongue in that tiny, well-tied knot of flesh. Has his son tongued that navel, or gone even further? Was that why Pigeon has been so concerned he not "tell" Junior about their little game, or about some of the other games they have played? Were he and Junior, the son he despised, cursed, the daily object of his enmity, actually involved in a triangle with this very same pretty young girl?

A pink and white triangle passes through Johnny's mind, traveling within the code of signals, her sex concealed by the hoop of color at the intersection of her legs. Is he a living thing? or a demon? an incubus sprung from the soul of his dead father, soaring above Old Eastlake, looking for intercourse with any woman, young or old, that he might catch off guard.

"Here, take this five dollar bucket . . . on me," Johnny says thrusting the balls at Pigeon. "Go hit! But keep your top on. . . ."

"Thank you . . . Mister Foozler, sir. I'll be a good girl. . . ."

The frisson has passed—for both of them. With Pigeon gone, Johnny begins to fill the empty buckets. He does it by weight, not number. Who has the time, or patience to count out 100 golf balls? He uses a scale his father had bought at the auction when Mickey's Meat Market finally closed for good. Maybe I should change my sign, Johnny thinks: RANGE BALLS/ ONE DOLLAR PER POUND. Then no one could complain, but maybe they would. In his mind's eye Johnny sees some old hacker taking his bathroom scale out of the trunk to weigh his bucket of balls.

One of the many ironies of this story is that while I have attempted to make it clear that Johnny has a certain appreciation for women, his own statements would imply just the opposite. In Foozler's own words:

"All my life I have been afraid of girls, or women, afraid of being rejected by them. When I was a boy, and then later, I feared being rebuffed because I thought I was not physically attractive. I also wondered if I might be a homosexual. . . ."

Perhaps this fear of being rejected was why Johnny always resorted to proposition by ambush—the risk being much less. He preferred to rely on success by numbers. If he seduced enough women, maybe one would love him in return. So he rarely passed up an opportunity.

John Foozler carried in his wallet a folded and yellowed newspaper article about a woman who had been arrested for cutting off her husband's penis. He had underlined the statement this feminist "heroine" had made to the police officer, a man, who arrested her: *He always has an orgasm, and he doesn't wait for me to have an orgasm. I didn't think it was fair; so I took out a knife, and while he was sleeping I just did it.*"

This would never happen to an incubus. Johnny never exploits; he always waits for the woman to come—perhaps that is his charm.

Business at the range drops off by mid afternoon. All the older folks stay home to watch the soaps and talk shows. The people who work—Johnny wonders if anyone really does work anymore—are usually trying to put in an honest hour or so before going home. The hackers will be out again in force come evening. Johnny is thankful the days are starting to get shorter. He says that everyone asks him when he is going to install flood lights, as if this costs about as much as going down to the Home Depot and buying a few clip on lamps and extension cords. If Johnny had his way he would have a giant window shade, painted with a *trompe l'oeil* night sky, that he could pull down over the range about six o'clock.

There are only three people left on the line now, two cash customers and Pigeon. Everyone else tips their buckets over, spilling out the balls, which they tap into position with their foot or club. Not Pigeon. She keeps her basket upright, and bends over, no discreet stoop, taking the balls out one at a time, providing a full view of her sweet little bum, her miniskirt riding high up her thighs, and her bikini panties pulled up into her crack.

Pigeon has carefully positioned herself so that with each bend-over her back faces the road, and Johnny's shack. From the highway her pink and white undies must appear like nothing at all. Johnny hears the odd squeal of brakes, and the trucks seem to pass at a much slower rate of speed. Having filled all the empty buckets, and stared Pigeon's bum to boredom, Johnny decides it is a good time to read his book. Reaching under the counter, he finds his well worn copy of "The Flame of Life" by Gabriele D'Annunzio. He does not have a page marked; he opens the book at random. He has read this book many times before.

Johnny is a man who does not read just for the story. He savors the words. He chews them. He interprets their meanings, finding wisdom in the smallest sliver of emotion. A glance at a paragraph can lead Foozler to hours of speculation. After he reads a page he presses his hand upon it, as if to feel its possible deeper message.

After the death of its lead singer—when The Artful Foozler broke up—Johnny had resigned from the world. For six months he did nothing but read and play golf. It was the first time in his life that he had actually enjoyed golf. This had been a wonderful time for Johnny. He had found a calmness in words, in golf, and in all things, including himself. This period had spoiled him. Then his money ran out, and he returned to the reality of his everyday existence, and the need to find a job.

Nevertheless, during those six months he had arrived at the recognition that he would never be as important in the world, at anything, as he once thought he would become—a wisdom that comes high among the comforts of aging, and the consciousness of early failures.

"Like what'ch reading?" It was Pigeon, she had finished hitting her balls, and brought back the empty wire basket.

"A book. . . ." Johnny says, annoyed at being interrupted in his thoughts.

"Like, I can see that it's a book. What's it about?"

"Italy. . . ."

"So why are you reading about Italy? Like, is it for a class you're taking, or something? . . ."

"I'm reading it just because I like to read. Don't you? . . ."

"No. I never read anything unless I have to. I want another bucket of balls . . . small size."

"Don't you ever say please? . . ."

"Please, may I have another small bucket of balls, Mr. Foozler, sir?"

"That's better." Johnny says, handing her the bucket. "Here...."

"Like, don't I have to pay you?"

"No, I'll get the money from your mother . . . tomorrow."

"Oh no you won't...."

"Why not?"

"Because my mother doesn't pay you with money, ya know...."

"How do you know that?"

"Like, she lets you screw her, that's what...."

"What makes you say that?"

"I just know...."

"Know what?"

"Like she came home today without her underpants on . . . after she had been here supposedly hitting balls . . . ya know what I mean."

"Oh yeah, and how do you know that?"

"We went to the pool together at the country club before I came here. We changed in the cabana. When she took off her shorts she like wasn't wearing any panties, but she was wearing them when she left this morning. I saw her come out of the bathroom with red ones on under her robe, like those there lying in the corner...."

"They're not anybody's underpanties, just an old rag I use for cleaning clubs."

"They were my mother's panties this morning...."

Johnny gets up and reaches for the balled up cloth in the corner. Pigeon has moved in the same direction at the same time. Johnny puts his arms around her to avoid a collision.

"Touch me, Johnny," she says, holding on to him.

"What!?" He pushes her away.

"Put you hand inside my panties...."

"Why should I?"

"Like, I want to pay you back for the bucket of balls."

"Look, you can have the damn balls, free, on me. You can even take them home and keep them if you want."

"Aren't I as pretty as my mother? . . ."

"You're prettier...."

"Then why won't you touch me?"

"You're too young. . . ."
"I am not . . . I've been with boys."
"Who?"
"A couple. . . ."
"My son Johnny?"
"Yeah. . . ."
"Then go home and tell your mother that my damn son takes after his father, and his grandfather . . . in one way at least."
"Like, I think she already knows that, ya know. . . ."

SIX

THE BLAZING SUN presses down on the horizon, not yet ready to give up its grip on the landscape. The hint of rain that had come with the afternoon clouds has vanished into the empty sky.

After supper it is as if the whole town turns out to hit golf balls, or to watch and eat ice cream at the stand next to the range. There isn't much else to do on a summer evening in Old Eastlake. Preparing for the rush takes up most of Johnny's supper hour, so his meal is more often than not a hot fudge sundae from next door, which is now melting on the counter as he counts change and fills buckets.

The range has taken on a festive air, almost like a carnival. There is little serious practice going on, the real golfers being out at Wilbender County's three golf courses playing in the leagues. In the evening no one warms up by hitting a few wedges, and then working their way up through their bag. In the evening everyone brings out the driver.

"The game is to see who can hit the ball the farthest," a young man explains to his date as the two of them watch while sipping orange smoothies.

And some of the evening crowd can hit the ball far, if not straight, nor consistent. Watching the mayhem with mirth, Johnny gulps down another spoonful of the soup that his hot fudge sundae has turned into.

"Just look at that sucker go!" shouts a hulk of a man, his tattooed arms bulging from under a Harley-Davidson t-shirt. Having caught his friend's attention, he promptly tops his next ball, and dribbles it out about 50 yards. He is ready with his excuse. "Damn range balls . . . half of them are fucking dead. . . ."

Yes, Johnny thinks, overhearing him—it's all my fault. If they happen to be hitting them good it's their skill, but let them mishit one and it's my defective range balls. I will not disabuse anyone of this notion. It's all my plan, me! . . . the shaman . . . who by skillful legerdemain manages to slip in that "bad" ball when they least expect it; when they have just said "look at me," when they're showing their girlfriend how it's done, when they are demonstrating to their young son the "right" way to hit a ball—oh if only I had such command.

The sun is sinking rapidly now, tired from its day. Foozler watches as one of the last of the big hitters pounds balls into the twilight, sailing them over the 300 yard sign, out of the ranges boundaries into the bosky property beyond. Johnny hates this. The range was laid out before the age of the oversized metal driver. In years past only the best players might occasionally hit a ball out. Now there are young gorillas, who probably can't break 100 on a course, who can stand there and knock half a bucket out. Johnny will have to go in there tomorrow morning with his shag bag, amid the briars, and poison ivy, and deer ticks, and pick the balls up one by one.

Three days have past since Johnny last visited his mother. This evening promises him an opportunity. The earlier blue sky has turned into an ominous dark ceiling, now and again streaked by frightened white flashes on the dull horizon. The air is cooling rapidly, becoming windy. A tincture of rain begins to permeate the grass. Buckets of balls abandoned half full, lie on their sides half empty. Golf bags are being hastily loaded into car trunks. Johnny smiles—the last of the players is departing.

The lack of electricity in Foozler's shack, which denies him air-conditioned relief from the hot summer sun, creates another obstacle for him at night. Johnny sits at the open window counting up his receipts by the illumination provided from the neon sign of the ice cream stand next door. It has been a good day. He wads up the dollar bills and stuffs them in his right front pants pocket. He closes the plywood window, steps outside and locks up. Johnny breathes deeply. The air is fresh now, invigorating. The rain seems to have passed. He will walk the short distance to the nursing home where his mother is staying.

Through the lighted window of the Donbar Restaurant, he can see Barb wiping off the counter, a few customers still sitting there, like figures in a Hopper painting. He should stop and have some supper; he hasn't eaten, but decides not to. He knows Barb would be glad to see him, she always is. He continues walking on.

Johnny loves the night. With few cars on the road now, he can walk the periphery, scanning the dark landscape. The clouds have begun to part. Here and there stars are beginning to show themselves, fragments of a greater universe. He stops to watch a shooting star, gauging its arc in terms of the space it gathers away from the earth. As he walks up the road his eyes roam the shadows, trying to see everything.

The Old Eastlake Retirement Village isn't really a village, just a former motel that has been converted into a place for old people when too many new motels—mostly franchises—had sprung up out on the bypass. Wilbender County had gone from a place with a serious room shortage to a place where the motel rooms couldn't be filled even if both local colleges held their graduations on the same day, which they by mutual agreement did not. Thus the failed Sunset Look Motel had become a home for retired people, or more accurately, a home for those who had retired from being retired, and were quietly awaiting their final call.

Foozler strides in through the front door, boldly ignoring the thought looming in his mind that in the not too distant future—he figures that he has more years behind him than in front of him now— he may come through this door and only leave again by the back door; feet first and on a gurney.

"Good evening, Nurse Madeline. How's your golf game coming along?" Johnny says, applying a generous pat to her white-clad bottom. One of the things he likes about Madeline, besides the fact she has kept her figure well into middle age, is that she still dresses like he remembers nurses dressing, in a prim, white uniform. The rest of the staff at OERV waddle around garbed in colorful outfits that look like they could be their kid's pajamas.

"Oh you, Johnny!" Madeline says, feigning embarrassment.

"Remember . . . it's all in the hips. If you want power, and distance, you have got to develop those hips. . . ." Another pat, this time more of a full-hand grab.

Nurse Madeline is bent over the front work station, writing on a clipboard, her bra and panties embossed into her thin Dacron uniform. During the hot weather she does not wear a slip. The light from a floor lamp has turned her thin, white nurses' outfit almost transparent.

"My hips are developed enough . . . as you well know. That gives you your power and distance, your balls? . . ."

Putting down her clipboard, Madeline makes a playful, grabbing motion in the direction of Johnny's crotch. Instinctively, he backs away, surprised by her boyish gesture.

"Genuine, long distance. . . . I'll let you play with them sometime," Foozler sasses back.

"Oh, goody. Maybe I'll do better than last time."

"Maybe you'll be good enough to make a sixty-nine. . . ."

"It depends on what you shoot. . . . How's that little putter of yours doing tonight?"

"I can always knock the ball into the hole. . . ."

They are both beginning to feel the heat generated by the gross mimic of their conversation. It occurs to them to look around to see if they are being overheard.

"Ah huum. . . ." A frail woman in a pale blue terry-cloth bathrobe is standing behind them. "Good evening, Nurse Madeline," she says, ignoring John Foozler completely.

"Do you need anything, Ma'am?" Madeline asks.

"I was just going down to the TV room," the woman replies, and then continues to paddle her chrome walker down the hall.

"Gotta be going. . . ." Johnny says, giving Madeline a kiss on the lips. Her tongue darts into his mouth. She makes a face. Is it the flavor of hot fudge?

"Do you have time to play a few holes?" Madeline asks, jesting. She looks around and, seeing no one in the area, rubs her knee across Johnny's testicles.

"Stop it! None of that. I'm here to see my mother. Is she in her room? . . ."

"Yes . . . but Doctor Sangam told me if you came in to ask you to see him first. . . ."

"Oh . . . what's he doing here so late? . . ."

"Now that he's also the administrator he spends a lot of time here in the evening . . . he never seems to go home. He's over in his office."

"In the Recovery Wing? . . ."

"The same place it's always been. . . ."

In a concealed corner of the former motel is an area redesigned to have the look of a hospital, this is the Recovery Wing. Johnny heads in that direction. He knows that no one ever recovers in the Recovery Wing, only waits in pain until they die, or their money runs out, and they are allowed to stop suffering. For some reason he feels he should thread softly, but his steps echo down the dim hallway. The gray doors begin to pout and wink at him, as if beckoning Johnny to enter.

From behind one of the doors he hears a sobbing, and faint screams, the sound of someone who is no longer a person, but only a chemical experiment that can have but one final result. Johnny sees himself in that bed, engaged in an endless conversation with someone who looks just like him; however he never gets a word in edgewise. Why is he here? He is in good health, full of plans. He scratches at the scarred veins on his arms; they have no feeling. He has come in high spirits, to put himself entirely at the doctor's disposal. He has a progressive mind and no prejudices. His only passion is to serve science. He has an excess of time, sterile and without use. No, it is not for him that he has come here—not this time, he says to himself, relieved.

Johnny knocks on Doctor Sangam's door.

"Come in."

"The nurse said you wanted to see me. . . ."

"Yes. Sit down, Mr. Foozler. It's about your mother . . . she's not getting any younger. . . ."

A pretty lame observation from someone whose parents have obviously spent a great deal of money on his education, Johnny thinks. "Don't suppose any of us are. . . ." he says, trying not to sound sarcastic. Johnny broods on his own childhood, deliberately cut out of his life by himself and his father. Now, as a grown man, he is trying to give his youth a comeback.

"I mean . . . she's not a well woman . . . and her medicines are getting rather expensive. Some of her treatment is taken care of by Medicare, and her insurance . . . however, these payments are hardly enough. Now, I know how much you are already contributing," Dr. Sangam is fidgeting, tapping his pencil on his brown palm, "but, I am going to have to ask you for an increase of . . . let's say $900 per month."

"Another nine hundred a month!" Johnny exclaims, quickly rounding out the math in his head. "That's almost eleven thousand dollars a year."

"I know it's going to be hard on you . . . but I hear the range is doing well. . . . So if you can see your way. Otherwise we are going to have to be a little *careful* with the treatments your mother receives. I mean you want the very best for your mother, don't you? . . ."

'Careful?' Johnny chokes on Sangam's euphemism. He looks across the desk at the short brown man, with the trim little mustache. They must be about the same age. Where is this man's mother? Back in India or Pakistan or wherever. Who is taking care of her? Does Dr. Sangam send money for her care? From what he has read there are millions of people dying in India and other countries from lack of proper medical attention; what is this greedy, little wog doing here medicating American old ladies?

"Look, Sangam," Johnny says, purposely omitting the honorific, "I'll have to talk this over with my wife . . . she's the one who handles the finances. I'll have to get back to you. Can I see my mother now? . . ."

"Of course, Mr. Foozler, the doctor says, emphasizing the honorific, "She is in her room; you know the way." He pauses, folds his hands in front of him: "God bless you, Johnny . . . you are a very good son."

Johnny wonders at the appearance of the deity that has just been invoked to consecrate him. Does it have a beard and long flowing hair, nailed to a cross by its hands and feet, or does it perhaps have six arms, and an eye in the middle of its forehead, or maybe an elephant's trunk.

"Hello, Momma. . . ."
"Who's there? . . ." the frail voice of Mary Foozler asks.
"It's me Mom . . . Johnny."
The old woman's brittle figure lies stretched out on the bed, heavily covered despite the heat, her gray eyes, embedded deep in her skull, are dully studying the water-stained, painted blue ceiling above. The stains have taken on the shape of clouds, giving the flat plane the depth of sky. In her mind it is a preview of heaven.

His mother's fingers clutch at a rosary; as her lips move noiselessly in prayer. Mary Westcott had not been very religious when she was young, but was beautiful, the prettiest waitress at the Blue Coral Country Club in Zephyr Hills, Florida.

The man she would marry, the only man Mary would ever sleep with, had been an assistant pro at Blue Coral. She had watched him through the windows of the club house giving lessons as she scurried about balancing a tray of Manhattans and martinis.

On his free time her assistant pro would practice putting on the green out front, and she would take her break to have an excuse to talk to him. He was going to go on the tour, he told her, and make a lot of money. In the evening Mary watched him hit bucket after bucket of range balls into the fading sunset.

Then one day her assistant pro, he said his name was John Foozler, announced he was leaving. He had saved enough money and was going to try the tournaments. And she told him she had been saving her money too, and would leave with him, and be his caddie, if he wanted her to. Mary said that she didn't want to live at home with her parents and sister all her life. And he said that he would only agree to have her as his caddie if she would also consent to be his wife. So they married and bought a twelve-year-old red Ford convertible and just took off.

At first it was fun, driving all over the south. She had never been anywhere north of Orlando. Everything was a great adventure, a new town, with a different golf course, each week. Then the sameness began to set in; long drives down long highways that all looked alike, to small towns that could have been the last small town they were just in. And they were spending more money than they were making, which was easy because Johnny hadn't won anything. In fact he had yet to make it past the qualifying rounds.

When they ran out of money they would just stop in the town they happened to be in and take odd jobs, until they had saved enough to be off again. There was always a tournament somewhere, which Johnny had heard of—that he was sure he could win this time.

Then their son was born, and after a while John Foozler's wife couldn't take the traveling anymore. They moved back to Eastlake to live with his parents, "just temporarily." Mary thought they were set for life when her husband was appointed head professional at the local country club.

A faithful wife, she suffered terribly, and prayed and lit candles to the Virgin Mary, when her John was fired from his job because of his womanizing. The newspapers, eager as always to sell copies, and sparing no one, had been filled with the prurient details.

"How are you doing, Momma?" Johnny asks. He touches her hand. The skin is frail, almost transparent, drawn tight over her bones, looking almost like an x-ray. "Dr. Sangam said he's giving you a new medicine. How's it working? . . ."

Not without a struggle, his mother turns her grayed head toward him, the pillow enveloping her face like a nun's wimple. He can see in her eyes the senile intemperance of her winter. She tries to smile, a hopeless spurt of vitality. She is in the thirteenth month of her final year, the old trick of time kept alive by the chemicals flowing into her body. Johnny takes her hand, fingers spouting uneven and formless, stumps folded into a fist.

"Is that you, Johnny? . . ." His mother fights against herself, and the fluids holding her together, trying to accomplish a simple task. She does not desire to dance, or to walk, not even something as elaborate as to sit up, all she wants to do is think. "Hah . . . how . . . are things . . . at the range? . . ."

"Things are fine, Momma."

"Da . . .they . . . haven't been . . . trying to buy it . . . have they? Your father would never sell it . . . you know . . . how, he loved that range . . . he wanted it for you. . . ."

"No, Momma . . . I'm not planning to sell."

"Ya, ya . . . your father wouldn't like that. . . ."

Outside the window a neon flash of lightning forks across the sky, momentarily illuminating the ceiling. There are cracks he has not seen at first. Does water drip in when it rains? Johnny wonders. The room smells of mildew, and urine, and chemicals, and dying flesh. There is another flash, farther away; tonight it will not rain, not here anyway. He senses his mother has fallen asleep. He is about to make his escape when she speaks:

". . .Hah . . . how's Junior?"

"Fine, Momma . . . he's just fine."

"Hah . . .has he got a job yet? . . ."

"No, Momma . . . but he's been looking . . . not much work out there these days, especially for drama-ramas. . . ."

". . .and how's Anna?"

"Fine, Momma . . . she's just fine."

She takes a sagacious pause, something his mother has always been capable of, or perhaps it was just a habit, or maybe now it is the medicines. Her fingers move faster on her rosary beads, she seems to be holding back. There seems to be something she wants to ask, but cannot. She begins to speak, her breathing, slow and irregular:

"You . . . you're not cheating on Anna now . . . are you, Johnny?. . . Your father cheated on me . . . you know . . . and it ruined everything we had. . . ."

"I know, Momma . . . no, I'm not cheating on Anna. You know I wouldn't do anything like that. . . . I gotta go now. The nurse is here. Visiting hours are over, Momma." Johnny leans over and plants a kiss on his mother's forehead; the woman has fallen asleep.

"Are you hungry, Johnny?" Madeline says. She is standing in the doorway. "I bet ya haven't had any supper. . . ."

The light from the hallway passing through her thin dress outlines her body, making it appear as if she is naked. Outside there is a rumble of thunder. Inside, Johnny hears the sound of his mother's breathing, a kind of snoring, not unlike the sound his cat makes when it sneaks on his bed while he is sleeping.

"She's asleep. . . ."

"It's her medication," Madeline confirms. "Let her be. There are some left-over dinners in the kitchen. Would you like me to heat something up for you in the microwave?"

Thunder continues to roll in over Old Eastlake. The wind is brisk, from west to east, but no rain falls. Lightning dances across the ridge, searching for any metal object bold enough to rise above the landscape. The lights flicker once as Johnny follows Madeline down the hallway.

"This place must have a back up generator," Johnny says as they enter the empty kitchen.

"Don't worry," Madeline answers with a wink, "the lights never go out around her unless I flip the switch. . . ."

She takes two frozen dinners from the refrigerator and pops them into the microwave, hits some number, and the thing begins to hum. Madeline sets two place settings, but with paper towels folded for napkins. There is an urgency in her preparation. As if she is eager to be done with these preliminaries. Does Johnny even want any supper? Madeline wonders.

Foozler sits in a chair studying her movements as Madeline darts about a kitchen that seems to him too small to be used to feed the large number of people he imagines must reside here. She is humming a tune he does not recognize. Anyway, it isn't anything from The Artful Foozler. Madeline's body moves under her nurse's frock as if it were under shallow water. Through the gossamer top, and through her bra, he can faintly make out the darker form of her nipples, and the shadow cast by the volume of her breasts. A little farther down the overhead lights find the deeper shadow of her navel, and below that, through the skirt, the shape of her bikini panties. Does she always dress this way? Johnny wonders. Or is it only the lights? It is almost as if she is parading around with nothing on. Is no one here embarrassed by her immodesty? Or is it that being so close to death such things no longer matter? Are our bodies merely vessels that temporarily hold a life waiting to be emptied? Foozler wonders to himself.

Lightning flashes nearby; the lights flicker off momentarily and then on again. Johnny is not looking forward to a dinner of reheated hospital food, but he needs to eat. The hot fudge sundae has left an empty feeling in his stomach, and there would be nothing waiting for him at home. Nurse Madeline goes over to a closet and produces an electric candle, apparently left over from a former Christmas display. She plugs it in and sets it on the table between them. It begins to glow, casting a red light on the room.

"It won't help us if the power goes out. . . . But when the generator comes on the lights are much dimmer, so we'll have a nice atmosphere."

"Wine, too?" Johnny says, seeing Madeline produce a bottle from a cupboard.

"We don't serve it here," she laughs. "It was a gift for Mrs. Delaney, but she couldn't drink it. Then she died. . . ."

Madeline pops the cork and then pours them each a water glass full. As if on cue the microwave dings three times.

"Don't you have any work to do?" Johnny asks as she sets their plates on the table.

"I was signing out when you walked in. As you can see not much goes on around her at night. The bedridden ones are usually drugged up by around 7:00, and sleep through until 7:00 the next morning. The ones who can walk are down at the other end, watching TV or playing bingo. So I'm all yours. . . ."

She raises her glass and toasts Johnny; then he toasts her. They eat and drink, the unexpected richness of the Merlot turning their leftover dinners into an intimate banquet. They toast each other again, and then his mother, and Doctor Sangam, "the great brown healer," and the rest of the people in the home. They were getting silly in their toasts.

Johnny can hear the oxygen being sucked in and out of the old woman's nostrils, fast and hard, like a piston. Madeline has chosen Mrs. Wainwright's room because it has an empty bed, and she is the one closest to death, the one least likely to be disturbed by their passion. On top of Madeline, their bodies lathered, Johnny strokes on, unaware that he is keeping time with the labored breathing in the next bed.

They roll apart, their moist bodies sucking coolness from the heavy air. The night is still. The threatening storm has passed. Johnny can hear the faint cry of a barking dog, and a truck passing on the highway.

"Was it good for you?" she says.

"Yes. Was it good for you?" he says.

"It's always good for me with you. . . ." she says.

"I'm glad it was good for you. . . ." he says.

"I'm glad that you're glad it was good for me. . . ." she says.

In the darkness they can hear all the delicate noises of a dying woman.

SEVEN

ITS SINGLE PISTON moves up and down, gathering fuel and air at the bottom, compressing and exploding it at the top, creating the power that drives the little tractor forward, its headlights piercing the night, reflecting off the hundreds of tiny, white globes scattered around the field. Left and then right across that gentle slope Johnny goes, riding on the hard seat, in the protective cage not needed now.

After his visit to his mother Johnny has returned to the range, and not just to pick up his car. Foozler cannot go home until the entire field is swept clear of range balls. Right now his precious balls are protected by the light of the ice cream stand. If he should leave them out overnight, they would not be there the next day, gone, picked up by neighborhood kids to sell to his competitor three miles farther up the highway.

Tomorrow morning early, if it does not rain, he will ride the same machine, dragging a different device, across the same field, until every single blade of grass has been trimmed to the exact same height.

Then he will fill the buckets with balls, and line them up on the shelf. And the people will come and hit them back into the field, if it does not rain. If it rains, John Foozler will be happy to sit in his shack and read D'Annunzio.

There is only one light on in the trailer when Johnny arrives home, the light over the kitchen stove. Anna always leaves this light on for him when she goes to bed. She thinks it does not use as much electricity as the others. Most of the time they leave it on all night, so you can see your way to the bathroom. John Foozler has reached that age where he is certain to need at least two trips to the toilet every night.

He opens the refrigerator door, the light inside momentarily adding its brightness to the dim room. Taking a swig from a half-full bottle of cranberry juice, Johnny sits down at the table to finish the rest. He hates the taste, but drinks it because his wife says it's good for his bladder.

Down the dim, narrow hall, in the larger of the two small bedrooms, Anna stirs from her sleep. She senses another presence in the trailer. Looking at the glowing dial of her clock she sees that it is too early to be Junior. She gets out of bed. After the brief rain the night has become hot again. Without bothering to put on any clothes, Anna walks to the kitchen.

"Oh, I thought it must be you. You're rather late tonight."

Johnny averts his eyes. After all these years, Anna's casual attitude toward nakedness still embarrasses him. He can stand to see other women undressed; he rather enjoys it—but she's his wife. Lifting his head he steals a quick glance at her body. In this faint light her figure is young, sensual. Despite her age, Anna is still an attractive woman.

When it's warm enough she walks around naked all the time, indoors and behind the trailer where he has built a fenced area so she can sunbathe. Anna claims she can't stand the heat, nor the air-conditioning, so prefers to have nothing on. She says it makes her feel free.

When they first met in Florida Anna hadn't been wearing much either, only a halter top and cut-off jeans. She had been a band groupie, and just took off with him. Johnny had not even known how old she was, or who her parents were. Anna never bothered to tell him. The motels they stayed in on tour were always dingy, and too hot, so she always sat around the room nude, even when the other band members were there. But although Anna liked to show herself off she was committed to Johnny, and never had sex with anyone else after she met him.

Foozler had not minded her walking around without any clothes when Junior was a baby, but when the boy started to grow up Johnny used to urge her to "put something on." He said she was embarrassing her son. However, Junior didn't seem to mind as he ran around naked himself most of the time, even when he was a bit too old to do so in public. Anna told Johnny she thought it was good thing for a boy to see a naked woman at home as it took the mystery out of it, and he wouldn't have to go chasing around after them like his grandfather and, she added with a smirk, his father.

"I went to visit my mother," Johnny says. He takes another gulp of cranberry juice. "Then I had to stop at the range to pick up the balls. We had a pretty busy day . . . and I need to mow tomorrow, if it doesn't rain."

Anna turns on the small burner at the front of the stove. The blue circle of flame illuminates her face as she bends over to light her cigarette. She inhales, coughs slightly and blows smoke at the ceiling.

Johnny frowns, coughs, fans his hand in front of his face, then gets up to open a window. However, they are all already open. He hates Anna's smoking. He gave it up in the rehab clinic, along with his drugs and alcohol. Her smoking brings it all back. When they first moved here he told her to go outside, and she did, sitting on the front steps with nothing on while he begged her to come in. The next day his neighbor had asked Johnny sarcastically if things were so bad at the range that he couldn't afford to buy his wife any clothes.

"Did you have any supper? Want me to heat up something for you?" Anna asks, hoping her husband says no.

"No thanks. . . ." Finished with his juice, Johnny gets up and rinses out the bottle. "I ate some leftovers at the nursing home. It's the least they can do . . . considering all the money I pay them. And now that bastard Sangam wants more. Mom never eats anything . . . always blown away on drugs. She mustn't weigh more than ninety pounds. I don't know why I bother to go there . . . she hardly knows who I am. . . ."

"I'm sure she's glad to see you . . . even though she doesn't show it," Anna says, unconsciously reflecting her own feelings toward him.

"Then I wish to hell you'd act more like my wife and come along with me now and then . . . she's your relation too. . . ."

A bead of moisture has formed in Anna's clavicle. She takes a deep drag on her cigarette, holds the smoke in for a long moment, and then exhales. The drop of sweat trickles down the valley between her breasts.

"Maybe if you acted like a husband and came home sometime."

"Maybe if you stopped smoking those goddamn ciggies so I could breathe around here. I gave up cigarettes, and drugs, and booze...."

". . .and sex?"

"What? . . ."

"You heard me! If there's any fucking going on it's certainly not going on around here...."

"Look, Anna, I love you," Johnny says, sitting back down at the table. "I'd do anything for you. I've been under a lot of strain these past few years . . . ever since the band broke up. And then Dad dying, and now Mom like this...."

Anna glares at him, and takes a deep drag that lights up the end of her cigarette. Defiantly, she blows the smoke across the table and into Johnny's face. "So that's your story...."

In his head Foozler can hear the breathing in the dying woman's bed, the oxygen being sucked through the plastic tube, fast and hard. Turning his face from Anna's smoke, he takes a deep breath. It is as if all the winds of the world are being sucked through Johnny's brain. His best defense is offense: "And you and that fucking kid of yours . . . neither one of you can keep a goddamn job. What the hell do the two of you do all day long here in this fucking, stinking, dirty trailer?"

Anna crushes out her cigarette butt in the empty tuna can that serves as an ashtray. A thin sliver of smoke rises toward the ceiling. Finding no place to go, it curls back down on itself. She gets up from the table, her motion causing some hidden glass object to tinkle in anxiety on its shelf. Johnny's eyes hungrily follow his wife's nakedness as Anna retreats down the hallway, but he does not get up from his chair to follow after her. A few moments pass. Then he hears her bedroom door slam.

Johnny sits at the table, his head in his hands. He loves the day, but nighttime has become unendurable. A flash of headlights on the window pane tells him Junior has driven up. Peeking out he sees that there is someone with him—a girl. The kid will want his own bedroom. Tonight Foozler will sleep on the couch in the kitchen.

EIGHT

SIX MONTHS HAVE passed. That terrorists have crashed two hijacked airliners into the World Trade Center buildings, toppling them to the ground, didn't matter too much to Johnny, who hasn't been to New York City since his band lost its record contract. He never watches television, and doesn't believe what he reads in the newspapers, except for the *Weekly Guardian*, which he gets by subscription from the UK. Although he probably is more aware than most Americans, Foozler has become quite unconcerned with what is going on in the rest of the world. The War on Terror is, to him, just something invented to justify the Republican's military spending. He has his own litany of grief. To him "homeland security" is keeping the neighbor from knocking over his garbage can when he backs out of the driveway in his pickup truck.

It is snowing in Eastlake. Snow covers the ground. It is that time of the year when the sun is not seen for days, and when it does vaunt itself it does not travel very high above the horizon— the period of the shortest days and longest nights. There is snow on the highway, snow on the range, snow on the top of the shack. There is crusty snow everywhere. It has blanketed the landscape for weeks, not a delicate snow, but deep, frozen. The overcast sky and the horizon seem to have coalesced into a singular dull whiteness.

A car slowly pulls into the snow covered parking lot of the New Old Eastlake Driving Range. It is not a new car, rather a big, old American car, with its rocker panels, fenders, and door bottoms crenulated with rust. A rear wheel drive, the vehicle does not get very far into the lot before its balding tires are spinning in the deep snow. The thing whirs to a halt, hopelessly stuck. The driver gets out, turning the collar of his thin raincoat up against the cold made even colder by a brisk wind. He is wearing neither hat nor gloves. He stands in snow up to his knees, over the tops of his low shoes, filling the cuffs of his trousers. He looks about furtively, like a dreamer who has fallen into some snow white kingdom when he meant to be home in his bed.

John Foozler takes a shovel from the trunk of his car, not a snow shovel, or a garden shovel, but a deep scoop, the kind of tool once used for loading coal. Ignoring his stuck vehicle, Johnny tramps, with drum major steps, through the high snow out to the hitting area of the driving range. Working with considerable effort in the bitter cold, his feet sliding, he clears a six foot square space, revealing the bare, frozen turf. He returns the shovel to the trunk, the blustery wind catching the lid and holding it for a brief moment as he struggles to slam it down.

Foozler tries his key on the shed's padlock but it is frozen. He fishes a cigarette lighter, small and pink the kind a woman would use, from his jacket pocket and begins applying a flame to the lock, shielding it from the chilling gusts with his body. The inscription on the lighter reads: To Anna from Johnny, with love on our First Wedding Anniversary.

Finally thawed, the lock gives itself up. Foozler opens the door and goes inside. Feeling the stillness almost like a thief, he is grateful for the faint warmth of being out of the wind. In the half light, he slowly fills a wire bucket with golf balls from the large barrel. The balls are ice cubes; his hands burn with each touch. The bucket filled, John slides a club from the tattered golf bag lying in the corner and goes outside. He does not bother to shut the door, which bangs and hammers behind him, breaking the steady sound of the howling wind.

Out in the spot he has cleared, Johnny takes a handful of snow and pats it into a small mound, the way they used to make tees out of sand in the early days of golf. He balances one of the balls from his bucket on the snow mound and takes his driver, the old one with the wooden head, and without any warm up swings pounds the ball out into the frozen air. It is like hitting stone. The ball goes out straight enough fighting the crosswind, and then, at its apogee, as if confused to be out in such weather, dives back down, arcing into the snow, disappearing just in front of the post that in summer would hold the 150 yard sign.

Johnny is cold, stiff. He rubs his hands together for heat, and sets up another ball. His stroke was sure, but flawed. Muscles not warmed up, flexed, were being asked to do something they had done many times before—but not recently. Foozler paces about, his head down, describing a small circle in his tiny space; pondering, turning his wrists over, visualizing his shot. He will try another ball.

Johnny takes the club back, slowly, smoothly making a good shoulder turn, pauses an instant at the top, starts his weight forward, and then throws his full body into the swing. His foot, shod only in low, leather-soled dress shoes, slips on the frozen ground and slides out from under him. Foozler goes down on one knee. The mishit ball slices out a scant 50 yards and buries itself in a vanilla drift. There is a sharp pain in his ankle from the twist, and in his knee from making contact with the frozen earth. He stamps his feet up and down to shake off the pain, and to try to bring back some warmth. With his hands in his pockets, he again hobbles in circles around his cleared space.

"Swing smooth . . . smooooth . . . keep your balance . . . not hard but smooth . . . swing through the ball, not at it . . . slow and smooth," the snow golfer mutters to himself underneath the wind, trying not to remember the advice as that given to him by his father.

Despite the passage of time, and the old man's death, Johnny cannot forget. He feels his father watching him, pacing back and forth as he hits, studying his swing from every angle. He remembers the occasional sharp sting as the rubber grip of a golf club was applied to some offending part of his anatomy.

"Keep your head down, son," he hears his father say.

"Screw you . . . you old drunken letch!" Johnny shouts into the howling whiteness, words he thought back then—but never dared to speak.

His father had always had a curious influence over Johnny, and the relationship existing between the two had been even more curious. The elder Foozler had taken very little interest in his son, and allowed him considerable freedom in all activities but golf. And while he was careful never to purposely hurt the boy's feelings, he never let his son get really close to him.

Johnny tries another shot, and then yet another, with better results. He is warming, the activity bringing the heat of pounding blood. The sun appears occasionally, briefly through cracks in the frozen, scudding clouds. His movements have thawed the ground under his feet, and ripped the grass. Mud clings to his shoes, and shows in splatters on his trousers where he went down.

Johnny's attire is not what he usually wears at the range. Under his thin, tan raincoat he has on a dark suit and matching vest, bought from a thrift shop, a white shirt, and a dark blue, almost black, necktie, knotted by a man not accustomed to tying ties. His dress is more appropriate for where he has just come from than where he is now.

Foozler is almost finished with his jumbo bucket. Nearly 100 balls have risen into the air and then fallen to bury themselves to various depths in the white field. Numerous cars have passed on the slick highway. A few have slowed out of curiosity, while most have gone by without even noticing. One car slows, travels up to the clear parking lot in front of Donbar Restaurant, makes a u-turn and returns to the range, being careful to pull into the tracks made by Johnny's car, but not going in as far. The car is a new four-wheel drive SUV. A man gets out. Stepping delicately in the tracks made by the Johnny, even though he is wearing high, insulated boots, the man makes his way out to the range.

"Johnny! I was just passing and I though I saw you; so I turned around. What in heavens name are you doing out here in this snow and freezing cold? . . ."

Startled at hearing his name Johnny looks up. The man he sees is Randolph Benson—Joanie's husband. Not the same svelte Randolph, who dressed so neatly in high school that it made everyone think he was gay, but a later version. Porcine from his success, he has taken to wearing his flannel shirts out to conceal his paunch. Johnny figures he and Joanie don't have sex anymore because he can't find his penis underneath the mountain of flesh that has become his abdomen.

"What the hell does it look like I'm doing, Benson . . . I'm hitting fucking golf balls. What the hell do you care? It's not your goddamn range . . . at least not yet . . . not until the first of next month. And I'm not stealing your fucking balls . . . as if you cared about them. They'll be here when the snow melts, and your bulldozers come to turn this place into a mini-mall. Or you can just plow them under. Most of them are dead anyway. I would have had to replace them in the spring." Johnny interrupts his screed just long enough to send another frozen sphere groaning into space. "I guess that's the advantage of golf balls . . . unlike people, you can just replace them when their dead." He quickly hits another ball. "Well . . . I suppose you can replace people too. . . ."

"It's freezing out here," Benson says, for something to say. He rubs his hands together.

"I hadn't noticed. If you keep moving you stay warm . . . that's the secret. It's just like life . . . if you're moving you're warm, and alive . . . when you stop you're cold and dead."

Johnny hits another ball. His hands are red and swollen. His activity has become a ritual—a self proclaimed sacrament. It is as if having suffered through his wife's Extreme Unction, the ultimate of the seven sacraments, he has invented one more. His confused, over-determined mind has pared down his emotions, and sifted them through a small-grained sieve, causing them to emerge all neat on the other side. He is performing his own eighth sacrament. He can not speak directly to God, but with each ball hit he is sending his message to heaven.

"I'm so sorry about your wife," Benson says. "It was a beautiful ceremony. I feel badly that Joanie and I couldn't go to the cemetery . . . but it's so cold, and Joanie wasn't feeling very well . . . I'm so sorry."

"It doesn't really matter. Nobody came except me and the damn undertaker and pallbearers . . . but they were paid to be there. Anna really didn't have any friends. . . ."

"I'm so terribly sorry . . . you must be under a tremendous strain, losing your wife only three months after your mother."

Foozler continues to drive balls out into the field. He is getting slower with each stroke. There are long gaps between each swing. The skin on his hands has begun to crack and bleed. He has lost the feeling in his toes. He pauses:

"I didn't lose my wife, or my mother," Johnny replies sarcastically. "I know exactly where the hell they are, Benson; which is more than you can say for your wife half the time. They're dead, lying next to each other in Saint Anselm's Cemetery. Only Anna isn't even buried yet. They couldn't get the damn backhoe started . . . too fucking cold. So they just left her there . . . in her box . . . in her hole, covered by just a few flowers. I couldn't even throw in a handful of dirt . . . everything was frozen. They said that they'd get to it tomorrow . . . maybe."

"They will, Johnny . . . I'm sure of it."

"And my damn kid. He didn't even come to his mother's funeral. He said he couldn't get leave . . . said he was training troops about to be sent out to Iraq. It was just an excuse . . . he didn't want to come. My damn son . . . after all the money I spent to send him to college, he winds up running off to join the fucking Marine Corps. . . ."

Johnny abruptly halts his hitting ritual, and fumbles at his zipper; his frozen, battered hands making a simple task infinitely difficult. The consumption of a great number of jars of cranberry juice has not cured his urinary problem, yet he does not wish to see a doctor, who he fears will no doubt run a rod of some sort up his penis. He barely has his member out before it begins to spray.

"What are you doing?"

"Watch your fucking feet, Benson . . . I wouldn't want to piss on those fine, leather boots of yours. I bet they must have cost you a bunch of money. . . ."

"Heavens . . . Johnny, you can't just urinate out here in the open on the range like this."

"Why the hell not? It's still my range . . . isn't it? At least until the end of the fucking month anyway. . . ."

"I meant that you can't just expose yourself. . . ."

"Why? Who the fuck's going to worry about seeing my little dick . . . especially on a day like today. In the summer I got young ladies out here in miniskirts, with no underwear, bending over and waving their asses at all the passing traffic and nobody gives a shit. Who's gonna worry about seeing me?"

The limpid yellow stream sprays about in a way that is not random, Johnny directing the flow of his urine carefully, left, right, across, back again, and then in a long arc. Foozler steps back, like the artist he once wanted to be, and admires the design he has etched in the frozen surface.

"Look! Benson," he exclaims. "It's Pinehurst Number One . . . seen from the air!"

Johnny has never viewed the famous golf course from the air, nor from the ground either for that matter. Foozler, who takes perverse delight in being denied anything, had gone there to play the private course once, when the band was on tour in the Carolinas, only because he heard he would not be allowed on.

Benson looks at the yellow pattern rapidly disappearing in the snow, studying it as if it were a course diagram on the back of a scorecard. A golf snob himself, he has traveled widely to play many famous courses, including Saint Andrew's in Scotland, Benson hesitates to admit he has never played Pinehurst Number One. "Really," he says. "Myself, I think it rather looks more like Pinehurst Number Two."

Johnny bends over, staring hard at the pattern in mock seriousness. "No, it's definitely number one. . . ."

"What makes you so sure? Have you played there?"

"Look closer, Benson. . . ." Johnny pushes Randolph's head down near the snow. "Remember when we were little. Pee pee was number one, and cockoo number two. Now if you look close, Benson, you can clearly see that it's number one."

"Huuumph. . . ." is all Benson can manage.

Johnny zips up his pants and goes back to hitting balls.

The clouds are lower to the ground now, obscuring the tops of the trees in the field behind the range. Overhead they hear the drone of the incoming commuter flight, lower than it should be as it searches for the airport hidden over the next hill. On clear summer nights one can see the airport beacon's flashes from the range. This afternoon with the poor visibility, and ice building on the wings, the pilots will not see the comforting light until their airplane is about to cross the threshold.

Benson stands with both his hands in his pockets. Johnny's absurd comment has caused him to temporarily forget his mission. As he watches he is awed by the smooth fluidity of Johnny's swing. If only he could hit balls like this, he thinks. He is taking a lesson. For a moment Johnny is god; his hubris can be excused.

Benson shields his eyes from the frozen precipitation, watching the balls fly out effortlessly, as if being launched from a catapult. Here, on this bitter cold and windy day, wearing ordinary shoes on frozen turf, with swollen hands grasping an old wooden driver by a worn-through grip, John Foozler is hitting balls farther, and straighter, than a man should be able to—certainly farther than Benson can with his new, high-tech titanium driver under the best of conditions. He hates Johnny for his skill, which seems to have come naturally to him, and which he regards so lightly, even rejects. Benson watches enviously, yet he is a man of modest goals. If I could ever hit like that I might even become the club champion someday, he tells himself.

Foozler strokes out another drive. Climbing out steadily, it disappears into the overcast and does not immediately reappear. Squinting into the flurries that have turned into freezing rain, Johnny waits for the ball to arc back out of the mist. Frozen droplets of water land on his viscous eyeballs, thawing into liquid prisms, a momentary, multi-faceted vision of the world that exits as tears in the corners of his eyes. That tragic stillness which always seems to precede sublime events falls across the range. Even the wind appears to have stopped. Johnny hears his breathing, and the raucous explosions of his cough. His arms are shot through by muscular contractions. He feels twitching in the tendons of his legs. He waits, looking up, prepared to receive his blessing from the hands of God. He raises his arms. An unintelligible babble comes from his lips, as if the words have been frozen to the mucus clinging to his tongue: "Aaaaaaaaahhhhh!"

"Johnny! Johnny! What's come over you?" Benson asks. He gazes with concern at the bluish pallor on Foozler's face, the icicles hanging like tiny crystal flowers from inside his nose.

Clearing his throat with a great hack, Johnny's words come freely again: "I did it! I fucking did it! . . ."

"You did what? . . ." Benson asks incredulously. Johnny's last shot seemed to him no different from the one before, and the one before that.

"I hit a damn golf ball right out of this fucking world!"

"Johnny! I think you're hallucinating. . . ." Benson says, worried now. "It must be the cold has gotten to you. Let me take you home, it's getting late and I think you're getting sick . . . besides your car is hopelessly stuck."

"You go home, Benson. Get into you goddamn fancy SUV, where it's nice and warm, and drive the hell home. I've got balls to hit! I've got it; I've discovered the secret of the perfect swing. I've got the move . . . infinite distance. No one can stop me now. I'm going to hit everyone of these damn balls right out of this fucking world. . . ."

"There are no more balls," Benson says pointing to the empty bucket. "You've hit them all. Let's go . . . I'll take you home." Benson puts his arm on Johnny's shoulder. He can feel Foozler's muscles trembling under his thin coat, his body shaking.

Johnny looks down at the container, then out at the glaring whiteness. His eyes strain through pupils burned from the freezing rain. A thin layer of new snow has filled in the tiny dots where the golf balls have punctuated the field. "There are no more balls? . . . I've hit them all out of this world? . . ."

"There are no more balls, Johnny . . . you've hit them all out of this world. Now let me take you home."

Delighted to find the spot of soil cleared of snow, and dug up by Johnny's footwork, a flock of slate-colored Juncos, which has apparently arrived from nowhere, begin pecking at the turf.

NINE

THE CAR'S HEATER hums confidently, set to High on the little symbols for floor and defrost, not quite warming their feet, while it struggles to open an arc in the moisture condensing on the inside glass. Through the growing clear space the early evening sky can be seen beginning to appear in dappled luminosity. Outside the wipers echo the effort of the defroster, working with brutish pleasure at their task of carving a precise fan shape in the falling snow trying desperately to cling to the windshield. Considering the conditions, and perhaps because he is a lawyer and mindful of any action that might involve him adversely in a legal situation, Benson turns on his headlights, and carefully checks for other traffic, before he slowly pulls out onto the highway. He flicks the beams to low. The cascading snow crystals seem to disappear from their view.

Feeling is returning to Johnny's feet. He tries to match his toes to the indentations on the insides of his shoes. They are good shoes; comfortable, they take the pattern of his foot. Foozler huddles his hand inside his coat, giving and receiving warmth at the same time.

"Nice car you got here, Benson . . . safe. You ride up nice and high. I can see why all you rich dudes drive these SUVs . . . gets you up here, above all us common shits. Must have cost you a bundle, though; probably about as much money as you paid me for the fucking range. . . ."

Eager to avoid a subject they had discussed too many times before, Benson turns on the radio. The voice of a popular, local Evangelic talk show host, who had been an automobile parts salesman before he heard the call, was consoling a caller: "Jesus tells us in the Bible. . . ."

"The Bible! Jesus didn't write the Bible. . . ." Johnny rants. He holds down the seek button while the little, Asian electronic marvel nibbles at the content of every radio signal being beamed out from every tower in the surrounding three counties. "Damn shit . . . goddamn call in talk shows are nothing but a babbling brook of shit. . . ."

"Then find some music."

Johnny lifts his finger off the button. The little green numbers stop their parade. The lyrics of a popular rap song rattle through all four speakers.

"I'm gonna blow you away, man . . . I'm gonna blooow you aaaway, man . . . I'm gonna blooow you the fuck awaaay!" Johnny voices his own lyrics over the song. His hands thawed now, Johnny begins pounding on the dashboard. He is once again the young Johnny Foozler, drummer for The Artful Foozler on all three of their albums, more recently filling in with the local band Stash Yankowski and the Polka Dots. He abruptly stops his rhythm and hits the radio's off switch. "Rap music isn't music . . . it's god damn fucking shit. The early rockers . . . Buddy Holly . . . now that was music. . . ."

The after a while the inside of the car goes silent. Benson has been concentrating on the frozen highway, ignoring his passenger's comments. Wishing to avoid any more of Foozler's epigrams, he circles the conversation back around to the topic he had been trying to avoid, a sore point between them: "I paid you a fair price for that range . . . it was twice what your father was offered three years ago. . . ."

"Yeah. But that was then, and now is now. . . . The land is worth four times that much today."

"Then why did you take my first offer? My partners and I were prepared to go a little higher."

Johnny pauses for a moment, realizing that he did jump at their deal. He was so eager to sell the range after his mother died, and his wife had become terminally ill with lung cancer, and to get out of this lackluster town, that he had not even considered holding out for a better price. He had accepted their offer as if there would be no other offers. He hadn't consulted a real estate agent or gotten his own lawyer, but allowed Benson to handle all aspects of the transaction. Despite all his sarcasm and rough talk, Johnny was basically a trusting person. He always held a human bond to be higher than the law, more often than not to his own disadvantage.

"I'm not some fucking horse-trader, Benson . . . I don't like all that wheeling and dealing shit. You made me an offer, and I accepted it . . . That's all there is to it. . . ."

"Well, that's settled then. Maybe now you can stop hating me for buying the range. If I though you really wanted to keep it open I would be more than happy to cancel the deal . . . and even lend you some money until you got things organized again. . . ."

"No. I'm through with the range." Johnny responds without the slightest hesitation.

"What are you going to do then? We may not have paid you all we might have but you ended up with a good bit of money . . . considering there were no liens or mortgages on the property. . . ."

"Yeah, my father sold the house to pay for the range. That's why we lived in a trailer. . . . But I still owe that bastard Sangam a bunch of money for my mother . . . and Valley General and all those doctors for Anna . . . and two funerals. Do you know that it costs a fucking lot of money to die these days?"

Using four-wheel drive, Benson's SUV has plowed its way down Johnny's unplowed street. The snow is falling heavily now in huge white clumps that look to Foozler like a million golf balls being dumped from the sky. As they pull up in front of his trailer, Johnny wipes the side window with his sleeve. Through the damp, cleared spot, he sees a dim glow coming from the kitchen window.

"There's no one home. I always leave the light on over the stove for myself . . . it was something Anna taught me. She said it was the light that used the least electricity. . . ."

"You don't have to go in Johnny . . . you can come home with me. Joanie said she would be happy to have you for dinner. She's always talking about you. She said she's really going to miss her afternoons at the range. You know her game really has improved since she started taking lessons from you and hitting balls regularly. She was so sad when she heard you were planning to leave town. She said that she's really going to miss you. . . ."

Johnny just sits there. The car's big engine idles, the exhaust sighing out a gentle cumuli behind. It is so quiet, Johnny thinks, not like my old heap. All that power harnessed not to make the car go, it could get by on a motor half the size, but to run the accessories: automatic transmission, CD player, global navigation system, power windows, power door locks, power sunroof, power brakes, power steering, power seat; this was a power car. Foozler looks over at Benson, his alpaca scarf, leather trench coat, dark blue suit, with a lighter blue shirt and paisley tie. Here is a power guy, in a power car, Johnny muses—something I will never be.

"I'm sorry Joanie's going to miss me," Foozler says, breaking the silence. "Tell her I'll miss her too . . . thanks for the invite though, Benson." He shakes Benson's hand and then turns and opens the door.

"Johnny . . . we've know each other all these years, don't you think it's time you started calling me Randall . . .after all we are soon going to be grandfathers-in-law. . . ."

Foozler stops half way out the door, his foot halted in space by the words he thinks has just heard: "Grandfathers-in-law? What the hell do you mean by that, Benson?"

"Yeah! Us! Grandfathers! Hasn't Junior told you . . . he and Pigeon are going to have a baby? "

"A baby! . . . No shit! That sly bastard! He never tells me anything. . . ."

"Maybe he didn't want to worry you . . . I mean with everything you had on your mind. That was one of the reasons they couldn't come up for the funeral. Pigeon is in her ninth month. Joanie and I thought you knew."

"That sly bastard," Johnny repeats, pulling his foot back in out of the darkness. "I didn't know . . . . He never calls, never writes. I wonder if Anna knew about it, and never told me . . . she was suffering so much. But at the end she seemed almost happy, as if she knew everything was going to be all right." Foozler closes the door and leans back in the seat. He stares out through the beating wipers. The melting flakes have bedecked the windshield with a thousand tiny lights. "You know, Randall. . . ."

"What's that, Johnny?" Randall says turning to look at him. Their children have been married almost two years, and this is the first time he has heard Johnny call him by his first name. In school he had always been called Randy, but he knew that behind his back an expletive was always added; Randy the pansy, the queer, the faggot, the fruit, the fairy.

"...I've been thinking of moving someplace south. Now Florida's too damn hot . . . I've lived there. Maybe somewheres in between . . . the Carolinas. I was thinking maybe Turtle Beach. It's not that far from Parris Island . . . I could stop down and see the kids from time to time . . . and now that I'm gonna be a grandfather. . . ."

"Turtle Beach's a great place, Johnny. A lot of fine golf courses there."

"I don't need golf courses, Randall, just a driving range . . . some place where I could get a job . . . and maybe get into a band. . . ."

"Johnny, I've watched you hit balls many times. You have got to be one of the finest natural ball strikers I have ever seen. Even today, in the snow and all that . . . you were hitting unbelievable drives. Maybe you should try playing again. You must be over fifty . . . did you ever think of trying to make it to the Senior Tour? I know your father played on the regular tour."

"You're fucking nuts! Benson!" Johnny jumps out of the car, slamming the door behind him. The thing he doesn't like about Benson is his way of thinking he can always arrange other peoples lives for them better than they can. And how can he destroy his father's legend by revealing that the man never played on the PGA tour, just showed up at tournaments on Monday mornings and tried to qualify—but he never did.

TEN

THE NIGHT AIR inside the trailer is heavy and damp, almost as if Johnny has brought the snow storm now raging outside in with him. He sits brooding at the kitchen table, the light bulb over the stove the only illumination, alternately soaking one hand and then the other in a shallow pan of warm, salt water. The back of his hands seem to him to be sprinkled with more small brown spots, not exactly freckles, than he remembers from last week. The hand not in water at the moment tips up Johnny's glass of cranberry juice.

Foozler sees—or does he only think he sees—a whitish figure, a woman, standing in front of him naked, in a room that is cold, smiling, scarred holes of flesh where her chest should be. Smoke, clouds of smoke, pour from her lungs, and surround her like a halo. His cracked hand trembles in the salty water. Johnny is at first filled with dread, then suddenly overcome with an effusion of tenderness.

The memory of their celibacy is turbidly reawakened in Foozler's mind. He forces his thoughts back to their earliest years, the good old days, when their feet never touched the floor in the morning before their bodies had joined. Compelled by an instinctive impulse of his spirit, Johnny returns to seek refuge at the source. A sudden flood of joy bathes him, as if in a single instant their entire relationship has streamed back into his heart. He sees lightning flash jubilantly into Anna's body, joining it with his. Foozler blinks his eyes, looks again. There is no one there, only a trick of the snow falling past the halogen lamp illuminating the trailer park courtyard.

Taking three of the darkest towels from the bathroom cabinet, Johnny goes about the trailer and covers the mirrors. He doesn't know why he should do this; just that it is something he is supposed to do. He remembers his grandmother doing it when he was a little boy and his grandfather died. She told him that the dead returned for nine days and wandered about saying their farewells, and that if you looked in the mirror you would see them over your shoulder. His mother had not covered the mirrors when her mother died. He had asked his mother if they should cover the mirrors, and she had replied: "It's a stupid old world custom . . . nobody believes in it anymore."

Before draping the bedroom mirror Johnny sits at Anna's dressing table. Her things are all around him, woman's things: hair brush, nail file, and dozens of mysterious little boxes and bottles containing creams, and potions, and ointments, all things meant to restore her aging beauty. They had divided their world. The bathroom was Johnny's; his things filled the shelves in the cabinet behind the mirror. The bedroom was Anna's space.

Johnny turns on the lamp and studies his face in the mirror. He is no longer young. His head is patched with a wild and recalcitrant shock of gray. He wets his fingers on his tongue and tries to pat his hair down, the way his mother used to do it. His face bristles with stubble, longer and more irregular around the wart on his chin. He picks at his nose. The hair hangs too long from his nostrils. Why doesn't it grow like that on the top of his head? he wonders, only where he doesn't want it to. The image that stares back at him is not the same face that has appeared on three record jackets, the image of himself he carries in his mind. There is a childlike expression of helplessness on Johnny's face, a curious sort of dreaminess. His eyes seem to be looking beyond the glazed surface, as if he is trying to see through to the other side.

A morning sun arcs through the window, slanting on a mound of blankets that moves from time to time, stirred by the fit of Johnny's coughing. The snow has stopped falling sometime during the sleepless night. On the white roadway a plow works at clearing the way for the endless file of yellow buses that will soon descend on the high school down the hill. The first sunlight in several days searches for the room's immobile inhabitant the way one might search for a fish in an aquarium that has hidden under a rock. Only Johnny's nose, emerging from the swathed nest, reveals that someone is awakening inside.

To Johnny's eyes, someone far from loved—or no longer loved—the light seems to be different. The beams enter his room like the day waiting for all other lights to be extinguished. The bare window frames a cloudless sky. The outside is cold. A thin sheet of glass separates Johnny from a frozen death. Even his painfully swollen fists could easily smash this glass, Johnny thinks. I could just lie here, uncovered, and hang around for what comes next.

Foozler turns over on his right side. His left arm hurts from lying on it. He tries to sleep. He sees a young boy and girl behind a cabana next to a pool. They are laughing. From the main building, the sounds of a waltz float on the warm night. The boy puts his hand on the girls hand; it feels soft as velvet. He can feel her heartbeat in the pulse of her fragile white skin. Johnny strains, something he cannot bear to see is blocking his memory. All his life Johnny has been a deeply divided man. The shadow of what has been confounding him has not been dispelled by his past wanderings, or by his recent years of immobility. Were they friends, or lovers? an unfulfilled relationship now grown up into adultery. A thousand kaleidoscopic solutions pass in an instant. The boy and girl part, waving to each other—turning away from their unlived lives.

Johnny's mind is a fragment of moments from the past which he delivers to himself piece by piece. Yet when each scrap of time is fully discovered, it proves to be something he has not known.

Fully awakened by the alarm clock, Johnny stumbles automatically out of bed. He pauses to wonder who has set the clock? It is the middle of winter; the driving range is closed. The owner of a driving range in the North is a bear. He sleeps through the winter months, at least during the day. In the night he plays in a band, if he belongs to one. But The Artful Foozler is long gone. Drumming with Stash Yankowski and the Polka Dots on alternate Thursdays at the Eastlake American Legion Hall is not the way he wants to finish out his life.

Johnny stares at the glowing green digital numbers. He is befuddled. He did not set the clock to go off at 9:00, in fact he doesn't even know how. The buttons on the back are a modern technology he has not yet fully grasped. Setting the alarm was something Anna always did. And why hadn't it gone off yesterday, or the day before that?

Wide awake now, Johnny makes himself tea and buttered toast. Anna might have made him eggs. He knows how to make eggs, Johnny's not a bad cook, but he's not hungry. This is his first day really alone. For the past three days Anna has been here with him, well not actually; but he saw her, her face wearing more makeup than she ever wore when she was alive. He didn't know why he had the casket left open, or held a three day wake. Perhaps he was hoping someone would come, but his wife knew few people in this town, had no friends.

The green rubber cup squats on the floor at the end of the hallway. Johnny stares at the cup exactly twelve feet away. He has paced it off, the longest unobstructed distance in his trailer. Foozler has been hitting golf balls at this cup off and on for the past six days. At first he missed a few putts; however, now he has his best ever streak ever going—999 tries without a miss.

He stopped his practice early last night, when he made number 999, and watched television, something he never did. He thought about the 999 previous putts, and the upcoming number 1000. Foozler considers this might be the most consequential putt he will ever make—if he makes it tomorrow.

The alarm clock goes off at nine again. Johnny has tried to change the time, but can't figure out how. Nor can he find the instruction manual that came with it. So he just gets up every morning at nine when it goes off, as if someone else has decided that is what he is supposed to do.

Foozler takes his half of a grapefruit, toast and tea. Yes, he has added grapefruit to his diet for the Vitamin C, and is even doing an hour of exercises now, stretching and push-ups. A back issue of the PGA magazine is open on the table next to him—they still come to the range in his father's name, no one having bothered to report to the organization that the man was dead. While he eats Johnny studies one of the pages carefully. It is an article about qualifying schools for the Senior Tour.

Finished with breakfast, Johnny washes his hands at the kitchen sink, and then wipes them dry on the dish towel. He is ready. His putter is leaning against the wall in the hallway waiting for him. He puts down a ball, and lines up his putt, just as he has done the previous 999 times. Foozler doesn't bother with a practice stroke. He brings the putter straight back, pauses for a microsecond, and then brings it forward. The stroke must be on the same line, square, moving toward the target as if there is no ball there, the contact must be incidental. The ball must roll, not slide or hop.

The white globe starts on its way down the worn carpet, the equivalent of a fast green. Once started there is nothing Johnny can do to change or alter its path. Bumps in the floor, tufts of carpet, external things might change its course, but not him. It is like life, once begun you must see it through to the end.

The green cup catches the ball, and holds it, in the strangely magic way that rubber cups do.

"One thousand . . . damn!" Johnny says to no one but himself. "Hello, Senior Tour . . . maybe that Benson had a good idea. He can't be that dumb, after all he did marry my best girl. . . ."

Outside the snow is beginning to fall again. Johnny goes into the bedroom and pulls his small suitcase from under the bed; he is only going to need his summer clothes.

ELEVEN

THE SNOW IS falling steadily now; not the soft fluffy kind that usually falls in novels, but real snow, those tiny annoying flakes that fall for days, nonstop, from low gray clouds in no hurry to pass across the skies of the Northeast, now deserted of even the departing flocks of geese. The clouds, which have lapped in low over the icy waters of the Great Lakes to the north glutting themselves with water before becoming humped up against the slopes of the Appalachians like a giant herd of confused white buffalo, must relieve themselves of their moisture so that lightened they might climb over the undulating ridges, leaving the little towns of Wilbender County covered with a frozen white crust.

This swirling gray snow morning marks the beginning of Shove Tuesday, the last day of Mardi Gras. Tomorrow is Ash Wednesday, the first day of lent, that season of fasting and self-denial. The faithful who have not yet suffered enough can begin tomorrow to deprive themselves of whatever earthly pleasures they still may enjoy, and feel virtuous in their deprivation.

In the predawn light we can see Johnny Foozler attempting to back his big old Buick, the car that belonged to his father, into the parking lot of what used to be his driving range. The lot has not been plowed all winter. The rear tires whine in the deep snow, spinning first one than both of the wheels. Determined to get as close as possible to his shack, Johnny guns the motor, his near bald tires propelling the car sideways as much as rearward.

Considerably short of his destination, Johnny gets out and looks about helplessly, like a stranded traveler meant to be somewhere else. He takes a shovel from the trunk and begins clearing a path to the small wooden building. While Foozler has on a hat, and gloves, the rest of what he is wearing might be called "summer clothes." He is dressed, perhaps prematurely, for where he is going, not where he is now.

Finally inside the boarded up shack, Johnny feels a bit warmer. Dragging a battered golf bag from the corner, he counts the clubs. There are thirteen. One is missing, the driver—the club he last used out there on the frozen range, hitting balls into the crusted snow, on the way home from his wife's funeral. In the semidarkness he searches for the club. Has he left it on the range? Johnny looks out the door. The snow is so deep it covers the poles for the yardage signs, the surface having become a level playing field, a nirvana for hackers now, if they would come, for deprived of the perspective of numbers all golfers would be equal.

Foozler finds his driver behind the door, its head still caked with ice, where Benson put it when he finally got Johnny into his car. He slides the driver into the bag and, stepping lightly to keep his tattered, white sneakers dry, loads the bag into the back seat of the car next to his small suitcase. Foozler opens the trunk, which is empty. The lid rocks up and down, a huge metal wing wanting to take flight in the swirling breeze.

Back inside the shack, Johnny stamps his feet and rubs his hands together for warmth. He is wearing a blue and gold bomber jacket with tan leather sleeves, the kind of jacket that sells for a lot of money these days as a retro replica. But his is an original. The fit is tight, and it smells of mothballs, nevertheless Johnny is pleased to be able to get in to it after all these years.

He found the jacket when cleaning out things his mother had left when she died. This is what we have mothers for—he had thought digging through the boxes of stuff he planned to throw away, but found himself mostly keeping—not only to give us birth, but to save things we think we do not want, until we realize that we do. On the back of the jacket, embroidered in a circle of gold thread are the words: Eastlake High School Golf, and a number, the year Johnny would have graduated had he not run away.

Johnny wrestles a metal drum over on its side. The floor of the shack is immediately covered by the barrel's contents, thousands of red banded golf balls. Slipping and sliding on the rolling objects, Foozler makes his way to the door. He knocks the snow from his shovel, and scoops up some balls. He carries the load, trying not to spill too many, to the trunk of his car and throws the balls in loosely on the floor.

Freed from the confines of the cramped barrel, where they were prepared to stay all winter, the red and white globes rattle around their new space. This is not the wire baskets they know, nor the hot grass of the range, where they are often forced to lie in the sun for hours waiting to be returned to the coolness of the shack. This is a new place, strange and alien. Johnny shovels another load of balls on top of them, then another and another, in rapid succession.

"Damn! I didn't know it was going to be so much fucking work," Johnny says to no one but himself as he throws another shovelful of range balls into his car trunk. Johnny has reread his real estate contract. It says nothing about the balls. He is not going to leave them behind for Benson's men to plow into the ground when they build his shopping mall.

A golf ball weighs 1.6 ounces. With each shovelful the springs of Johnny's old Buick sag lower, and lower, until the bumper backs down into the snow.

"Traction," Foozler mutters. There's a big storm coming up the coast. By the time he gets to Pennsylvania the snow will be really deep. His tires are a little bald, but he can't afford new ones. He doesn't want to wait a day or so until the snow is gone; he's afraid he might change his mind and chicken out. He's ready to go now, so he's going to go. With all this weight in the back, Johnny reasons, his Buick will ride like Benson's big, expensive four-wheel drive. Besides, the balls are his balls.

Johnny slowly burrows out of the parking lot. The bumper is dragging low but his car does appear to have more authority in the snow now. He pauses for a second, only one brake light flashes, before pulling out on the highway, turning left, heading south. Although he does not look back, there is a slight dampness in his eyes and a lump in his throat as he drives along the familiar road. Despite its heavy load the Buick seems to skim along, its wheels barely touching the frozen pavement.

The snow has become heavier now than when Johnny began his journey over an hour ago. Through the barren trees Foozler catches a glimpse of a white valley in the middle of which a frozen river meanders widely. He crosses an old girder bridge, and then turns left and follows the Susquehanna downstream, retracing the twists and turns that have been etched into the land over thousands of years.

After another thirty miles, on a road cleared of snow by the heavy traffic, Foozler merges onto the Interstate. In twenty minutes he passes into Pennsylvania. Although the snow is falling heavily, his worn wipers have filed themselves somewhat even and are doing a spirited job of keeping the windshield clean. In his travel towards the Poconos, John has gained 1300 feet of altitude. While outside the terrain appears level the performance of his Buick—with the accelerator pressed to the floor he can barely maintain the speed limit—tells him otherwise. He wonders if he should stop and unload the golf balls rattling around in the trunk.

Despite the drama of the conditions: the road iced over in spots, and the constant buffeting his car takes from being passed by tractor trailers traveling at twice his speed, Johnny finds driving on the big highway tedious. Foozler hits the radio button, and then remembers that it is broken. Steering with one hand, he fumbles a cassette player from a bag on the seat next to him, and slides the earphones on his head. Johnny had found the device, probably abandoned by his son, in a box of junk when he cleaned out the trailer. There were a few cassettes with it, music he hadn't heard but wouldn't listen to anyway, and a book on tape, "The Great Gatsby." It is a book that he has never read.

The wipers continue their ritual. Johnny is enjoying the sound of Gatsby, if not the story. It is the first time he has ever listened to a book on tape. Foozler is having difficulty keeping up with the text, which just continues on when he would have liked to stop and gone back over a sentence or paragraph to consider the meaning, or the beauty of the words. Basically a visual person despite having been a musician, although then he always "saw" the drum beats rather than heard them, Johnny is also having difficulty creating mind images from sounds, rather than from perceivable symbols on a page.

Halfway across Pennsylvania, while the tapes narrator is limning Jay standing on his dock looking for Daisy's light across the water, the stream of traffic Johnny has been following slowly grinds to a halt. As he inches forward in falling snow the size of golf balls, Foozler can see flashing lights: red, yellow, and blue, coruscating through the crystals of moisture clinging to his windshield.

"Must be an accident. . . ." Johnny says to himself, holding in the clutch, at the same time twiddling the recalcitrant heater up to its ultimate detent.

Someone is tapping outside his window, and shining a flashlight in his face. Dutifully, Johnny rolls down the glass, the cold and blowing snow immediately attack his nose.

"Excuse me, sir, because of the poor road conditions we are closing the highway to all traffic, except four-wheel drive vehicles, or vehicles with chains or studded snow tires. . . ." A tall man wearing a yellow raincoat made official with reflective tape is apparently saying something to Johnny.

"What? . . ." he says pulling "The Great Gatsby" from his ears.

"Sorry, sir . . . but it's against the law in Pennsylvania to wear a headset while driving. I won't give you a ticket though, just a warning."

"I wasn't driving. I'm just parked here on the highway . . . where I have been parked for the past half hour. . . ." Johnny, habitually no friend of the law, replies in a mordant tone.

The officer, tired and cold, and probably having heard the same comment numerous times already today, chooses to ignore Johnny's sarcasm: "I'm sorry, sir, but due to the worn down treads on your tires, which I doubt would even have passed inspection here in Pennsylvania, I am going to have to ask you to leave the Interstate at this exit. . . ."

Johnny can see the cars in front of him moving faster now, urged on by an officer wielding a baton flashlight. The lights of a single anomaly seek their own way down the off-ramp and disappear into the blowing snow. It looks dark down there; no friendly lights from service stations or motels—or anything.

"But I don't want to get off here! I'm headed south. Look! There isn't shit down there," Johnny argues pointing to the ramp.

"Sir, if you turn left under the overpass, you will come to a small town. There are several motels there. The crews will have to work all night but . . . the roads will be cleared by morning."

The cars behind Johnny are being waved on. A second tall silhouette walks up from behind and appears at his window.

"Chuck . . . this here car has a taillight out. . . ."

"Sorry sir, this time I'm going to have to give you a citation . . . for the defective taillight. May I see your license and registration?

Johnny fishes in his wallet. He looks at the man's face, wondering if he should slip him a twenty dollar bill. Thinking better of it, he just passes over the requested documents. The two men look over Johnny's papers, deciding who gets to go back to their nice warm cruiser somewhere up the road to write out the ticket. The outside air seems colder to Johnny now. Snow is blowing in on his jacket and pants. He wants to roll the window back up and go away, but the window has become stuck. And he has become awash in some absurd official police theater that he doesn't understand, but must play his part until the end.

"Look! Officers!" Johnny shouts into the blowing snow, using his best rock-n-roll voice. "I just drove over 200 miles on these damn tires, through the mountains in freezing rain and snow, because they're the only tires I've got. And I don't have the money to buy new ones. But I got here safely. And I drove over 200 miles with one taillight. And nobody crashed into me and I didn't crash into anyone else. Back there I was the only one going the fucking speed limit. Those bastards were passing me like I was parked . . . did any one of them get a ticket? The answer is no!

"Look, I've got thousands of golf balls in my trunk. Their weight gives me more traction than most of those goddamn cars you're letting through. From here to the border is only sixty miles of level land. I got no business in your goddamn state . . . just let me go on, and I'll get the hell out of here . . . and I swear, I'll never come back to fucking Pennsylvania ever again . . . never!"

Alarmed by Johnny's raving descant, the two police officers quickly step back from the car door, as they are trained to do, and draw their guns, as they are also trained to do.

"Step out of the car, sir. Now! With your hands over your head. . . ."

Johnny stands facing his car. His hands on the roof slowly melting their shape into the covering of snow as he is patted down. The second officer lifts the lid of the car's trunk. People in the cars that are being waved on, fine people in fine cars, with deep treads on their tires and four-wheel drive, gawk at the dark tableau. Their police are protecting them on this snowy night they reassure themselves. Perhaps they have caught a would-be al Qaida terrorist, or at least a drug dealer.

    Steadying the trunk lid against the blowing wind, the officer shines his flashlight into the dark cavern: "Cripes!" he exclaims. "The guys not lying, Chuck. The trunk is filled with golf balls . . . hundreds, maybe thousands, of them. They're not in boxes or anything though . . . just kind of spread out rattling around back there. . . ."

TWELVE

"BEST RESTAURANT AROUND these parts. . . ." the man behind the desk in the tiny, smoke filled motel office boasts, pointing to a picture of the place on the calendar hanging behind him. He should have added that it was the only restaurant, at least in walking distance.

A huge green dragon winks on and off, alternating with the words GEORGE'S in red neon and RESTAURANT in blue neon. This must be in some reference to Saint George, Johnny supposes, or perhaps there are dragons here in this Pennsylvania wilderness that he is not aware of. High stepping in his low sneakers, Foozler has made his way through the quarter mile of wet snow, suffering the splashing of the eighteen wheelers rushing past on the roadway. While these monsters are dressed in enough lights to illuminate a small city, only the usual two headlights in front are useful as an aid to the driver's forward vision. Not expecting to see anyone tramping along the highway in the snow, Johnny has received several snow baths along with his close shaves.

Not wanting anymore traffic violations, Johnny has left his car at the motel. He felt the walk would do him good. The moisture working its way through his thin canvas shoes tells him he has made yet another wrong decision.

"Aachoo!"

"God bless you, honey. . . . Are you catching a cold?" the waitress says, returning with Johnny's cup of tea. He had rejected her earlier offering of coffee. Coffee always appears automatically in these truck-stop diners; asking for tea means you are different, deserving of a good wait.

"Aachoo!" Johnny sputters again, covering his mouth with his hand. "It's not a cold. I just got my socks wet. . . ."

"Better take them off then," the waitress suggests to John's surprise. "I wouldn't want you to catch a cold. Give me your socks then. I'll hang them over the grill there. They'll dry off while you're eating."

Perhaps he is old-fashioned, but Foozler still appreciates the constraint of manners. Despite all the other odd things he may have done before, Johnny never takes his socks off in a restaurant.

Foozler looks around at the men sitting around him at the counter—tired truck drivers, stocky, mostly bearded men, wearing baseball caps turned around the correct way with words like MACK and PETERBILT printed on them. The drivers' inevitably overweigh midsections are wrapped in wide, black elastic belts designed to support their backs and kidneys. The sour odor of sweat, from long days of fatigue and fear, radiates off their bodies.

The truckers snap-inhale their cigarettes, then exhale the smoke out their nostrils in twin plumes. Are these the dragons of GEORGE'S? John wonders. With elbows digging into the Formica counter top, the drivers sit there staring into their black coffee with glazed eyes, a base, almost bestial expression on their faces. Having eaten, they have attained one of the few goals in their daily lives, and are quietly waiting for their dinner, and their Quaaludes, to digest so they can get back on the road.

"Woowoo! Hey Marie . . . how come you never offered to dry my socks?" the big man sitting next to Foozler says, winking at him. Johnny hopes the man is only winking at his own joke.

"Aaachoo!" Johnny tries to stifle his sudden sneeze into a handkerchief, not so much out of politeness, as no one here seems to care much about being polite, but rather not to draw anymore attention to himself.

"Hey dude, give Marie your socks . . . next it'll be your shirt and your pants . . . then who knows . . . har, har, har," the man next to him says, jabbing his elbow into Johnny's ribs with a force that surprises him.

Tossing wrinkled dollar bills on the counter, the MACK and PETERBILT hat wearers get up to leave. They suck on toothpicks as they swagger toward the door: "Watch yer socks, buddy . . . don't let Marie put them on the grill . . . she might just serve them up to the next customer that comes in here, har, har, har, har. . . ."

With a roar of exhaust and a grinding of gears the two truckers rattle off into the still falling snow. Six other chrome and steel leviathans idle in the parking lot under the amber floodlights. The diesel engines are never shut off on cold nights like this for fear they will not restart, and also to keep their drivers warm, who are sleeping in the bunks behind the cab.

The temperature outside has fallen to the lower double figures. Cold air, blown in through the open door, runs across the floor, finding Johnny's feet.

"AAAaacchhhooooo!" Johnny sneezes again, louder than before.

"Really! You better take those socks off, honey, and let me dry them before you catch your death." Marie says. She puts her hand on Johnny's arm, leaving her touch linger longer than just a casual contact.

Wanting to avoid any further comment, and perhaps because he is beginning to fear he may actually be catching a cold, Johnny reluctantly removes his foot coverings and hands them over the counter.

Marie wrings the damp fabric into the dish sink, then moving aside a few hand towels, hangs the socks on a small rack below the grill. She wipes her hands once on her apron, picks up a breaded fish fillet that has been thawing on the counter, pats it three times, and then plops it into a pot of boiling grease.

Well at least it's my fish sandwich, Johnny thinks.

"So . . . what brings you out on a night like this, honey?" Marie asks, trying to sound off-handed. "I mean, I can tell you're not a driver . . . and you're not from around here." Marie stirs the fish patty with her thongs. A white cumulus of grease escapes up the vent.

"I'm from New York."

"New York! Wow, that's a great town."

"Not the city . . . upstate. My tires are worn down; they made me get off the Interstate. I was heading south."

"Jeez . . . my tires aren't too good either. I hope I am going to be able to get home. The cook and the other waitress have already left . . . they're all going to a Mardi Gras party. Another girl was supposed to come in, but she hasn't shown up. It must be the snow."

Marie places Johnny's fish sandwich in front of him, her head leaning closer to him than necessary. "You enjoy your dinner now, honey. I'll be right back to see if you need anything else. . . ." she says, patting his hand.

Marie makes her rounds of the other customers, asking the ubiquitous question: "Is everything okay here?"

One of the truck drivers mutters something to the waitress that Johnny cannot hear, and laughs, a vulgar kind of laugh. Paranoid, Foozler wonders if something might have been said about him.

"Oh, you get otta here. . . ." Marie responds, dismissing the man with a wave of her hand and walking away.

The fish burger actually tastes good. But then Johnny has not eaten anything all day. He covers the fries with ketchup, trying to conceal their origin as flavorless potato pulp forced into crinkle shaped molds.

"God! It's too quiet around her . . . especially since it's Mardi Gras," Marie announces, leaning over the counter to get to the jukebox selector mounted in front of Johnny. Her body is so close to his that he can smell her scent. She flips through the selections, brushing her arm against Foozler again, slowly, purposefully. John can see her breasts, squeezed together, creating a white valley in the pink V of her uniform. She presses the letter C, and then the number 9. "Now here's one I really like. . . ."

Signaled from this remote source the huge juke box at the end of the room, the kind you don't see anymore, a real classic, all glass, and chrome, and neon lights, begins its robot-like action of spinning the disk.

Na, na, nah. Now baby, I may be lower than a green snakes belly . . . but you could carry a jar of jelly . . . underneath me while standing up wearing your high-heel sneakers. . . . Na, na, nah. Now baby, I may be lower than a green snakes belly. . . ." The song blares on, bouncing out lyrics from another era, a sensibility that has passed.

Johnny's mind gropes back to a dingy recording studio in New York City. Marijuana smoke fills the room, empty Scotch bottles line the counter tops. He has been there for the past twelve hours, with only cold pizza to eat. The band was arguing. They didn't want a song—the one that was being played on the jukebox this very moment—on the album that they were making.

It was not a song they had written. Nevertheless, the producer wanted it included; he owed a favor to the songwriter, or was screwing him, or something like that. Their manager had compromised, claiming the song was not really that bad, actually rather kind of *catchy*. They had tried six or seven versions of the song, about 36 takes, each one more pitiful than the last. But the song "Snake's Belly" arguably one of the worst songs ever written, somehow had caught on, and became The Artful Foozler's only runaway nationwide hit. Johnny has not heard the tune played on a jukebox in a good many years.

"That's The Art Foozler!" Johnny blurts out.

"Yeah . . . I love 'em," Marie says. She is doing a little dance, a kind of twist, between the counter, getting into the music, shaking her body, feeling the beat, lost in the rhythm, no longer a middle-aged woman, but a teenager again.

"Woo! Wooh! Go for it Marie!" someone shouts. Other customers are clapping their hands.

Johnny can see Marie's nipples standing out on her shaking breasts. He feels a firmness growing between his legs, a heat he has not felt since his wife's death. Marie keeps bouncing, smiling; she is dancing just for him.

". . .snake's bbeellllyyyyyyyy. . . . Yeah!!!"

The music stops; the frisson passes.

"Whew!" Marie says, wiping her hair from in front of her face.

The truck drivers applaud politely, and then go back to smoking and staring at the dregs in their coffee cups.

"Oh god. . . . excuse me," Marie says to Johnny. A ripple of sweat runs down her neck and disappears into the crevasse of her breasts. "I just got carried away there for a moment. It's The Artful Foozler . . . they are my favorite-ever group. Actually, they're still pretty popular around here, the jukebox plays "oldies." But you don't hear anything about them anymore. I read years ago that the lead singer killed himself, and then the group broke up. Have you ever heard of them?"

"Heard of them," Johnny replies. Although he fancies himself a humble man, Foozler is vainglorious to the point of wanting to be envied. "Hand me two of those spoons there. . . ."

Tapping the spoons on the counter top, Johnny beats out the exact drum solo that they just heard on the record.

Marie tilts her head and listens intently. "Hey! You are good. Then you have heard The Artful Foozler before. . . ."

"Heard them! I was one of them!"

"What do you mean?" Marie says, placing her arm on John.

"I'm Johnny Foozler . . . I started the group, and was the drummer!" he exclaims.

"Ya don't say?!"

Marie places both her arms on Johnny. Close up, almost intimate, she stares into his face, trying to recall an image from a record jacket, a group of carefree young boys, with long hair and sun glasses. They were trying to look arrogant and self-confident, when in reality they were actually diffident and insecure. Marie superimposes the various images over Johnny's no longer young face, his head bristling with a short and unkempt shock of gray hair, tufts bristling too long on his eyebrows, and from the openings of his nostrils.

"Jeez. I know which one you are," Marie exclaims, stepping back from John. "Like, you're the one with the big nose!"

"The big nose? . . ." Johnny repeats, sounding offended. Yes, his nose did appear a little too large back then, however, over the years his face has grown up to match his nose, and there are women who think him even more handsome now than when he was younger.

"Oh! I didn't mean it that way," Marie retreats. "I mean your nose wasn't ugly big, it just was . . . well . . . bigger than any one of the other guys in the group; if you know what I mean. Oh god . . . what am I saying, eh . . . anyway, I'm really pleased to meet you. What did you say your name was, again?"

"Johnny . . . Johnny Foozler, the one with the big nose. I was the drummer."

THIRTEEN

BEHIND THE MOTEL the snow covered fields stretch out frozen and barren, the dead corn stalks seeming incapable even of the possibility of decomposition. The night air is crystalline, almost absent. Johnny opens the trunk of his car and scoops about three dozen golf balls into a wire basket. He slides his pitching wedge from his battered bag, and walks to a clear spot in the deep white carpet left by the departed car of a couple who hadn't planned to stay the night. Standing in the center, he mounds up a handful of snow to make a tee and sets one of his range balls on top of it. Foozler takes three loose swings, and then sets up, aiming at a light stanchion at the other end of the parking lot. He opens his stance slightly and flattens the club face. In spite of his jacket, which is too tight, and the coldness of the night, his swing is flawless. He lofts the ball into the frozen air, the light catching its whiteness as it melds with the steadily falling snow. The shot starts off straight, heading for the stanchion. Halfway there, as if guided by the magic of the night, the dimpled ball cuts to the right, neatly clearing the pole by three feet, before disappearing into the darkness.

Johnny rubs his cold hands together, blowing on them for warmth. He sets up another ball, still aimed at the light stanchion. This time his stance is closed, the club slightly hooded. Glowing in the halogen rays, the red and white globe starts out straight, and then curves gently to the left, passing the pole on the side opposite the first ball.

Our snow golfer sets up a third ball. This time his stance and club are square to the target. He swings, and lofts a ball directly at the pole's light fixture. The dimpled missile seems on a destruction course, then the aerodynamics of flight take over giving the ball lift. It carries over the Lucite dome, again by a scant three feet.

Johnny turns his head and listens to the cold night air. He hears the air horn blast of a freight train moving somewhere out there in the darkness, not far, but beyond his circle of light. A treasury of memories unlocks in his mind.

* * *

The boy and his father were standing in a summer field full of clover and dandelions. The milk cows at the other end, in the shade of trees, were purposefully ignoring them.

"Don't swing at the ball, Johnny," the father barked. "Swing through it; like its not there at all. Swing smooth . . . smoooooooth. . . ."

The boy stroked his wedge, sending a chunk of sod, and a ball scurrying into the sky. The ball vaulted the railroad tracks that paralleled the field, and came to rest within six feet of the telephone pole the father had designated as the target.

The father picked up the displaced turf and waved it angrily in his son's face. "Not a bad result, John . . . but a bad shot. A good shot will always have a good result. With a bad shot you have got to trust to luck," the man said replacing the little clod of soil, stamping it down hard with his foot as if he bore some grudge against the offending piece of earth. "Now . . . show me where you hit."

"Right there. . . ." the boy said, bending over and pointing to the beginning of the tear in the soil. He felt the sting of his father's pitching wedge on his backside and quickly stood up, his bottom smarting.

"Now show me where the ball was lying."

The boy bent over again and pointed to a spot about a eighth of an inch in front of where he had previously pointed, and received another, harder blow for his effort.

"So, tell me what you did wrong, John. . . ."

Johnny thought of the many answers he might have given to this question: I was born; you are my father; you make me hit golf balls when I would rather be doing something else. John's behind was a star of pain. He wanted no more blows, so gave the answer expected of him: "I hit behind the ball, Father."

"Is the function of the stroke to produce a divot?"

"No, Father, the divot is only the incidental result of a well executed shot."

"Good boy, John . . . now try the shot again."

The train whistle blows again. John's memory is closing in on him, afraid that he will actually see his father standing here watching him with scorn in his eyes.

"The train is early today," his father said. "Hurry . . . we've got to prepare for the game. . . ."

What was the game?

As the freight train approached each player, father and son, dropped twelve of his opponent's balls randomly along the edge of the field. Johnny's balls had three blue dots, his father's two red ones, as identifiers. The balls had to be dropped properly, according to the rules of golf, from shoulder height with arm extended. They could be dropped wherever one wished, as long as the lie was playable, and all balls were played down.

Then they began back to back, like duelists, holding their wedges aloft. When the train reached the edge of the field, they broke and ran to find their respective balls. The object being to hit their balls over the moving train to the same telephone pole they had been using for their practice.

The engineer eagerly anticipated the father and son's game, and usually gave a sharp blast at the beginning of the field to start the match. He then continued with a steady cacophony of horns and shouts, intended to destroy the player's concentration, until the trip passed. The other trainmen were also known to get into the sport by hurling rotten cabbages, pumpkins, and other missiles at the two players as they scurried about the turf finding and stroking their golf balls.

All shots had to pass cleanly over the train. Hitting a ball into one of the freight cars made you an automatic loser. The game had been invented by Johnny's father. It was supposed to develop the skills of: finding and identifying your ball, playing out of various lies, usually roughs, and hitting high, lofting shots under pressure.

The father and son worked vigorously, sweat running off their bodies, setting up, and without delay, stroking off their shots, amid shouts, horns sounding, and tomatoes flying. As the target telephone pole, which had a nine foot circle drawn around it, was rather close to the tracks on the other side, and only balls within the circle counted, the players had to hit high lofting shots that came down quickly once they cleared the train.

The caboose clattered past, its bell ringing; the man on the rear platform waving and yelling: "Hit those dumb balls . . . you damn idiots!"

"Red dot, red, red, red . . . a blue, red. . . ." Johnny's father tallied up the results. "Aaah! Its a red dot. I get closest to the pin . . . and another red. That makes my six red to your two blue . . . I win!"

"Congratulations, Dad . . . you always win."

"I know, John. I'm older and more experienced . . . you've got a long way to go to catch up to me . . . and if you ever do it won't be because I gave up."

"Someday I'm going to beat you, Father . . . and it certainly won't be because you gave up. . . ." Johnny said mechanically, saying what he was supposed to say, suppressing the nervous desire to tell his father that he had no regret at loosing these games, which he regarded as a dubious and empty exercise, played not so much for his education in a sport for which he had no interest, but apparently great talent, but rather played to display his father's prodigious bravura.

Johnny listens to the train disappearing in the distance, stepping back from the memory as if it were an event that has occurred in someone else's life.

* * *

"Hello . . . it's me," Marie whispers into the telephone. "How's the baby? And Brad, did he do his homework? . . . No, I'm still at the restaurant . . . everyone else has gone home. There are no customers here so I'm going to lock up . . . the radio said that all the roads are closed, and it looks pretty bad outside, so I'm going to stay here . . . George has a little bed in the back room, I'll sleep there. . . . No! George is not here. He left earlier; they're all going to a Mardi Gras party . . . I am telling you the truth . . . I know he screws all his waitresses back there, but not me. Have I ever been unfaithful to you? Well that was a long time ago . . . and we were both drunk. Look, if you want me to come home so bad, you can come and get me . . . I can't drive in this. Okay, I'll stay here . . . no you can't call me later . . . because the bed's in the back room, and there's no phone in there. No, I can't hear the one out here . . . I know because I've been back there. No, not with George . . . I have to go back there to get stuff sometimes . . . look, are you drunk or something? They keep the extra paper towels and things back there. Don't worry, I'll be fine . . . I could use the peace and quiet . . . you too. Okay, get a good night's sleep . . . I'll see you tomorrow, after I finish my shift, the roads should be clear by then. . . . I love you too . . . don't let the kids stay up all night watching TV . . . and give them a kiss from Mommy . . . Good night."

Marie locks the back door of George's and gets into her car. The car's front end slides a little, making her uncomfortable, but she only has a short drive to the Wayside Motel. It is dark, but she can see its lights through the blowing snow. She is not sure he is staying there, but she did watch him walk down the road in this direction, and it is the only place he possibly could have gone in his light-weight varsity jacket and canvas sneakers, unless he is lying dead, frozen to death somewhere.

Having navigated the desolate stretch between there and here Marie skids her old Chevrolet into the Wayside's driveway. At her arrival the neon sign blinks out. The office light switches off; the NO VACANCY sign lights up. She wasn't going to ask in the office anyway, people know her here. Marie drives slowly past the row of rooms. She remembers Johnny said that he was from New York, but there are no New York license plates. Marie is beginning to think that perhaps this was not a good idea. Spinning the rear tires, she heads around the back. There is a car from New York, but it's a rusted out, old Buick. She studies the car. It can't be his. A rock star, even an aging, washed-up one would have some kind of limo, a Lincoln or Caddy, maybe even a Rolls-Royce. Then she catches a glimpse of someone standing out in the lot under the lights. That's odd, she thinks, the man is hitting golf balls out in the snow. It's him! She pulls up beside Johnny, and slowly rolls down her window, blinking as a frozen white crystal lands on her freshly mascaraed eyelashes.

"Hi there. . . ." Marie says.

Johnny looks around surprised. The wind had masked the sound of her car's arrival. "Hi there yourself," he says rather stiffly, resenting this intrusion into his privacy. Foozler was content with his solitude, which he never confused with loneliness.

"Whatchya doin?. . . ."

"What does it look like I'm doing? I'm hitting golf balls."

"Are you crazy . . . out here in the cold and snow?" Marie brushes a snowflake off of her lips, or is she perhaps just calling attention to their newly painted-up form. Her tongue darts out and licks the unseen flake off the tip of her finger. She smiles.

"I can't very well hit them inside the room, can I?"

"Why do you have to hit golf balls at all?. . ."

"Because I like doing it . . . it's kind of like using drugs . . . once you get into it it's hard to stop."

"Are you any good at it?" Marie asks. She turns up the car heater to its highest detent. The open window has brought a chill to her bare legs. Her panty hose, having too many runs in them to be seen, have been removed and left back at the restaurant.

"Good at golf?" Johnny says, assuming that's what her question was about, although he's not quite sure. "I'm damn good, ya know . . . better than my father, and he was a professional."

Marie looks around. "I bet you can't hit that there light pole that you've been aiming at. . . ."

"Bet I can."

"Nobody's that good. . . ."

"Want to put money on it?"

"Hey, I'm only a waitress . . . and there weren't that many tips today. But I'll bet you a dollar."

"You're on for a dollar. . . ." Johnny says.

Foozler tees up another ball, lower this time. He squares his stance, and shortens his grip, for a three-quarter knockdown shot, the kind you hit when you want to keep the ball down out of the wind; or when you are in the woods and want to hit out between some trees. He stares at the pole, getting its image firmly in his mind. "Never look at the trees, his father always told him, not even a glance. You must only look at the spaces in between, because that's where you want your ball to go. The reason people hit a tree is because it was the last thing they looked at before addressing their ball. They had the image of the tree in their mind, and that's where their subconscious told the ball to go." Johnny never believed the reasons behind it, but the technique always seemed to work for him.

Johnny strokes his ball out, a low trajectory, straight at the light stanchion. The shot slides left, missing the pole by about six inches.

"Hey, not too bad . . . but you didn't hit it, so you owe me a dollar."

"Okay . . . let's bet again, double or nothing."

Foozler studies the snowflakes slanting through the light, checking the wind, which seems steady now. He sends off another shot, this time starting it slightly to the right of the target. The ball goes out straight, and stays straight, passing the pole by three inches, this time on the right side.

"Hey, you owe me another buck . . . keep trying. I'll make up what I didn't make in tips today. . . ." Marie jokes. She laughs, her face mottled with melting snow. She feels a crazy joy, a lightness she has not felt much of these past few years.

"Here we go . . . only this one is for fifty dollars," Johnny announces, rashly raising the ante.

"Wait! Don't hit it. . . ." Marie screams. "Like I don't have fifty dollars."

"Well then, what do you want to bet?" Foozler is rubbing his hands and stamping his feet—suddenly cold he is eager to get the game over.

Marie ducks back inside the car, checking her lipstick in the rear view mirror. Satisfied, her face comes back to the open window; she speaks in a voice soft and caressing, almost lewd: "I'll bet you my body."

Johnny hesitates. He has not had sex with anyone since his wife's death. And before that, he and Anna had lived in celibacy for nine years. The doctors said it was normal, quite common for men over forty. There were treatments, perhaps an operation would cure him; otherwise there were pills. Yet, while he was impotent with his wife, with other women he had become a demon, an incubus, sprung from the soul of his own dead father, roaming the night looking for intercourse with any female, young or old, that would have him.

However, after John learned his wife was terminally ill with lung cancer, he had become unable to produce an erection under any circumstances. It was as if he too were ill. He had a finite sense to his body. He cried easily—like a child. He cried to himself, without sobs, or outward signs, so as not to be heard, so as not to trouble the woman he loved, the woman he had made suffer so much. He had become filled to the brim with the guilt that was troubling him. He felt he was unthinking and had done his wife a great injustice, for which it was now impossible to make amends, an error that clung to him to this day.

Wiggling his feet down into the wet puddles he had created, Johnny sets his stance. Everything must be slightly to the left of his previous shot. The wind was not as much a factor as he had anticipated. He moves his hands farther down the grip. He will play a lower shot, hitting the ball firmer, keeping it under the wind. Where the ball will land is not the consideration, rather the line of the ball's flight. He stares at a spot half way up the stanchion. The ball will hit his target while still climbing, accelerating through the wind driven snow. John takes his swing.

Clang! The ball hits exactly in the center, about six inches from where Johnny had aimed, and then ricochets off into the darkness. Someone will find it in the cornfield next spring and wonder how it got there.

"Wow! You're good," Marie squeals, "really good. . . ."

"Well then, let's see what else I'm good at. . . ." Johnny says walking in the direction of his motel room.

FOURTEEN

THE IRISES AND daffodils that had been planted in an attempt to landscape the row of battered and rusted mailboxes are overgrown with thistle, a nasty weed that can neither be pulled out nor easily dug up, and which, if left to go to seed, will spout up in every place where it is most unwanted. Its coarsely divided leaves, blue-gray above and white underneath can grow up to six feet tall, and in midsummer send up branched stalks topped by prickly ball-shaped flower heads of metallic blue.

There are no flowers on the thistle today. It is not summer, although the mild temperature, and the bright sun, might confuse someone arriving from the North. It is the month of February; the first day of lent, the day after Mardi Gras.

MAGNOLIA ESTATES the sign proclaims, revealing a realtor's marketing fantasy. There are no magnolias, nor estates; only run-down trailers and a few double-wides, surrounded by chicken wire fences and abandoned cars. Things of some value are covered by flapping blue plastic tarpaulins.

A smaller sign directs the passerby to CAPTAIN'S DRIVE. The sign notwithstanding, the young man turning into the road in a middle-aged, middle-priced, middle-American car, is only ranked a corporal. He pulls over and, leaning across the seat, looks to see if there is any mail in his box in the long row. Finding nothing, he swerves to miss a red plastic tricycle that has somehow found its way into the road, and continues on into the compound.

The corporal parks his sun-faded blue Malibu on the gravel street in front of his immobile mobile home. Stepping around the empty beer cases, and a broken lawn mower crowding the small wooden platform that poses as a porch, he goes inside.

"Hi, Pigeon . . . I'm home."

"Hi, Johnny."

He gives his wife a quick kiss on the forehead, and heads for the refrigerator.

"Want a beer, Hon?"

Not now, Dear . . . I gotta nurse the baby."

Sitting cross-legged on a rather battered green plaid couch, his wife is suckling a naked baby. The wife is also naked, except for a long faux pearl necklace around her neck, a thin gold chain around her waist, and a half dozen or so silver bracelets of various sizes on both her arms. Pigeon's body is young and lean, her skin slightly tanned, even the pubic region, which had been shaved for the childbirth. After she came out of the hospital she had looked at herself in the mirror and decided she liked herself better "without all that fur down there."

Leaving his cold beer on the kitchen table, Corporal John Foozler, Jr. USMC disappears down the hall, slipping out of his boots and his camouflage fatigues as he goes.

In the living room the mother and child watch cartoons on television. The baby, its brain not yet formed enough to interpret the pixilated characters disporting themselves on the cathode-ray tube, concentrates on his mother's nipple. In the background we can hear a shower running.

The shower stops. Corporal John returns to the kitchen area, drying himself with a towel, dripping water on the cracked and peeling linoleum floor. He takes another sip of his beer, then puts his foot up on a chair and begins to rub the towel vigorously around his penis and testicles.

A large black and white cat comes in through a hole in the bottom of the screen door. It greets Johnny Jr. by brushing up against the leg he is balancing on, and then runs and squats in the cat box between the stove and the refrigerator. Why it always does this is something he can't understand. It is an outdoor cat. Why does it come in the house to do its business? But then there is a lot in this world that the corporal does not understand.

"Was there any mail, Hon?" Junior asks.

"Only the usual stuff, catalogs and bills . . . I put them there, on the table by the door."

Pigeon removes the sleeping baby from her breast, and places it carefully in a crib. The child makes a small cry, and then goes back to its sleeping. The mother goes over and retrieves the pile of mail. Opening the screen door a crack, so as not to display too much of her nakedness to the street, she scurries the cat back outside with the side of her foot.

John throws his wet towel over the back of the sofa and sits down. "Cartoons! How can you watch this shit all day?. . ." he says, and begins surfing through the channels.

"There isn't much else to watch but soaps and talk shows," Pigeon replies, shuffling through the mail. "Hey! Here's something from your father. . . ."

"My father? What in hell does he want? He never writes . . . open it up and see what he says."

"Listen to this!" Pigeon reports. "He says that he's sold the driving range to my father. . . ."

"Which we already knew from your father's letter. . . ."

"But wait. . . . He's keeping the range balls. He's going to take them with him . . . when he heads south. . . ."

"South?"

". . .south to try out for the PGA Senior Tour."

"SeniorTour? Are you making that up? Gimme that letter . . . my father hates to play golf. He was supposed to be pretty good at it when he was in high school . . . but hasn't played since then. What the hell could he do on a professional tour?"

"Well, that's what he says he's going to try. And he says he is going to stop here to see us and the baby. And he wants you to be on the look out for a van that he can trade his car for. . . ."

"This is crazy," Junior says, reading over the letter. "My old man must be doing drugs again . . . or something. He took it pretty hard when Grandma died, and then Mom so soon after."

"Like your father does drugs? . . ."

"Yeah . . . when I was a little kid, and we traveled around with his rock band, he was into all kinds of shit. They even put him away two or three times. I think it really fucked up his mind. I mean later, when he was off drugs . . . he didn't even drink or eat meat . . . he was still kind of crazy. We never knew what he might do. He wouldn't sleep with my mother, yet he was fucking every other woman in town . . . including your mother."

"I know John, don't bring that up again."

"Yeah . . . and he even had the hots for you."

"Like, I told you! . . . . He never touched me, ya know."

"He says he's coming here! When did he write that letter?"

"The post mark is smudged."

"And he didn't put a date on it. . . ."

"He did say he was leaving on Mardi Gras."

"Mardi Gras! Cripes! Unless he somehow got lost, or got in an accident, he should be due here any minute now. . . ."

Pigeon picks up the military garb scattered by her husband along the hallway and deposits it in the washer. She takes the wet towel from the chair and sticks her head out the rear door to see if anyone is around. The backyard is fenced for privacy, but for a brief moment at the top step she can be seen by anyone passing in the street. Pigeon pops out and hangs the towel on a line to dry. She has been in the house all day taking care of the baby—the sun feels good on her naked body.

Reluctantly she brings herself back inside: "We had better clean the house," she announces, "if your father is coming."

"If my father ever arrives. . . . You never can tell what kind of shit that old fool might get into between Eastlake and here."

FIFTEEN

YELLOW STREAKES OF sunlight mark the end of the snow, a condition which happens gradually between Washington, DC and Fredericksburg, Virginia. The grand white tablecloth that had covered the land becomes threadbare, and the rust-colored earth reveals itself through the ragged holes. The painted tin roofs on the old farmhouses now show their true colors of black, or brown, or orange.

    Johnny drives along. He is finding it interesting to be out and about once again. In recent years he tended to hibernate in the winter, rarely leaving the trailer. He spent most of his time in front of the kerosene stove they used for heating studying the ever-elusive flame. Or, he applied himself fastidiously to the cleaning of rooms, which he did with great importance and ceremony, much to the distress of his wife who had just finished cleaning the same spaces. Foozler did not reprimand his wife when he found hidden, missed, balls of dust. His cleaning was conceptual, and had a deeper, symbolic meaning, a function which often drove him to spasms of delight.

    Now free of the snow, Johnny Foozler slows his pace. We notice for the first time Johnny's ardent interest in the landscape, the passion of an artist and a golfer wrapped up into one. A silent laughter transforms Johnny's face as he drives along having vivid conversations with himself—tickling his imagination.

    Now there's a beautiful tree, he thinks to himself pointing out the window. If I were an artist, I would come back here in the summer and paint it. And a little farther down the road: There are some mighty fine fields. If I had the money I would buy them and build a nice golf course there.

    Yet while he passes through it, and makes plans for it, the countryside, indeed the world in general, seems to Johnny indefinably far away, separated from him by an incalculable gap in his understanding.

Foozler drives along with lazy indifference at exactly the speed limit, ignoring the tailgaters, as well as the drivers that blaze past, glaring and honking their horns. He has nowhere to go, and no time in particular when he must be there. He has written to his son that he is coming, but purposely not given a specific date for his arrival. Foozler, absentmindedly, has even grown remote from practical matters. Although it is well past one o'clock, Johnny has not had anything to eat since early this morning when Marie served him his going away breakfast at George's. She started work at 6:00. He didn't have to pay, and promised to stop on the way back. The sign says there is food and fuel at this exit. Johnny turns off the Interstate.

The "food" is a Burger Baron, perhaps a bit lower priced than a Burger King, John reasons. He drives up to the takeout window and orders a fish sandwich and French fries.

Three hours later, still nibbling on his cold and soggy fries, Johnny discovers a driving range apparently closed for the season, or perhaps gone out of business. No matter, he has his own supply of balls in the trunk. In the sky the shadows of an undulating end of winter night are beginning to hide the tinted colors of Ash Wednesday. He has only a short while to launch his balls into the deserted landscape before the curtain of night descends.

Foozler labors at his hitting, seriously, as if he has a plan, maybe even a goal. Beginning with his wedge, he works his way up to his driver. He hits some balls right, some left, longer and shorter. The stripped globes are not sent out at random, but seem to be part of some grand design. The maestro is not just stroking the balls, he is composing them—placing the white and red globes at will around the field as if they were Pointillist dots flying off the tip of a paintbrush.

He goes back to the trunk for another bucket, and then another. Johnny sees that he has not made a dent in his cache; if anything the supply appears to be growing. Perhaps, left to their own devices, he thinks, or prodded to an eroticism by the swaying of the car as he drives along, the balls have begun to breed.

His task completed, Johnny deposits the wire basket in the trunk. He pauses for a moment and listens, thinking he hears the sound of applause. Foozler takes a bow, and slams down the trunk lid. Pleased with his effort, Johnny is laughing now, a hard conspiratorial laugh, as if he has played some grand trick that only he is aware of, something which will perhaps be discovered later on, if and when the range opens again. He is laughing so hard, holding his stomach, that he begins to blow wind. Farting wildly, Johnny hastily gets into his car. The last day of Mardi Gras, and the first day of Lent have had a lightness for Johnny that has consoled the sadness of his wife's death, and made him aware of his own rebirth. Foozler takes a nostalgic look at the darkness descending over the range like a scenic backdrop. There must be driving ranges lining the entire route, all the way from here to Florida, he tells himself; he will test every single one of them.

Pine trees! Pine trees, pine trees, pine trees, pine trees, pine trees, pine trees, pine trees, pine trees, pine trees, pine trees, pine trees, the next day begins totally covered by pine trees.

Ahead the morning road shimmers and ripples with the coastal sunshine slanting between the tall evergreens. Johnny drives along scanning the spaces in between; the duff covering the forest floor, the fields lined with baulks of red clay, the blue sky. He is looking for a place where he can stop and hit his golf balls.

By mid afternoon Johnny has arrived at the north end of Turtle Beach, a settlement of country and western bars, gospel churches, sporting goods stores, condos, and topless dancers. In the midst of a row of honky-tonks, he finds the first driving range that is actually open. Although Johnny had stopped earlier to hit balls into a random farm field, he is once again beginning to feel symptoms of withdrawal.

Turtle Beach is a golfer's Mecca, the grand daddy of the golf holiday, that traditional rite-of-spring that brings legions of duffers down from the North to get a head start on the season. With its more than 90 golf courses, the place is a golf addict's overdose, where the player can wallow in his sport from dawn to dusk. Evenings can be spent in one of the many golf-themed restaurants recapping the days round, and planning tomorrow's challenge, while dining on seafood "Low Country" style.

But Johnny is not yet ready for fairway golf. First, he must replenish his capital which after only three days, and despite his frugal habits, seems to be diminishing more rapidly than he anticipated. Standing behind the line of hitters, he chooses his mark carefully, checking his ability to strike the ball by the quality of his swing, and his ability to pay by the quality of his equipment.

Foozler sets his bucket down at a station next to a man in his early thirties who seems to fit the sucker profile he has defined during the many hours he has spent in his shack observing the various hitters. He has taken little bits of money at ranges now and then, but this will be his first try as a "professional." Johnny hits a few wedges to warm up, watching the man next to him, waiting for him to hit an especially good shot before he speaks—trying to sound offhanded, casual.

"Hey, nice shot! Great swing you got there. . . ."

"Thanks," the man says with a smile puffing up his face.

Johnny hits an easy 8-iron, out in the center, but not wonderful on distance. He knows his neighbor is watching him. "Damn," I didn't get all of it," he mutters.

"You need to make a bigger shoulder turn," his neighbor, an expert now, volunteers. "Here, watch me."

"Wow! That sure went nice and high . . . and you're right out there, almost to the 150 sign. Let me try again."

Taking a three-quarter swing, Johnny quickly strokes a ball, out in the middle again, but short of the 150 yard sign. "What club did you hit?" he asks shaking his head.

"Seven."

"Oh . . . I tried an eight."

"Not enough club for 150 yards."

"Oh yeah," John says, feigning bravado. "Bet you five bucks I can get it past the 150 with my eight."

"No way. Not with your swing. You're on for a fiver. . . ."

Johnny takes a fuller turn and strokes his eight. The ball goes out straight, but lands short, lacking six feet to the sign.

"Damn! Well I was close . . . here's your fiver." He pulls the bill from his wallet and hands it to the man. "Look, gimme a chance to win it back. Hit your best six. Ten bucks says I'm past you with my seven."

"You're on again . . . for a tenner."

The mark hits a good six, but not as good as he might have. Johnny has to be careful to lay up a bit with his seven.

"Jeez, short again . . . I'm usually much longer. Here's your ten spot, Dude. Achooo! I got a bit of a cold. It must be affecting my game."

"Maybe, but I still say you need more shoulder turn . . . and your stance is too narrow. And you're under-clubbing yourself."

"No, no. . . . I know what I'm doing. I'm usually longer than this . . . must be the humidity. Hit your best 5-iron."

Johnny works the man up through his bag. By the time they reach the 3-wood, Foozler has lost $100. The mark is into it now, marveling at how lucky he is to have found such a stubborn fellow so eager to loose money.

"Okay," Johnny proclaims, spitting on his palms and rubbing them together. "I got the feeling for it now. Let's hit drivers even, for . . . let's say $500."

"Five hundred dollars? . . ."

"Look, I really wanted to spend my vacation in Las Vegas . . . but I'm afraid of flying," Johnny explains, putting a little seasoning on his charade.

"Well, eh. . . . I don't have $500 on me.

"Shit! How much do you have, Dude?"

"I can go for two, plus the hundred you already lost to me."

"That's good by me. Here's my three," Johnny says. "Lay yours on top of it." The mark complies, and Foozler puts his bucket of balls down on top of the money. "You got the honor, Big Guy. Remember we're playing even this time . . . so give it your best shot."

The younger man does have good form. He takes his graphite-shafted driver back smoothly, making a big shoulder turn, pauses briefly to get his weight shifting forward, then pounces on the ball. The over-size titanium club head contacts the ball squarely on the face, sending it out sharply, with that sizzling sound a good shot makes. The ball lands abeam the 250 yard marker and rolls forward another ten yards.

"Acchooo! Sniff. . . . Nice ball," Johnny says. He pulls his wooden, metal-shafted, battered relic of a driver from his bag.

"Isn't that persimmon?" the mark asks incredulously.

"Yeah, genuine," Johnny replies sarcastically. "The only place you can get drivers like this these nowadays is in an antique store."

Johnny sneezes again. He shuffles through the bucket, squeezing and rejecting various balls, like he was picking grapefruit in a supermarket. He has handled enough range balls in his life to recognize a dead one. Selecting one to his liking, he puts it on the tee.

"Boy! You really got your ball out there," Foozler says. He wipes his nose with the back of his hand, and then wipes his hand on his pants. "Maybe I shouldn't have bet so much. . . ."

Johnny is not looking at the 250 sign, but staring beyond, at a point over the fence, out of the range. His father had drilled into him that the reason people have so much trouble with their drivers is that they stand there without a target in mind. With all their other clubs they have a clear idea of the distance they can hit, so form a mental picture of the shot in their mind. With the driver most people just stand up there and try to hit it as far as they can. You have got to have a plan, a target. Johnny concentrates on the cord grass beyond the fence.

"Give it a whack, old-timer," the mark smirks. "This ones for all the marbles. . . ."

Old-timer? Johnny is annoyed by the man's words. "I've only just turned fifty," he says. He thinks: maybe it's my hair, when I get to Junior's I will have Pigeon cut my hair. In all the years they had been together his wife had always cut Foozler's hair. He has not had a haircut since her illness and death. He had thought to go to a barber, but had been afraid he would not know what to say.

"Okay, so you're only fifty . . . hit the ball already. I gotta get back and wash up so I can take my wife out for dinner . . . I think I'll take her to a fancy place with all of your bucks."

"I hope you saved enough for a pizza. . . ." Johnny mutters as he takes his driver back. His mind is in a field covered with snow; his hands are bleeding; he remembers a swing key—hit the ball out of this fucking world.

Johnny's grip is gentle, like when he is holding his drumsticks. His stroke is smooth, like stroking a paint brush. His shoulder turn is not excessive, deceptively simple, so as not to upset his balance. His weight is on the balls of his feet. His club comes forward on the exact line on which it went back. His contact with the ball is firm, right on the sweet spot. His club goes out at the target. His finish is high, but controlled, not overly dramatic. His ball is turning over, starting out to the right, catching what little tail wind there is, then drawing back to the left.

Passing high over the 200 yard sign, Johnny's ball reaches its apogee, and begins a graceful descent. The red and white projectile is still thirty feet in the air when it clears the fence at the end of the range and disappears into the cord grass in the decaying marsh beyond.

"What the fuck?. . ." is all the mark can say. His eyes wide in disbelief, he stands in a torpor watching Johnny pick up his money.

Stuffing the bills in his pocket, Johnny hands the almost-full bucket of balls to his crestfallen opponent: "Here kid, you can hit these before you meet your wife for dinner . . . it looks like you could use a little more practice."

Johnny sits in his car counting his money. He is tired, and has come far enough for today. He decides to stay in Turtle Beach tonight, in a nice motel, not a mildewed, 1950s cabin like he slept in last night.

SIXTEEN

TURTLE BEACH IS an onion, a sixty mile long stretch of white sand and kitsch with no center. Continuing his drive down the traffic jam that is Route 17, Johnny passes an endless repetition of amusement parks, water slides, surf centers, golf shops, video game arcades, souvenir shops, restaurants, high-rise hotels, low-rise motels, and fantastically gaudy miniature golf courses.

The can-you-top-this miniature courses, with their giant elephants, mechanical lions, windmills, and talking Captain Kidds, fascinate Johnny, despite the fact that he has never been much of a fan of putting. A putt was just something you did to finish off a hole, preferably once, and certainly not more than twice on each hole. The reason Foozler hit his approach shots so close when he was on the high school team was that he hated putting. The only thing he hated more than putting was practicing putting.

Johnny's father had invented another of his sadistic games, this one to teach his son how to putt. He called it "21." The game's rules seemed to be very flexible, and changed every time the son showed the possibility of winning. Foozler recalls the rare day when he was leading by a score of 20 to 19.

* * *

The father was obviously the finer putter, in style as well as result. His many years of experience showed in the graceful manner in which he moved his club, straight back, and then straight forward, striking the ball as if the contact was only incidental to the clubs movement. Whereas, Johnny's pinched stabs always seemed to cause the ball to break right, or left. His father attributed this problem to his son's tendency to decelerate the putter head just before making contact with the ball.

Johnny disagreed. He felt his problem was reading too much into each putt. When he had begun playing he had just stroked the ball however he felt, and it went in most of the time. Then his father made him analyze each putt until he was bored. Always the teaching professional, his father not only explained the topography of the green, but included such details as when it had been cut last, the direction of the grain, and how a ball traveling from sunlight to shade might have its roll effected. Faced with such a surfeit of information, Johnny's mind went into overload, causing him to stroke out his usual little jab. The more he knew, the poorer his putting became, and the poorer his putting became, the more his father loaded on him.

Johnny remembers the time when sinking his three foot putt would have given him a victory, the first time ever to beat his father at "21." The man's putt had come up three inches short, and lay on his son's line.

"Putt out, or mark your ball," Johnny said eying his putt.

"We don't mark in '21,'" the father replied. "We're playing *stymies*. You've got to go around me . . . if you knock me in I get the game."

"What! This isn't Croquet," the son protested, something he never did. His father's word was a law to be obeyed. "We've never played *stymies* in '21.'"

"We always do. . . ."

"We never have. . . . You're always changing the rules."

With a breath laden with whiskey, his father began to recite in Johnny's ear: "These are the rules, as I explained them in the beginning, and they have always been the rules . . . only you are too dumb a kid to remember them."

"I'm dumb!" Johnny didn't give his father a chance to finish his screed. He gave his ball a mighty whack. His plan was to drive his ball into his father's with such force that it would fly over the cup. The scheme worked perfectly, except in reverse—with his father's ball spinning into the hole while Johnny's trickled by.

"Hey! That's '21.' I win! Nice game, Son. You almost got me . . . maybe next time." He shook Johnny's hand. In the old man's mind the contest was over, there was no room for protest.

* * *

Sitting in his car, munching on the last of the two large orders of French fries that was his dinner, Johnny watches and listens. Through his front window the arc lights reveal a capricious world of fake and real people playing at a game that loosely resembles golf. To get to their goal, the real people must hit putts under, around, or through the mechanical monsters, who resemble in some why or other the creatures loaded into Noah's Ark, and who whistle, flash lights, close doors, and operate other devious devices designed to impede a golf ball's progress. Seen from the wordless darkness of his car, the brightly lit miniature golf course is a screaming, kaleidoscopic, child-like scene; a place that unlocks the shadows of Foozler's memory.

In his early years, perhaps because of his parent's frequent traveling on the pro golf circuit, Johnny had had no friends. He was a social isolate, a child who felt different from everyone he knew. He took this sense of being different into an imaginary world, a world he could not share with the people around him. In bed at night, under the covers with a flashlight, he would secretly read whatever books he could get his hands on, often books too mature for him which his parents had put down. Early on, Johnny had begun a dialogue with fantasy, the characters in his books becoming the inhabitants of his real world.

Johnny kept notebooks then, hidden from his father, filled with stories he had written and illustrated with his drawings. He drew tiny people on cardboard, and then cut them out to act in the improvised plays he staged in the shoe-box theaters he constructed.

As a child Johnny had always wanted to play miniature golf, but his father would not allow him to, telling him that he was going to grow up to become a real golfer, and real golfers didn't play on miniature golf courses. Now Foozler realizes that if he was going to make it on the Tour he would have to be able to putt, something he had not practiced, except in the hallway of his trailer, in thirty years. But he hated the look of practice greens, with their multiple holes dug out all over, with little flag sticks sprouting out of them. No longer in the shadow of his father, he would practice wherever he liked. On a miniature golf course at least he would have fun.

Stuffing the change from a Twenty dollar bill into his pocket, Johnny heads for the first tee. He is waiting for the group ahead to finish when a rather attractive middle-aged woman seems to appear out of nowhere.

"Hi," she says. "Do you-all have a partner?"

"No," Johnny replies, looking around to be sure she is addressing him.

"Want to do around together?"

"Why not. . . ."

"Do you-all come here often?"

"No, this is my first time. What about you?"

"You might say I'm a regular. I live here in Turtle Beach. What else is there to do in the evening if you don't like country music, or play video games?"

"Oh, by the way . . . my name's Johnny . . . Johnny Foozler."

"Please to meet you-all, Johnny. My names Tridance . . . but my friends all call me Tridy."

She has neglected to give her last name. Johnny wonders if this is just southern informality, or does her remissness have a hidden meaning.

"Looks like it's our turn," Johnny says. "You go first. Since I've never played here before I'll watch what you do. . . ."

"It's simple. Like, all you-all have to do is hit your ball between the legs of those two turtles. But watch out. See . . . when one of the turtles' legs are open the other's are closed. So you've got to hit it just right or you'll get stuck."

The turtles must come first because they are the symbol of Turtle Beach, Johnny considers, or perhaps it is because they are the slowest, and therefore the farthest from Noah's Ark, which must be the final hole.

Tridance bends, rather than stoops, to place her ball. Behind her, Johnny observes the smooth roundness of her bottom, two cheeks peeking out daintily below her sheer white short-shorts, which are pulled up tightly into her crack, and that from the front clearly reveal the contours of her pudendum. She does not appear to be wearing any undergarments on her lower or upper body.

Though sprightly, Tridance is not young, middle-aged if you consider the average American woman lives until 79. Since the average American male is supposed to die at 72, Johnny, at fifty, is well past middle age. Nevertheless, since Tridance is apparently younger than he, in Johnny's eyes she is young, but too old for the heavy makeup on her face, and the extra long earrings that dangle under her teased out, bleached-blonde hair. Even in this artificial light Foozler can see clearly that the woman's legs are firm, slender, with no cellulite, and only the slightest hint of varicose veins. He wonders how she can walk in her high-heeled clogs, but agrees that they do turn out her calves nicely.

"Oh, darn. . . ." Tridy says, as the first turtle closes its legs, preventing her ball from passing under it. The ball rolls off to the side. "I'll never get it in from over there. Go ahead Johnny . . . *see if you can get it all the way in. . . .*" she says winking at him.

As Tridance turns toward Johnny the glare from an overhead light passes through her tan tank top, for a second it is transparent, providing him a glimpse of her breasts cantilevered beneath the thin fabric.

"I'll give it my best shot. Don't forget . . . I've never played this course before." Johnny, the drummer, is counting the rhythm of the mechanical creature: feet open-one-two-three, feet closed-one-two-three; with the sequence just the opposite for the far turtle. He will strike his ball at "closed-two" on the nearest tortoise. Foozler strokes his putt smoothly, no stab or jab, surprising himself. Concentrating on the slow motion of the turtle's feet, he has brought the club back in one, natural movement.

The ball clears the first turtle's legs and enters the carapace, emerging just in time to find the second turtle's leg-doors opening. Johnny's ball exits the second shell, and rolls past the hole. It ricochets off the sideboard and comes back to within six inches of the cup.

""Whooee! You-all did it!" Tridy shouts. "I've never seen anyone do two turtles before . . . and I've been coming to this here course since I was in junior high."

She takes two more shots to get through the first turtle, clears the second in one, and three more to finish, for a seven. While she is wiggling around, Johnny taps in for a two.

"You-all did it in two! That's an eagle . . . this hole's a par four," Tridy announces, using the little pencil to mark the card. "I've seen people make birdies before . . . but never an eagle. You are good. And you said you never played here before." She takes

Johnny's arm and leads him to the next hole, pressing her breasts firmly up against his elbow.

They play the subsequent holes with similar result, Johnny usually making par or birdie, and Tridy two or three over. Although Foozler does mess up on the hole with the alligator and takes a double. Tridy is delighted when she beats Johnny with a bogey, and gives him an unexpected kiss.

Foozler is pleased with his new companion. A vain man, he takes vicarious pleasure in the admiring glances she gets from the other men, especially when she bends over to place her ball, which she always does, presenting an ample view of her bum to those waiting behind, and a generous décolletage to those passing in front. However, the response to her attire is far from unanimous. One woman drags her husband away sibilating: "Shameless hussy. . . ." And a little girl is heard to whisper: "Mommy, I can see that lady's titties through her shirt!"

Despite the distractions going on around him, Foozler is putting well. He keeps reminding himself that it is the stroke that matters. If he keeps consistent his intuition, he hopes, will guide him when he arrives on a real golf course. With no mechanical alligators between him and the cup, he tells himself, putting should be a piece of cake.

The final hole is Noah's Ark, the supreme challenge. Not only must the player hit the ball up a steep ramp, but must also avoid the outstretched arm of a fearsome, motorized Noah, who guards the entrance to the vessel determined that golfers, or at least their balls, should not be allowed an easy survival of the flood. Behind this biblical robot, neon lightning bolts flash off and on, while recorded sounds of rain and thunder blare from a hidden speaker. Johnny is so taken by the fantasy that he holds out his palm and looks up at the sky.

"It's only a recording, silly. . . ." Tridy says, nudging him, never missing an opportunity to make body contact, her whole demeanor a semaphore of blatant sexual signals.

Tridy takes nine tries before getting to the top. Four times she is short, and four times she finds her ball batted back by Noah's karate chop.

"Oh, Johnny, I'm so bad . . . it's never taken me so long before. I bet you can get it up just like that," she squeals, rubbing up against him again, her breasts soft on his arm.

Her many tries has caused the group behind, a born-again Christian family, to have to wait. The father has been studying Tridy's "form" out of the corner of his eye; while the mother has self-righteously turned her two children around and, pointing to the night sky, is giving them a lecture about "our Lord Jesus in Heaven." They all turn back to watch Johnny putt, a person who has impressed them on the previous holes as being a true master of the game.

Not wanting to disappoint, Johnny has been carefully studying the robot Noah's karate chop. He not only intends to get up the ramp and past the descending hand, but plans to do it with such force, and at such an angle, that he will get around the corner, leaving himself a clear shot at the hole, which is up another level in the prow of the boat.

Johnny takes the putter back and through, sending the ball up the ramp at a fast pace. However, he has overestimated the needed force, and the ball arrives too soon. Striking Noah's lowered hand, it is repelled back down.

A shocked, "Ooooh!" goes up from the watchers.

Johnny steps back to appraise his mistake. Tridance moves away—no one snuggles up against a loser.

"I must have hit it too hard," Johnny says, scratching his head.

He tries again, the same angle, but with a little less force. The ball runs up the ramp, skips neatly under the descending hand, then bounces off the sideboard and disappears around the corner.

"Nice comeback," the Christian man says smiling.

"My hero. . . ." Tridy coos, giving Johnny another squeeze.

Holding onto Johnny's arm for balance, Tridy starts up the steps on her high-heel clogs.

Mr. Christian man bends over to place his ball. Though his head is down, his eyes are up, firmly focused on the ample cheeks displayed below Tridy's short-shorts.

"Keep your mind on the game, Maynard," his wife says, grabbing him by the collar and pulling him upright.

Once inside the ark, Tridy is even more impressed by Johnny's last shot. His ball has not only made it around the corner, but somehow managed to make it up the short ramp to the next level, where the cup is waiting.

"Wow! That was some shot . . . you *are* my hero. You-all deserve a big reward!" In the privacy of the ark, Tridy throws her arms around Foozler and presses hard against him. She puts her lips on his and, when Johnny accepts hers, darts her tongue into his mouth, rolling it around three times before pushing him away. "You sly devil," she says, as if Johnny had instigated the action.

A ball rockets up the ramp and lands at their feet. Could it be a warning from the Christian family?

"Well, I'm already lying nine . . . so I'm going to pick up," Tridance says. "You-all can play out if you like."

Johnny stands over his putt. Looking at the frayed carpet, he is reminded of the hallway in his trailer, where this all began not that many days ago. The distance is about twelve feet. He strokes the ball smoothly, almost casually; the ball finds the cup.

"Oh my gosh! That's a three. You made birdie after hitting Noah's hand! I can't believe it . . . you are good," Tridy proclaims, loud enough so that the Christians on the lower level can hear. "You-all deserve a reward after that. I know . . . let me buy you a drink," she says, trying to sound as if that had not been her plan from the beginning.

Johnny hesitates and then nods, as if it had not been his plan all along.

SEVENTEEN

BARRELING ALONG WILDLY in his huge, old Buick, Johnny is attempting to follow Tridance's sleek, white Porsche 911 down an inky two-lane highway. The evening sky has become cloudy, bloated, darkening and shutting out the light from above. Tridy is driving at great speed; she knows the road. His accelerator to the floor, Johnny is barely able to keep up with the fleeing vehicle ahead. He curses the weight, and the rattle, of the golf balls in his trunk. No longer seeing Johnny's headlights in her rearview mirror, Tridy slows her pace. Having found her man she does not want to lose him, at least not at moment.

Sudden flashes of light, heat lightning out over the ocean, illuminate the sky. Johnny catches fleeting glimpses of the landscape, its subtle beauty muted in grays and browns, and patches of dark green, hidden by jasmine, and honeysuckle, and oaks draped in Spanish moss.

Speeding past them, mansions built long ago appear as only a ghostly lighted glow at the end of a tree-lined driveway. The names on the gate signs hint at their historical importance: Ashley Hall, Brigade House, Charlotte Manor. A red light blinks on the left side of Tridy's car; then the entire backside lights up. She turns into a driveway marked "Sea Wind." The large, wrought-iron gate swings open automatically, and then closes behind them.

"Like my house?" Tridy asks, mixing herself a martini on the rocks. "Sorry I took so long, but I had to forage the kitchen for your cranberry juice, I never go in there, and it's the housekeeper's day off. In fact no one is here for the rest of tonight but us. . . ."

Foozler catches the gist of her remark. He is looking at the Picasso oil painting over one of the couches. It is real. He ran his hand over the surface when she was out of the room. The collection of modern paintings and the contemporary furniture seem out of place in this antebellum structure.

Sensing Johnny's question, Tridy supplies the answer: "The house has been in my family for generations, but the Yankees took away all the furniture during the war. My mother left it to me because I was the only child. She was married to a contractor from New York City. And I don't mean a contractor like we have down here . . . where you-all buy yourself a pick-up truck and hire a couple of coloreds and call yourself a contractor. My daddy built skyscrapers. His men even worked on The World's Fair out in Flushing. I remember going up there to see it. But mostly I stayed down here in the South . . . going to fancy boarding schools."

Tridy sits down on a black leather couch, stretching out her lean brown legs. Johnny notices she has changed out of her previous outfit and is now wearing only a red silk robe, and no shoes. The lacquer on her toe nails matches her robe.

She gives her martini a final stir with her little finger and raises her glass to Johnny: "Cheers!" With her free hand, she pats the couch next to her: "Stop looking at the pictures . . . come sit down here next to me."

Johnny complies, but his eyes are still on the artworks covering the walls. "Nice paintings you got here. I really like art. When I was a kid I thought maybe I was going to be an artist . . . I even won a contest. But my father told me that all artists are fags. These pictures are all real, aren't they?"

"I should hope they're the genuine article . . . my daddy's brother was an art dealer in New York. He used to take my parents to auctions, where they bought all this stuff. My father didn't care much for it then, but his brother convinced him it was a good investment . . . so he just kept buying. Mostly he had everything in storage. When he died my mother and me moved back down here. Mother had the pictures packed and sent down, and then put them up all over the house."

Tridy takes a sip of her drink, sets it back down, and then swivels her body around, depositing her legs on Johnny's lap. She gives her robe a half-hearted tug closed. "Oh Johnny, my feet hurt so much . . . would you be a dear and massage them for me?"

Foozler sets down what's left of his cranberry juice and begins to rub Tridy's feet. They feel cold. He notes her toenails not only match with her robe, but also her fingernails and lipstick.

"Ooooooh . . . that's so good," she purrs.

Johnny is in no hurry to get to what seems like the obvious conclusion to the evening. He is enjoying the paintings, if only from a distance. He will prolong the conversation: "I'm sorry about your father. How did he die?"

"My father? Did I say he died? . . . I should have said he was murdered . . . at least we think so, but no one has ever been found guilty. There had been trouble brewing over the years between him and some of his workers, and the union. Some people said my father was involved with the Mafia. One day he went out to inspect a job, and a whole hopper of cement fell on him. After that his brother told mom and me it would be safer if we moved back down here, to what used to be our winter home."

"Oh, I'm sorry. . . ." Johnny says, embarrassed he asked the question, but unwilling to leave the subject. "So what happened to your mother?"

"About a year after we moved here she was killed by a hit-and-run driver. They never found that person either. That's when I got married. It was either that or live in this big, old house with my crazy aunt." Tridy realizes now that she has mentioned she is married; something Johnny has suspected from the beginning. Nervously, she takes a pack of cigarettes from a cabinet next to the couch and puts one in her mouth, offering one to Johnny.

"No thanks . . . I quit years ago."

Tridy lights up and takes a long, deep drag. She exhales, letting the smoke curl around her tongue.

Johnny sneezes.

"I'm sorry," Tridy says, snuffing out her cigarette in the ashtray.

"Oh, you didn't make me sneeze . . . I'm just getting over a cold."

"That's okay. I shouldn't be smoking either. It's just that around here everyone does it . . . we grow the stuff down here you know. It's almost as if you're unpatriotic if you-all don't smoke."

"What about your husband?" Johnny asks—tiptoeing back to the subject she was hoping to avoid.

"What about my husband?" she says, a hint of anger in her voice.

"...Does he smoke?" Johnny asks, retreating.

"Don't worry . . . he's not about to come barging in on us, he's out of town. Besides, there's an alarm on the gate."

"That's not what I meant. . . ."

"He's a state senator. He stays in an apartment over in the capitol when the legislature is in session. He fucks his secretary, and I give the servants time off so they can't spy on me."

"Well that's nice to know. When you said to follow you I thought we were just heading for a bar . . . or someplace like that," Foozler says, feeling more relieved now that he understands the situation.

Tridy again rummages in the little cabinet: "Want to do some coke?"

"No thanks, but I'll have some more cranberry juice . . . if you have anymore."

"Don't be silly," Trudy says, producing a plastic bag of white powder. "I meant cocaine . . . ever tried it?"

"Yeah, I've tried it, I've tried everything, I used to even shoot heroin," Johnny says resignedly, turning up his sleeves to reveal his scarred arms, blue veins still bearing the traces of needle marks. "I used to tour with a rock band . . . we did everything. I've been through three rehabilitation programs. That's why I don't do anything now."

"You still fuck . . . I hope," Tridy says coyly, swinging her legs back up on Johnny's lap.

"Oh yeah, sometimes . . . with the right person," Johnny replies, mimicking her coyness. "And there are those who have said that I'm very good at it . . . maybe even better than I am at miniature golf."

"That I will have to see for myself. But first, let's have a swim," Tridy says. She jumps up and, taking his hand, leads him out a set of French doors to the pool.

The wind waves the water in the illuminated pool, causing the tessellated animal at the bottom to shimmer and dance.

"Gross isn't it . . . the tiger I mean. My husband had it put there. It's his university's mascot. He even had the tiles made up in a special shade of orange to match the school colors."

Foozler turns back to look at Tridy, but she has already doffed her robe and is standing naked on the edge of the diving board, the blue from the waves reflecting on her body.

"Well . . . come on, take your clothes off. You didn't think we were going to swim in bathing suits did you?" With a perfect dive, Tridy knifes into the water.

Johnny sits on a chaise lounge and tugs off his sneakers. He undresses slowly. Despite all his bravado and vanity Foozler is a shy person. His manners have always made him uncomfortable, about appearing naked in front of other people, the same reserve that caused him embarrassment about taking his socks off back in George's Restaurant. When he was young his mother had always walked around the house in the nude, and later so had his wife and son. He had always undressed in the bathroom, and worn pajamas or underpants to bed, even in the hot summer.

Johnny sits on the edge of the pool, his legs crossed, with one foot dangling in the water. He is also afraid to admit that he is not a good swimmer, and never goes in over his head. He watches Tridy glide through the water, an excellent swimmer. She jackknives under the water and splashes up in front of him.

"Aren't you coming in?" Tridy asks, standing on the bottom. Her breasts bob in the water about even with Johnny's legs; she begins rubbing them on his knees. "Well . . . I showed you mine . . . aren't you going to show me yours? If you-all got one," she says, affecting a coquettish, little girl's voice. Tridy grabs Johnny's legs, prying them apart, revealing his organ. "Wow! Look at that . . . I think I've hit the jackpot! No wonder you keep it hidden, if word got out every horny woman in the Carolinas would be lined up outside your motel room."

The size of his nose and the size of his penis are two things Johnny has always been self-conscious about. Age has filled out his face, seeming to reduce the dimension of his nose. However, the years have also caused his hips to disappear and his testicles to shrink, leaving his penis a giant sausage protruding from his midsection. Tridy is fondling this thing, licking the end with her tongue. It is beginning to swell. She takes it in her mouth. The nipples on her wet breasts, pressing into Johnny's legs, are becoming hard.

"Not yet!" Tridy pulls away. "You've got to swim first," she says pulling him into the water.

Taken by surprise, Johnny goes down, under. Despite his arm flailing, he keeps going down, his lungs filling with water, the taste of chlorine in his mouth, chlorine burning his eyes and nose. He trashes about, struggling, fighting for his life. His knees hit the bottom. Tridy's hands are under his armpits, her supple body pressing against his, lifting him out of the water. Johnny is coughing, fluid pouring from his mouth, nose, and ears.

"Stand up you silly goose!" Tridy exclaims, pounding him on the back to help drain the liquids. "The water here is only five feet deep on this end. Why didn't you tell me you can't swim?"

She wipes his eyes with her wet hand. Johnny has stopped coughing now, breathing deeply. She takes his head in her hands and places a kiss on Johnny's open mouth. Her tongue finds his.

The diffuse whiteness of a coastal morning filters through the white lace curtains. As often happens after a lustful night, the participants are not too eager to get out of bed. Everything is quiet and cozy. Tridy lies there discovering parts of Johnny that she overlooked in her rush to get him upstairs. Amidst sleepy talk, time passes unnoticed. Then the telephone rings.

"Hello, Dear . . . Yes, things are fine over here; how are they over there? I mean are you getting all you legislations passed, or whatever? . . . They didn't pass your damn extension bill? . . . oh, your Dam Extension Bill. Well that's too bad, maybe next session . . . No, I'm okay . . . of course I miss you . . . No, you know I don't like it over there, besides the apartment's too small, and you're always at some meeting or other . . . No, I don't want to go to the university on the weekend for a basketball game, you-all know how I hate basketball . . . besides, I find it rather silly, all those old men dressed up like tigers . . . No, I'm fine. I'm always fine . . . This afternoon? I'm playing golf . . . Yes, I like golf . . . No, that's because you and your friends take the game too seriously, and they always cheat, and so do their wives . . . No, not at the club, someplace else . . . I don't know where yet . . . No, just by myself . . . No, really, I just decided to go, to get out of the house . . . Okay, I gotta go too . . . What? . . . Yes, I love you too, Dear. Bye."

Tridy hangs up the telephone she has been holding with her left hand, all the while fondling Johnny's member with her right. "Let's fuck one more time before we go," she says. Rolling her naked body on top of his she fumbles with Johnny's half-erect penis, rubbing it up and down her moistening slit.

She dangles her breasts in Johnny's face, the flesh shifting and swaying as she moves on top of him, drawing one, then the other of her nipples across his mouth. Foozler's tongue darts in a circle around the areola, wetting the pigment with his saliva, watching it darken, and become erect.

Lovemaking in the daytime can be a real test for two older persons living an illusion. Darkness is flattering and can hide a multitude of faults, both physical and emotional. Nothing can be hidden in the cruel, analytical light of morning. Suddenly, as if for no reason, the frisson passes. Tridy breaks off her encounter, rolls over on her back, and stares at the ceiling. After a moment she gets up and opens the door to the bedroom terrace. A gentle breeze rustles the curtains. Beyond is the sun-dappled ocean, and the cloud bloated sky teeming with gulls.

"I live here," Tridy blurts out, "at the top of the pyramid in terms of comfort and privilege . . . but what is the point of the whole thing?" Without warning, she begins to unpack her bag of emotions. "A woman can survive anything . . . accept anything. She can learn to be content, or at least to exist without the need to shout and rebel, in almost any circumstances."

Her voice is chocking. Johnny can see tears forming in Tridy's eyes. He was not expecting this gigantic mood swing. He wonders what has brought this on. She is not the laughing, flirtatious, free-spirit he met yesterday.

"Most women in this world are prisoners," Tridy continues, "living lives of misery, boredom, degradation, frustration, and unhappiness. Yet, we don't have the energy to crawl out of our own personal cells. We dream of escape. But to where?"

Outside the clouds have backed up, blotting out the sun. The breeze blowing in has become colder. Lying on his back next to her, Johnny wonders why Tridy's emotions are suddenly being unloaded on him. Does she see him as a way out? He is just a passerby, a traveler with his own journey, his own problems to solve. He does not see her appearing anywhere later in his story.

EIGHTEEN

FOR MOST OF the past week Johnny Foozler has been dallying here in Turtle Beach, hustling marks at the driving ranges in between servicing the senator's wife. You ask what has happened to his goal. Wasn't he on his way to Florida to try out for the Senior Tour? The truth is Johnny has become faint-hearted, painfully aware that the 78s and 82s he has been posting while dabbling at golf with Tridy are hardly the numbers that would get him past all the other "mulligan boys" trying to qualify for the tournament on any given Monday morning.

Moreover, at this moment Foozler is more concerned with his heart than his golf game; not his physical heart, but his emotional one. Johnny's heart beats for everyone. Yet, in his heart of hearts, he fears that in this whole wide world there is no heart that beats for him.

From that very first evening he met Tridance, Johnny had felt tied to this woman—that they were more than just casual acquaintances having an affair. He had told himself that he was merely a passerby. But what was Tridy's mysterious affinity? Perhaps their vice was beginning to overpower him. Or was he attracted to her unhappiness, without hope and without possibility of escape, a situation which was not unlike his own.

They see each other every day and every evening. Tridy comes looking for him everywhere. She waits for him outside his motel. She waits for him in the parking lot of the driving range. She does not ask for anything, merely speaks with her eyes. It is enough for him to look at her to understand. Johnny smiles his usually silly or convulsed smile; and never asks for anything either, just waits. Tridance pouts, that sullen kiss-trap she must have learned from watching the movies popular when she was a little girl. He is unable to resist her, and she cannot send him away.

Johnny's presence acutely complicates Tridance's social situation. They frequently are spotted by many of her husband's friends, to whom Johnny is introduced as an "old classmate from high school." Despite the raised eyebrows, Tridy does nothing to rid herself of Johnny. She has taken to saddened effusions of love, which wrench Foozler's heart. Wrinkling up her mouth as a child might do when it was about to cry she would plead with him: "If you loved me Johnny you would take me away with you. . . ."

Having spent the morning hustling hackers, Johnny returns to his motel to shower. He is meeting Tridy for lunch. He heads for the office to tell the clerk he plans to stay yet another day. In a rack out front he sees a copy of the local paper, The Turtle Beach Times-Leader. It is the headline that has caught his eye: Is Senator Tied In With Mafia? There is a picture of the senator, the same face in the photograph next to Tridy's bed. He buys a paper and goes back to read it. The phone rings. He knows it is Tridance, so does not answer. When he finishes the article, Johnny begins hurriedly packing his bags. He knows that it is too late in his life to accomplish all that he would yet like to do—nevertheless, he would still like the chance. After loading his car, he stops at the front desk and checks out. The clerk hands him a telephone message, which Johnny puts in his pocket without reading it. He gets in his car and drives quickly out of town.

A glance in his rearview mirror confirms what Johnny has suspected for several miles. The car he believes to be following him is still there. Foozler has never had the occasion to be tailed before, only seen it done in movies. Should he speed up, or wait until he is temporarily out of sight and swerve down a side road? When would they start shooting? So far they, whoever they are, were acting with professional discretion, staying just far enough back to not be observed, yet close enough so he is aware that they have been following him.

Although the highway still displays the same route number as the one he drove into town on, the way out has turned into a shoulder less two-lane road, closely lined by pine trees, and totally devoid of amenities. The strip malls and surf shops have been replaced by small towns composed mostly of mobile homes, and shacks with front porches jutting onto the roadway where people sit watching the traffic pass by. The towns appear to be populated with whites on one end and blacks on the other, the only common point being a combination grocery store and gas station.

For the past half hour Johnny has had a growing urge to pee, a persistent problem he suffers despite his religious consumption of cranberry juice. Also, the car's gas gauge is nudging empty. He hadn't planned on leaving town just yet, so hadn't filled the tank. However, the small grocery, gas, and fireworks stores, with the hangers-on sitting out front, which are all that he has been passing, seem to him distinctly hostile. Perhaps it is just his imagination, a Northerner's paranoia. He wishes his license plate did not read NEW YORK, or at least had an asterisk that said "upstate" below it. Moreover, the large black car with the darkened windows, the kind the Mafia guys always used in gangster movies, was still following him. No matter how much he slows down, sometimes as low as thirty-five, it continues to trail behind. At stop lights it lurks back two or three car lengths, so that he is unable to see the occupants inside. As best as Johnny can make out, there appear to be two men in the front seat. They are wearing sunglasses, even though the day has become quite gray and clouded over.

At last he spies a likely place up ahead. Not only does it appear a little cleaner, it doesn't have a fireworks sign, and there is a sheriff's car parked out front. No one is going to harm him in front of a sheriff—or are they? Tridy's husband is a state senator, Johnny remembers, don't sheriffs work for the state; or is it the county? It is too late; he has signaled his turn and started to pull in. He can't change his mind, it would look too suspicious.

Johnny rolls up to the pump and gets out. It is self-service. Not being very mechanical, he hates to pump his own gas. All these pumps seem to operate differently and confuse him, even under normal circumstances. Fiddling with the lever, Foozler tries to bring the pump to life. Across the street, the black car has pulled over and parked quite conspicuously, its dark windows closed, the motor running to keep the air conditioner working. A stocky man, in the sharply pressed, tan uniform of a county sheriff swaggers out of his car. The radio on his belt crackles as he walks slowly over to John Foozler.

"You-all from Nooo Yawkh?" the officer asks.

Johnny sees his face reflected in the sheriff's mirrored sunglasses; he tries not to look terrified. He wants to answer: No, I just borrowed this car from a friend in Nooo Yawkh, I'm actually from, Birmingham, or Beaufort, or Biloxi, any place farther south that would turn this cracker into a Northerner. He wants to get in one smart aleck remark while he can. They're not going to kill him for screwing a senator's wife are they? Or maybe it's that ticket he skipped out on in Pennsylvania? They have all that stuff on computers nowadays, and they're all connected aren't they? "Yes, Officer," Johnny responds guardedly. "I'm from New York," adding, "*upstate* New York."

"Well now, maybe you-all don't do that back up there in upstate Nooo Yawk . . . but down hair we-all have a law that says you're supposed to signal before you-all make a turn . . . now when you-all turned in hair I didn't see no light flashin' on the front a yer car. . . ."

Johnny glances across the highway. The black car is still waiting for him. It is not as big as he first imagined it to be, not a limo or anything but a mid-sized American car. "Oh, I'm sorry, officer . . . I thought that I did signal . . . maybe the light is broken, or something."

Johnny reaches in turns on the key, and them presses down the turn signal. He walks around front with the sheriff. "Well . . . look at that, it isn't working. It must have just happened. . . ." Johnny lies.

"It's probably just the bulb . . . you're not illegal during the day . . . if you-all use hand signals. So I'm gonna let you-all go without giving ya a ticket," the friendly sheriff says, adjusting his sun glasses, and stuffing his book of citations into his back pocket.

"Oh, thank you, officer." Johnny starts toward the pump. He's in a hurry. His need to urinate has become urgent.

"Hold on there just a minute, sonny . . . you-all know yer hand signals don't ya. I just wanna make sure," the sheriff says. He holds out his left arm straight up. "What's this here one mean?"

"Right turn," Johnny replies eagerly.

"Okay . . . now what's this here one?" the sheriff asks, holding his arm straight out.

"Left turn."

"Well . . . you-all sure are a smart fellow. Now there's one more you gotta know before I let you go. . . ." The sheriff holds out his hand, palm upwards.

Johnny thinks for a moment: speed up? It's raining? What can it mean? Then the correct answer flashes in his mind. He reaches in his wallet and takes out a twenty dollar bill.

"It was only a ten dollar signal, son," but we don't make no change down hare," the sheriff says, smiling and crumpling the bill into his pocket. "I notice though that all you fellers from Nooo Yawk are big spenders, must be the high price of things back up there. You-all have a nice day now."

Hurrying through the store, Johnny is pointed to the toilet in the back. It is not as clean as he hoped, but he is not planning to spend much time there. It has a window up high that looks out onto a wood. For a moment he thinks to jump out; to make a run for it, but the window is painted shut. Someone knocks on the door. "Just a minute," Foozler says. When he comes out there is no one there.

Johnny picks up a bottle of cranberry juice on his way to the counter. A man in a shiny suit, wearing sunglasses is heading out the door, unwrapping the cellophane from a pack of cigarettes he has just purchased. He heads for the black car across the road. Foozler pays the cashier, a huge black man, affable, but he notices a shotgun leaning next to him under the counter.

"I see Sheriff Stuckey done got you-all good. . . ." he chuckles, handing Johnny his change.

"Yeah . . . my turn signal light is broken. . . ."

"Don't make no difference . . . he seen you-all comin' down the road with yer out-o-state license. He was fixin' ta follow ya until you done somethin' . . . probably would of stopped ya for speedin' before ya got to the county line . . . if you-all were or weren't. Business is slow. Not many strangers passin' through here anymore since they finished that Interstate."

"Oh, thanks, makes me feel better knowing it was nothing personal," Johnny jokes. "Say, see that there car across the street . . . have you ever seen it around here before?"

"No, can't say that I have . . . like I thought at first they might be friends of yourn. Don't look like they's up to no good though . . . that's why I got out the shotgun, ya see. . . ."

Johnny pulls his old Buick back out onto the highway, after a few seconds the black car follows closing the space between the two vehicles, apparently wanting him to be sure they are still there. Foozler thinks to head west, and pick up the Interstate. There would be more traffic, and he would feel safer, but that would be a little out of the way to his son's house, which is where he is headed.

Foozler is beginning to feel hunger pains in his stomach. He also has the nervous urge to hit golf balls. Lately the two needs seem to come together—the need to hit oftentimes being greater than the need to eat. He sees a sign for a driving range, but it is off the main road. Johnny decides to pass it up. He is not about to turn down a side road with the black car still following him. He is starting to get nervous, not about the thugs, but because he has not had his morning fix, that is, his morning bucket of balls. Johnny is having that same withdrawal feeling he used to have when he was a junkie; only now he needs to hit golf balls, a small bucket in the morning, a large in the afternoon, and a jumbo before going to bed. Jeez, Johnny thinks, if only I could pull over and do a small bucket in that field. His hands are beginning to shake.

Outside Georgeville Johnny takes a left at the steel mill, remembering to signal with his hand out the window, and detours through the historic downtown. He rolls the window down. The tree-lined streets are rich with antebellum mansions whose well-manicured gardens give off the sweet smell of magnolia, damp with the ozone from a brief thunderstorm that has recently passed through. The temperature is nearing eighty. Johnny finds it hard to believe that just a few days ago he was driving through a blizzard. He is not a snow-lover by any means, and would be happy here, if it weren't for the hired killers he is sure are chasing him.

Left at the paper mill, his hand signaling out the window again, he takes in the pungent smell of pulp as he heads over the causeway. Past the airport the road widens into a dual four lane highway with a concrete divider, but there is little traffic. Johnny remembers the road from another time. It goes for a long way, through a national forest. The black car is still behind him. Foozler regrets not having stopped for something to eat in Georgeville. If he is going to die, he should at least die with a full stomach. He remembers a half-eaten bag of popcorn underneath the seat. He pulls the bag out and takes a handful.

Fifteen minutes pass. Johnny has been driving at 55MPH; maybe the speed limit here is 65, but there are no signs. A few cars and trucks have passed him by, but his stalker always remains back a few car lengths.

Watching in his rearview mirror, Foozler sees his pursuer suddenly speed up, closing the gap between them. Have they grown tired of shadowing him, or was it their plan all along to wait for this relatively deserted stretch of road? The other car is in the fast lane now, passing him. Do they mean to run him off the road? Or will it be a bullet through the window to the brain? Johnny jams on his brakes, ducking down below the window ledge. His car slides off the roadway, spinning into a ditch, its rear tires wallowing in the soft mud. Lifting his head cautiously above the dashboard, Foozler watches as the dark vehicle rapidly disappears down the highway.

Clearly shaken, Johnny gets out and surveys his situation, keeping one eye on the road in case the black car should return. His own car has carved a deep grove in the wet shoulder, and is quietly sinking even deeper into the quagmire. He calculates it will take him some time to get it out, especially with his bald tires—if he can get it out at all.

Out on the highway cars speed by in blissful indifference. To their occupants Johnny is just a man with an urgent need, which is what he has. He jumps across the watery ditch and finds a bush to relieve himself behind. Standing there, with legs apart, carefully spraying downwind so as not to wet his trouser legs, Johnny peers over the foliage, watching the road for the return of his stalkers.

He hops back over the ditch to his car. His fear of the would-be assassins has passed. If they were coming back, he reasons, they would have done so by now. The brief time that has gone by has already made the incident seem like a fantasy in his mind. It was all merely coincidental, Johnny tells himself. The men in the car were not following him—they just happened to be heading in the same direction at the same time. The man in the shiny suit just happened to need a pack of cigarettes at that moment. Why would a state senator be concerned about a nobody like him? To think so is just to flatter himself, Johnny rationalizes. Tridy is probably, at this very moment, screwing some other passerby she picked up at lunch when he failed to show up. Why are his hands still shaking then?

Looking around, Johnny sees that he is standing near an open field. There are trees at the other end. He has tied a white handkerchief onto his antenna; someone will report his distress somewhere up the line, and a tow truck will soon appear to tug him out. All that he has to do now is wait. He opens his trunk and unloads a small bucket of balls. What better way to pass the time. The field is relatively short, so he takes his wedge and begins to hit.

Returning to his stuck car, his craving satisfied, Johnny is disappointed to see not a tow truck standing next to the old Buick, but a large dog. As he comes closer Foozler is surprised to find the animal is not a dog but a small cow, a calf. The bovine creature tries to poke its nose into the trunk when Johnny opens it. Foozler has no knowledge of cows, so has no way of judging the calf's age, or sex. However, even to his untrained eye, the animal looks very young, almost as if it has only been born a short while ago. Johnny steps out on the road and looks up and down. There are no farms, not even houses, as far as he can see. He wonders if the animal might have fallen from a truck, although it doesn't appear to be injured.

"Hey, little fellow . . . or girl? Where did you come from?" Johnny says to the calf using a baby-talk voice, the way one talks when trying to be understood by the young of any species—be it kittens, puppies, or human beings.

The calf does not answer. It lifts one of the range balls out of the trunk with its mouth and begins to chew.

"Hey . . . bad! Not good for cows . . . give it here," Johnny says trying to wrestle the ball from the calf's jaws. He has never put his hand in any kind of animal's mouth before.

The calf, either understanding Johnny or realizing that golf balls are hard and do not taste very good, lets the red and white pill drop from its mouth back onto the pile, and starts licking Johnny's hand with its soft pink tongue.

"Hey, are you hungry there? . . ." Johnny hesitates; the animal will need a neutral name as he doesn't know its gender. "Bovie!" he announces to no one, considering himself clever for having concocted this name from the word bovine.

"Here Bovie, try some of this. . . ." Johnny says, pulling up some grass and dandelions from alongside the road, he holds it out to the calf, who takes it from his hand.

Foozler has just committed the two cardinal sins one can make when meeting with stray animals—rules that I must admit apply mainly to dogs and cats, but also can be fatal when dealing with cows. Having named the animal, and given it food, it is now his until, hopefully, the creatures true owner can be found. Johnny, unfortunately, is not aware of these consequences.

Slamming down the trunk lid, Foozler pats his animal on the head: "Sorry, gotta go now, Bovie . . . you'd better stay away from this road . . . go on, go back to where you came from. . . ."

Bovie follows Johnny around to the driver's side; the white handkerchief is still tied to the antenna. No one has stopped, no tow truck has come. He wonders if it is his New York license plate. He will have to drive out himself, after all he does have the weight of the golf balls in the trunk. As he starts to get in the driver's seat Bovie sticks his/her head in after him.

"Go, Bovie! Scoot! I told you to stay away from the road." Johnny gets out and pushes and tugs the recalcitrant ruminant around to the other side, where it stands looking into the passenger side window.

Back in the car, Johnny starts the engine and pops the transmission into drive. All this manages to do is produce a banshee-like whining from the right rear tire. He rocks the car backward and forward using his best Yankee stuck-in-the-snow technique. This causes little progress in Carolina mud—convincing Johnny that he is hopelessly stuck.

Intent on freeing his vehicle, Foozler does not notice the large, black limousine appear in his side view mirror. Approaching Johnny's car, the limo slows imperceptibly, as if the driver has momentarily taken his foot off the accelerator, and then speeds off down the highway.

The attractive, smartly-dressed woman in the back, seated next to the distinguished-looking, but portly man, had involuntarily blurted out a name, which had caused the driver to decelerate momentarily, causing her husband to ask her what she meant.

Quickly catching herself the woman had replied: "Oh, it's nothing. . . ."

Being that they were running late, and the driver had received no other instruction he hurried on.

"Are you sure it's nothing? You said the name Johnny. We don't have any friends in common named Johnny," the man seated next to the woman muttered disdainfully. Putting aside the newspaper that had occupied him ever since they left Turtle Beach—after all the headline article was about him—the senator poured himself a bourbon from the bar. He did not offer his wife anything. He took a sip from his drink, placed it back on the little shelf, and picked up the receiver of his car phone.

At that moment the wheels of Johnny's stuck vehicle, having dug a channel down to firm gravel, begin crawling forward. Foozler, who has been looking rearward, intent on the sounds the wheels were making, turns around. Standing in front of the car, its little head barely visible above the hood is Bovie. He slams on the brakes. The Buick grinds to a halt and instantly sinks back into the soft swale.

NINETEEN

SENATOR WILLIAM ROBERT Plantigrade, better known to his constituency as "Billy Bob," had not planned to return to his house in Turtle Beach on this day. His wife had told him earlier she had no interest in accompanying him to The Fortress Military College for the annual review of the cadet corps, at which he was to be the guest of honor. He had been awarded this distinction for having pork-barreled a good sum of taxpayer's money to the college for a new stadium, part of a plan to revitalize the school's football program and "put The Fortress back on the map."

The drive from the senator's apartment in the capital to Charlesboro, where the college is located, was a little over two hours. Detouring over to Turtle Beach would add another hour. The distances were too close to make his airplane useful, as the trip would actually take longer when you added in the time spent driving to the airport and boarding the plane.

Years ago Billy Bob Plantigrade would have flown anyway, just to make a show of his importance. But the voters weren't buying that program anymore. They wanted economy, cut-backs, and lower taxes. When you went out to the hustings these days you had better take a bus, and bring a few country-western singers along with you. Billy Bob had let his full-time pilot go three years ago. Since then, some of the replacement pilots he had hired looked like they weren't old enough to drive a car, and flew like they had learned on a videogame, which they probably had.

The senator had a pilot's license, and in the old days it was good for at least one news story every election: "Former War Hero Plantigrade Flies Around State Campaigning." Yes, that was the way the papers wrote about Billy Bob back then. He had flown observation planes in Viet Nam, even been shot at once. However, he never mentioned the fact that on one mission he fouled up so badly that he almost got a whole platoon wiped out by friendly fire. Fortunately his mistake was discovered before the jet fighters he had summoned dropped their napalm bombs, but not before they had strafed the area, killing three Marines.

After that Plantigrade was assigned to flying VIPs and newspaper columnists back and forth to the front. It was at this duty that he developed his skills working with politicians and journalists, an ability that served him well in his later political career. Billy Bob can legally still fly, although his skills have deteriorated considerably. He even has a current Airman's Medical Certificate bestowed on him by a doctor who is an old fraternity brother. However, he has a hard time complying with the "eight hour from bottle to throttle" rule.

The newspapers these days were less kindly to Billy Bob. Today's front page article alleging that he was tied in with the mob, had sent him scurrying back to Turtle Beach, where the story had come from, before heading down to Charlesboro for the military review.

The senator had been blindsided by the allegations in the newspaper. The fact that the Times-Leader was owned by a close friend of his biggest rival, who he had beaten in the last election, did not make what little information they had dug up any less credible. He had already talked to his lawyers about a possible lawsuit. The biggest item on his mind at the moment was "damage control."

Several of Billy Bob's aides had warned him about an out-of-town reporter, who had been hanging around for the past month, asking questions, and doing a doing a lot of research in the public records over in the capital. It had something to do with an investigation going on in New Jersey. But the senator was sure he was above reproach, or at least had carefully covered his tracks. He may have taken a little payola now and then from the wrong people for the wrong reasons, but everybody in politics did it. He would get this flap behind him. He was popular with the voters. There had even been talk about bigger things—perhaps sending him up to Washington.

The plot of Senator Billy Bob's life so far had followed that progression from fantasy to reality that has been portrayed as "The Great American Dream." A Christian young man of promise, from good, but humble origins, works his way through college, The Fortress, and then joins the Marines, returns from a bloody war, finishes law school, assails the halls of the capital, climbs the ladder of politics, and gives form to his image of government. Then, after years as a notorious bachelor, marries a young, rich, and beautiful woman, and makes his way in the best society. In his own lifetime his name has been placed on bridges and public schools. And now this happens—some muckraking journalist from up north, no doubt hungry for a Pulitzer Prize, is trying to take him down.

As soon as Billy Bob had finished reading the article this morning in his office over in the capital, he had telephoned Tridance to tell her he was coming for her. He needed her at his side. He needed her to show the voters that although they had no children, they were still a family: that the rumors his wife was sleeping around back home while he was seducing his female staff were not true. He also needed her at his side because the president of the college had specifically asked that he bring along "his beautiful wife." The Fortress had been getting a lot of bad press lately, especially in the Northern papers, because of the harassing given to the first female members of the corps of cadets. The president wanted a few women up there on the reviewing stand alongside the "good old boys."

The senator especially needed Tridance now that the papers were claiming he had links to organized crime. It would hurt her, he knew, but he would have to drag out her past, to spread it in the papers. A husband who has a wife whose parents were murdered by gangsters didn't play ball with the mob. This was something the voters would believe, a melodramatic fact that if played up correctly could overshadow any other things that might be dug up to the contrary. However, when Billy Bob had called home early this morning the cleaning lady had answered and told him his wife had already gone out.

The senator sent two of his men ahead in another car to find Tridance and bring her home. They had done this before and knew the places she frequented. And Billy Bob had many friends among the bartenders and restaurant owners who were more than happy to inform him on what Tridy had been up to. Checking around the two men learned that she had made a reservation for two at the

Blue Dolphin. They reported this to the senator, who tried to call Tridy on her cell phone, which she refused to carry, saying that she didn't want to be bothered all the time. The men learned from the headwaiter that Tridance had been in several days previous with a rather scruffy man with a New York accent. He had seen the two of them leave in separate cars, the man driving a beat up old Buick, with a New York license plate. On his way home the headwaiter had noticed the same car parked at the Sea Mermaid Motel.

Contacted in his limo, the now en route senator ordered his men to go to the Sea Mermaid, and if they found the fellow from New York there to follow him and see what he was up to. Billy Bob was convinced that this stranger had perhaps played fast and loose with his wife so that he might obtain information about his dealings from her.

Arriving home, the senator had not found his wife there. He called the Blue Dolphin and was told she had left some time ago, without eating, after apparently waiting for someone who had not come. He walked around the house but none of the staff were there either, Mrs. Plantigrade having given them the rest of the day off as she was planning to bring Johnny back for a swim.

Slightly panicked, but more annoyed, Billy Bob poured himself a bourbon. He sat down and mentally began to draw up a list of his virtues. This was a technique he had acquired early in his life at a tent prayer meeting, and always found helpful when he was feeling down. Like a child, he took joy in what he regarded as his small, but certain riches. He knew he was facing a crisis in his life, but was confident that he would—as he had done so many times in the past with the help of the Lord—come away renovated, refreshed, and released. He was sure he was entering a new period in his life. He had a bird-witted, or so he thought, but attractive wife, who despite her occasionally sleeping around, worshiped him, or so he believed, which gave him carte blanc to do whatever he felt like when he was over in the capital.

His health was good, except for his stomach. His doctor had told him to cut back on his drinking. Billy Bob thought perhaps he should give up his cigar smoking too—but the tobacco companies always contributed so heavily to his campaigns. He believed that there was an author still lurking somewhere inside of him. He had published a short story in his college magazine. If he was forced out of office, he would have time to write his memoirs as he had been planning to, albeit with a slightly different ending than he had intended. In the back of his mind Billy Bob secretly dreamed of inhabiting the White House some day.

His commercial interests were doing very well, the two shopping centers and the bowling alley. However, Billy Bob found the thought of having to deal with the day to day details of running a business rather grim. It was mostly his wife's money that he had invested anyway, which made it all the more imperative he overlook her indiscretions. He knew that she was very unhappy; nevertheless, the possibility of a divorce was completely out of the question, especially at this time.

Billy Bob poured himself another glass of bourbon from his wife's bar. It was then that he noticed a red striped range ball mounted in a shot glass, and set like a trophy on the counter top. He could not recall ever having seen it there before. Telephoning his driver, who was waiting in the hall downstairs, he instructed him to tell his wife to come up to her bedroom as soon as she arrived. From his next call, made to the men who were tailing Johnny, he learned that the fellow from New York had checked out of his hotel. The senator cursed into the phone, telling them their man was probably planning to slip out of town. He told them to keep on his tail, and to call him as soon as anything new happened. Looking out the front window, Billy Bob saw his wife's white Porsche sports car coming down the driveway.

"So just where the hell have you-all been? I telephoned the restaurant where you were supposed to have lunch and they said you left more than an hour ago." Billy Bob snarled at his wife the moment she came in the door.

"I had to eat didn't I. . . ." she lied.

"They said you-all left without eating."

"I went somewhere else." She could not reveal that she had been driving around town looking for Johnny Foozler. "And just what do you mean by having your goddamn goon downstairs order me to go right up to my bedroom. And this is my bedroom . . . what the hell are you doing in it anyway?"

"Look, like I told you on the telephone . . . I need you-all to come to Charlesboro with me today. For the next few weeks we have got to stick together . . . until this here thing blows over."

"Until what thing blows over? . . ."

"Didn't you-all read the story about me in today's paper?"

"No. You know I don't buy the newspaper. I never read it so it's just a great big waste of money . . . you're the one always complaining about my spending too much."

"You'd think them reporters would have more important things to do than to snoop about in my business. Like who's looking for them damn A-rab terrorists who are supposed to have targeted the naval base?"

"What has Arab terrorists got to do with you?. . ."

Damn media . . . panders to the lowest common taste. A good scandal is what most people want. Goddamn reptiles. Don't appreciate anything what's been done for them. Shit . . . they got Medicaid and Social Security, cheap gas, and free schools for their kids. Always wanting something else. Nobody wants to struggle anymore . . . like I did, ya know what I mean."

Like marry a rich woman, Tridance thought. "So stop your ranting already, and tell me what this is all about. . . ."

"Okay, okay . . . I'll tell you in the car."

"The car? . . ."

"You'd better get dressed . . . you're coming with me."

"Coming with you? Where? And I am dressed."

"You're not coming like that! Put something decent on. But I still want you to look sexy . . . I'm the guest of honor; so we're going to be up on the reviewing stand."

"What? Am I just some goddamn baby-doll that you dress up and carry around with you? If that's all you want get yourself a fucking inflatable." Going over to the bar to pour herself a glass of gin, Tridy saw the red and white range ball on top of the counter. The memento brought a quick smile to her face, which she made sure was gone when she turned back to her husband.

The senator was wildly rummaging through Tridy's closet, throwing clothes off hangers, kicking shoes out of the way: "Don't you-all have any decent clothes? This here looks like the wardrobe for a goddamn whorehouse."

"You picked them all out for me, remember . . . but I paid for them." Tridy said, finishing her drink. She sat down on the bed, kicked off her shoes, and lifted her pink silk tank top over her head. She was not wearing a bra. Her breasts stood out, firm despite her age. He anger had made her nipples hard. Tridy walked over to the mirror and began admiring her breasts. Women who were proud of their breasts always undressed by taking off their tops first, as she had. Those who thought their breasts inadequate removed their bottoms, keeping their shirts on until the very last. Tridy was admiring herself in the mirror, squeezing her breasts and pinching her nipples.

"For cripes sake . . . will you-all stop playing with your goddamn titties and come here and help me pick out something for you to wear. We've got to leave in five minutes or we're going to be late . . . and we've got to be there on time. We can't hold up the whole damn corps of cadets. Besides we're gonna be on TV . . . live!" her husband shouted. His vandalizing had moved over to her second closet.

"Those are winter things in there," Tridy said, unzipping her skirt. Sliding the sheer fabric down her hips, she caught the elastic of her bottoms with her thumbs and removed her bikini panties at the same time. She tossed the clothes on the bed and strode over to the bar, where she refilled her glass and lit a cigarette. She stood there naked, laughing lightly at the senator's mayhem.

Finally finding an outfit he considered acceptable, Billy Bob pulled it from the hanger and turned back to his wife. Her nudity startled him. He had not seen his wife naked for some time now. He knew she swam naked, and sat around the pool with nothing on, even when some of the male staff members were around. In the beginning he had found this behavior arousing, however, as he became more politically prominent, it had become embarrassing. When they had stopped sleeping together, she had stopped displaying herself to him, and put on a robe when he was around. Seeing her in the mirror manipulating her breasts had begun to arose him, but it was not until he turned around and saw her full nakedness, the pose—legs spread, balancing a drink in one hand and a cigarette in the other, that Billy Bob felt a hardness growing for her that he had not experienced in a long time.

Noticing the bulge in her husband's pants, Tridy smiled. She took a, long deep drag on her cigarette, let the smoke curl out around her tongue and mocked: "We need to go. I had better get dressed . . . we can't keep the whole damn cadet corps waiting.

Besides, we're going to be on TV . . . live, or as live as a phony like you can be."

Billy Bob's blood was pounding in his head. He wanted his wife, wanted to throw her on the bed and force his way into her, fuck her until she screamed—like they used to do. He held the skirt and jacket up against her naked body, the back of his hand brushing up against flesh it no longer had access to. She was right. They didn't have time, but maybe they did, he thought. If he was subtle, it had always worked in the past.

"Hey, this outfit looks good. A nice conservative image is what we need now," he said turning her to the mirror, "but still smart looking."

"Cripes! This is the suit I bought for your Aunt Sadie's funeral," Tridy said, clutching the clothes to her body while studying her reflection. Billy Bob's face leered over her shoulder like a dog in heat.

Sliding his arms onto her bare shoulders, Billy Bob began to message them slowly, deeply. Tridy rolled her head ever so slightly. He could feel her tension breaking. His tongue traced a wet pattern around the back of her neck. Furtively checking in the mirror, he could see her face relaxing. He ran his fingers down Tridy's spine and she gave a slight shudder. The senator was pleased with himself. He knew what buttons to push. He was an expert at rousing a crowd—or a woman. His left hand went around front and slid under the jacket she was holding to herself. He fondled one breast, and then the other, while his right hand released his penis from its zippered storage and was rubbing it up and down the fleshy crack of his wife's buttocks.

"Uhmmmmm. . . ." Tridy murmured. She had dropped the skirt she was holding. Her fingers had found her clitoris. She was smiling, but her smile was for the fool that was her husband.

The telephone rang. Responding to Billy Bob's orders to let him know whenever they knew anything, the men following Johnny Foozler had called in. The senator, his hard cock dangling out in front of him, hopped over to the phone.

"Hello, yeah . . . no, no, it's okay . . . what? . . .what? . . . Wait, hold on a minute. . . ."

Billy Bob was waving at his wife, trying to get her attention. She was standing in front of the full length mirror, manipulating herself. He held his hand in front of the speaker: "Dear, we don't have time . . . could you-all come over here and do me while I take this here call. . . ."

"Just who the hell do you think I am? Your goddamn secretary!" Anger flashed on Tridy's face. She picked up a bottle of nail polish and threw it at him. The missile narrowly missed, and splattered on the wall behind, leaving an obscene red gash. Her feeling of loathing had taken on a renewed strength. "You pig! You goddamn fucking pig . . . suck your own cock. And you be careful . . . some day I might just cut the fucking thing off!" she screamed disappearing into the bathroom.

The senator's member began its retreat, the soft folds of skin curling in on themselves. Moments earlier it had been rampant, ready for battle, now he cupped his hand around it, just glad it was still there. He knew his wife's threats were not to be taken lightly. Then he remembered he was talking on the telephone. He removed his hand and spoke into the receiver. His voice was unfamiliar to himself, a kind of whimpering.

"Hello . . . you-all still there? You say he's just passed through Georgeville, headed south . . . okay, well then forget about the bastard. It's probably just a lot of rigmarole anyway. I don't think he's the reporter we're after. . . . Look, I need you-all to hurry on down to Charlesboro to make sure everything's set up for me. Oh . . . and my wife will be with me . . . she doesn't have time to pack . . . so I'll need you-all to get some things for her . . . you know, tooth brush, hairspray, stuff like that . . . we'll be leaving here in a few minutes . . . see you-all there in a couple of hours."

The senator hung up the telephone and considered his now flaccid penis, a parody of what it had been. He stroked it briskly with his hand, hoping to finish what he had started, but although it still tingled he got no response. He stuffed the sore sausage back into his pants.

Tridy stepped out of the bathroom perceptibly changed—an unexpected smile on her face. She had put on the gray pin-stripped suit jacket, but wore no blouse underneath, displaying a generous bit of décolletage. The matching knee-length-for-the-funeral skirt had been rolled up under the jacket so that it was now mid-thigh. In the brief time the senator was on the telephone, she had teased up her hair and applied a makeup job that could best be described as high-class tart. "I'm ready," she said striding past him toward the door. "Let's go . . . we can't keep the whole damn cadet corps waiting. Besides, I'm going to be on TV . . . live."

Out of the corner of her eye Tridy caught sight of a cockroach scurrying past the door. They weren't supposed to have cockroaches. She would have to speak to the housekeeper about this when she got back. And then there was the matter of the nail polish splattered on the wall.

TWENTY

WHAT UP UNTIL now Foozler had considered a mere folly has been elevated to the level of a serious problem. The calf will not move. Just when Johnny thought he was about to get his car free of the mud, he has slid back into it again.

"Hey you, Bovie! Stupid! Get out from in front of my car!" Finding yelling does no good, Johnny blows his horn: Beep Beep!

The shrill cacophony of sound accomplishes nothing. The cow stands there looking at Johnny out of one eye. Foozler considers this for a moment. I suppose that's normal, he thinks. How could it look at me with two eyes, if they are on opposite sides of its head? He recalls something he learned in school before he dropped out: There are two kinds of creatures; runners and hunters. Tigers are hunters; they have their eyes in the front of their heads. He imagines a prehistoric cow, bending over eating grass. A tiger, probably saber-toothed, sneaks up from the side and kills the cow. His teacher had told him that over the years the cows with their eyes more to the sides, who saw the tigers coming and got out of their way began to mate with other cows who had their eyes more to their sides, until cows ended up with their eyes where they are now. A reasonable enough explanation he assumes.

Beep! Beep! Beep!

A family of doves that has been making its way along the shoulder scatters for cover. The cow still does not move. Johnny looks in the rearview mirror. His eyes are in the front of his head. He should be a hunter, a killer, yet he is clearly a runner—has been all his life. He wishes he had eyes in the side of his head, and maybe the back as well. "Maybe even in my asshole," he says to his mirror image. "You gotta do what you gotta do to survive."

Foozler Runs

Foozler gets out of the car. He has decided to push the calf out of the way. He estimates that it can't weigh more than 100 pounds.

"Go on Bovie, go on boy . . . or girl. Get over there to the side of the road. Go on, that's a nice cow."

The calf does not budge. Johnny realizes it is heavy for such a small animal.

"Go on . . . move!" He gives the calf a slap on the rump. It skitters from in front of the car. "Well, that's a nice Bovie. You just stay over there by the side. Better yet . . . why don't you go back to wherever you came from?"

Johnny quickly hops back into his car, starts the motor and pops the clutch. There is a loud whirring sound as the Buick digs itself deeper into the ditch.

How in hell am I going to get out of here? Johnny thinks. He doesn't remember passing a telephone booth for miles, and no one has shown the slightest interest in stopping. What he takes for a lucid thought forms in the gallimaufry that has become his brain. It worked in the snow, why not here? He needs more weight in the back. The calf! It's small but must weigh a good hundred pounds. Foozler sets about clearing out the rear seat, putting his things into the trunk. There is plenty of room back there despite all the golf balls. Why hadn't he loaded his stuff back there in the first place? He could have been sleeping on the seat, the way he did in the old days when he traveled with the band.

"Go on, Bovie, in you go . . . go on now, be a good little cow. I'm only going to take you for a short little ride . . . not far . . . just a couple of hundred feet up the road. Up there to where it's dry."

The calf is stubborn and will not move. Johnny couldn't blame it though, remembering that when he was as young as this calf must be in cow years, his mother had told him to never get in a car with a stranger, even if they offered you treats. Wait! That was it—treats. Foozler digs under the front seat for the half-eaten bag of popcorn.

"Hey, Bovie . . . check this out. That's a good little cow." The calf eats some of the popcorn he has sprinkled on the ground. "Here . . . come over here and I'll give you some more." Johnny puts a handful of the buttery stuff on the edge of the rear seat."

Bovie, obviously hungry, laps it up. "Good cow, eat that," Johnny says, running around to the other side and opening the door. He puts another handful on the middle of the seat. "Yeah, you like this . . . well here's some more. Come on stick your head in . . . and now your legs." The calf is in. He dumps the rest of the bag on the seat and slowly closes the door. The calf is eating and doesn't notice his actions. "Don't be afraid, Bovie . . . I'm not going to hurt you. I'm just going around the other side to close the door. Go ahead, eat the whole bag. . . ."

Great, Johnny thinks, as he looks at the back end of the Buick sagging into the dirt. He will ease his car out of here and be on his way. He can't believe that he thought a car full of bad guys was actually following him. If they had planned to kill him they surely would have come back by now. Dozens of cars had passed by, no one stopping, no tow trucks, nothing.

The next sounds we hear are: the whir of tires spinning, the crunch of a car being rocked back and forth as it carves its way through a channel it had created earlier, the slap of mud and gravel hitting the undersides of the fenders and being filtered out through the rust holes, and a calf, frightened by the noise of its new confinement, bellowing at the top of its lungs. Its wheels alternately grabbing and spinning, the Buick gradually works itself free of the slough that has been holding it prisoner. On dry gravel again, Johnny brakes to a halt.

Foozler leaps from the car and opens the rear door on the passenger side. "Okay, Bovie! You're out of here!"

The calf looks at Johnny. Terror shows in its eyes. The animal has crouched down on the seat, and does not move. Johnny goes around to the other side and opens that door also. He tries to push the calf out.

"Go ahead cow! Get out of there. It's time you went home. I know that seat is comfortable . . . I've slept on it myself . . . and you just ate all my popcorn . . . but I gotta go. . . ."

A short time passes, during which Bovie appears to sleep, and Johnny paces up and down, trying to think of a plan.

"All right," Foozler says to the calf. "I've decided to take you to the nearest house . . . maybe someone there will know where you came from, or at least be able to help me drag you out of my car."

Having not yet gone completely irrational, Johnny spreads newspaper under the calf's back end. It is the paper with the story about Tridy's husband, Billy Bob and the gangsters. "The paper is just in case you have an accident," he tells Bovie. He gets in front and starts the motor. "Just relax and enjoy the ride," Foozler says to the startled animal as he pulls back onto the highway.

The feverish activity of the past half hour has revived Johnny and postponed the almost complete collapse that he had been on the verge of when he feared he was being stalked by paid assassins.

The highway runs straight. Sunlight peering between the departing cumulonimbus filters through the scruffy pine trees, the tops of which have taken on a calligraphy that reads as if they might have been cleared by a blight, or perhaps a hurricane. Bovie sleeps quietly. The animal has complete confidence in her new master. She has no way of knowing the insecure and questionable state of Johnny's mind as he plunges farther down the highway without seeing any habitation.

"Hey! Look up there, Bovie," Johnny shouts over the wind noise as he slows down. He has had his window open for obvious reasons. "I think it's a store, or something. It isn't much . . . but there's been no place else for miles."

Pulling his Buick up to the front of the clapboard shack, Johnny is careful not to block the one, ancient gas pump, although it looks as if it is little used. He opens the battered screen door, and steps inside of what he takes to be the office. His senses are immediately assaulted by the darkness, and the musty smell, the stale odor of dead things.

"Hello! . . . anybody here?" Johnny asks before taking another step, waiting for his eyes to adjust to the dimness.

"What you-all want here, mister?" A voice comes from somewhere. Then Foozler spots a grizzled, old black man, hardly as high as the counter, almost invisible in the tenebrous space.

"Oh, ah . . . I don't want to buy anything. I . . . ah, just found a cow back there on the side of the road," Johnny says, trying his best to sound convincing. "I have it in my car. I was hoping you would come out and take a look at it. Maybe you can tell me if you might know where it comes from?"

"What you-all tryin' ta pull, mista? I done heard some tall stories in my day, but dis here one does beat all. You-all tellin' me ya got a cow in yer car? And you-all want me ta come out dar ta take a look? You-all tryin' ta have some fun with a dumb old nigger? Well let me tell you . . . I ain't dat dumb. And if yer fixin' ta rob me . . . let me tell you I got a gun in my hand right now . . . under dis here counter. . . ."

Johnny holds up his hands: "Look . . . take it easy."

The man says something that is blocked out by the noise of a tractor-trailer roaring by on the highway.

"I'm not planning to rob you . . . and I'm not making fun of you. I need your help. I really do have a calf in the back seat of my car. . . ."

"Mista, let me tell you somethin'. The way you-all done come from, der ain't nothin' but pine trees fo ten mile. An da way you-all is a headed, ain't nothin' but pine trees fo another ten mile. Out back of dis hare place be more trees, fo ten mile. Now across the road be trees fo a mile, dan dare be da ocean. Ain't no farms hereabouts nowhere. So where's dis hare cow o' yers supposed to have come from? You-all spect me ta believe dat God Almighty jus put down a cow alongside the road fer ya ta find. Now you-all jus better git otta hare. An the next town ya come to why don't you-all tell yer story ta da police. If day look in yer car and find no cow . . . I spect day's gonna put you-all away fer bein' crazy . . . and iffen day look in yer car an do fine a cow . . . I spect they's gonna put you-all away for cattle rustlin'."

"Cattle rustling . . . you're joking," Johnny says nervously.

"Happens down hare all the time. It's a serious crime . . . in dis hare state day put ya away fer life. If I were you-all I'd git back in my automobile an fergit about yer cow story."

Back on the highway, boredom is beginning to overtake Johnny despite the presence of his new friend. An article he had read in a magazine a few days previous comes to Foozler's mind. Normally a vegetarian, he has been living on fishburgers, French fries and chocolate bars, unable to find anytime he can eat in the fast food /grocery store /gas stations he has been stopping at on the way. A fact pops into his head: the average human consumes more than a ton of fat in a lifetime. The image of a block of fat as big as his car sticks in his subconscious. No, it would be bigger, heavier.

He sees himself sitting there with a spoon, slowly nibbling away at this huge mountain of fat. He has not eaten his share of the world's fat, and will not be allowed to die until he does. He feels sick to his stomach—has for several days.

Perhaps it is his diet that has gotten his stomach off, Johnny ponders, or maybe it's the traveling. His digestion was never that bad when he traveled with The Artful Foozler, but then he was much younger. He considers going back to eating hamburgers and hot dogs. There isn't supposed to be that much meat in them anyway, mostly fillers like soy products. Not very efficient use of the land though, growing cattle, he reminds himself. The trivia slot in his brain pops out the fact that it takes 900 pounds of plant protein to produce 50 pounds of beef protein. In an average year the US cattle population consumes 145 million tons of grain and soybeans to produce only 21 million tons of meat.

"Don't you worry back there, Bovie . . . you're my friend," Johnny says over his shoulder. "Nobody's gonna eat you . . . at least not while I'm around." The calf is sitting up, looking out the window, occasionally giving its new owner a lick behind the ear.

Johnny has come up with a new plan. He will take his calf to his son's house, and give it to their new baby as a present. Perhaps the kid could ride around on Bovie's back when it got older. Or, if it's a girl cow it could give them milk. He reasons that they must have some kind of a backyard where they can keep it. If anyone asks he will tell them he bought the calf from the old man at the store back there, but didn't get a receipt. Yes, that's the plan—he will drive straight through to Junior's place, only about six more hours away.

At that moment Bovie makes what sounds like a giant burp, then passes what smells like a giant fart. Johnny leans over and rolls down the window on the passenger side. The odor does not pass quickly. Foozler is not sure when his calf has last eaten, or what it has eaten, except for the bag of popcorn he lured it into the car with. One thing he is sure of is that his calf is not house-broken, or should we say car-broken. What he is not sure of is where he might be when his pet decides it is time for a bowel movement, nor what kind of warning the animal might be expected to give.

TWENTY-ONE

THE WESTWARD MOVING sun appears like a luminous smudge beneath a departing body of cumuli. Warm air gasps in through the open windows. Johnny has been heading south. It is warmer here than in Turtle Beach, which was warmer than the town before that, which he can't remember because, although it has been a little less than a week since he left New York, it now seems like a long time ago.

Foozler has driven from winter to spring, a spring that has become more real, and dazzling than any other spring he has known, a spring that takes it's presence seriously, seen in the postcard landscapes framed by the becoming more frequent strip malls and service stations, a spring full of enthusiasm far beyond the calendar—when his old home lies barricaded by snow. A spring that, seen through the window of his car like a moving picture, was at any given moment capable of producing in Johnny an infinity of emotions which take permanent shape in his mind as sadness and delight.

Across the river, spanned by a colossus of a bridge, is the City of Charlesboro. Bovie has been sleeping peacefully, without a doubt enjoying her ride, showing no sign of discomfort. The calf has not even made the slightest moo for the past half hour. The bridge catches Johnny's interest. He has crossed it once before. Built tall enough to allow battleships and aircraft carriers to pass beneath it to the naval base beyond, the bridge's massive, gray steel girders span the sky as well as the land.

Named for an obscure Civil War general, the structure stands higher than the highest church steeples, and so dominates the landscape that at its apogee it presents a vista unmatched in this flat part of America. This view, with its attendant, sensation of flying, is something Foozler cannot resist. He opts to take the bridge, rather than the longer, but probably faster, by-pass.

"Look at it Bovie! Wake up and look at the view . . . isn't it great! Look! Off over there you can see the ocean. . . ."

BBeeepppp! BBeeepppppp! A car honks behind Johnny.

"So, go ahead and pass asshole!" Johnny cries, waving his arm out the window at the tailgater. His hand a momentary airfoil, the warm air catches it and lifts it aloft, proving once again Bernoulli's principal.

The following car beeps again. Johnny is going the speed limit. He checks his rearview mirror to be certain it is not the mysterious black car, which in his present exhilaration he has temporarily forgotten about. Seizing an opening in the traffic, the car behind Johnny speeds up and passes him.

"What's your problem, Buddy?" Johnny shouts at the fleeing automobile. "Don't have a cow!" He smiles at the cleverness of his remark—he does have a cow. He wonders at the origin of the phrase, what does it really mean? Foozler repeats the phrase as a question: "Don't have a cow?" For a moment he is a deconstructionist philosopher. He wonders if those fortunate people who do have cows are the ones who experience true happiness and understanding—maybe in India? Enough, he tells himself and goes back to observing the landscape.

Intent on the scenery, Johnny is taken by surprise when the bridge comes to an abrupt end. Banking like a peregrine, he careens down the off ramp, and is immediately deposited in the middle of the downtown on a street named Confluence. Jarred by the sudden turn, Bovie has begun to howl in protest. The calf nuzzles its snout out past Foozler's head and continues bellowing, as if calling to some long lost relation it has just recognized passing in the street.

"For god's sake Bovie, sit down!" Johnny cautions his calf, using his free hand to try to push the animal back into the car. "Do you want to get us in trouble?"

"Look, Mommy!" a child in the SUV next to Johnny says pointing. "That man has a little cow in his car!"

"It's only a stuffed animal," the mother replies knowingly.

For a reason unknown to Foozler, the traffic has come to a complete standstill. This lack of motion has confused Bovie, who has ceased his/her baying.

The cars begin moving again. Johnny can see a police officer, wearing white gloves, directing traffic about three cars ahead. There appears to be a parade. A military band, dressed like faux West Point cadets, is turning into a park.

Bovie has gone back to making nonstop noise. Johnny has come to the conclusion that the calf needs to perform some bodily function, which it thoughtfully has not done since getting into the back of the Buick.

"Sorry, Bovie, it seems there's nowhere to go. There must be some kind of holiday, or something."

The traffic inches forward a few cars. Johnny is abeam the entrance to the parking lot of the Dixie Boys Hotel. Remembering to make a proper hand signal, he pulls out of the line of cars clogging Confluence Street and into the lot.

"You-all a guest at this here hotel, sir?" the black lot boy, curiously dressed in a Confederate general's outfit, asks.

"Ah, no . . . just parking for a while. If that's okay."

"Dat's fine . . . hare's yer ticket, sur." The man has notice Bovie in the back, but is telling himself that he is not seeing what he thinks he sees. "You-all ain't plannin' ta leave dat dare cow in yer car now, are ya?"

"Is there a problem with that? . . ."

"Jest read yer ticket, mista. It says ware not responsible fer thangs what's left in da car. . . ."

"I'll have you know that this here little critter is a celebrity. . . . This little calf is Flosie, haven't you seen her on television? She's valuable. I've got to take her with me wherever I go!"

"Well then I'm sorry dat I didn't recognize yer cow, sir. You-all can park over dare in da front row . . . it's reserved fer V.I.Ps."

The car is parked. Johnny fears he will not be able to get Bovie out. As soon as he opens the car door, however, the calf rushes from it on its skinny little legs. Apparently confused by the sleeping herd of mechanical monsters it has suddenly been dropped in the midst of, the calf wanders about looking for a familiar form. Finding nothing it recognizes, the calf deposits a cow pie next to a black Mercedes and then produces a puddle that runs underneath a white Lexus. Finished with its business, Bovie looks at Johnny with an expression that says: Now I'm hungry.

Taking a length of rope from his trunk, rope he had been carrying around for years but did not know why, Johnny reclaims his calf and ties it on a lead. Tugging it by the head, the way he's seen cowboys do it in the movies, Foozler starts down the street. "Okay, Bovie . . . let's go and find some fresh grass someplace for you to eat."

From down the colonial, antebellum, not quite burned by Sherman and authentically restored for the tourist trade, street comes the sound of drums—the marching figures Johnny had caught a glimpse of while waiting for the traffic light. Trees wave at the end of the block. There is a park, with grass, and a parade. Johnny loves parades. He skips to get in step with Bovie, who is marching alongside. Confused by Johnny's action, or not used to being on a lead, or never having been downtown before, or perhaps a combination of all of the above, Bovie balks and lags behind. Johnny skips again, the drums' beat has opened a long closed track in his brain.

* * *

The Eastlake Pioneers Drum and Bugle Corps was where Johnny had learned to march, and to play a drum. Well, actually he first learned to play a bugle, or learned that he couldn't play a bugle. But the only choice given him was a bugle as the girls played drums—the less pretty ones. The better looking ones were given flags or banners to carry. The real beauties, which seemed to mean nice legs and big boobs, were taught to twirl batons.

A short man, of Italian extraction, everyone called "Pithy-Pithy," however not to his face, was the director of the Pioneers. He had been christened Giuseppe Verdi, after the great composer, as a child in, Italy. But his parents had changed his name to Joe Green when the immigrated to America. Pithy was called "pithy" not because he was terse, which he was, but because he began each musical piece by shouting: "Okay, let'sa go now . . . and a one, two, three, pithy, pithy. . . ." In his ear pithy was the sound the bugles made, and he did have a good ear for sound.

Although Johnny wore a uniform and carried a bugle, and even held the bugle up to his mouth as he marched along, so bad was his playing that he was expressly forbidden from blowing one single note. He and the other three members of the last row were there mainly for show. Nevertheless, caught up in the excitement of the parade, usually at the moment the group was passing the judge's stand, young Foozler could not constrain his enthusiasm and would begin blowing wildly, as if some Aeolian goddess was guiding his flowing windpipes. Whereupon Pithy-Pithy, on hearing Johnny's sour notes, would rush to the back row and shout: "Hey! Who'sa da wise guy that's a makin' noises backa here. I tolda you . . . no pithy pithy inna da last row. . . ." It was after the Pioneers had just missed winning the Back Mountain Marching Band Competition, losing points for their musical renditions, that Johnny was given a drum, an instrument for which he showed an immediate talent—a move that would shape his life.

* * *

"Let's go, Bovie!. . . There's some nice grass down there . . . and a parade too," Johnny says, tugging the calf's rope.

"Look, Mommy! That man has a calf on a lead," a young girl shouts pointing.

"Well . . . so he does," the mother answers noncommittally.

"Why's he taking his calf for a walk, Mommy?"

"I don't know, dear. . . ."

"Hey Mister! Why are you taking your calf for a walk?"

"Why not. . . ." Foozler replies, waving cordially.

"Come away, Brittany," the mother says grabbing her daughter's arm so hard she makes the girl wince. "I told you never to talk to strangers. . . ."

A man walking a small cow on the Charlesboro Common is not right. In fact no one has walked a cow on the Common since just after the Civil War when freedmen kept their newly acquired animals there. The mother, a good mother, must protect her daughter from this man. There is no telling what is wrong with him; besides he sounds like he is a Yankee.

Foozler Runs

Something festive has entered Johnny's life, an eager enthusiasm, an importance that pervades his gestures and swells his chest with cosmic pride as he marches toward the center of the green field. Maybe it is the music, the beat of the drums. Or is it Bovie, his new friend.

The band plays "Dixie." The earthy campus seethes with the unanimous ecstasy of the hundreds, maybe a thousand, of people assembled there. The sun is brighter in this open space, and vast. The nebula of grass under Johnny's feet becomes denser, the earth giving up its dusty yellow opulence. In the dark spaces between the green blades of grass whole worlds live, imparting the flat ground the importance of a cosmos, an immense ant heap of planets.

Foozler hovers above this infinity, lost in the finite. As he trots over this other alien world under his feet, he has become disoriented, losing his bearings. His head hangs down like an antipode over the upturned zenith. Leading his calf, he wanders over the trampled turf, Bovie's wetted snout ruminating across maps of another sky, devouring star after star. Thus the two meander after the marching military procession, in orderly single file, snuffing out those remaining survivors of the first onslaught, who had scattered in all directions at the corps' approach.

The last human barriers fall. The marching column parts, upperclassmen to the right, underclassmen and underclasswomen to the left, leaving Johnny and his calf perpetuated in immobile flight, caught in an interplanetary vacuum, revealed to a new constellation—the reviewing stand. Circling in an endless holding pattern, Johnny and his calf mark the path of an unknown cosmography; while in reality, innocent as babes, they have succumbed to a planetary lassitude—and have surely put their heads into the fire.

The dust has begun settling over the column standing at attention in the Town Common, a yellow film sinking into the perpetual grayness of the faux Confederate uniforms worn by the honor guard. The folds of their genuine battle flags ripple in the slight breeze, giving off the fluffy smell of mildew. Only the Old Glory is new, a gift of Senator Billy Bob Plantigrade, who had received it from the White House for his outstanding efforts at campaign fund raising. The waning sun glints off the pressed white pants of the rigid cadets, brilliant white worn under off-gray tunics copied from West Point. Today, for the first time, young women have also marched down Confluence Street, the long way from their fortress on the hill. The whole column stands at rigid attention in front of the plank of the dignitaries, eyes straight ahead. Yet in their ears they hear laughing. Chins tucked under the straps of their headgear, they hear laughter coming from behind them, and they wonder what the cause is—but their discipline prevents them from turning their heads.

Holding his microphone to his mouth much as he must have held an ice cream cone when he was a child, a TV announcer speaks to the waiting Southland: "Hi you-all . . . this is Jobe Wagg, back with you live from the Town Common here in downtown Charlesboro, where my partner Kissey Brown and I are covering the annual presenting of the colors by The Fortress Corps of Cadets. And we're also keeping an eye on that other breaking story, the hunt for the Arab terrorists believed to be somewhere in the area planning to blow up the Charlesboro Naval Base. We'll let you know as soon as anything develops. . . . . It sure is a great day for a parade," Jobe concludes nodding at Kissey, indicating it is her turn to speak.

The camera pans around the park, and then to the face of Ms. Brown. If your TV set is tuned to WCBR, you will have noticed that except for Ms. Brown there are few people of color presently to be seen on the Town Common for this pompous occasion, although on an ordinary day it is usually a bustling rainbow of races.

"It sure is. . . ." Kissey says smiling. Jobe points his finger to the scene now appearing on the monitor. "And it sure has brought the folks out," Kissey says picking up on Jobe's cue. Her job is to provide the color, in more ways than one.

"Well would you-all look at that," Jobe says startled. "Something strange seems to be going on. . . ." He tosses a cue to Kissey.

"Yeah . . . something strange," Kissey says.

The TV viewers haven't yet been shown what is going on, but can hear sounds of laughter in the background. Jobe waits to deliver the punch line—the camera is still on his talking head. "Would you believe that here, in the middle of all the pomp and ceremony of this 150 year old event . . . we have a man walking a calf on a rope?"

The cameraman is finally allowed to segue from Jobe's face, with its feigned look of incredulity, to a wide angle shot of Johnny and Bovie circling in front of the reviewing stand. The camera begins to zoom in on the two, but it is just a tease. Jobe is on the screen again: "We'll find out what this is all about in just a moment . . . but first, a word from our sponsor . . . the Reconstruction Bank and Trust Company."

The viewers are treated to a scene of a distinguished-looking older man and his much younger trophy-wife happily motoring in a 36 foot power yacht on the Yesitsme River. They are carefree, or so we are meant to believe, because their financial worries are being taken care of by the Reconstruction Bank and Trust Company. The couples smiling faces, wind ruffling their well-groomed and slightly graying hair, fade into a RB&TCo logo.

Meanwhile Jobe Wagg, off camera, has been yelling at his producer: "Who the hell's this here guy with the cow anyway? And where did he come from? It's not in the script. I mean do we just ignore him . . . or play up the human interest angle? I don't want to get sucked in if this is just some kind of goddamn publicity stunt for a dairy bar or something . . . and then catch hell for it later on." He turns to Kissey. "Get on your cell phone and call the station. Ask them if they know what the hell's going on with this here guy and the cow."

Kissey shakes the phone, and then taps a few buttons. "Can't call nobody . . . phone's dead . . . battery must be gone. Went out while I was talkin' to my momma."

"What the hell were you-all doing talking to yer momma on the station cell phone?"

"My momma axes me ta' call in from time ta time. . . ."

"Jeez . . . . how much time do we got?"

"We're live again in one minute," the cameraman replies. He has been taping Johnny and his calf should something happen while they went to their commercial break.

The TV viewers are watching car dealer Sam Hill gesture at the thousands of quality vehicles, new and used, that he has, every day, at huge discount prices, "rite hare at the southland's largest auto discount center."

"The guy's moving," Jobe shouts. "He's pulling the damn cow right up to the stand . . . get that camera rolling?"

"This is Jobe Wagg back live from the Town Common . . . where a strange man leading a calf on a rope has just showed up in the middle of the presentation of the colors. No one seems to know who he is or where he came from. We are trying to find out what this is all about. . . ."

Not good enough, Jobe thinks; he needs more of an angle. Who will be watching "Talk of Charlesboro" on the local channel when they could be viewing Fox or CNN? He needs something big, exciting, like the time he discovered Lindbergh's kidnapped child, alive and living right here in Charlesboro. So what if the person turned out to be a hoax, born ten years after the real child had disappeared. The story had gotten a lot of coverage, even gone national. He had been noticed up at the network. A few more stories like that and Jobe Wagg could say goodbye to this jerkwater rebel town and hello Big Apple.

"Hold everything!" Jobe tells his viewers. "I've just had an anonymous caller on my cell phone inform me that the man with the cow is part of a terrorist plot to kill Senator Plantigrade!" The viewers out there in the southland will be glad their screens are locked on to him now, not Fox or CNN.

"But the cell phone ain't workin'. . . ." Kissey says off camera.

Seated above him on the stage, the senator's eyes are focused on Johnny and his calf now, as are the eyes of the president and provost of The Fortress, as well as their wives, and General Charles "Charger" Frump, the Commander of the US Forces in the Carolinas, and Admiral Forsythe Stumper, USN, retired. In fact, everyone in the surrounding crowd, which has grown considerably, is looking at the strange man who has wandered into the middle of the ranks of cadets with a cow on a lead—astonished, suspicious, not believing what they are seeing.

"Have you been able to learn anything more about the identity of the caller, Kissey?" Jobe asks, passing the mike over to her while he tries to untangle the cord that has become wrapped around his feet in his excitement.

"No Jobe . . . I have not been able to ascertain any new information," Kissey says, not knowing what else to say, but trying her best to sound official. "However, I have observed that at this very moment every police car in Charlesboro seems to be arriving on the adjacent streets...."

"What?"

"Like I said, look around and you-all can see that police cars are coming from everywhere."

"Every police car here in Charlesboro? . . ." Jobe says incredulously.

And so they keep arriving, disgorging dozens of officers, who push through the crowd to get to the parade ground. Has there really been a phone call, Jobe wonders, or had the entire police force just been watching "Talk of Charlesboro?"

TWENTY-TWO

IT IS NOT what Johnny Foozler had anticipated, leading his calf into the glare of the late afternoon sunshine slanting low through the trees on the crowds of people circling the Commons. Turning from the street Foozler has entered a different climate—there are different currents of air, the cool and unfamiliar regions of a different world. He had seen her when he first entered. Johnny thought it was her, Tridance, seated next to the man that must be her husband, the senator. But he wasn't sure. The park is not that large, the distance not that far, but his eyes not what they once were. As he gets nearer, he can see that it is her. He doesn't know what she is doing there; however, she is on the reviewing stand, so must have some official part to play. Johnny's plan is to get up close, staying behind the marchers, and when it is all over maybe he could get to talk to her, show Tridy his new pet, perhaps even give it to her. Since she is going back that way, he reasons, maybe she could arrange to have it returned to its rightful owner.

Foozler had not expected the column to part, and that he and his calf would be left exposed, standing in the middle, the center of attention.

"What the hell is this all about?" Vito Vitello, the wealthy casino developer sitting behind Billy Bob asks leaning over the senator's shoulder. It is not Johnny and his calf that worries him, but the sudden appearance of all the cop cars. Vito's bodyguard jumps up from the seat behind his boss, his hand on the Glock pistol inside his jacket.

"Damned if I know. . . ." the senator says, reaching for the flask of bourbon in his jacket pocket.

"It's Johnny!" Tridance shouts, unable to hide her elation.

"This is Mains Hampton, Charlesboro Police Chief," a voice reverberates through a bullhorn. "Don't anybody move. I repeat. Stay where you are . . . by order of the Charlesboro police. Stay where you are. . . ."

Bovie has begun bellowing, which is why Johnny does not hear the chief's warning.

The Charlesboro swat team has sealed off the open end of the park. Three expert riflemen have their scopes zeroed in on the back of Johnny Foozler's head.

"What the hell is that guy doing here?" Billy Bob asks.

Turning her back to the stand, Bovie drops what Kissey calls a "damn cow pie." The station will later regret it was not able to bleep out her remark.

Johnny tugs Bovie forward. He wants to be free of the dung. He wants to be away from here. Out of the corner of his eye he spots three black-helmeted, policemen stalking him from the side of the reviewing stand. His self-confidence is hemorrhaging. He will give the cow to the senator and get out of here. But he can't just hand Bovie's rope to Billy Bob and Tridy and be done with it. He needs some kind of ceremony. For his sake, and the senator's, Johnny supposes, he must make a good show of it. Another group of policemen have appeared on the other side of the stand.

"Don't anybody move. . . ." the bullhorn growls again.

This time Johnny hears the warning, but his mind does not register that it applies to him. He is the central figure—everyone must hold still, but not him. He must do his part. Johnny takes a step toward the senator, who towers above him on the stand.

The three snipers reposition Foozler in their sights.

Johnny thinks a salute might be appropriate, after all this is some kind of military ceremony. He raises his right hand.

Three riflemen begin to squeeze the grips of their rifles. They are trained; you don't pull the trigger, your whole hand contracts equally, smoothly, without jerking. They are ready if the order should come.

Chief Mains Hampton sees Johnny's hand moving upwards, a threatening, terrorist-like gesture from where he is positioned. He has no way of knowing the man is merely preparing to give a salute. The chief must make his decision now: "Fire!"

Three bullets are sent on their way.

Johnny's plan had been to salute the senator, and then make a graceful bow to his beautiful wife, which he does.

Two bullets pass over Foozler's head and splinter into the red, white, and blue bunting decorating the stand. The third bullet finds the back of Bovie's head, a portion of the cows skull flying forward, its blood splattering Johnny's arm. With a mournful bellow the calf falls down, rolls over on its side, and begins the process of dying, an ending not that different from what Bovie was destined for, but at least this time the animal's life will have finished with a walk in the park instead of down a slaughterhouse ramp.

Screaming now, not sure where the shots have come from, or why, people are jumping off the reviewing stand and running in all directions. The police marksmen cannot fire again. Vito has fallen on top of Tridance to protect her. Or is he dry humping her? Tridy has taken advantage of the situation to work her skirt up, and is rubbing her bum hard against her protector's bulging member.

"Johnny! Johnny! What in hell are you doing here?" Tridy yells between her stolen moments of pleasure.

Military discipline, never very much at this faux West Point for Southern boys, has broken down. Heads ducked, the corps of cadets is scattering in all directions. The members of the honor guard, seizing their moment in history, have knelt down, mimicking positions they have seen in Civil War picture books, and are firing their rifles at the terrorist, in their excitement forgetting that their ceremonial guns only contain blanks.

People are shouting and pointing every which way. Later on, at a closed hearing, Chief Mains Hampton will deny his men opened fire first. Shots will have come from the grassy knoll, the railroad overpass, and the book depository across the street.

Johnny kneels and strokes the young cow's head, smelling of hay and infancy, the parts that remain, awkward, and still unformed, too round, the shattered skull, parts that should be central spreading to the sides, blood dribbling down a silky soft nose, breath coming in pained gasps.

Johnny sees the swat team moving toward him, to the spot where he was, where he remains.

"There he is! Careful men. . . ."

Threatened, Johnny's mind seeks for answers in another state, to a memory of an existence as a lower animal, when he like Bovie had eyes in the side of his head—when he was a runner.

Foozler Runs

Whatever he had been in the past, Foozler was human now, with binocular vision, eyes set together in such a way that he could see his pursuers with total clarity. But to see his enemy is not to understand him. Every promise is a loss, every discovery a threat. Johnny's panic denounces the possibility of any other reality; out of his delirium emerges another kind of reason.

Johnny looks up. The danger is moving closer. His identity is not a static display, crouching there stock still, but rather an endless synthesis of the contradictions of his life. Foozler believes in fugitive faith, the only faith he finds believable for its great likeness to the animal. He sees the policeman reaching for him. He backs away from his dying friend, slowly, very slowly; then he turns and runs. Johnny runs as fast as he can.

"Grab that mother-fucking terrorist! He's getting away!"

Two policeman lunge at Johnny, but he evades their grasp.

Foozler runs. He has done nothing wrong, he reasons, why then is he fleeing wildly through the crowd?

"Hold it! Don't shoot! We might hit somebody...."

TWENTY-THREE

ALTHOUGH CHARLESBORO IS well south of the Mason-Dixon line its clocks still keep winter time; that time of the shortest days and long cold nights, when the city, even one as lively as this, slips early into the labyrinth of darkness. Its downtown, abandoned by the daytime inhabitants, surrenders itself to another sphere, opening up streets that are reflected images, make believe. These are the normally proper places, with the usual names, which have assumed new, and fictitious, configurations brought on by the inventiveness of the night.

In his rush to evade his pursuers, Foozler has become hopelessly lost. Normally possessed of a keen sense of direction, in his flight he has panicked, running down streets with no names, across anonymous backyards, through empty alleys and full parking lots, all left behind in a blur. Out of breath he can run no more so, like a trapped animal, he crouches under a bush hoping to avoid capture. He has done nothing wrong he reassures himself yet another time. He should have just stopped, put up his hands, and surrendered. Perhaps it was all a mistake, but they had shot at him with real bullets. The police would find something to charge him with. He had stolen the calf. It was called cattle rustling. They hung people for that in the early days. This is the South; perhaps they still do that here.

Johnny rubs his hand over the stubble on his face. He is tired and worn out. He has thrown away his golf hat, with Eastlake embroidered across the front, as being too recognizable. Now his gray hair stands out wild like a porcupine. He is hiding between a wall and the hedges that border what appears to be the campus of an urban college. As we can see by the expression on his tense and silent face, Johnny's lack of visual references has heightened his senses of smell and hearing. He remains in touch with the unseen world around him, its dark corners, shadowy quadrangles, and dusty cobbled alleyways. From somewhere not too far away there is also the scent of flowers, daffodils. He thinks of home, now called home, when before it had been merely "the trailer." Just a few days ago, when he had left that snow-covered place where his wife is buried, there were no daffodils; they would not appear for another two months. He had been glad to leave. Now, crouching in fear under a bush in this strange city, he wonders if he will ever see Eastlake again.

Rising from under his cover, Foozler discovers it is now very dark. He is cold and not wearing a coat. Johnny's first instinct is to return to his car and get his jacket. But he has no idea in what direction to head. And if he did find his car, his wisest choice would be to get out of town fast—if he could. Then Johnny realizes he is not cold at all. On the contrary, he can feel waves of unseasonable warmth, a spring night. As he approaches the street corner, a fitful evening breeze wipes gently across Johnny's damp forehead. John Foozler realizes that if he needs anything now it is to eat.

At this finicky time of night it is impossible to walk down Confluence, or any of the other streets which radiate out from the Town Commons, without noticing that it is the most attractive shops and restaurants that are still open, places that, because of their small size, one might overlook in the light of day. I must be careful though, Johnny tells himself. He must find just the right place. He has seen no policemen about. Perhaps they have discovered the folly of the whole incident and given up on him. Nevertheless, he cannot take any chances.

"The Odyssey," a gaily decorated sign proclaims in what a local sign painter has imagined to be "Greek-style" letters. Johnny loves Greek food. He would love any food now. He has not eaten since breakfast. Peering through his reflection, Foozler studies the menu in the window. It is pricey, but not more than he can afford. However, it appears expensive enough that people would dress up to go there. He is filthy. Johnny's clothes, dirty from his travel, were not clean when he put them on this morning. In the meantime, it has been a long day. He has been stuck in the mud, hit golf balls, wrestled with a cow, ran from the police, and hide under a hedge. Looking down he sees for the first time that there are a few splatters of Bovie's blood clearly visible on his shirt and pants. He would be immediately noticed if he walked into The Odyssey. Maybe no one would recognize him as a fugitive, but people would surely wonder what he was doing there. Johnny needs a more casual place, somewhere a not-to-clean working man, one doing landscaping or something like that, might stop on his way home.

Foozler continues down the empty streets. It is a nice night for a walk. He must not look in a hurry, just out for a stroll. But why then is he so dirty? Perhaps he should shuffle a little, with his head down, as if he is a street person. No, bad idea—Charlesboro is a tidy town. He has not seen anyone who might pass for a homeless person, at least not in this section of the city. A police car cruises past on the cross street, going very slowly. Have they noticed him?

Johnny turns and looks at a display of TV sets in a store front, pretending to be interested. He is just out for an evening of window shopping. There are nine sets stacked in the window, all tuned to the same channel. On nine screens, some clearer than others, nine couples are happily motoring their yachts on the Yesitsme River, their financial worries happily taken care of by the Reconstruction Bank & Trust Company.

Turning his head, Foozler risks a quick glance down the street. The police car is gone. He wonders if the officers have recognized him. Are they circling around the block to come up on him from behind? Have they radioed other cruisers who are at this very moment on their way to surround him? He looks back at the display. It is the nature of a television set that if it is turned on you will watch it, no matter how preoccupied you may be with something else, even something that may be threatening your life.

* * *

Johnny was sitting in a hospital room with his mother. They were both watching Jeopardy on the television. A nurse had come into the room to check on the old woman, but found her dead. She had passed away sometime between the commercial break and the final question. The category had been Sunspots. The answer was: a vague, indefinite, or borderline area.

Johnny believed he had the correct response, even shouted it out to display his knowledge, phrasing it as a question which you had to do. His mother had not said anything. But then she rarely did, even if she knew the answer, which she usually forgot to phrase as a question anyway.

The nurse had walked into the room at the moment Johnny had shouted: "What is a penumbra?"

The woman had had a moment to read the question on the screen, paused and then replied: "I'll be damned if I know. . . ."

They waited, staring at the three commercials that must be endured before Alex reveals the correct response. None of the three contestants got it right. But Johnny had.

"I got it! I got it!" Johnny screamed when "What is a penumbra?" had flashed on the screen.

"How much did you bet?" the nurse asked.

"All of it!" Foozler boasted, jumping up.

"Your son's a rich man now," the nurse joked turning to the mother. It was then that she noticed the old woman had no breath, no heartbeat, no pulse—nothing. There was only the dull humming, and pumping, of machines that no longer had any purpose to what they were doing.

* * *

In a window in a store on DuBonnet Street, nine TV sets flash nine images of Johnny leading Bovie happily behind the parading Corps of Cadets. There is a quick flash to another scene, Johnny and the fallen calf—crowds of people are running in panic in the background. Then the talking head of Jobe Wagg urging viewers to "tune in at eleven to find out more about the man with the cow, and the two Arab terrorists believed to be somewhere here in Charlesboro."

Foozler considers returning at eleven. He is curious to find out why his simple act of walking a calf in the park has created such a disturbance, and why he is being linked to terrorist activity. The final shot of the news teaser is Police Chief Mains Hampton speaking to reporters. "We-all have learned that the calf was stolen from a farm upstate. Patrols are out looking for the suspect. I am certain we will have an arrest by morning. And we are following up several leads on the two Arab terrorists."

Then it's Jobe Wagg again, telling his listeners he: "will be back at eleven with a complete summary of all the news . . . plus any late breaking developments."

Johnny stands there pondering how a summary can be complete and reveal "all" the news, and yet be a summary. He has another reason to come back at eleven, unless his capture is one of the late breaking developments. The screens now all repeat the familiar image of the couple happily boating up the Yesitsme River.

Foozler studies his image reflected in the window. He is about the same age as the man in the yacht. But the man at the helm looks younger. He is happy, smiling. Johnny looks old, tired. He wonders if it is because he has lived too long in the cold of the North. Perhaps he should not have gone back to Eastlake to take care of his ailing mother, and his father's failing driving range. Maybe his wife would still be alive. Maybe his son would not have run away and left him—the way he had left his own father. If only he had put his money in the Reconstruction Bank and Trust Company, he thinks.

A police car appears behind him in the glass. A cold chill goes through Foozler's spine. He does not move. The cruiser passes slowly down the street. Johnny decides it would be best to leave this well-lighted section and find his way on the darker streets of the town.

As he walks along, Johnny tries to piece together the details of his flight. His memory is slowly returning. According to his calculations, he ought to turn here, into a narrow lane that should take him past two or three side streets, to a row of small restaurants. He fears this is taking him even farther from his car, but Johnny's desire for food has become acute, and he has no faith that his car will be where he left it anyway. He needs to find Salt Street. He remembers this is the street the old church is on. He had hid there behind a stone in the old cemetery until by chance a funeral party arrived, and he fled over the back wall. Salt Street would take him all the way to the river. From there he is sure that he will be able to retrace his way to the Dixie Boys Hotel, where he hopes to find his car still parked.

Foozler Runs

Johnny turns into a street he thinks he knows. He begins to run, anxious not to lose his way. He passes three more streets, but there is still no sign of the turn he wanted. The appearance of the way is completely different from what he had anticipated. Nor are there any signs of the small restaurants he was expecting. He is in a narrow street of old row houses, with no porches, and doors very close to the pavement. Their tightly shuttered windows allow very little light to filter into the street. The moon has appeared overhead, and the moonlight reflecting off these mostly white buildings is all that illuminates this close quarter. His footfalls echoing too loudly, and fearful he might turn an ankle on the cobbled pavement, Johnny has stopped running. He was walking fast, rather carelessly. He has given up on the idea of finding the small restaurants. All Foozler wants to do is get out of this dark section quickly, and back to an area with which he is familiar.

He reaches the end of the street, unsure of where it has led him. Turning the corner there are street lamps, brilliant, but of an old-fashioned design. Our fugitive finds himself on a broad, tree-lined avenue, expansive and straight. The slight breeze carries the hint of water across the open space. Picturesque villas stand in the midst of their gardens, and back from the street, the houses of Charlesboro's old rich. In the gaps between are small parks with bubbling fountains and rows of flowers. The whole area looks like the postcard of Charlesboro he remembers someone bringing to class when he was in sixth grade.

This is Rampart Street, a street which at one time had guarded the river. The fickle waters have moved two blocks east, but will doubtlessly return this way again sometime in the future. The heavy cover of the tall trees spreads out in all directions, their limbs swaying with muted gestures. Moonlight filters through the branches overhead, the parks and gardens standing black in a silvery landscape. The glow of the antiquated street lamps creates a fictitious world echoed on the mottled pavement.

Halfway down the block Johnny espies a building standing closer to the sidewalk, and without a garden in front of it. It is smaller, and plainer, than the rest, but more brightly lit. It looks like a shop, perhaps a food shop. Lent wings by his hunger, Johnny hurries toward the glow.

Arriving at the source of the light, he sees that it is a coffeehouse, an anomaly in this neighborhood of grand residences. Through the large front window he can see that the place is open, but devoid of customers. A lone woman, who appears to be a waitress, or perhaps the proprietor, stands behind a counter talking on a telephone.

Johnny waits, his heart pounding, rooted to the spot by curiosity. He is reluctant to take the two steps down to the entrance, ready to flee at the slightest noise. How can he, a stranger, justify his visit to this place so far removed from the tourists' route? Overhead the moon slides behind a featherbed of clouds.

Two circles of light loom at the end of the street, growing in size. There is another light on top. A police car? No a taxi. Johnny's hand starts up as if to hail it. What would his destination be? And what cabby would stop for someone looking like he must look now? Did cabs even pick up fares in these small towns? They probably only respond to telephone calls. The cab rushes by.

Johnny turns around and runs down the two stairs. Finding himself at the front door, he notices the name for the first time. It is familiar, a name he remembers from a story he has reread many times, by the Polish author Bruno Schulz. The place is called The Cinnamon Shop.

Johnny stands at the door. The woman inside has hung up the phone and is arranging pastries in a glass case. This is mainly what she has to sell, along with a selection of books and audio-cassettes, mostly written or recorded by people who he has never heard of, probably locals. In an hour the coffeehouse will be quite crowded. Now is too early. Johnny remains outside looking in. Although he is very hungry, Foozler is reluctant to be the only customer in the place.

TWENTY-FOUR

HURRYING IN THROUGH the door out of the darkness, the stranger arrives, disheveled and dirty. The waitress, even though she is in the shop alone, does not find him threatening. He comes in quickly, which alarms her only so slightly. Then he stops and hesitates, as if about to turn and leave. For reasons she cannot imagine, the woman becomes concerned that he might go out. She is curious. What is he doing here? The man is dressed in "casual clothes" that might have come from a thrift shop, unlike her regular customers who wear "smart casual," outfits assembled with considerable care, and expense, at the Gap or from a L.L. Bean catalog. This newcomer even smells bad, as if has been sleeping with the cows in a barn.

"Oh . . . Excuse me," Johnny says, sensing the woman's response to his appearance. He turns and begins to leave.

"Yes! Can I help you?. . . Are you lost?" the woman, asks. She wonders if she has said the wrong thing. What better way is there to make a man feeling lost more uncomfortable than to ask him if he is lost. Men are never lost, or if they are they never admit it. "I mean . . . would you like a cup of coffee . . . or something?"

The wood paneled shop smells heavily of cinnamon. Johnny scans the room. There are no other customers, and no television set. Good. He does not want to see Bovie dead, and himself running, again and again, just to stir up interest in the late news. Perhaps this woman hasn't even heard of the incident. She seems vague, like someone who does not care too much about what goes on in the world—or at least what goes on in Charlesboro.

Johnny is hungry. He will have a quick bite to eat, get directions, and then reclaim his car and head out of town. "Yes, I'll have something," he vaguely responds to her vague question. He quickly sits down at the table in front of him, purposely facing the door. "Can I see the menu?"

"Oh . . . there's no menu," the woman informs Foozler. "All we have is what's there in the case . . . cakes and things. We don't serve lunches or dinners. We're just open in the evening. There's cinnamon cake, and cinnamon bread, and cinnamon rolls. Everything's made with cinnamon, what's why we call it The Cinnamon Shop."

Johnny gets up and looks at the pastries in the antique glass case. The woman wrinkles her nose. He does smell like a cow. She studies his face, an older man, but not that much older than her. She finds him attractive in spite of, or perhaps because of, his outrageous appearance.

"I'll take one of those, and one of those, and a round one," Foozler says, pointing. His fingernails are long, and unkempt, a half moon of dirt defining each end. And then he adds: "To go, please. . . ."

"To go?" the woman says, as if she has not heard him. She does not want this man to go, at least until she has figured him out.

"And I'll have a cup of regular tea," Johnny says, looking at the blackboard behind the counter chalked with teas from Asparagus to Zinger.

"Just plain tea? . . ."

"Plain tea," Johnny says, but does not leave it there. "When I want a cup of tea, I want a cup of tea . . . not a cup of hot water that has had some kind of flowers washed in it. And with cream and sugar too, white sugar, please." He smiles at her, a broad smile, referred to by some as a "shit-eating grin." Foozler has gone through this screed before. He knows how proud these new-age places are of their choices of teas, half of which no one ever orders anyway. He feels the old Johnny returning—smug, wise-cracking.

The woman smiles back at him. She likes his smart-aleck remark. She misses the bumptious conversations she remembers from New York City. Everyone here is too Southern, too polite. To be a liberal here is to be politically correct. At her other job—she teaches art part time at the college—she has to be constantly on guard of what she says, especially when criticizing her students work. She has to be circumspect. She would like to tell these flowers of the Southland what their precious little pictures are worth, what art up in The Big Apple is all about. However, she holds her tongue, because they hold the ax of student evaluation forms over her head. She does not have tenure, only an instructor's rank. If she doesn't dance a soft shoe, and keep everyone happy, she will be on her way out. She has fallen far enough just getting where she is. She does not want to fall any lower.

"I'm sorry," she says. "I just used up the last of the hot water brewing this coffee . . . it will only take a minute to heat some more." The woman is happy to have him trapped here for a short while longer.

"Okay, then put the buns on a plate. I'll start eating them here." Johnny's stomach is ravenous. He cannot wait. He looks around the room selecting a new table, one less visible from the window. "I'll sit over there. And can I have a glass of water, please. Oh . . . and do you have a men's room?" he asks diffidently, looking down at his hands, noticing for the first time that the days events have stained them with dirt, tar, and even blood. "I've been working in my garden."

"It's back there, to the left," she says, knowing he is lying. This man is not from around here. She has been working here long enough to recognize that. And the way he said "water." It's the way people pronounce it in New York, not how they say it down here in Charlesboro.

She waits until Foozler has emerged from the unisex toilet and reseated himself before she brings his water. He doesn't look up at her. In fact Johnny has not looked this woman directly in the face since he came in. He shifts and turns toward the window. She has also brought a newspaper. "Here's today's paper . . . thought you might like to read what's going on in Charlesboro. You're not from around here, are you?"

Johnny grunts a noise that could be a yes or a no, but he does not take the paper, or the bait.

She puts the paper down on his table. Johnny stuffs a bun into his mouth, bites off a piece and chews, ignoring the newspaper.

"Lots of excitement downtown today," the woman goes on, "well for Charlesboro anyway. Some guy with a cow busted up The flag ceremony. Pretty absurd. I mean the ceremony is silly enough, without the cow business. And then there's those two

Arab terrorists on the loose, I mean, I can't imagine any al Qaida terrorist even knowing where Charlesboro is."

"Umhum. . . ." Johnny says, licking cinnamon off his fingers.

The woman heads back for the tea water, which has begun to boil.

"That was regular tea you said?" she shouts from behind the counter. The woman has not forgotten—she just wants to rouse him, to be a bit smart-alecky herself.

"Yes," Johnny says, without turning around, "regular tea, with milk and sugar."

"Here's your tea," she says, placing the cup beside him. She moves the newspaper, flipping it open as she does. "Look! Here's a picture of that guy with the cow!"

Johnny notices the photograph is slightly out of focus, but it does look like him. He is wearing his white baseball hat. The picture is in color. Thanks to the wonders of digital technology the smallest, even give-away, newspapers have color on their front pages these days. There is no mistaking his yellow polo shirt. He crosses his arms in front of his shirt, hoping she will not notice it.

"Yeah, pretty dumb," Johnny says, refolding the paper and pushing it away from him as if he is not interested. "I heard about it earlier. I mean . . . why is everyone so worked up about a man with a cow? And how do they know he has anything to do with terrorists?"

"I hear they shot the cow," she says. "It was stolen from a farm up near Turtle Beach. But they're still looking for the guy . . . at least that's what I heard earlier. Maybe they've caught him by now. . . ."

"Yeah, maybe. . . ." Foozler grunts.

The waitress goes back behind the counter. Has she made the connection? Johnny watches her out of the corner of his eye. If she picks up the telephone he is prepared to run. He takes a sip of his tea. The too hot fluid sticks in his throat, seeks for his windpipe. He begins coughing violently.

The woman puts down the pot of coffee she is holding and hurries over to the stranger. "Are you okay? If you're choking I know what to do . . . it tells you on that poster we have up over there," she says pointing. She looks back at him. It is the first time their eyes have actually met.

"I'm okay," Johnny gasps. "It just went down the wrong pipe."

"That's funny. . . ."

"What's funny?"

"You saying 'down the wrong pipe.' I haven't heard that saying in years. We used to say that back home . . . when I was a kid."

He was supposed to say: Back home where? And she would tell him, and then ask: Where are you from? But Johnny has again not taken her baited hook. "Well, it wouldn't do nowadays, would it?" Johnny cracks, his breath coming back to normal.

"What wouldn't do?" she asks. He likes how she scrunched up her face when she said it.

"Down the wrong pipe. . . ." he says, pointing to the sign. "I mean, can you imagine millions of posters in restaurants all over America reading: What to do if food goes down the wrong pipe!" Johnny laughs. He realizes he has not laughed in some time, not that he ever laughed that much, at least not at what most people thought was funny.

The outside door opens. Johnny jumps. But it is only a young couple, obviously in love. They smile at each other and hold hands, while they point in delight at the display of cinnamon cakes in the glass case.

The waitress goes over to the couple to take their order. When she looks back in his direction, the stranger in the dirty yellow shirt is gone. She feels a curious sadness. She did not see him leave. He had not said anything when he departed, just disappeared, leaving his money, more than enough, on the table.

Unsure of what has happened, the waitress becomes preoccupied with the arriving customers. She tells herself that she has no proof he was the man with the cow. He sure smelled like it, however, and his shirt was the same color. She begins to brew another pot of coffee. Should she call the police? And say what? that she thinks the man they are looking for was just here. They would ask why she hadn't called while he was still there, and how long ago had he left, and which way was he headed? all questions that she couldn't answer.

They would send an officer out to question her—maybe even reporters would show up. Perhaps they would take her down to the station to assemble a composite photo from one of those god-awful computer programs police use nowadays, where every black male comes out looking like every other black male, and every white male comes out looking like your uncle George. It would all be a big waste of time. She would miss out on an evening's work, and most of her tips, which she certainly can not afford to lose.

Then they might even send over Ken Beaugard, she thinks, a police detective she has dated, and certainly doesn't want to run into again. What had she seen in him anyway? But then there aren't that many single men her age in Charlesboro, not decent ones, anyway. Not that Kenny wasn't married; at least he said he wasn't. That was until his bleached blonde, pink pants-suited wife had grabbed at the artist/waitress coming out of a Laundromat. Freshly washed clothing flew all over the lot, scattered by the wrath of a hysterical Barbara Beaugard. Her friends called her Barbie. The two of them together were Ken and Barbie, just like the dolls. They even looked like the dolls. After the Laundromat incident she had told Ken she didn't want to see him anymore. But the handsome police detective persisted on calling her. He even took to parking in front of her house in his unmarked police car—a stake out in heat.

In a free moment, the waitress stops to catch another glance of the newspaper. She reassures herself that the picture does look like the guy who was in here earlier. What has he done any way? She reads the list, right there on the front page. He was being sought in suspicion of stealing a cow, creating a disturbance, destroying public property, fleeing from the police, and threatening the life of Senator Billy Bob Plantigrade.

Nonsense, she thinks. A person planning to kill someone doesn't lead a cow in a parade in front of his intended victim. And the article doesn't say a thing about a weapon, no gun or knife, or anything. What was he going to do, throw a cow pie at the senator?

She keeps rereading the story between customers. The information is there, but obfuscated, as if it is purposely meant to be unclear. The whole story is too absurd to make sense of. And they have nothing that ties the cow man in with any terrorist group.

Foozler Runs

She wishes she could forget the whole thing, wishes the stranger had never come into her shop. She is afraid she has become infatuated with this man, perhaps even attracted to this alien person who has passed so briefly through her life. She tells herself that she should forget about the whole incident. It's not her business. She will not tell the police, nor mention it to anyone. Anyway, she is positive she will never see him again.

"Hi, Joan. How's it going?" It is Tommy, one of the regular customers. He startles her at first, walking in wearing a bright yellow polo shirt.

"Hi, Tommy . . . the usual?"

"Yeah. Weird night out there. . . ."

"Why do you say that?" Joan asks, pouring his coffee.

"I got stopped by the cops while walking over here . . . just three blocks away. They thought that I was the man they're looking for. It was my shirt. The guy with the cow, who is in with the terrorists, is supposed to be also wearing a yellow polo shirt. While they were checking out my ID they got a call that the actual guy had just been spotted down by the parking lot where he left his car. They handed me back my wallet and took off . . . sirens blaring. They probably have got the guy by now. . . ."

A chill runs through Joan's body, her hand shakes. The coffee she is pouring misses the cup.

"I'm sorry . . . I'll get a towel."

"Are you okay, Joan? I've never seen you spill coffee before."

TWENTY-FIVE

THE LIGHTS OF the Dixie Boys Hotel are disappearing over his shoulder. Running in panic, Johnny follows his nose, hoping to reach the river. He is sure that he can find his way out of town once he gets to the water. He feels colder. The temperature must be dropping, or perhaps his body, heated by the three blocks he has just run in fright, is cooling down now that he has slowed to a trot. Foozler rubs his arms together. He wishes he had on a warmer shirt, any kind of shirt, not just for the warmth, but to cover this once bright yellow thing he is wearing.

The yellow polo shirts had been his father's idea. He had planned to get them screen printed with the range's logo. He figured people would buy anything with a name on it. But his father had died before he ever had the shirts printed. His son had boxes full of yellow polo shirts to wear out.

Johnny always hated yellow. Blue was his color, dark blue. Why had he brought along the yellow shirts? probably because they were new. He didn't have that many new clothes. He figured they would look sharp in the tournaments he planned to enter. They were the only real golf shirts he had. He wishes he had on a dark blue shirt right now.

It had been a close call. Foozler had managed to find his way back to the lot where he had left his car only to find it gone. He reasoned a towing company had probably taken it away because his time had elapsed or something. Johnny had started into the lobby to ask after the vehicle when he spotted the policeman. Running, not casually turning and walking back out as if he had accidentally come into the wrong place had been his mistake. Scrambling over a wall and through a narrow hole in a fence had enabled him to elude his rather overweight, and out of shape, pursuer. It had not occurred to Johnny that they might have the lot staked out. The parking attendant must have recognized him. After all, not many people park their car and then walk away leading a cow on a rope, especially people with a New York license plate. Johnny figured that he must have been the only one today.

But where is he now? Johnny has arrived at an empty part of town. There are no rows of brightly-lit mansions like that other neighborhood, but only sullen, one-story warehouses behind which he can hear the lapping of the river. Faintly, like something just emerging, the low-tide smell wafts in from the water, giving a putrid odor to these dark streets hugging its banks. Towering above him is the massive bridge he had crossed so excitedly this morning, with Bovie as his back seat driver. An endless stream of traffic floats overhead with a dull roar, lights streaking higher than the tallest water towers.

Low, sparse clouds seem to sit on the edge of the steel structure, their grayness disintegrating in the white lights. The fickle night threatens the atmosphere with an inaudible thunder, making cowards of the passersby below.

Down here the air is heavy with exhaust and mildew. This once powerful center of business, the gem of the city, is in decay. These worn, dark fronts, devoid of commercial activity, reveal only the "& Company" where once proud Southern names like Butler, Calhoun, and Davis could be read. The late night gulls have mutated into bats, flying rats, circling and careening under every lamppost.

The mist Johnny has taken refuge in is dissipating. He continues on, chasing his ill-starred hopes, born of the flight he has made the mistake of taking. The building fronts become newer, with new goods, unloaded daily in containers and crates. The way now seems to be crowded with men who look like they might be stevedores who, their work done, seem to have nowhere to go. They shuffle through the darkness, exuding an aura of stale gin recycled as sweat.

Voices tremble under the dim glow of the street lamps. Their words resonate after Johnny as he runs along, an intruder in a now-empty house that still smells of its previous occupants. He catches the echo of his feet on the cobbled street, the clatter biting into the coolness of the night, into the evening of his memory.

"Hey man . . . like ware you-all goin'?" a voice sibilates at him from the dark of a doorway. "You-all lookin' fo a good time?"

There are no policeman chasing Johnny now, he is alone. He wonders if he has given them the slip—or is this just a part of Charlesboro where they are not brave enough to venture.

"Twenty-five dollar . . . and I'll do it any way you-all like. . . ." a shadow whispers.

Johnny wanders sing-song down the grim streets, past the faceless doors. He is tired. He needs to sleep. At the end of a murky abyss a huge, white capsule yawns before him. Bathed in fluorescent light, and incandescent light, and neon light, and halogen light, the night gives way to an artificial day.

A light rain has begun to add its flourish to the newly revealed brightness. As on a summer night in New York City, the drops slant silver across the lights, peppering Johnny's body with coldness, a wretchedness that darkens his bright yellow polo shirt to ochre, sticking it to his body. The wetness brings black to his matted gray hair. Like a moth he moves toward the whiteness. He stinks horribly. Foozler wants to be out of this damp and murky background scenery. He wants to be warm—and to sleep.

The rain is falling a little heavier now. Johnny has arrived at a small plaza filled with parked cars and feral cats. His passage arouses a once-loved, but presently cast-off, black tom who, distracted from cleaning itself in a doorway, abandons its place to scurry around a puddle and disappear into the darkness under a car. A scruffy calico, displaced by the scouring tom, slips three cars away. Looking down, Foozler treads lightly around the fragments of a mottled, matted, mutilated gray cat, sleeping permanently in the gutter.

A late-model Ford Mustang pulls into an empty space. Its occupants scurry out into the rain. A small ginger cat hurries for the warmth of the Mustang's engine. Another car arrives; they keep coming. All the cars appear to be occupied by Marines, and their wives or girlfriends. He remembers when Marines used to dress up, even wore medals on their chests. Now they are all clad in camouflage combat fatigues, even though any war is far away. It is as if battle gear has become smart casual for a night on the town.

Seeking refuge from the rain, Johnny hunches down in a doorway with a one-eyed ginger cat and a black man in an out-of-

Foozler Runs

season Santa Claus suit. The cat nuzzles up against the fugitive and rubs its face dry on his leg. Across the square is Foozler's goal. Bright neon circles enclose the entrance to "The White Whale." Invisible currents are drawing him, signals spelling out warmth, pleasure. To be inside in a crowd, listening to music, the thought brings a smile to Foozler's face, remembrances of his spent youth. He waits, reconnoitering. Johnny needs just the right moment, a group going in. He can not go in alone—after all he still is a wanted man, as far as he knows.

"You-all ain't planin' on goin' in dare, r' ya?" The man next to him says, handing him a piece of folded paper.

Johnny sees the Santa Claus suit for the first time. A little late for that, isn't it? It's February, or March? He seems to have lost track of time. The blank spaces in his calendar have gone unchecked. It was Mardi Gras when he began his trip. Was that a day ago, maybe a week ago, or was it longer?

"Why shouldn't I go in there?" Foozler asks. He wants to inquire why the man is wearing a Santa Claus suit, but decides to take it one question at a time.

"Dare's evil in dare, brother . . . evil and sin."

"Evil and sin?"

"Yes, brother . . . evil and sin. You-all jes take a look at dat dare paper I jes gave you. It tells all. Praised be da word o' da Lord. Hallelujah brother! . . ."

Johnny unfolds the paper. It is too dark in the doorway to read the damp missive. A crowd has gathered at the door of The White Whale, the moment he has been waiting for. Foozler starts toward the glowing white building. A powerful hand seizes his wrist, holding him back.

John Foozler feels the weakness in his body. His impulse is to break free, but he is held fast by the black Santa Claus, a man stronger and more powerful than he first appeared.

"Da Lord spoke ta Jonah," the black man begins. "He told him to go to Ninevah, and to cry against it, for dare wickedness is come up before me. . . ."

Johnny struggles to release himself, but Santa Claus tightens his grip. His face is so close to him, Johnny can smell the odor of the man's rotting teeth.

"Jonah sought to flee da presence o' da Lord by ship . . . but a great tempest arose, an da frightened mariners cast Jonah overboard."

"But it was at his own request, wasn't it?" Johnny says, recalling the story from his youth. He tended to like best those stories from the bible where people were responsible for their own destiny.

Johnny again tries to pull free, but the man's uncut nails draw welts of blood on his wrists.

". . .and Jonah is swallowed by a great whale. . . ."

Johnny stops struggling. Accepting his impuissance, he resigns himself to hearing out the whole story. Perhaps when it is ended the man will release him. He can see tears forming in the black man's eyes.

"But Jonah prayed to da Lord from the belly o' dat whale . . . hallelujah, brother! And he was vomited up on dry land. And he is commanded again ta go to Ninevah, and ta preach unto da people. Jonah preaches, and da people repent. Hallelujah, brother! And God, seeing Jonah's good work, spared Ninevah."

The man is crying openly now, sobbing almost hysterically. He releases Johnny's wrists to wipe his eyes. Johnny breaks free, and runs for the door of The White Whale.

"Beware! Dare in are more dan three hundred people who do not know da difference between dare right hand and dare left. . . ." Black Santa shouts biblically after the fleeing Johnny. A covey of pigeons that has been sheltering from the rain under a nearby façade bursts into flight.

Drawn to the light of the glowing edifice, Johnny scurries, head down in the rain, across the small, cobbled square, and into the path of an oncoming car. The driver, peering through his breath fogged windshield, brakes hard, and leans on his horn. Stopped, he rolls down his window, sticks out his closely-cropped head and yells after Foozler's fleeing figure:

"Hey! Fuckin' asshole! Watch where the fuck you're going. What are you, fucking drunk or something?

At that moment, the driver of the car behind, also a Marine, finding his way blocked, blows his horn, and then rolls down his window and shouts:

"Hey! Fuckin' asshole! What the fuck do you think you're doing? Move your fucking car!"

The Marine in the first car responds to the Marine in the second car: "Shut the fuck up, you fucking asshole. It's none of your goddamn fucking business!"

The Marine in the second car to the Marine in the first car: "Oh yeah, Fuck-head! Like I'm making it my fucking business. Now move your goddamn fucking piece of shit car before I come out there and ram my fucking fist down your fucking throat."

First Marine, "Oh yeah!. . . . Up a pig's gigee. Stick it up your goddamn fucking ass!"

Second Marine, getting out of his car and rushing toward the first Marine: "Fucking wise-ass fucking piece of shit! Like I'm going to teach you some fucking manners. . . ."

A small crowd is beginning to gather, huddled under the arcade of The White Whale. The two Marines are out of their cars now, standing in the rain, jostling one another.

"Fuck you, buddy! . . ."

"Shut the fuck up . . . you fucking asshole!"

"Fucking scumbag piece-of-shit. . . ."

In the meantime, the Marine's girlfriends, in ready reserve, are applying war paint in their car mirrors, while at the same time lending support out of their open windows.

"Don't take any shit from that guy, Randy!" Randy's girlfriend shouts. "Who the fuck does he think he is?. . ."

"Don't take any shit from that guy, Joe!" Joe's girlfriend shouts. "Who the fuck does he think he is?. . ."

They continue applying lipstick, at the same time balancing nervous cigarettes on the dashboard.

A third car pulls up behind the first two, its windshield wipers clearing a spot through which the driver, apparently another Marine, can observe the two combatants going at each other in the rain. He leans on his horn.

"Hey! You two fucking assholes . . . move your fucking cars!" the new arrival shouts giving his horn another long blast.

The sound waves, amplified by the raindrops, fall on the ears of our first two heroes, who interrupt their brawling and turn their attention to the newcomer.

"Who the hell's that fucker blowing his fucking horn?" shouts the first Marine, wiping blood from his nose.

"Fuck if I know. . . ." says the second Marine, spitting blood from his mouth. "Some fucking wise-ass fuck head that ain't got no fucking manners. . . ."

"Like, then let's teach that fucking prick some fucking manners!" announces first Marine, pounding his fist into his palm.

"I'm fucking with you, buddy. . . ." vows second Marine. He puts his arm around the shoulder of his new found friend and the two advance toward the interloper, who has gotten out of his car and is standing in the rain facing his two challengers.

"Don't take any fucking shit from those two guys, Mark!" Mark's girlfriend shouts. She has taken out her lipstick and flipped down the mirror behind her sun visor.

A fourth car pulls up behind the newly stopped car, followed shortly by another. The cars are all occupied by Marines, who are all now spilling out onto the street, all ready to join in the fight if for no other reason than that they have nothing else to do. These angry louts are by and large the bottom rung of the corps. Trained to kill—the idea so firmly fixed in their mind it takes away any bother of thinking—when there is no killing to be done, they perform their other duties in a lackluster way, and then moon about the base eager to be set free.

The crowd has gained in size. One can sense the excitement in the air. The people are ready for a big brawl. Even the ticket taker and the bouncer from The White Whale have joined the group of rubber-neckers. Lurking at the rear of the group, Foozler takes advantage of the distraction to slip through the entrance; unnoticed and without paying.

TWENTY-SIX

INSIDE THE WHITE Whale is another kind of chaos. What was once a tobacco warehouse now scintillates with hundreds of pulsating lights, and an equal number of pulsating bodies. The place is done in a nautical style, with what is commonly assumed to be nautical decor. The windows have been blanked over and turned into portholes. Decorative fishnet drapes over silver painted wooden dowels meant to be harpoons. Stuffed swordfish share wall space with white plastic whales executed in a cartoon style, the club logo. Crowding the center of the great space is a large plywood pylon, striped in red and white diagonals. The light from the rotating beacon on top coruscates off the walls. A replica lighthouse Foozler supposes.

Model schooners of various sizes and shapes abound, and more plastic whales. A blue neon sign with the words: "Thar he blows!" hangs over the door to the men's room. A similar sign, in pink, "Thar she blows!" indicates the entrance to the ladies'.

Above the clamor, repeating every three seconds, so loud that it blocks out all the other sounds, even the blaring of the band, comes a strange electronic baying noise, a foghorn perhaps, Johnny thinks, or maybe a simulacrum whale song.

The sign out front had announced: Tonight Only! Welcome Back Charlesboro's own "Blower and the Hootfish." The small print informed that the group was back in town after successfully completing their first national tour.

With the breakup of The Artful Foozler, Johnny had lost interest in the music scene. He no longer read the pop music magazines, keeping up with the numerous groups that come and go like leaves in the fall. He has not heard of Blower and the Hootfish but, judging by the crowd, in Charlesboro the Hootfish are big. The group is playing mainly songs written by other artists, but the leader Bobby Blower, is quite novel. He plays a wide variety of wind instruments, which he keeps stacked on a table in front of him, choosing one or the other seemingly at random. The band has a kind of eclectic, hard rock-jazz sound, which pleases the mix of young and old, civilian and military. Blower and the Hootfish are not disappointing their fans. If they don't play well—they play loud.

Johnny mingles among the crowd, seeking his coign of vantage, safety in numbers. The men were mostly military personnel from the nearby bases, which surround Charlesboro on the three sides that are not on the water. Their companions sound local, wives and girlfriends, and maybe a hooker or two.

Without saying a word a woman, perhaps a little older than most, begins to gyrate in front of Johnny, shaking her enormous breasts, bra-less under her red tank top, drawing him out onto the dance floor.

Foozler doesn't want to dance, at least not now, not with this woman. He is hungry. He wants to find the food, if they have any food here. So far all he has been able to do is to grab a handful of snacks, goldfish crackers in keeping with the nautical theme, as he walked past the bar.

"What's the matter? Ya-all got two left feet?" the woman asks, shaking her hips. Her tight blue jeans tuck up into the crack of her pudendum.

Johnny twists around once, swinging his arms the way dancing was done in his day. When he twirls back the woman is gone. She doesn't want to dance with someone with two left feet when the place is filled with sailors and Marines who perform with casual military precision. The prophet in the Santa Claus suit has warned him this place was filled with people who "didn't know their right hand from their left." However, he failed to mention anything about people not knowing their right foot from their left.

His partner gone, Johnny turns to leave the dance floor, but a navel catches his eye. It is an exceptional navel, exposed in a field of bronzed flesh, about three inches above a pair of black, hip hugger jeans, and six inches below a lime green halter top. The owner of the navel, about the age of the daughter Foozler never had, smiles at him and keeps wiggling and giggling.

Blower is blowing a saxophone now, wild animal notes. Johnny is trotting, turning to the stimulation of the tunes, concentrating on the navel. The girl keeps smiling, perhaps not aware of the less than chivalrous thoughts forming in Foozler's dancing mind—lust not love. He imagines his tongue exploring the road map of that tiny, perfect knot of flesh, the scar of the first violation of her infant body, the moment she was separated from her mother. He sees his hand undoing the bright metal zipper, sliding down the skin of her jeans, her scanty undies, revealing the fleshy, rounded elevation of her mons veneris. He sees his tongue seeking that spot which gives her the greatest pleasure. Foozler is not too old for such things as her taunting pelvis would imply.

"Hey! Watch it, buddy!" A male person, possibly a Marine in mufti, or maybe a skin-head, has taken offense at Johnny's accidental collision.

The belly-button is gone, replaced by a slim thing in short shorts. As she spins around the waxing and waning crescents of her buttocks bared below catch the phosphorescent light. Johnny has the urge to bite them, like twin apples in the Garden of Eden. But it is food he really wants. His head is swimming from the lights, the music, his fatigue, his hunger. He needs to sit down, but cannot. Foozler is in the middle of the floor, being carried along by the swaying throng. He shakes his head, trying to focus his eyes. A girl in front of him is wearing a T-shirt with the words "Fuck Me," on the front. Blinking his eyes, his head spinning, Johnny steps backwards, stops.

"Hey! Watch what the fuck yer doin', Bozo!" another short haircut spats at him.

Foozler just stands there.

"Like get the fuck off the fuckin' dance floor if ya don't want ta fuckin' dance, asshole!"

Johnny is pushed aside by a boy wearing full leather, a biker perhaps, or trying to look like one. He is shoved again, by a tattooed arm, snakes, flames, "Mother," protruding from under a black leather vest. Foozler has staggered from the ephebric section to the province of the punkers. No barriers are broken down here in this pulsating fantasy world, the separations mimicking the real.

Johnny shuffles along, half dancing, half stumbling. He finds a corner where his group, middle-aged men, sit and drink, while they exercise their voyeuristic prerogative by staring at the diaphanously dishabilled damsels disporting on the dance floor. Suddenly, Foozler is face down on that same floor. Has he fallen—or was he tripped?

He looks up at the table he was approaching. Actually, due to his vantage point, Johnny's view is under the table. The three middle-age men have their penises out and are discreetly diddling their dorks.

"Jeez!" Foozler groans at the sight.

Three half-hard-ons are quickly retracted into their pants. However, to bear witness to this perversion is not the reason Johnny has been brought down. He was tripped. The booted foot that did the tripping now finds Foozler's bottom, with extreme force.

"Surprise! Like you're that fucking piece-of-shit that started it all out front!" a Marine with a swollen face growls at Johnny, giving him another kick, this time in the ribs, as he tries to get up.

"I don't know what you're talking about . . . see the waiter if your service is slow," Foozler defends, trying to make a joke out of it. He is on his feet now, his chin is bleeding where he hit it on the floor. He wants no trouble, especially with a big, angry Marine. He wants only to eat something, and then find a place to sleep. He is so tired.

"You're the fucking asshole that jumped in front of me and almost made me wreck my fucking car. . . ."

The Marine is holding two mugs of beer, one probably for his date. Johnny's febrile eyes examine the limpid amber liquid, the fluffy foam. The man's angry words hang in the air, never quite reaching the exhausted Foozler. The shadow that has been the day is passing in front of his face.

"I'm sorry. . . ." Johnny says.

"Fucking sorry don't make it fucking okay . . . fucking jerks like you need to be taught a fucking lesson. I bet you were probably in the fucking Navy . . . weren't you?"

Blower and the Hootfish are doing another appropriation of an old favorite in their particular way, the sound never quite succeeding, never reaching a definite conclusion.

"Navy?" Johnny says incredulously. The man's words are imprecise to Foozler's fatigued mind, their meaning indefinite. All he can think of to do is repeat the word: "Navy?"

"Fucking 'A,' man. . . . All you fucking, goddamn, cocksucking faggots are in the fucking Navy."

A sudden clearness comes to Johnny's head, the sounds of Blower and The Hootfish floating over the feverish crowd, the shiver of a familiar tune breaking the tension of his misfortune. He is no longer threatened by the possibilities, but faint with the delightful rigidity of a realization.

"Listen!" he tells his tormenter. "They're playing one of our songs, that's Snake's Belly . . . by The Artful Foozler."

Na, na, nah . . . Now, Baby I may be . . . lower than a green snakes belly . . . but you could carry a jar of jelly . . . underneath me while standing up wearing your high-healed sneakers. . . . Na, na, nah, now Baby, I may be . . . lower than a green snakes belly. . . ."

The man opposite him swears and glares, a look that says: One, two, three, four, I'm in the Marine Corps. Johnny, unsure of what comes next, begins to back away, one small step at a time, not a false move, but planned and deliberate. His pulse quickens with the approaching danger. He is master of his own fate. He can end this unhappy situation by running. But Foozler believes in rules, invisible rules that two people who do not know one another have nevertheless agreed to, the gooseflesh of his convulsive dreams. He will stay on his side and his antagonist will—he hopes—stay on his.

Blower and The Hootfish are still playing "Snake's Belly." Through the fog of memory, Johnny hears his band again, sees them; not nearby, but far away, the wretchedness of a wasted youth, the nonsense of their splendidly colored cardboard life.

* * *

The Artful Foozler was playing in a club near the Marine base at Parris Island, South Carolina. The dingy hall was filled with blue smoke, pink women, and green Marines who have been preparing to go to Iraq.

Solo, the groups lead singer had begun one of his anti-war songs, "Must we go on dying . . . and crying?" Songs the band had been told not to play, because the club owner had warned them the crowd would be mostly military personnel. Johnny, on drums, did not know what to do. He just kept beating out a rhythm to the lost syllables of the song.

A confusion of silence came over the room. People stopped talking and turned around and listened to what they normally did not hear. Johnny's exaggerated hopes were that Solo's song was transforming the troops, which was why they had become silent. A few of the men began laughing and jeering, and making obscene gestures. The confusion that had quieted the room was giving way to ugliness. Foozler could smell the hate spreading through the room like spilled gasoline.

A beer can rattled onto the stage. The men at the bar had begun throwing bottles and cans, their drunken aim causing some of their missiles to fall short, landing on their comrades at the tables out in front.

"Goddamn fucking liberal, towel-head-lovin' queers! Get the fuck off the fucking stage. . . ."

A bottle arched past Johnny's head and crashed into an amplifier, sending up a shower of static and sparks.

"Killers! Goddamn fucking, murdering baby killers," Solo screamed. He was grabbing things off the stage, returning the troop's fire. "Goddamn fucking, baby killers!"

The fusillade of taunts and projectiles crisscrossed the hall. Most of the patrons had dived under the tables. From the back corner a small group, its strategy quickly worked out, prepared to charge the stage.

"Goddamn fucking paid assassins!" Solo shouted, hurling a mike stand at the attackers.

"Let's stomp that fuckin' cock suckin' faggot bastard!" A burly sergeant rallied his troops.

Like a cat pouncing on a mouse, Solo leapt to his guitar case, producing the small automatic pistol he always cached there when the band was traveling. "Stand back you fucking assholes . . . if you don't want to die!" he shouted waving his gun wildly about. He fired two shots randomly at the ceiling, shattering one of the lights. A rain of glass fell on the tables, along with some of the red, white and blue crepe paper decorating the hall.

Silence overtook the room, punctuated only by the whirring of the ceiling fans, and the faint sounds of the paper streamers swaying in the artificial breeze. Advancing to the center of the stage, Solo sat down on the edge, his naked knees shining through the holes in his worn denims.

"Let's get the fucking police!" a corporal shouted, starting for the door.

"Don't anybody go anywhere!" Solo cautioned, pointing his gun at the head of the nearest Marine. "Or this poor fucker gets his skull blown open. So everyone sit down. I don't want to hurt anybody . . . all I want to do is talk."

There was some grumbling. Johnny sees himself getting up from his hiding place behind his drums—he still doesn't know what he should have done—and sit back on his stool. Then a tense stillness came over the room, a nothingness, the quiet of the dessert.

For the next quarter of an hour, although it seemed like an eternity, Solo, his gun trained on the man in front of him, lectured to the group. The troops listened intently. They had been indoctrinated to listen, and to obey, and not to feel, nor think beyond the confines of what was needed to do the job. Intimidated by this crazed, potential murder in front of them they did not even sip the warm beer going flat in their glasses, or draw on their cigarettes growing long ashes in the trays.

Joe Normaneski, known as Solo, the gone mad lead singer of The Artful Foozler, described his childhood in Iowa: the family farm, fishing in the creek, Junebugs, his mother and sisters, and his father, who had died in another war. Then he told them a little about American history, and what democracy meant to him; and how we weren't really liberating anybody anyway in Iraq, only fighting a war for the oil companies. He reminded them that there they would be required to kill innocent people. He told them that if they didn't go, just went home, and everyone else did the same, there would be no more wars.

The men at the back were becoming anxious. The rocker wasn't talking about himself anymore, but about them. It wasn't they who were doing the wrong thing, it was him. They were defending freedom, and their country, and the American way of life. Where did he, this dope-taking, flag-burning, liberal faggot, think he was coming from telling them what was right or wrong.

"Yeah! Ya think yer so fuckin' tough because ya have a fuckin' gun on someone. . . ." A thick-necked lance corporal, his white face standing out from his camouflage uniform, yelled a challenge at Solo.

Scanning the room, Johnny noticed for the first time that all the Marines in this Southern bar had white faces, despite the large number of black Marines he had seen passing in the street earlier. Even the topless dancers, cowering in the corner their arms folded over their breasts like bullet-proof vests, or perhaps a sign that they are temporarily off duty, were all young, white girls, probably only in their teens. The other women in the hall, wives, girlfriends, and perhaps a few hookers, were also all white.

The corporal's remonstration had broken the silence. The troops began to murmur among themselves. Some cautiously lifted warm beers to their lips, refreshing their false courage. Solo, the performer that he is, sensed he was loosing his audience.

"Put that fucking gun down . . . and take me on hand to hand. Then we'll see who's tougher!" a voice shouted out.

The challenger's dare gained momentum. There was a chorus of: "Yeah! Yeah!" The idea had the support of the crowd. The battle cry, "Let's see how tough you are without that fucking gun. . . ." began to echo around the room.

Jumping to his feet, Solo fired another shot at the ceiling. Once again he shattered a light fixture. Again shards of glass came tumbling down, quieting the protesters.

"So you're finally getting my point," Solo said, striding up and down the stage, his rock-star cowboy boots making the only noise. He was strutting in that way pop singers usually do. "Might makes right . . . I've got a gun, and you don't . . . so I'm tough, and you're fucking nothing." Solo's feet were moving faster, it was almost as if he were dancing with himself. "So, who is man enough to come up here and take this gun away from me?"

Solo stopped his pacing. He held the gun in both hands and took careful aim at a man in the front row. The man did not move. Johnny saw sweat beading on his forehead.

"Bang! You're dead!" Solo said playfully, mockingly.

"He's fucking crazy!" a sergeant shouted from the middle of the room. "He doesn't have enough rounds in that gun to shoot more than two of us. Some of you run out and get the police!"

"Is that an order, sergeant?" a private with a sugar-cured Virginia accent questioned from down front. "You're closer to the fuckin' door, why don't you-all go . . . I don't want to be one of the two that gets his fuckin' ass blown away."

A nervous laughter scurried around the room, momentarily easing the tension. Annoyed by the levity, Solo fired again, shattering the mirror behind the bar. Johnny watched the topless dancers scatter in a flurry of shaking breasts and sequined g-strings. The laughter stopped.

"Courage depends on what end of the gun you're on," Solo continued. "In a few days from now you'll be in Iraq with a gun in your hand. And you'll be staring down at some poor slob of a local, who doesn't have a gun in his hand, so you'll be brave. But now you're all chicken-shit . . . afraid to move your fucking asses because someone might get shot . . . and it ain't gonna be you, because you're too shit-scared to die."

An undertone of reluctant agreement passed through the crowd.

"You are all probably sitting there thinking I'm some cowardly, drug taking, rock musician piece-of-shit," Solo went on. "Well you may be right on all these things, except one. I'm no coward. . . ."

Solo was pacing again, his snakeskin boots beating a little tap on the surface of the stage. Tears could be seen defining the corners of his eyes. His voice had gone dry, his speech soft, as if he was coming to the end of what he was going to say. "You see, unlike you poor mother-fuckers, I'm not afraid to die. And when I die it will be by my own choice, not because I was sent out by some fucking politician to kill someone who has done me no wrong. I'm not going to kill somebody I don't even know . . . but someone I know very well. . . ."

Johnny watched in horror as if in slow motion Solo raised the gun to his temple. He gave a slight nod, almost a bow—and then emptied the remaining shell into his brain. Foozler had leapt up from behind his drums, but too late. He caught the falling body, the head tilted, a spot of red growing on the temple. Johnny stroked the dying Solo's head. "Was it worth it?" he whispered.

* * *

"Was what worth it, fucker?. . . What the fuck are you talking about? you goddamn cock-sucking sailor boy."

Foozler shakes his head. The White Whale ebbs and flows around him. His antagonist has guzzled down one of the two glasses of beer he was carrying, passing the fluid directly to his brain. He is starting on the second beer, and shows no signs of going away. Johnny would like to move on but the Marine has hold of him with his free arm.

"I wasn't in the Navy," Johnny replies, trying to remember what the question actually was.

"Then what were you in, fucker? . . . the fucking queer-ass Air Force."

"What's wrong with the Air Force?" one of the middle-aged men who have been watching from the table says, rising to his feet.

"No body's talking to you. . . . I asked this smart-ass fucker here."

"I wasn't in anything," Johnny reveals, instantly realizing he has said the wrong thing. He should have said the Foreign Legion, the Green Berets, CIA, something.

"So you what are you, too good to serve your county? You-all must have been one of them goddamn liberal, abortion-loving, dope smokin' college kids," he says, firmly drawing the battle lines.

TWENTY-SEVEN

WHAT HAD BEGUN as a casual imbroglio blossoms into a serious brawl. A bloody donnybrook follows. It is not merely a bar fight. Most of those present, men and women, civilian and military, were combating one another for reasons that had nothing to with anything at all—knocking each other wildly about the room, crashing into tables and breaking chairs. After feebly trying to defend himself, Johnny is knocked down and kicked in the face, causing his left eye to become swollen. With whistles blaring, the police finally arrive. Foozler tries to slip out wearing a borrowed raincoat over his yellow polo shirt. The owner sees the coat and claims it as his. Johnny is arrested and carted off to the station in a police van filled with brawlers.

Johnny sits, cowering, in the crowded holding tank among the other perpetrators. He is sure he will be found out. Here is the attempted assassin, a member of a terrorist cell, the cattle rustler, subject of a state wide manhunt, just sitting here, bloodied, in this sweaty and urine smelling cell, waiting for the police to realize his identity.

"Okay, you're next," a policeman says dragging Foozler before a man sitting behind a desk.

"All right . . . would you-all state your full name?"

"John Franklin Foozler. . . ." Johnny hesitates. He was about to add "sir" as all the other men had referred to the man behind the desk as "sir." But they were military men, or Foozler supposed them to be. He does not want to be taken for a military man. If he is going to go down it will be as he is, whatever that is. At this point he is not sure.

"Can I see some ID, John? . . ." the man says, giving Foozler's swollen face a long and curious look.

Johnny reluctantly hands over his driver's license. More than the fear of being found out, he now resents being called by his first name by someone he does not know. Even during his rock-n-roll days John Foozler always preferred the formality of proper address.

"Huum. . . . Says here you-all are from Noo Yawk, son. . . ."

"Yes, I am . . . Sergeant Atkins," Johnny replies with emphasis. He has counted the stripes on the officer's sleeve for the honorific, and read his name off the man's tag. Foozler is about to add, and I am not your son, my real father is dead, but he restrains himself.

"No need to call me Sergeant Atkins, son, my first name is Monmouth . . . most people here jus call me Moo," he says, grinning at Johnny.

On hearing the word "moo" Johnny's heart flutters. He raises his eyes to meet the sergeants. The sergeant smiles again. Is it just a coincidence? A firm believer in telepathy, Foozler forces his mind to go blank. Do not even think of cows he tells himself—thinking of cows.

"So. . . . Jus what you-all doin' down here in our fair city, John?"

"Just passing through . . . I mean visiting the, eh, historic sites."

"Our city is kinda different from back in Noo Yawk . . . ain't it?"

"I'm not from *the city*. . . ." Johnny says, emphasizing the words. "I'm from upstate."

"Well, Noo Yawk is Noo Yawk, up or down. And you-all is in Charlesboro now. And we're right friendly down here. We got what they call 'Southern Hospitality.' So we don't take kindly to no Yankee comin' down here and startin' trouble. . . ."

"But I didn't start any trouble, Sergeant Moo," Johnny protests, realizing no one has yet figured out who he really is, even though he is wearing a bright yellow polo shirt and a face that, before his beating, matched the wanted man they have been showing on television all night long.

"We got witnesses that say it was you-all that started the brawl."

"That's not true . . . I was just taking a walk around town, and it started to rain, so I went into The White Whale to get a drink. . . ."

"One drink?"

"I didn't even get a drink. I mean I don't drink liquor. I was looking for a cup of tea or something."

"Then you-all should have no trouble walking straight down that there white line there, should you?" the sergeant says pointing.

This has been the sport Johnny has overheard, but not been able to observe from the holding cell. It provides entertainment for the officers waiting around the squad room, who are reforming now, making a gauntlet of sorts. The accused is made to "walk the line." If he succeeds, he is not charged with anything, and set free. Those who fail, in front of so many witnesses, are booked for drunkenness, and sent to the city jail for the night to "sleep it off."

"Well, go ahead, Yankee. . . ." one of the officers says. "It shouldn't be no trouble for a sober fellow like you-all. . . ."

The beating he sustained has transformed Johnny's face to a petrified and tragic mask—perhaps the reason no one here has recognized him as the hunted man. The pupil of his left eye hides behind his swollen eyelid. His right eye lays in wait, tense, rotating around the room in a frenzy of permanent suspicion. Pale and faint, his head pounding, no longer possessed with the powers that protect a perfectly healthy person from failure, Johnny watches disconcertedly as the spidery, white line zigzags down the gray industrial carpet. A cockroach emerges from a chink in the floor, its path mirroring the movements of the stripe. Trying to focus his one good eye, Johnny watches as the white line explodes into a bolt of lightning. The panic of the real possibility of spending the night in jail, where his true identity would surely be revealed, seizes at his brain. He hesitates, reluctant to begin walking. One of the officers at the end of the row appears to be holding an arrow in his hand. Foozler stares hard. It is not an arrow, but a golf club, a putter.

Suddenly grasping an idea, a way not to have to walk the line, Johnny addresses the group of police officers. "Hey! Are you guys sporting fellows?"

"Now are you-all gonna walk this here line . . . or what?"

"Any fool, drunk or sober can saunter down a twelve foot line," Foozler says. "If you've got a ball, and a water glass to go along with that putter . . . I'll bet you I can sink a put that long."

"Damn fool Yankee must be crazy," one of the officers says to the group.

"Just walk that there line, fellow," Sergeant Moo urges.

"Hey! Let him try it," the owner of the putter chimes in. "You-all can give it a try . . . I got some balls and a practice cup in my locker. Some of us practice here when we don't got nothin' better ta do. . . ."

"And even when you-all do have somethin' better ta do," someone interjects. They all laugh heartily.

Johnny tests the weight of the club in his hand, feeling the straightness of the shaft and the smoothness of the face. "I'll need two practice putts to get the feel of the club, and the roll of the floor," he says, "and then the third one goes in . . . dead center."

The policemen look at one another, they want to laugh, but are intimidated by Johnny's hubris.

He feels confident with the man's putter in his hand. It is something, the first thing today, that he can relate to, something anchored in reality. Johnny is taking a calculated risk, but he knows that with his vision blurred the way it is he would have had a difficult time walking a straight line. The odds are in favor of him making the putt, since he normally putts with his left eye closed anyway.

A dull green, rubber practice cup is brought out, the kind where the sides gently fold over to accept the ball, the kind he practiced with in his trailer. Johnny likes these. He does not like the electric powered cups that shoot the ball back with a pop when you make a putt—too much distraction.

The floor should be fairly true, he thinks. The building is rather new. It is impossible to read any break, although there is sure to be some. He studies the nap of the carpet. It looks to be worn right down the line, which appears to have been recently repainted, brushed not sprayed. He imagines the hundreds of drunks, possibly thousands, that have staggered down that three inch wide stripe, some successfully—others not.

The green cup at the end has become an anchor that keeps the white line from swaying in his Cyclopean vision as he takes his practice swings.

"At least he knows how to hold the club," one of the officer's remarks observing Johnny's overlapping grip.

"He don't look like no country club type though . . . I'd say he was a public course player," another adds.

Johnny raises his hand for silence. "It's rude to talk when someone is putting," he reminds them, placing down the first of his three balls.

Taken aback by the serious tone of Foozler's remark, the officers fall into a desultory silence.

As is his habit, Johnny takes two practice strokes, then steps up to the ball. He tilts his head, and lines up the putter with his right eye, keeping his left eye closed. By now he could not open his left eye if he wanted to. His method is not so much to strike the ball, but to allow the club to push the round object to its target. Foozler determined that as he could see no break, his best plan would be to roll the ball straight down the white stripe, directly at the cup.

The ball is on its way. Straight out, tracking so nicely along the line that one of the coppers shouts out: "Damn . . . he's got it on the first try!"

However, it is not to be. The ball begins to slow down and then, hitting what must be a slick spot in the paint, speeds up and falls off the line, pin high to the right.

"Not bad," someone remarks. "But not in the hole, although I'd say the rest of that is a gimme." He picks up the ball and pitches it to Foozler.

"I said two practice balls," Johnny reminds them. He will have to start the next ball a little to the left, he tells himself; which he does.

But the second ball falls off farther to the left and, catching the loose nap, slows dramatically, ending up about a foot short.

"If we were having a match I'd say I gotta see the rest of that," the man who owns the putter says.

The trip to the ball, taken with a long arc, is more difficult than the putt, which Johnny cleans up with apparent ease. But the activity was not as casual as Foozler had made it appear. Johnny's good eye had not just navigated him to the ball, but also rotated wildly around the floor as he walked, taking in the grain of the carpet, how the paint was worn, the slight dip on the floor he had not seen at first, and a myriad of other details his brain is now processing.

"Well, buddy . . . this one here is for all the marbles. Knock it in and you-all can go home. Miss it and you-all will be staying here for the rest of the night. . . ."

The coppers are all laughing as Johnny walks slowly back to the other end, deliberately circling, hoping they don't notice his one-eyed wobble.

"I wouldn't give you a nickel for this guy's chance of going home tonight. . . ." one of the younger cops ventures. There is more laughter.

Standing up from the crouch he had assumed to study the putt, Johnny reaches for his wallet. "A nickel! Anybody want to put some real money on it?" he asks. "If I'm not out of line. I mean I don't know if they allow gambling in police stations in this state. . . ."

"They only allow gambling on Injun reservations," a short, fat policeman offers, adding: "If they're Injun reservations that belong to the Mafia. . . ."

"Which will be everywhere, if Senator Billy Bob has his way," another officer observes sarcastically.

"Damn fool politician near got his head blown off this afternoon," another voice says. "Any news on that there terrorist guy we're supposed ta be looking for?"

"Last word I heard they-all seen him up in Bullham Township. He ain't no A-rab though, but he sure is a damn ugly looking fellow, got a real big nose. . . ."

Hearing this Johnny crouches down and puts his hand over his eyes, shielding his face. Nothing unusual about that, the pros always do it on TV.

A large cockroach dashes across the white line, sprinting for safety, only to be flattened by a size twelve police boot.

"Goddamn cockroaches . . . come down here from the nigger neighborhoods."

"Yeah . . . goddamn niggers got them in their fuckin' pants. When we lock em' up the damn critters sneak out in the cells."

Foozler Runs

Glancing around the room, Johnny observes there are no black men among the officers. If there are any on the force they don't hang around here. He shifts the dull, gray cast iron putter to his right hand, trying to get back into himself. He regrets his rashness at having suggested a bet and slides his wallet back into his pocket.

"Woah. . . . Don't you-all put that billfold away there, Yankee. How about it Moo? Let the man put up a little bet . . . kinda like makin' bail," the policeman who stomped the cockroach says.

"Well, I got five bucks I'll put in myself," Sergeant Moo announces somewhat jovially. "What's the bet?"

With megalomaniac exaggeration, Johnny takes 103 dollars from his wallet, all the cash he has, and throws it down on the floor. "Here . . . even money. You guys can cover that with your donut fund."

"Well at least we know we couldn't get him for vagrancy," one of the officers says. "I'm in for a tenner."

"Yeah, but when he misses we can get him for vagrancy as well as for drunk and disorderly."

They all laugh.

The money is counted and neatly piled in the middle of the floor.

The convulsion of laughter trickles to silence as Johnny approaches his putt. It must be the time for the change of shift, as the room is filling with fresh blue uniforms. The odd petty criminal, newly apprehended, has been left to sit off to the side, still handcuffed. The thin white line running down the floor has taken on a deeper meaning as Johnny watches its now more subdued movements with a mixture of apprehension and pleasurable excitement. With a firm, yet gentle, grip he runs the short-handled club along the floor. He takes two practice strokes before stepping up and addressing his ball. He feels fluid, draining from his swollen left eye, running down his cheek.

Johnny has decided he will not play any break, but go straight at the hole. The speed is critical. Too fast and the ball might skitter off to the right. Too slow and it will die to the left. His stroke must have the passion of the artist and the huntsman melded into one. The ball is on its way, slowly tracking along the slick line toward its goal. Decelerating slightly, as if to add a touch of melodrama to the scene, the ball slowly drops into the cup.

The police officers stand there in stunned silence, and then reluctantly hand over the pile of money.

Pushing open the door and stepping out of that caged capsule of fluorescent light, Foozler quickly pockets his newly doubled cash. In his haste to be gone he did not bother to count it. However, if you can't trust the coppers, who can you trust? Echoing in his ears are the alarmed words that the fugitive they are on the lookout for has been spotted on the north side, out near the motel where the senator is staying. All cars in that vicinity are being sent to that area.

Behind him the bright lights of the station house are fading in the spring-like rain. Rubbing his bare arms for warmth, Johnny smiles, and quietly disappears into the thick, damp darkness.

TWENTY-EIGHT

THE POLICE STATION six blocks behind him now, Johnny slows from his triumphal striding to a more sedate walk. His wallet bulges fat in his pocket with his newly won money. The moon rides high in the heavens. Like a shaken snow globe, the night sky reveals the metamorphoses of its multiple configurations.

Foozler has, by chance, returned to the Town Common. Rain is no longer falling. The air is light to breathe. It shimmers like silver gauze. He can smell daffodils and wet grass. Proceeding in a luminous journey across this vast expanse, Johnny cannot believe the events of this afternoon. It is as if the day had been the nightmare, and this trembling night the real day.

Johnny hesitates. There are some people moving across the Common toward him. He thinks to run. Then he sees that they are merely people out enjoying an evening walk, a strange situation in a city where a mad assassin, who also kidnaps cows, and two al-Qaida terrorists are supposedly on the loose. The passersby do not even look at him, a sorry sight with his swollen eye, but merely mumble a hello, as they pass with uplifted eyes, enchanted by the starry displays.

On such a fresh night as this, Johnny cannot help having happy thoughts and inspirations. He mind is refilled with his ideas and projects. He has completely forgotten about his cow, and the senator and his wife, and the police. He wants to be on his way to he's not sure where. Florida had been his destination. Then he remembers his missing car, and how tired he is. And where is he going to sleep tonight?

Across the park, then along the river, through back alleys and down well-lighted streets, Johnny walks unnoticed. He is retracing now, without realizing it in his fatigue, his journey of an earlier hour. He finds himself on a familiar street. A diffused whiteness glows at the end of the block, although not as bright as earlier. He can read the letters on the glass clearly: The Cinnamon Shop. Then the window goes dark. His heart stops, only to start again when a familiar figure emerges from the darkened space. The person turns and fumbles with the door.

"Excuse me," Johnny says. "I was here earlier. . . ."

"Oh yes. You're the person from New York. . . ."

"Did I say I was from New York? I don't remember. . . ."

"No . . . but I lived in New York long enough to recognize the accent. However, you're not from the city, or if you are you didn't grow up there."

They are walking together, side by side. She was walking quickly, as if she wanted to get away from something, but not him; for whenever Johnny slowed his pace she slowed hers so he could keep up.

"Hey! What's the big rush?" Johnny asks, sounding so tired.

"Oh, it's nothing," she says, pausing as if she was about to add additional information he does not need to know.

"Nothing?"

"I thought you were someone else. . . ."

"Disappointed? . . ."

"No. Actually I was rather glad to see you . . . there's a guy who follows me around, a real creep. He won't leave me alone. I thought at first you were him."

"Why don't you report him to the police?"

"I can't. . . . You see he is a policeman, a detective. We had, well, a sort of affair . . . and then I found out he was still married. I told him to stop bothering me . . . but he won't."

"Where's your car parked?" Johnny asks. They have already traveled three blocks.

"Oh, I don't have one. I live in an apartment downtown, so I can walk everywhere I want to go."

"And where are you going now?"

"Home," she answers, considering him rather forward. "And where are you going?"

"I don't know. . . ." Johnny stutters. "Would you like to go somewhere with me? I mean for a cup of coffee or something. I just won a lot of money playing golf with some policemen. . . ."

John Foozler's remark causes the woman to stop short. He realizes he has said more than he should have. Overcome by pain and fatigue he is babbling.

"Playing golf with policemen?. . . At night? . . ." she says, skeptical of his story. "Surely you're joking. . . ."

"Well, I was only putting," Johnny replies.

They are standing under a street lamp. The woman looks at him, noticing his swollen eye, seeing it clearly for the first time. "Oh my god! What happened to you? You didn't look like this when you came in earlier. Did they beat you up?"

"Who?"

"The police. . . ."

"Oh, no. It wasn't them," Johnny says, deciding the truth, as bizarre as it seems is his best course. "I got a in a fight with some Marines, and got taken down to the station house. I had to sink a twelve foot putt to prove I wasn't drunk . . . or they were going to lock me up. But I wasn't drunk . . . I haven't had a drink in years."

The lights of a car are slowly making their way down the deserted street, too slow to be someone going somewhere. Pulling him into the shadows, the woman puts her arms around Johnny and presses her lips to his mouth. She watches over his shoulder as the car creeps by. She realizes that she is somehow attracted to this man, in spite of, or perhaps because of his outrageous appearance. He had looked pretty bad when they first met, and now he looks even worse. He must be delirious, she thinks, making up a story about playing golf with the police, in the nighttime yet. She is not sure why she is doing what she is doing. She wonders if she might be heading for big trouble.

"What was that all about?" Johnny asks, pulling his head back, but in no hurry to leave her arms, enjoying the feel of her breasts soft against his chest.

"It was a Charlesboro police car. They were probably looking for you. . . ."

"Me? Why would they be looking for me?" Johnny says, unwilling to give up his identity.

"Maybe to get the money back you won from them playing golf," she chides him. "Or maybe because you're the man who stole the cow, and tried to kill Senator Billy Bob. . . ."

"What makes you think I'm someone who has stolen a cow?" he says, avoiding speaking about the senator. Johnny cannot believe what he heard on the television. He has no idea of what happened this afternoon.

"Well . . . for one thing, when you came into the shop earlier this evening you stank to high heaven. I thought at first you just needed a bath . . . then I realized you smelled like someone who had been sleeping with a cow."

"First of all . . . I didn't sleep with the cow, and it was only a little calf. I named her Bovie. I don't know why everyone keeps saying I stole a cow. And I didn't *steal* her, not really. She just sort of got into my car."

"Got into your car!" the woman says incredulously.

"Yeah. . . . She just got in . . . and then she wouldn't get out; that is until we got to Charlesboro."

"And why did little Bovie want to go to Charlesboro? To help you kill the senator?"

"I didn't intend to kill the senator . . . I mean that's a totally crazy notion that someone must have made up. I didn't have a gun or anything, just this calf, which I was trying to give to his wife."

"Give to the senator's wife! Why on earth would you want to give something to that tart?"

"Tridy! She's really nice. . . ."

"Tridy? You know her then . . . Tridance Plantigrade?"

"Eh. . . . Yes, we met back in Turtle Beach. . . ."

"Turtle Beach? How long did you live there?"

"Oh, I didn't live there . . . I was just passing through. . . ."

"I'll bet you were. . . ." she comments with a slightly sarcastic tone.

They are under another street light now. She is beginning to wonder if he might have injured his head. He does not seem to be making complete sense.

"Here let me take a look at that eye," she says, turning his face to the light, holding it with her hand.

Concealing nothing by his expression, Johnny watches her through his good eye as she probes the injured one.

"Ouch!" Foozler says, grimacing.

"My god! It's oozing pus. . . ."

The woman takes out her handkerchief and touches the cloth to her tongue, moistening it with her spittle. Looking up she catches Johnny's one good eye staring lustfully at the tip of her pink tongue. She sticks the moist organ out farther, rolling it luridly around her lips. She smiles, and then takes the damp handkerchief and begins cleaning around Foozler's eye.

"Be careful. . . ." Johnny urges.

"Where are you staying?" she asks, going at her work with enthusiasm.

"I don't know. . . ." is Johnny's curt reply. "The police have taken away my car, with everything I own in it. All I have left is the money I won from them."

"Then you're coming home with me," she says putting the finishing touches to his eye. "By the way . . . my name is Joan, Joan Tray. What's yours?"

"John. You can call me Johnny," he says, instinctively shaking Joan's hand. He does not voice any resistance to her suggestion since it is the best offer he has had all day.

As for Joan Tray, she has decided that this man, despite what she does not know about him, and what he might or might not have done, and the sorry state of his appearance, is the most interesting male she has encountered since arriving in Charlesboro some three years ago.

After a considerable bit of walking, they finally arrive at Joan Tray's street. It appears to Johnny they may have taken a devious route. Although unfamiliar with the layout of Charlesboro, Foozler does have an adept sense of direction. He has the distinct feeling they doubled back and retraced their tracks several times. He had watched the moon through the trees lining the streets, sometime in front of him, and sometime behind.

Joan makes a signal for him to be quiet, and they stop. She whispers to Johnny to wait in the shadows while she goes ahead. Joan is especially concerned about the presence of a black car in front of the antebellum house she lives in on the second floor rear. She points out two windows. Joan will turn on a light in the one nearest the street if all is clear. Then Johnny should come up the back stairs, where she has just disappeared.

If she turns on a light in the rear most window, he is to go around the corner and wait for her in the darkness of some bushes.

If a car is following her when she walks by, he is to stay hidden until both she and the car are out of sight, and then go up the back stairs, where he will find her apartment door unlocked.

Johnny crouches in the shadows, heavy with sleep, waiting for what seems like forever. He hears himself start to snore, and his stomach rattle. Only his hunger, and the ever increasing pain in the side of his face, keeps him from dozing off. He is beginning to forget which window is supposed to mean what. Then a window lights up, the one nearest the front. Crouching slightly, he hurries toward the back stairs.

She must have left the light off on purpose, Johnny thinks as he gropes his way up the steps in darkness. At the second landing he is greeted by the glow from a door open just a crack. Then Joan's head appears. Holding her finger across her mouth to indicate silence, she lets him into the apartment.

"What's all this spy stuff about?" Johnny asks once inside.

"Take off your clothes. . . ."

"What! Like we've only just met. Don't you want a little foreplay or something, and I could use some food. . . ." Johnny says facetiously. "By the way, my name's Johnny . . . what's yours?"

"I've already told you my name; I'm Joan," she replies, adding, "Joan Tray." She emphasizes her last name, noting it is the second time he has avoided giving his. What is this? she thinks, some kind of cheap pick-up date where no one gives their last names. Besides, she does not recall her saying anything about them having sex; although she has not ruled out the idea. "I told you to take off your clothes because you stink like a cow. I want you to go in the bathroom and take a shower. I can do your clothes in the washer in the basement. Didn't those policemen you supposedly played golf with notice you smelled like a cow?"

"I don't know," Johnny says fumbling with his belt. "It was pretty smoky in there . . . plus the coffee and donuts and all that." He starts to pull his polo shirt over his head. "Jeez! . . ."

"What's the matter?" Joan says, startled by his sudden, painful cry.

"Cripes! I think I must have broken a rib or something. It hurts when I raise my arm," Johnny squeals, discovering a new hurt in his body.

They struggle to get Johnny's shirt over his head without causing him too much discomfort. He sits on the bed and she takes off his shoes; then hesitates.

"Next. . . . Do you want to do your pants, or should I?" Joan asks.

Johnny begins to work down his trousers, tugging at his underwear with his thumbs at the same time. He is sure his jockey shorts are dirty. Always have on clean underwear in case you are in an accident, he remembers his mother telling him. Involuntarily he lets out another yowl. "I can't it hurts too much. . . ."

Freed of his fright, and the excessive adrenalin that has been sustaining him, the bruises acquired in his bar brawl have now become more painful. Or more accurately, Johnny now feels the extreme pain he has had all along. With a great moan he lies back on the bed.

"You do it . . . please. I hurt too much." It is the first time he has been able to lie down in some time. Foozler is comfortable now—all he wants to do is sleep.

"All right," Joan says, tugging at his pants. "Are you consenting? Or does this count as rape?" she adds jokingly.

"Whatever you do is okay by me. Besides . . . I'm old-fashioned. I don't believe a woman can rape a man. . . ."

"Oh, no! Can't they now. I've heard of cases. . . ."

"Is this my bedtime story?" Johnny interrupts.

"There is an island in the Pacific, Trobriand, where during the annual yam festival the women have permission to capture men, and then have their way with them."

"Have their way with them?" Foozler laughs.

Joan has caught Johnny's pants on his marbles, and is struggling to get the waist down. He lifts his bottom to help her and his organ pops free. She is surprised by its size, and quickly tries to suppress the expression of delight she is aware has spontaneously flashed on her face. Joan returns to the conversation.

"Yes, it's an ancient custom. The native women wait in the bushes and jump out on the men when they are passing by, and sexually assault them. Not with men from their own tribe, but from neighboring villages. It's a kind of ritual humiliation."

"You've been there?"

"No! I've only read about it in a book. . . ."

Joan has Johnny's pants down to his ankles and is struggling to get them off his feet. She keeps averting her eyes, which are constantly being drawn back to Johnny's member, which is growing as he lies there.

"Sounds like a good place to be, especially during the yam festival. If I ever get out of Charlesboro maybe I'll go there. I haven't got any better place to go. . . ." Johnny jokes. Perhaps he was sending her a signal, consciously or unconsciously, that he is a free man.

"Oh, I don't think you'd like it there," Joan assures him, pulling his pants free. She discreetly keeps his soiled drawers balled up inside, as she senses he would wish her to do.

"Why not?" Johnny asks. He absentmindedly scratches at his scrotum, and then checks himself when he catches her looking at him.

"Well . . . if a male is caught, but can't perform, he can suffer serious consequences."

"Really? Like what?"

"The women will hold him down and urinate on him."

"Urinate! ugh. . . ."

Out of his one good eye Johnny watches his once rampant penis begin to deflate. Joan notices it too; she goes on almost spitefully.

"Then they bite off. . . ."

"Don't say it!" Foozler says, with a pharyngeal moan.

". . .the poor man's eyebrows and eye lashes." Joan completes the sentence.

Johnny's organ is shrinking more, cowering back into his skin. He envisions himself, bedraggled and shaken, wandering about the streets of Charlesboro, eyebrowless and smelling of urine.

"Okay . . . off you go, to the shower," Joan says, neatly folding Johnny's clothes in her arm. "While you're cleaning up I'll take these downstairs to the washer. After that I'll fix you something to eat.

Helping Johnny up from the bed, Joan starts him in the direction of the bathroom. She watches his naked body disappear down the hall. He is on a beach on Trobriand Island, all around him women are dancing, making full play of the grass skirts slung low on their hips, kicking up sand and waving their hands from side to side, whipping themselves into a fever of excitement, their bare breasts glowing with coconut oil and yellow pollen. Joan hears drums, and a lewd, untranslatable chant. Padding down the flowered linoleum floor hallway, Johnny senses her fantasy and turns around. Thrusting out his pelvis, he smiles, and then shakes his penis with a gleeful vulgarity.

TWENTY-NINE

THIS IS JOAN'S home, not a whole house, just an apartment, only one third of the second floor of what must have once been a grand single dwelling. It is one of the few structures to have survived the Battle of Charlesboro, when most of the town was burnt by Federal troops during the Civil War. Joan mills about the kitchen, still a bit confused by the events of the evening, and the choices she has made. If what the media was saying about this man is true, she could be in big trouble—harboring a fugitive or something like that.

She can hear him in the bathroom, Joan thinks, but actually she can't. Johnny is not yet ready to run the shower. He is sitting on the toilet in a torpor, trying to remove from his bowels what little that is there. His business is completed, he guesses, but the pain has not gone away. He contemplates the three, tiny turds floating in the shallow water. This could not have been causing him all this discomfort, the three sweet rolls that he ate in The Cinnamon Shop. Then Johnny remembers the polished Marine Corps issued boot, stomping into his stomach and ribs. Gingerly, he lifts his leg into the shower stall. There is no tub. How Foozler wishes he could stretch out and soak in a bath of hot water.

Joan opens her refrigerator door. The light does not go on. It isn't the bulb; she has tried replacing that. The landlord, who lives downstairs behind a door with a plaque proclaiming his family has been here since forever, said he would fix it, but that was three months ago. Then this is the South. Time seems to pass unnoticed in Charlesboro. Joan always feels as if she is swimming against a tide. She wishes she could return to the faster pace of New York City. But how? She has a job here and lives on about half of what it would cost her back there.

Although brought up a Catholic, Joan never did quite understand the concept of Hell. But living in Charlesboro made her understand the concept of Purgatory—that is except for the weather. The weather in the summer was too hot; Hell. In the winter, on days like today when she found the temperatures pleasant, the locals thought it was freezing. As a consequence the landlord kept the heat cranked up so high she found it unbearable. If she was here alone, she would have been walking around naked, which was what she normally did. But she didn't know this man she had brought home, so was reluctant to just take off her clothes, although she had done so in front of plenty of other men. Why has she suddenly become shy about her body? Hadn't she just stripped him of all of his clothes? And he hadn't seemed the least bit embarrassed. In fact she had been rather offended by his rude gesture when he turned back to her before going into the bathroom. Yet his body had radiated a kind of spooky luminousness. Joan knows she wants to have sex with him. She will not deny that. However, for reasons she cannot fathom, she wants to go slow, to make it last, not only the sex, but the relationship. It is strange, Joan thinks, to worry about a relationship with a man she has only just met, a somewhat older man at that, and man about whom she knows nothing, except the bizarre story he told her, a will-o'-the-wisp who will doubtless be gone tomorrow—either safely on his way or in jail.

Having inventoried the contents of her refrigerator, and stood in its coolness as long as she could, Joan shuts the door. Turning back to the kitchen, she opens three more buttons on her blouse, then, reflecting, refastens the lowest one. But it is hot, she tells herself. And it is getting hotter now that the rains have past, or is it the humidity that is becoming so oppressive. She wants to open a window. However, to do that she will have to pull up the shades, which, as she isn't naked, she could do. But he is here. The last she saw him Johnny was naked, although he would probably find her bathrobe on the back of the bathroom door and come out wearing that. But if he is the man the police are looking for she can't let him be seen from the street. She might turn on the air conditioning, but then the landlord would hear it and come up and pound on her door complaining because she was running her air conditioner when he had the furnace going.

Joan looks around the kitchen, wondering where her cat, Pol Pot, is hiding. She is concerned because Pol Pot always comes running when the door to the refrigerator is opened. Maybe he is in hiding because there is a man in the house, a habit Pol Pot had gotten into whenever Kenny the Cop came over. Joan's cat had tried to be friends with Kenny, but the police detective didn't like cats, especially Pol Pot.

It was the mice Pol Pot killed, dozens of them. The cat caught them, played with them, and then laid them out on his killing field in the living room, which was why Joan had given him this name. Kenny had not understood Joan's New York accent.

"How come you-all named that scrawny little critter Polecat . . . it ain't no more a polecat than I'm John Wilkes Booth," he had chided.

"My cat's name is not polecat . . . it's Pol Pot," Joan had corrected him.

"And what the hell's a pole pot?" he asked.

When Joan realized he was not joking, she had gone on to explain about the Khmer Rouge and the killing fields. She asked Kenny if he hadn't read about it in the newspapers.

"I never read the papers, except for the sports," Detective Kenneth Beaugard, Charlesboro PD answered. "What the hell do I care if some goddamn foreign slops are killin' one another. I've got enough trouble just takin' care of things in this here damn town. The way I look at it, it was probably a good thing. I mean, the more those towel-heads knock each other off the less of them our boys will hafta' kill when they are sent over there to protect our freedom."

Whew! . . . Joan had thought to herself.

Pol Pot tried to be Kenny's friend. On one of the rare nights the detective slept over—he usually said he had to leave because he had the early shift—the cat had snuggled up under his chin. Waking up in the middle of the night, the startled detective had swept Pol Pot off his chest, throwing it up against the bureau. The frightened animal began to hiss and howl. Kenny took this as a sign that the cat was bewitched, and had been trying to kill him by sucking out his breath. This was a tale he had heard from an old black woman who had done some house cleaning for his mother.

Kenny threw one of his shoes at Pol Pot, and the cat took off, with the naked cop after it in hot pursuit. Joan, awoken by the commotion, had sat up in bed laughing hysterically at Kenny bouncing around the room bare bottomed, until he cornered Pol Pot behind a door and began kicking the poor animal so violently that he broke its leg. But not before Pol Pot, in defense, had taken six strips of bloody skin from Kenny's bare foot.

Joan had not appreciated the detective's angry attack on Pol Pot. She wrapped the creature in a towel and rushed off to the home of a vet she knew. She asked Kenny to drive her, but he refused, so she took a taxi, leaving him to bleed on her carpet. To Joan's surprise Kenny was still at her apartment when she returned with the bandaged and splintered Pol Pot.

"If that fuckin' cat ever scratches me again I'm takin' it down to the dump, and using it for fuckin' target practice," Kenny had threatened.

"Pol Pot! Pol Pot! Come out kitty," Joan cries. "That bad man's not here. This is a different man . . . a nice man. Come on out puss cat."

Walking down the hall looking for her cat, Joan passes the bathroom. She notices the door is ajar, and does not hear running water. She knocks.

"Hello? John, are you done in there? Is there anything I can get you?"

There is no answer. Cautiously she pushes the wooden paneled door open. The bathroom is small. It has probably been built into what was a maid's pantry when the grand mansion had been converted into apartments. Joan is startled to find Johnny lying there on the floor, still naked, curled up in a small corner. At first she thinks he might be dead—until he groans.

"I'm so tired . . . and my body hurts everywhere. I can't get into the shower. . . ."

At that moment Pol Pot scampers in, having abandoned his hiding place to see what creature has invaded his space. Or perhaps he just needs to use his litter box, which is between Johnny's head and the toilet. Its eyes wide, the big, scruffy gray studies Johnny, who is in a place he does not usually find humans. After sniffing him carefully, the cat begins to lick Foozler's feet.

"Hey! Puss cat . . . cut it out. . . ." Johnny says laughing as Pol Pot works his sandpaper-like tongue across the underside of his foot. Momentarily forgetting his fatigue, Johnny sits up and begins petting the cat and tickling it under the chin.

He likes cats, Joan tells herself, taking this as a good omen. "This is Pol Pot," she says, "and even he thinks you're smelly. So let's get you into the shower...."

"Pol Pot?" Johnny says, struggling to get up. "Why did you name your cat after the leader of the Khmer Rouge?"

Great, Joan thinks, helping Foozler to his feet, he not only likes cats but also reads newspapers. Pol Pot, having checked out the new person, scurries away. Johnny notices that the cat, while a large and handsome gray tiger, limps a little on a left rear leg that seems slightly deformed. He wonders what could have happened to the friendly fellow.

Propped up in the corner of the small shower stall, Johnny feels the water running down his body. Joan is only hands, turning the taps from behind the pink plastic shower curtain.

"Yoah! Too hot. . . ." Johnny yells.

"Shhh . . . not so loud," Joan cautions him, sticking her head in. "We don't want the people in the building to know you're here."

"Why?" he asks. "Don't you usually have men over?"

"Not ones who are fugitives from the law," she jokes—hoping that it is a joke.

Joan tries to get the mixture correct, as he tries to hold himself upright. The water is running down her arm, soaking her blouse, causing the wet fabric to cling to her bra-less breasts. She catches Johnny's eyes on her firm nipples.

"Shit! This is no way to do this . . . I'm getting my new shirt all wet," Joan says, pulling the curtain shut.

Johnny feels the frisson pass. He leans back against the stall. Then, in a matter of seconds, Joan reappears, throwing open the curtain with a magician's flourish, and revealing herself naked and holding a huge bath sponge.

"Move over a bit," she says, stepping into the shower. "I'm coming in there to give you a good scrubbing...."

She washes him carefully, cleaning behind his ears as his mother had done. Slowly the winter-like pain in his body becomes dull, warmed by hot water, and vanishes like spring snow. As if groping in the half-light that precedes dawn, his swollen eye gradually begins to open.

Working her way down his body like an explorer, Joan delicately probes his rib care until Johnny winces.

"I don't feel anything broken," she says, her voice a low murmur below the rushing water. "As far as I can tell everything is in good shape."

"And I find the same," Johnny says.

He has soaped his hands, and is working them slowly, and with pain and caution, up and down the sides of Joan's body. Johnny feels her shudder at his touch.

On her way down Johnny's stomach she examines a large bruise that matches the one on his ribs. He winces again. Joan moves her hand away from his body, but Foozler's expression indicates that she should not stop. There is something waiting just below his belly. Her thumb grazes the thick brown carpet of his pubic area.

They are functioning reciprocally now. As she slides her hands down he works upwards. Johnny cups the wet fullness of her soft breasts. He fondles the secret charm of her firm nipples. Having discarded their complicated personalities they abandon themselves to each others needs. Joan applies her soapy hand to Johnny's member, feeling the flex grow out of it as she increases her pressure. Without any scruples, Johnny takes advantage of her enthusiasm and reaches down, spreads her legs, and finds the entrance to that honeyed place which gives a woman the most pleasure. Armed only with water and their nakedness, they explore the frolicsome passage of their present existence.

She tries to mount him, but this is premature. His fatigue, his pain, the running water, all conspire to deprive his shaft of the firmness it needs for a forceful entry. She does not mean to seem impatient, but feels awkward. She wants him now. Sensing her urgency, he slides his face down her soapy torso.

Johnny Foozler is not a man to fail a woman—unless that woman was his wife. Painfully he crouches down and buries his nose in her wet mound, his tongue deftly probing the flower she has opened to him. Joan leans back, her head against the wall. She turns the water full hot on her breasts. Catching her excitement, Johnny bows to his task, slowly at first, teasingly, then faster as he feels the hot water cascading down.

"More, Johnny! More. Don't stop please . . . ." she says, digging her fingers into his scalp.

Their bodies speak in secret gestures. Joan's winter has turned into spring, a time of flourishing. In the damp, black thicket of her park, in the hairy coat of bushes, Johnny wanders alone among the nooks and niches. The sky, which had been full of dark hollows and gullies, is opening, revealing bright pink gashes that leak sunlight.

"Oh my god! . . . I'm coming! I'm coming. . . ."

Joan's body shakes. Her head comes forward, her open mouth taking in the full force of the spraying shower. For a moment she is without air. She feels as if she is going to drown. Then she regains her senses and turns off the water. Joan begins laughing.

Johnny feels her muscles relax. He slides down to the shower floor. He wants very much to sleep. His penis is still half-hard, but he is tired. He cannot control himself. He watches the milky whiteness of his semen as it trickles slowly down the drain.

They are both still naked and lying on her bed. Joan is feeding Johnny bits of scrambled egg, which he is trying to stay awake long enough to consume. A small, dark lamp glows on a table in the corner. Outside, the city gives off a solemn silence. The events of the past day return to Foozler's mind. Johnny realizes that he is backed into a corner. He has decided he has no other choice but to hide out here for a while, until the Charlesboro police either come to their senses, or decide to give up on him. However, he is not yet sure this woman wants him around for more than one night.

"You made me come," Joan says, an incredulous tone hinting in her voice. "It's been years since anyone has made me come. I mean it's usually . . . wham, bam, thank you, Ma'am . . . especially down here in Charlesboro. And you did it in the shower besides. . . ."

Joan had woken him again just before dawn, when they consummated their relationship for the third time. Johnny slouches over the breakfast table, a spent man. Three times that night he had been awakened from a restful, if fitful sleep. What fire he had had the night before was burnt out. He took this morning's scrambled eggs as he had taken last night's scrambled eggs—naked. She had removed his clothes to wash them, and they had not yet been returned. Johnny wonders if he will ever see his clothes again. Perhaps this is part of her plan, to keep him here, forever naked, forever her sex slave, forever eating scrambled eggs. He wonders if the eggs are a metaphor, or the only thing that Joan knows how to cook.

Getting up has cost Johnny a considerable effort. Mortally pale, laboring for breath, he wants no more than to be back in bed. His ribs and abdomen ache from the beating he received in the bar, and now his penis burns from the activities of last night. Joan stands by the stove cooking more scrambled eggs, also naked, yet her nonchalance is not without beauty. She is a woman who does not try to look younger than she is, nor does she know how. She just accepts gracefully what the years have given her, and goes on with what she has to do, which Johnny has learned is making art. Johnny regards her through his one lazy, good eye, the other having swollen back shut and giving indication it wishes to stay that way for several more days. He sits there studying her body, and groaning from his pain.

"Would you like more eggs?" Joan asks. When he declines seconds she finally joins him at the table. She smiles, and takes a bite of her food. Her face tells him what her words do not say. Joan looks down at her plate, takes another bite, and then looks up at him again. She positively glows. In her eyes Johnny sees discretion, and tenderness. Then Joan boldly responds to Foozler's impetuous gaze, trying at the same time to sound detached.

"God! It was great last night . . . I mean it was the best sex I've had in years . . . I mean really. I hope it was good for you too. . . ."

"Well . . . at least I still have my eyebrows," Johnny replies with a laugh.

"Eyebrows?"

"Yeah, eyebrows. I kept thinking about that story you told me about a Pacific island where the women raped the men during the yam festival, and how they cut off the men's eyebrows if they didn't perform. . . ."

"And you think I raped you? . . ."

"You woke me three times . . . out of a sound sleep! But I performed. . . ."

"You weren't asleep. You were telling me some story about hitting golf balls in the snow . . . you said you had hit them right off the face of the earth . . . or was it a dream you were having?"

"It was no dream . . . it really happened."

"Really happened . . . you hit a golf ball right off the face of the earth? What kind of a storyteller are you? Like playing golf in the night with the whole Charlesboro police force. Maybe you should become a writer."

"I mean I didn't hit a golf ball off the face of the earth . . . but I almost did . . . and in the snow too. I have a witness. . . ."

"I'll believe it when I see it. . . ."

Joan finishes eating and moves to the sink to do the dishes. Her full, firm behind is etched with a cross-hatch pattern from sitting naked on the caned chair seat.

"It was after my wife died," Johnny goes on with the story. "I was pretty broken up about it . . . although we hadn't been very close for several years . . . like we didn't have sex or anything, and I cheated on her pretty regularly." He isn't sure why he is telling her this.

Finished with the dishes, Joan walks around behind Johnny and begins gently massaging the back of his neck, and playfully nibbling at his ears. Chinks of sunlight shine in around the drawn blinds like a golden halo. From outside the noises of the occasional passing car, and the chatter of people on the sidewalk below, give testimony that the city has been lured awake once again by the warm spark of morning.

"When my mother died, it hit me harder than when my father went. I never liked my old man anyway, which was why I ran away in high school. I only came back there to take care of my mother. After that I began to think about how little time I actually had remaining . . . I mean my father and mother weren't all that old when they passed away. And so I thought I had better make up with my wife while we still had time . . . and before I knew it she was gone too. . . ."

Lost in the nostalgia of his reverie, Johnny has not noticed Joan's hands working their way down his body. Finding the object of her quest, she begins to gently tease his penis.

"Let's go into the bedroom," Joan whispers, increasing her stroke, while rolling her tongue in Foozler's ear.

Looking down Johnny sees that despite his fatigue and reluctance his member is responding to Joan's ministrations, swelling and growing in length. It is as if the thing has become a separate entity, with a will and mind of its own.

Joan leads him slowly down the hall. They make a strange procession, Johnny limping and holding his side, while the cat Pol Pot scampers along in the rear.

THIRTY

JOHNNY IS STRETCHED out on the couch, propped up by some pillows, watching TV with the sound turned off. Joan has produced some special, herbal remedy from the bathroom, which she is rubbing on his bruised and battered body. Perhaps it is the scent, or the coolness of the balm, but he feels somewhat better already. Looking around the apartment, which he had not paid much attention to when he arrived last night, Johnny observes the space is not filled with the usual female *tchotchkes*. Instead, the walls are hung with what he recognizes to be serious artworks, all in a similar style. He guesses that the pictures must be hers. Foozler recalls her saying something about making art. He had taken it to mean that it was her hobby, but apparently she is some kind of art professional.

The herb oil returned to its cabinet Joan curls up next to Johnny on the sofa. Today is one of the days she does not have to teach, one of the joys of working for a college, and the main reason why she is still living in Charlesboro. Johnny leans back on his pillows, supplying in his mind the dialogue missing from the soundless TV, a text he always finds more fascinating than what might be there. An image flicks on the screen that causes him to bolt upright. It is him, or at least a computer generated drawing of what he is supposed to look like.

"Quick! Turn up the sound!"

It is a teaser for the midday news, which is coming up next, more accurately next after three commercials and some chit chat by the local talking heads. Finally, emblazoned on the flickering screen, comes the full incongruity of Johnny's yesterday. The gaps in what happened have been filled in with that kind of fiction that sells newspapers and boosts TV ratings. But then what is the truth? Johnny thinks, nothing but personal experience take cabalistically.

He is finding it hard not to believe what is being said about him. And the journalists have been busy. Anchorman Jobe Wagg has the scoop:

"It is had been discovered that the man the Charlesboro Police are seeking in connection with the attempted assassination yesterday afternoon of Senator Billy Bob Plantigrade is from New York, and goes by the name of John Foozler. He is also suspected of stealing a cow upstate. His act, the police feel, was perpetrated to create a diversion, drawing the police to Town Commons, while his fellow terrorists planted explosive devices at the naval yard."

"A diversion?" Johnny shouts.

"Shhh. . . ." Joan says; her interest is riveted on the screen.

The scene shifts to an interview with Charlesboro Police Chief, Mains Hampton. Reporter Kissey Brown is holding the microphone so the WCBR logo is facing the camera. The chief looks like he has been over cast for a 1940s gangster movie in his dark, rumpled suit, wide necktie loosely knotted, and a tan snap brim hat.

". . . we-all are quite sure that this here attempted assassination was carried out in order to draw attention away from the groups main purpose . . . which was the destruction of one of our nuk–lee-ear submarines, which we have learned is secretly undergoing repairs at the local naval shipyard."

Kissey nods, smiles. It's her turn to speak: *"Do you-all have any confirmation to the story we've heard that the would-be assassin was also a member of the Mafia?"*

"Story you've heard! You mean the stories you've made up," Johnny grumbles at the screen.

Back to the chief. *"Well now . . . I can't say. But we're lookin' into that. But we-all think he is more in with the A-rabs we were warned were comin' this way. We-all do know that the fugitive was a member of a rock band called The Awful Fizzlers, when its lead singer committed suicide some years ago during a performance at a club near Parris Island, in connection with an anti-American protest. . . ."*

"Anti-American? It was an anti-war gesture. The poor bastard shot himself in protest. And it wasn't "The Awful Fizzlers," the band was named The Artful Foozler. Jeez! How did they find out about Solo's death?" Johnny says angrily.

"The FBI must have a file on you in their computer, or something," Joan ventures. "I am sure that they must have files on everybody nowadays. . . ."

"A file! Shit! They didn't even have computers back then. And what did I ever have to do with anything. I was never that political," Johnny counters sarcastically.

"Chief Hampton," Kissey continues, *"is there any truth to the story going around that you-all actually had this here John Foozler in custody last night when he was arrested for being drunk and disorderly following a bar fight at The White Whale. And that he was let go when he sank a twelve foot golf putt to prove that he was sober?"*

"Well now . . . I can't comment on that except to say that a man who bore a vague resemblance to the wanted man was arrested last night, and then was released when it was determined he was not intoxicated," Hampton replies officially.

"Hummm. So your cockamamie story is true," Joan says.

"Chief," Kissey digs in. *"Can you-all tell us something about the putting part of the story? I've heard that some of your officers put up a bet, and that the man in question walked out of the station with a great deal of money."*

"Well 'er . . . I can't comment on that, except to say that our officers are not allowed to practice putting while on duty. Now don't get me wrong. I'm not against the game of golf, in fact I play it sometimes myself, and it is one of our states leading industries."

"And what about the alleged gambling? . . . ."

"Well now . . . I can assure you that to my knowledge there has been no report of any gambling in Charlesboro's police stations last night."

"And is it true that you have discovered the fugitive is some kind of golf professional?"

"Well 'er. . . that has not been definitely established. However, when we found the suspects car in the Dixie Boys Hotel parking lot, which was how we established his identity . . . the back seat was filled with cowpies wrapped in newspaper." There is a muffled laugh from somewhere off camera. *"We also found the trunk filled with approximately 2000 range balls . . . you-all know them kind, golf balls with two red stripes they use to practice."*

"Finally, Chief . . . where do you think John Foozler is headed now?"

"Well 'er . . . we-all feel that the suspect is headed back up to Turtle Beach, probably to meet up with his A-rab buddies. We have put out an alert and the police up there are on the lookout for him. . . ."

"And why Turtle Beach?"

"Well 'er . . . we do know that Foozler stopped in Turtle Beach the day previous, where he attempted to contact the senator's wife . . . for what reason we do not know. Since he was unsuccessful, we feel he may try to contact her again."

"Unsuccessful!" Johnny storms. "I fucked the living shit out of her!"

Joan gives him an embarrassed glance.

"What I meant to say is," Johnny corrects himself, "we had a brief, but tender relationship. That's why I was trying to give her the calf, as a kind of going away present."

The chief is thanked for his helpful information. Kissey Brown sends us back to the station where Jobe Wagg announces he will be right back after a few short commercials.

A middle-aged man and woman appear on the screen. They are happily motoring their 36-foot power yacht on the Yesitsme River. They are carefree, or so we are meant to believe, because all of their financial worries are now being taken care of by the Reconstruction Bank and Trust Company. The couples smiling faces, wind ruffling their well-groomed and slightly graying hair, fade into a RB&TCo logo.

"Shit!" Johnny says. He is so angry his swollen eye is beginning to open.

"Let's see if you're on all the other stations," Joan says grabbing the clicker and surfing through the channels.

And there he is. Johnny's face appears in various forms on the three network affiliates, FOX, and CNN. *"Coming up next,"* One channel even promises, *"is an in depth report on the widespread manhunt currently going on in the Carolinas for a disgruntled golf professional and two al-Qaida operatives, after the golfer attempted to use a cow to blow up a state senator at a military parade, in order to create a diversion while the terrorists went after a nuclear submarine. . . ."*

"Murder! Blow up! Diversion! . . . ." Johnny shouts. "What kind of shit are they making up? I mean I didn't even have a gun . . . and now I am supposed to have dynamite or something. Where did I have it hidden, up my ass? This is all too bizarre. It's all lies, fucking lies. Is there so little of importance going on in the world that they have to make up stories about someone as insignificant as me? Al-Qaida? All I know about them is what I read in the papers. This is the most convoluted, concocted piece of bogus fiction I have ever heard. . . . ."

Johnny watches his tale unfold on the screen as naively as a child, wondering how the media has made up so much information about him in such a short space of time. He had been in the habit of reinventing his past as if to blot out his painful childhood, but now his most recent past is being invented for him. Foozler holds a formidable capacity for wonder in his heart, but even he marvels at the tabloid fantasy being fabricated around his innocent actions of yesterday.

"So now what do I do?" Johnny asks. "I can't stay hidden in your apartment for the rest of my life. . . ."

Joan had not believed him at first, even though her instincts told her to. But now she knows his story is true—more or less. What he told her corresponds with what she read in the newspaper, and heard on TV. Where, she wonders, is the line between what he claims is true and what is supposed to be an exaggeration? Maybe he really did have an affair with Billy Bob's wife, and wanted to kill the senator out of jealousy. Or may be he is some kind of maniac who planned to lead a calf loaded with explosives up to the reviewing stand just for the fun of it. And could the arrival of two Arabs in town on the same day as Johnny be a coincidence, if there even are al-Qaida terrorists anywhere nearby.

Joan tries hard to distance herself from her suspicions. A creative person by trade, her imagination is running wild. Last night Johnny's eccentricities merely seemed curious, perhaps a delirium from the beating he had endured. This morning, after watching the news, Joan has begun to question the accuracy of her observations. A profound change has begun to occur in her, in danger of undermining their budding relationship.

"You can stay here, Johnny . . . if just for a little while anyway. . . ." Joan begins hesitatingly; not exactly clear as to what she is committing herself to. "But you have got to tell me the truth . . . the whole truth."

"I have told you the truth, all of it . . . from the very beginning. And how am I to know that you are really offering to protect me? How can I believe that now you know I really am a wanted man, although for something I didn't have anything to do with, you won't slip out and turn me in to the police? We have nothing binding us together other than the three quick fucks we shared last night."

"Perhaps you should turn yourself in . . . they would realize it was all a mistake and let you go."

"I don't think so. You've seen the news. At this moment I seem to be the only rational person I know. Someone is somehow benefiting from all this panic and confusion . . . and I don't believe whoever, or whatever it is wants this all to end so simply. I am sure there is more to this than appears on the surface. . . ."

As Joan listens to him speak the balance of power seems to swing back in Foozler's direction. Convinced, perhaps, there is something snake-like in the way she moves closer and bends to his body. Johnny responds, stroking her with his hands, perception in his eyes. What reassuring words does he whisper in her ear? What secret doubts do both shake off as they come together—struggling against what or who they do not know?

Beyond the drawn shades the streets of the city are wide open now, traffic bustling, indifferent to the intense heat of midday. Fortunately for Joan it is one of those rare days when she neither has to teach nor hold office hours. No one will be looking for her. They have both showered. Joan has gotten dressed in her going out clothes. Johnny has on clean versions of the only wear he has.

"I'm going shopping . . . there's nothing left to eat in the apartment. I wasn't really expecting company." Joan announces, rummaging in her oversize handbag.

"You're going out shopping? . . ." Johnny says. He has to believe her. What else can he do? They can't both stay hidden up here forever.

"And I'll get you some different clothes . . . everyone in the world has seen you on TV in that yellow polo shirt, and stupid baseball hat. What size shirt do you take? Large, I suppose. . . ." Joan says heading toward the door.

"Yes . . . large," Johnny confirms, recalling the day he realized the stomach that had come with his age no longer allowed him to fit comfortably into a medium. "And it wasn't a baseball hat . . . it's a golf hat. That's my trade, or at least that's what it's gonna be . . . if I ever get out of this damn town alive."

Johnny is joking, but his comment sends an involuntary shudder through Joan's body. She stops and turns.

"Wait! You had better stay in this room while I'm out," Joan says, leading him down the hall to the one room of the apartment he has not been in yet.

"What's this?" Johnny asks, his eyes roaming the strangely cluttered space. "It looks like an artist's studio. . . ."

"It is an artist's studio," Joan replies, a strangely defensive tone sticking in her throat.

"Then are you an artist . . . or something?"

"Maybe I should say an 'or something.' I was an artist in New York once . . . rather well known . . . for a while anyway. Now I don't exhibit my work anymore. I just make things . . . and teach at the college."

"Hey . . . I wanted to be and artist once. . . ."

"So does my doctor and my dentist. . . ." Joan says dryly, and then is sorry that she made the comment.

"No, I mean when I was young," Johnny goes on. "But instead I ran away from home and became a drummer in a rock band. I was a sort of well known too, for a while, or at least my band was. I was the drummer. We played a lot of gigs in the Big Apple. Maybe you even heard us . . . The Artful Foozler. We played in several clubs that were supposed to be artist hangouts."

"Look," Joan interrupts. "Let's tell each other our life stories when I come back. Right now I've got to go . . . and you have got to stay in this room. I'll lock you in. I have the only key to the padlock on the outside."

"Why do I have to be locked in? You aren't going for the cops are you?" Johnny asks. In his mind he is not exactly sure that he is joking.

"Certainly not," Joan says sounding offended. "If I wanted to turn you in I could have called them while you were asleep. The problem is my landlord."

"Your landlord? . . ."

"Yes, the guy lives downstairs. He's a sicko. He comes up here when I'm not home . . . pretends he needs to fix the plumbing or something. But what he really does is go through my underwear. He especially likes the soiled panties he finds in the clothes hamper. I caught him in there sniffing them once. I can't make him stop."

"So why don't you move?"

"Good, cheap apartments downtown are hard to find in this town, at least in what they consider to be 'white' neighborhoods. Anyway . . . he doesn't have a key to this room . . . I put the padlock on myself. That's why I can only lock it from the outside. So stay in here until I come back . . . and if you hear someone rummaging around in the apartment . . . don't make a sound."

"But what if I have to go to the toilet?"

"Hold it in . . . or use one of those empty paint jars."

The padlock clicks a finite click, and Joan is gone. He can hear her footsteps on the stairs. Johnny moves to the window and fingers the Venetian blinds open a crack. Through the narrow slit he watches Joan disappear down the block—as does a man watering flowers in the front yard. As soon as Joan rounds the corner out of sight, the man turns and looks up at the window.

Taken off guard, Johnny steps back, letting the blinds bang forward. He has no way of knowing whether the man has seen him or his movement. He waits—sweating from what he is not sure is the heat of the closed room, or from fear. This whole thing is absurd, he tells himself. He has done nothing wrong. Why does he imagine that there is a conspiracy somehow going on around him? Joan is probably right. He has nothing to fear. It is all a big mistake. When Joan comes back he will have her take him to the police. Surely they will clear up everything and send him on his way. Or will they? There is the matter of the stolen cow. They will probably make him serve some time in jail just out of anger at his having made the Charlesboro PD look stupid in the national media.

Johnny goes to the window and cautiously pulls back the blinds again and risks a peek out. The man who had been working in the front yard is not there. A strange rubbing against his leg startles Foozler. Looking down he sees that somehow Pol Pot has been locked in the studio with him.

THIRTY-ONE

A GRIM SECTION of the downtown contains a collection of dilapidated brick buildings that had served as a hospital during the Civil War. Mostly abandoned and fallen into a moldy, mossy state of disrepair, this curious quarter serves as the nation to a minisociety of homeless, who have squatted here for as long as anyone can remember. One of the few edifices that is still being used functions as the site of the Charlesboro Morgue. During the battle for the city this wing was used as a surgery, and great quantities of blood, both Union and Confederate, had washed over the cracked tile-covered floors of the dark halls, and ran down the narrow stone staircases lined with wrought iron railings. Even in the brightness of midday the tall trees that surround this antiquarian structure blot out the sun, giving the place the atmosphere of being, part charnel house, part experimental laboratory, and part torture chamber.

The autopsy room is in the basement, reached by a series of tunnels through which the bodies are transported. The corridors are home to a colony of wild cats, whose purpose is to control the rat population. These felines are reputed to be direct descendants of the first cat installed here by the first medical examiner, whose name everyone reciting the legend seems not able to recall.

Johnny's cow, the little calf he named Bovie and driven half way across the state, had been brought here to die. More accurately, the poor animal had been brought here to be butchered before it had achieved the dignity of death.

The SWAT Team rifle shot meant for Foozler, that had brought Bovie down had not killed her instantly, as it had appeared on TV, just like a cow led to its death in the slaughter house does not die immediately—nor painlessly. Bovie had taken a bullet in the back that ran along the vertebrae before lodging in her skull. She had fallen first to her knees, and then over on her side, before letting out a great and horrible bellow sounding as if it were coming from an animal in hell. As she lay on her side shaking, the adrenalin rushing out of her along with blood, and sweat, and shit; she looked at Johnny as if to say: "What have you brought me to?" And then Foozler ran.

The police had no idea what to do with Bovie as she lay there dying. An ambulance arrived, but the eager paramedics, who had no experience with cows, just stood there and watched as the animal moaned and gushed out great quantities of blood. Finally a tow truck arrived. A chain was wrapped around Bovie's legs, and the still living, still bleeding, still bellowing calf had been pitched on a flatbed trailer and driven to the morgue. Dragged off the trailer by the chain, Bovie had been dropped outside the morgue door and left there while a plan was devised to get her inside.

"This here cow is important evidence. . . ." Chief Hampton kept repeating. "I want a complete autopsy on it."

Just what information he hoped to gain was never clearly established. But it is known that Bovie lay out in the alley for three hours, shaking in her own blood and filth, while the debate went on inside about what to do with the poor creature. Since the calf was obviously too large for the examining table, it was decided to cut her up outside and bring her in piecemeal.

As everyone stood around and watched, an assistant medical examiner took out a saw and began to slice off Bovie's hind leg. At the first cut, the moribund calf lifted up its sorrowful head and hissed a torrent of blood, drenching the man's smock. The examiner, seeing the calf was still alive, took out a huge knife and cut Bovie's jugular vein, catching the hot red fluid in a bucket. Then the calf ceased being, at least as we know it.

Early this morning Chief Hampton had been handed the bullet that had "killed the cow." When he learned that the cow had been shot by his own SWAT team, a fact that he knew but which in the excitement had slipped his mind, the chief decided the calf's pieces were no longer necessary as evidence. He ordered Bovie's remains disposed of. When asked how, Chief Hampton had pondered for a moment and then came up with what he considered a brilliant idea. He chuckled as he said: "Hell . . . this here's good beef, and the department picnic and soft-ball tournament is this weekend . . . let's barbecue the sucker."

And so, at the very moment that John Foozler is cowering in an artist's studio awaiting his fate, the examiner at the Charlesboro Morgue is busy cutting his former bovine friend into steaks, ribs, and hamburger.

THIRTY-TWO

MEANWHILE, JOAN HAS spent the morning shopping. Stepping out of the downtown branch of Horlbeck's Men's and Beach Wear, she runs into someone she would rather not meet.

"Good morning, Joan . . . how you-all this fine morning?"

"Oh!" Startled, she tries to regain her composure. "Ah, good morning Detective Beaugard."

"You-all don't call me Kenny anymore? . . ."

"Look . . . Kenny . . . I've told you I don't want to see you. I wish you would stop following me around. I mean, don't you have anything better to do? Or do I have to make a formal complaint to your superiors?"

"Well, Joan, or should I call you Ms. Tray, this here conversation is sort of on official business. . . ."

"Official?" Joan says, feeling a shiver pass through her spine.

"Yes . . . well sort of. We got a report that a stranger resembling the man we are looking for in connection with the attack on the senator was seen in The Cinnamon Shop last night, and that you apparently had a conversation with him. Now Chief Hampton is aware that you and I are . . . I suppose you would say sort of friendly. So he called me in and asked me what I knew about your background."

"Charlesboro is such a small town . . . isn't it?"

"He asked me if you-all had ever lived in New York. I couldn't lie. I told him, yes you had. . . ."

"And so did eight million other people, at least when I lived there, and that's just in the city. I have no idea how many more live upstate. Did you know that there are more people on welfare in New York City than live in the entire state of South Dakota?"

"The guy we're looking for isn't from South Dakota . . . he's from New York City."

"No he's not, he's from upstate."

"Upstate New York! So what makes you say that?"

"Well. . . ." Joan hesitates, fearing she has let something slip. "It said so in the papers didn't it?"

"Last night's newspapers made no mention of where our fugitive was from, as it had not yet been determined when they went to press. I know that for a fact. I was one of the officers who went over his car, and had already seen the newspapers."

"Oh! I must have heard it on television this morning then. Why are you asking me all this?"

"Did you-all talk to the man in The Cinnamon Shop last night?"

"What man?"

"A stranger that was reported to bear a resemblance to the man we are looking for. . . ."

"How should I know? That's my job. I try to be friendly and talk to everyone who comes in. . . ."

"But mostly it's the same people who come in all the time. I am sure you would have noticed a stranger . . . especially if you talked to him."

"Look, if someone thought that the man being sought was casually sitting in The Cinnamon Shop sipping tea, why didn't they phone the police?"

"They didn't realize that it was the fugitive until they went home and saw the police sketch on TV. You said the man was drinking tea?"

"I did? . . ."

"Yes you did. And that's what the couple who gave the report said the man was drinking. Now most people who come into your place drink coffee, don't they?"

"So. . . . Maybe this man, whoever he was, had coffee. I can't remember. We were very busy last night."

"The couple said that it was early, and rather quiet. They said they normally read your newspaper while they are there, but that last night the stranger had it. They were going to ask him if they could see it, as he wasn't reading it, but he had it rolled up under his elbow. Then you-all came and took the newspaper away and put it in the back."

"Oh . . . I probably thought it was the paper from the day before, and threw it away. Look, it's been interesting talking to you . . . but I have got to go. I've things to do at the college. . . ."

"As I recall, unless you've changed your schedule, today is your day off."

"Oh! Yes it is. But I've got to go in to my office to grade some projects."

"I see you-all were coming out of Horlbeck's. What were you doing in a men's store. I can't be your father's birthday . . . as I recall he's past away, and you told me you have no brothers. Can I see what you bought?"

"No you can't! It's . . . 'er, things for me," Joan lies. She can feel her face flushing. "Women wear men's clothes nowadays you know."

"Well I guess they do. I sure would like to see you-all in one of those sweat shirts . . . with nothing on underneath. How's about I come by sometime this evening?"

"No!" Joan is angry now, tired of playing at his game. "Look, I told you I don't go out with married men. You tricked me once. I've asked you many times to leave me alone. So please stop following me!"

"Well, this time I can't, *Ms. Tray*. If it's not me it may be someone else from the Charlesboro Police Department. We're checking with the other people who were in The Cinnamon Shop last night. You just may be coming in for questioning. . . ."

"I have no idea what you're talking about," Joan says. She turns and begins to walk away.

"By the way, *Ms. Tray*," Detective Beaugard yells after her, "This here John Foozler is not a married man . . . he's a widower. We learned his wife died just a few weeks ago. But you-all wouldn't sleep with no attempted murder, would you now?"

THIRTY-THREE

CROUCHED ON A stool in the dim studio, Johnny lets his eyes wander around the room, silently taking inventory of what it holds. Yes, she is some kind of artist, but her work is nothing he is familiar with. The smell of paint and glue brings him back to his grade school art room, but the images are unlike anything he has ever seen. As an artist this woman, who is presently hiding him, seems to be more interested in the written word than in visual icons.

He shuffles carefully through boxes full of magazine photographs, cut into objects and shapes that deny their printed image. Some are just little pieces of print and color, others scraps of deconstructed text. Johnny spreads a handful of these pieces of paper on a table, trying to make sense of why they have been cut the way they are. It is not a puzzle. The pieces do not interlock. They appear to have been cut at random, intuitively, and yet with great care. Also on the worktable are boxes of 3x5 index cards. In the first box all the cards contain only one line of text, taken out of context. Some lines make sense—having a completeness—others just seem to dangle on the page.

In the next box Foozler finds similar cards, but some of the cut up pieces have been added, stapled or glued into place. He is beginning to understand the methodology of her working. In the third, and final, box are cards that have had some hand work added to them, in colored pencils or watercolors, small drawings of volumes or cubes done in perspective, or crosses and other symbols traced through a plastic template.

What does she do with all these things? Johnny wonders. They don't look like anything anyone would want to put on their walls. Then he notices a cabinet of small drawers against the wall. He pulls open a drawer, and then another. They are all filled with these 3 inch by 5 inch artworks, each stamped on the back with a number and the date, and signed with the initials JT. He continues opening the drawers, like a man in a mausoleum looking for an empty vault, until he comes to one that is only half full. He pulls out the one nearest the end, and reads the number, 3333. The date is yesterday. Johnny turns the card over. A sudden chill runs through his body as he reads the phrase: "Coming from the North, he died in the South." Just a coincidence, Foozler tells himself. He puts back the card and quickly shuts the drawer.

Pol Pot rubs up against Johnny's leg and meows. The cat runs to the door, its tail bushed out; the hair on its back standing up in a straight line. Foozler listens. He can hear someone walking around in the kitchen. It does not sound to him like Joan's steps.

Crouching with his ear to the keyhole, Johnny tries to decipher the noise coming from the other side, but a throng of sparrows has convened on the roof above giving off a mind bending chatter. Foozler listens for the creaks and cracks he had made when he walked down the passage between the rooms, but hears nothing. He catches himself trembling slightly, his body cold despite the extreme heat of the closed up room. He is having difficulty breathing, unconsciously holding his breath, not wanting to make a sound. He wants to take big gasps of air, but finds he cannot. The air in the room seems heavy with a too rich, fermented atmosphere that provokes a constricting action in his mouth and nose, a sensation he connects all too clearly with his childhood.

* * *

Johnny remembers that in his youth he had experienced recurrent sore throats and respiratory infections, and chronic bronchitis. There had been little room for tenderness in young Foozler's family. He could expect no kiss, or hug, nor anything else that would express sentiment. His only means of gaining the affection he so badly desired had been through illness. Only then would his parents care for him. He loved these cozy times; his father's strong arms when he bent down to plump up Johnny's comforter, the sweet flavor of the cough syrup his mother spooned into him, the heat from the menthol she rubbed into his neck and chest. The family doctor recommended a tonsillectomy—a cure for everything in those days. Johnny was in terror at the thought, not just of the operation, but that its success would deprive him of all his pleasurable interludes.

Tiring of the medicines, gargles, and inhalants of his son's constant illnesses, Johnny's father decided the tonsils should come out. The elder Foozler arranged for the operation to be done at a private clinic, where he knew one of the nurses, having engaged in an adulterous relationship with her. He would be happy for a legitimate excuse to visit. Johnny had seen this woman taking a golf lesson. His father, turned into a giant insect, his long arms wrapped around the woman's body, ostensibly gripped the club while he demonstrated the takeaway and backswing, at the same time unrestrainedly brushing the sides of her breasts with his hands, while ramming his genitals into her buttocks.

The operation completed, a somewhat sedated Johnny lay in bed, the taste of blood and ether still in his mouth. A nurse was looming over him, a cone of ice cream in her hand. She was smiling. "Here Johnny, little boys usually get ice cream when they have their tonsils out. Your father went out and got it for you."

"I don't want it," he said, closing his eyes. Johnny did want ice cream, but not vanilla. He hated vanilla. His father never remembered that.

"He's a spoiled kid . . . he won't eat it. Let him sleep. You'd better eat it before it melts." Johnny's father said to the nurse with a wink. "Here, try it this way. . . ."

Out of the corner of his eyes closed to a slit, his throat burning with pain wanting the coolness of the ice cream, Johnny watched his father stick his index finger in the cone, watched the nurse take the finger in her mouth and suck off the gooey covering.

"Hey . . . I've got a better idea," his father had said fumbling with the zipper of his pants.

* * *

Johnny is suffocating, grasping for air. His throat burns. He wants to throw open the window and take in big gulps of oxygen, but he dare not. The birds have fled from the roof, taking their clatter with them. He wonders where they are going, and wishes he could have gone with them. In the silence Foozler can hear the footsteps in the kitchen, sounding close footed and shuffling, the way someone walks when they do not want to be heard. The steps are coming down the hall, heading for the bathroom. The confinement is overtaking him. He feels faint, his forehead beginning to sweat. The shuffling stops in front of the studio. A blot of gray interrupts the light coming under the door.

Unfortunately, Johnny is a person who cannot breathe holding his breath; he sneezes. AAaachooo!

"Hello . . . who's there?" A voice asks from the other side. "Is there someone in there?"

Foozler does not answer.

There is a knock on the door. "Is that you Miss Tray?" A hand rattles the knob, and then sees that door is locked by a padlock on the hallway side.

Johnny, breathing in silent gasps, spies Pol Pot at his feet, rubbing up against the door. Reaching down, he gives a good yank to the cat's bushy tail.

"YYooaaahh!" The startled animal lets out a loud and aggressive howl.

"Oh . . . it's only you Coal Spot," the voice says. "How in hell did you-all get locked in there anyway? Well . . . it serves you right. Yer old lady ain't give me no key fer that padlock. So's you'll just have to stay in there 'til she comes home and lets you out. Now don't you-all go messin' up the place, ya hear. I should never have let her keep you. None of them other tenants have pets. . . ." The footsteps start up again, retreating in the direction from which they came. "Coal Spot . . . damn fool name for an animal anyway," the man mutters to himself, "she says it's the name of some Jap general or something. . . ."

Johnny slumps to the floor breathing heavily. He had forgotten how much his body hurts from the beating he received yesterday. Perhaps the pain killers he took earlier are wearing off. He listens to the kitchen door close softly, and then the growing fainter sound of feet descending the stairs.

THIRTY-FOUR

AROUND THE CORNER from Horlbeck's, between the backs of buildings and fronts of dumpsters, is a blind alley that ends in a courtyard. This ultimate cul-de-sac is hemmed in between the smart section of the downtown, with its restaurants, coffee shops, and boutiques, where the white people go, at least in the day, and that section of crumbling row-houses and bars where the black people live. At the end of this land's end is a dull-red painted peeling door, desperately trying to hide its face in the blank brick wall that surrounds it. A small white card on the door reads: "Madam Boundrie, Psychic," and in smaller letters, "a direct descendent of the Fox Sisters of New York."

Joan carefully treads around the rivulet of black, stinking water that eternally divides the alley's cobblestone halves. The dismal door at the end is her goal, a last errand before returning to her apartment. Her mission will not take long. She only hopes that Johnny is not feeling too uncomfortable locked in her small, airless studio.

"What do you see?" Joan asks, as the wrinkled woman in front of her lays out her tarot cards. The elementary tricks of paranormal phenomena performed by this so-called spiritualist makes Joan susceptible to the silliest forms of transcendental surmise, and causes her common sense to shrug its shoulders in ignorance and gullibility.

"Be patient, my dear. . . ." the psychic urges.

Joan had initially come to the spiritualist as a lark with another faculty woman who was writing a book about psychics. She was surprised that Joan "being from New York" had never heard of the Fox Sisters. Joan explained to the woman she had lived in Manhattan, and that the small town outside of Rochester where these sisters grew up was as far removed from New York

City as the moon. But the Fox Sisters had worked in New York City, Joan would later learn, boldly calling back spirits of the dead for P. T. Barnum's Circus.

On Joan's first visit, Madam Boundrie had been completely convincing. Now she visited her regularly, or as often as she could afford to. Joan justified the expense as a replacement for the psychiatrist she had seen in Manhattan, which by comparison made Madam Boundrie's fees appear like a bargain. And Joan was also relieved by the fact that the psychic, unlike her psychiatrist, was not constantly trying to get into her underpants.

"Strange. . . ." Madam Boundrie murmurs, her voice ringing hollow in the brick-walled room that had once been home to a slave quarter, its ceiling taller than the space is wide or long. "The cards are trying to tell me a story . . . telling me to look inside myself for a story."

"A story?" Joan says disappointed. She has come here for specific advice, not to hear a story.

"Silence!" the woman says raising her hand. Then she places her palm on her forehead, as if she is experiencing great physical pain. "It happened long ago . . . someone is trying to get through to me . . . long before there was a United States. A man comes from the North. . . ."

"From the North? . . ." Joan repeats, her head filling with sudden recognition.

"Be quiet, Joan," the medium rebukes her. "You must not interrupt me when I am communicating with the spirits."

"I'm sorry Madam Boundrie . . . it's just that phrase. . . ."

"Shhh! . . . The man is seeking a favor from the governor. He brings the governor a present . . . I can see it now. It's a cow, no, a small calf. . . ."

"A calf!" Joan wants to laugh, but restrains herself. She thinks that perhaps Madam Boundrie has just been reading today's newspaper.

"The man gives the governor the cow and he is pleased. The governor grants the favor and the man goes away happy."

"And that's all. . . ." Joan says, disappointed.

"Patience, Joan . . . I must concentrate."

A faint knocking comes from somewhere inside the wall, or maybe from next door, or under the table. Joan knows this was the main contribution of the Fox Sisters to the spiritualist movement—the knockings, supposedly from the beyond.

"Wait . . . I see another man. He's shouting something. He claims that the cow the first man brought is his . . . that it was stolen from him. The governor consults with his captain-of-the-guards, who tells him the second man's story is true."

"How does the captain know this?" Joan asks.

"Don't interrupt . . . you are breaking my connection," the medium says, making a horrible face. "The spirits cannot tell us everything. We just have to believe. . . . It's coming back! I see the governor giving the cow to the second man. He tells his captain to go and find the first man and bring him in."

"Hummm," Joan says below her breath. She is on the edge of her chair, her hands on the table the way they are supposed to be, unable to decide whether to laugh or cry.

"I see the captain. . . . He is searching for the man. They find him sitting in a tavern where he has been bragging to all who would listen of how he outwitted the governor. The captain and his men drag the boastful man from the tavern to the town square, where they hang him from the tallest oak tree." Madam Boundrie, gasps and shakes her head; her spiritual phone link has just been disconnected.

"That's all. . . ." Joan says, nonplused by the whole thing.

"That's all," the spiritualist confides.

Joan pays her and walks outside.

After a promising start, the day has become gray and overcast. The sky is darkening, as in the cracking frescoes depicting "The Battle of Charlesboro" that adorn the rotunda of the old courthouse. Against the background of these leaden, ashen cumuli, the chalky whiteness of the antebellum houses lining the streets shine brightly, accented by the sharp shadows of their cornices and pilasters. Joan walks with her head down, her mood dark, as tense as the sky charged with electricity before the coming storm. The humid air seems to smell of danger. She crosses the street to avoid a group of students who are lounging in a corner of the park. At the next intersection she crosses back over to avoid two policemen parked in a car half way up the block. Then she crosses the street again to be on her side when she gets home.

The gray day is sinking even deeper into shadow and melancholy. The sun has blocked itself, and hangs low, swallowed by the dark of the threatening storm. Charlesboro, parched and motley, is holding its breath. Only the gardens, crazy and drunk from watering, continue to grow. A dog runs dizzily toward Joan, panting, its tongue out, and its tail between its legs.

Three black boys on skateboards roll round the corner. What are they doing here? This isn't their part of town, Joan thinks, as they rush at her laughing and joking. Nudging one another, they force her to step off the sidewalk. They can tell, she says to herself, they know I'm a Yankee. They wouldn't act like that if I were a Southern woman—nor would Kenny, or the landlord. Good god! I'm beginning to think like them, she tells herself.

However, her problem now is Johnny Foozler. Detective Beaugard had indicated that he is suspicious of her. Was he only fishing for information, Joan wonders, or perhaps he really knows something. He hasn't been following her, she is sure, or those black kids wouldn't have acted the way they did. She fears she might have given herself away by being seen coming out of a men's store. She should have gone to a big store in the mall, but without a car she would have had to take two different busses that never come on time anyway. She tells herself that if they bring her in for questioning she will not say a word.

Deep in her thoughts, Joan lets the wrought-iron gate to the garden clang shut behind her. She is in a different climate that she still is not used to, different smells, a green and unfamiliar season of the year. The bare branches of the trees point to the real time, their dark, forked tops outlined against the translucent gray sky. She listens to the voices of the birds, chirping under the peaks in the roof. Then from a shadowy corner she hears another sound, a voice silent and heavy:

"How'er you-all today, Miss Joan? . . ."

Startled, Joan turns her head, putting on a face of calm, trying to appear self-assured. The speaker is standing among the plants, watering. The hose held in his hand dangles between his legs like some giant penis that he wishes he had.

Joan froze momentarily at the sight, and then her eyes focused. She has often seen him in the shadows, or through the open door of the garage—stroking his member. Or at least she thought she saw him. She had always turned her head and hurried on. Joan knows he masturbates on her underwear when she is not home. He left her panties, spotted with his semen, spread out on her bed like some ritual object. She did not sleep for three nights after she found them the first time, not until she put the chain locks on the door herself. Has he been up to the apartment today? Joan forces herself to look at the man's face. She senses this prosaic fellow has risen above his triviality, and today has a clear goal in mind. She fears what that goal might be.

"Good morning," Joan says, purposely not speaking her landlord's name, and hurrying toward the stairs.

But he is ahead of her, blocking her way. "Just a minute Miss Joan, I think that we-all have got to talk about somethin'."

Joan can feel her nipples hardening from fear. His eyes are on her breasts. However, she is wearing a bra today, has taken to wearing one most of the time since she moved here form New York. The landlord's hand goes to her shoulder, his fingers feeling the straps of her brassier through her damp blouse. He seems to be steering her to the space underneath the stairs. Joan pulls away.

"Excuse me . . . I'm in a hurry!"

He blocks her again.

"You and I have gotta' talk. . . ."

"About what? My rent's paid up until next month," Joan says, hoping that is all he wants—plus an excuse to put his hands on her shoulders.

"There's somethin' I'm gonna say that I think you-all need to listen to."

"So get on with it! Say what you want to say," Joan blurts out, while trying to sound matter-of-fact. Possibilities are rushing through her head, each one more horrible than the next.

"You-all got a man up there in your apartment. . . ."

"So . . . I'm allowed to have visitors aren't I? He was there last night . . . but now he's gone."

"He weren't no local fellow . . . so where'd he go?"

"Yes he is," Joan says, trying to conceal her fear. The landlord is staring at her breasts again. She can feel the sweat running down her chest. She wants to reach up and close the top two buttons she had left undone.

"I know who that fellow is. . . ."

"It was Kenny . . . you remember Detective Beaugard."

"It weren't no Kenny. As a matter of fact, Kenny come by here early this mornin' . . . ask me if I seed you with anyone last night. He said it were official business. I told him I hadn't. I lied for you. . . ."

"What do you mean, you lied?"

"You-all came in rather late last night . . . and with a man. Momma and I seen you from the window. Then I heard the washer going in the basement, and went down to take a look. There was some man's clothes going round, some socks and underwear, and a pair of tan pants . . . and a yellow polo shirt."

"Those were my things. . . ."

"Oh, no, Miss Joan . . . I watch you coming and going, and have never seen you wearing such clothes."

"But they are mine. . . ." Joan's lie did not sound convincing, even to her.

"I'd seen those clothes earlier that day though." His eyes were beginning to look unexpectedly wild as he went on. "Momma always wanted me to graduate from The Fortress, it was a family tradition . . . four generations had graduated from there, and I was the first not to. I would have, but I got knocked down and hit my head during initiation. I was sick for a long time after that. I had a hard time thinking. . . ."

"Oh, I'm sorry," Joan says, beginning to understand his actions.

"Momma always likes to see the parade, so we went there yesterday, and were right up close when that there terrorist fellow with the cow tried to kill the senator . . . and he was wearing clothes pretty much like those I seen in the washer last night."

"But it was all a mistake . . . he wasn't trying to kill the senator!" Joan exclaims, realizing she would make a poor witness under cross examination.

"Then he is the one upstairs!"

Joan cannot reply. She is beginning to choke up. Her landlord takes this opportunity to place his hands on her shoulder yet again. She does not brush them away.

"Well . . . you-all know, we ain't no friend of Senator Billy Bob ourselves, in fact Momma says it's too bad he weren't killed . . . what with him being in cahoots with the Indians and the

Mafia . . . and havin' that whore of a wife. As for Kenny, he made plenty of trouble for us after Papa died. So I ain't inclined to tell him nothing either. . . ."

"Oh . . . I see," Joan says, regaining her composure. Maybe she has found the ally she needs to get Johnny safely out of town.

"So," the landlord goes on. "Seein' as how I've done you-all a favor by telling a lie for you . . . maybe you-all can do something for me. . . ."

"What's that?" Joan asks, an astonished suspicion in her voice.

"Won't you-all come to my room sometime, please . . . ." he says with an almost gentle politeness.

"Come to your room!"

"Yes . . . come to my room. You see, before I hurt my head I had never done it with anyone . . . and I still haven't. Momma says that there's no woman in the world who would want to go with me. And I guess she's right. But I see it on TV and in the movies all the time . . . and it drives me crazy. Sometimes I do it with myself so that you or some other woman can see me. Then it feels so good . . . but I want to really do it with a real woman . . . at least once before I die. . . ."

"You'll probably discover that it's not all it's cracked up to be," Joan mumbles, realizing she's made a bad pun.

"Whatever do you mean? . . ."

"Never mind," Joan replies. She is regaining her composure now. "What happens if I won't come to your room?"

"I don't know. . . ." the landlord says, taking his hands from her and stepping aside to let Joan pass.

Overhead the half-day-old clouds that covered the sky earlier have moved to one side of the horizon, as if raked there by some cosmic hand, piled in a dark heap, their anvil crown looming as a prelude to the storm that is to come.

THIRTY-FIVE

JOHNNY HEARS THE padlock being removed. Leaping from the room like a zoo animal just released from its cage, Johnny brushes past Joan and runs down the hall as if he has just discovered the rest of the zoo is on fire. Joan hears him coughing, and wheezing, and cursing. Then she hears the toilet flush. Johnny emerges, wrapped in his anger.

"Where the hell have you been? Christ, I was dying in there. I had to piss so bad . . . and I think I'm allergic to your cat. I couldn't even open the window."

Joan holds her finger up to her mouth as a sign Johnny should be quiet, but he ignores her and goes on.

"And then there was some goddamn pervert up here going through your apartment, so I couldn't even make any noise. Where the hell did you go? I though you were never coming back."

"I've only been gone for two hours."

"Let's eat, I'm starving. Then we can figure out what the hell I'm going to do. I've been thinking that maybe I should just give myself up."

"You can't."

"Can't give myself up. . . ."

"Can't eat. I didn't get any food."

"Why not?"

"I ran into Kenny . . . you know, my old boyfriend the detective. He saw me coming out of Horlbeck's men's store with the package of clothes I just bought for you. He told me someone had reported that they saw you in The Cinnamon Shop last night talking to me. He asked if I remembered you . . . and I lied. I don't think he believed me. He said that his superiors know that he and I had been together, and asked him what he knew about me. He said they were probably going to bring me in for questioning."

"They can't do that."

"They can . . . and they will. Besides it may be too late. The landlord knows you're here too."

"But I was quiet."

"He saw you come in, and also saw your clothes in the laundry room last night. He and his mother had been at the parade, up close to the reviewing stand . . . so they recognized you."

"This is all just too crazy . . . I'm going to the police and explain everything, the way I should have done in the first place."

"But you can't. . . ."

"Why not?"

"Because it's too late! Don't you see? It doesn't matter if you did or didn't do anything . . . they want you to be guilty."

"Who wants me to be guilty?"

"Billy Bob and his cronies. . . ."

"Billy Bob!"

"Senator Plantigrade. He is a very powerful man in this state. The opposition newspapers had just come out with an attack on him, charging that he was in favor of casino gambling because he is in the pay of the Mafia."

"Yeah, I read that. . . ."

"Now he's using his attempted assassination as a smoke screen. I saw him on television when I was downtown. He is claiming the fact that the Mafia, or al-Qaida, or whoever tried to have him killed is proof that he is not in league with the bad guys . . . but that they see him as a threat. If you came in they would never let you tell your story. If what you say is true, it would make this whole thing look foolish. They would lock you up somewhere and throw away the key. . . ."

"If what I say is true? . . . I thought you believed me."

"I do Johnny, I do. That's why you can't turn yourself in. I haven't lived in this town that long, but it's been long enough to know that things are different down here . . . or maybe it's the same everywhere. Things are never what they appear to be. And besides, you messed with the senator's wife . . . even you admit to that."

"But no one would believe I belong to the Mafia . . . first of all I'm Polish. Who ever heard of a Polish Mafia? Russian, yes, but not Polish."

"But Foozler isn't a Polish name. . . ."

"Look at my face . . . my nose. My grandfather changed his name from Fozylinski when he came over from Poland."

"But the word foozle means to bungle, doesn't it? A foozler is someone who does everything wrong."

"That's me! Unfortunately, my grandfather didn't have an English dictionary at the time. It also means to make a bad stroke in the game of golf. Imagine my father trying to be a professional golfer with Foozler for a last name. . . ."

"When you told me I didn't believe that it was really your name . . . just part of a crazy story, like everything else you were telling me."

"So what are we going to do now?" Johnny says, sitting down on the floor in the hallway. His body aches, he is confused—a fugitive. It was not that many days ago he sold his father's range and headed south, to find the sun, and to follow in his father's career. Now it seems to him years have passed, and that he has turned down some street which is leading him farther into some eerie, maddened world.

"We have got to get you out of here right now," Joan says, handing him the package she brought. "Here . . . put these clothes on."

"But I can't go now . . . I have no idea where to go. We have to at least wait until it gets dark."

"We can't. Police officers may be arriving here at any moment. My landlord stopped me when I was coming in. He threatened to call the police and report you if I didn't have sex with him. I gave him a vague answer . . . trying to stall him. But I can't trust him . . . his mind is not all there."

"So why didn't you fuck him?" Johnny says, pulling his new pair of pants up around his waist.

Joan's face flushes, there is anger in her voice: "Look, creep . . . there are a lot of things I would do for you . . . but fucking my landlord isn't one of them. What do you think I am, some sort of tart that fucks with every man that walks into The Cinnamon Shop? Well I'm not. I made a mistake with Kenny the cop . . . I didn't know he was married. But since then there has been no one. A grown woman can get very lonely in a jerk-water town like Charlesboro. I saw that you were different, and actually was attracted to you. How was I to know that you were some goddamn crazy golfing assassin with links to al Qaida?"

Johnny can see tears forming in Joan's eyes. He is truly sorry for his rude comment. He meant it as a joke, but it had not been taken that way. He tries to put his arms around her.

"No! There's no time for that," Joan says pushing him away. "Besides, we did enough fucking last night, and this morning to last me for a while." She winks hoping, he takes this declaration as the joke it was meant to be.

At the same time she has wiggled out of her Bermuda shorts, and her underpanties, and is rummaging in a drawer in the dresser. Taking out a pair of scissors, she begins hacking off the shorts rather modest length, leaving only about an inch between the legs, and carving deep slits invitingly up both sides.

"What the hell are you doing?" Johnny says, catching sight of her activity in the mirror behind him. He has been appraising the outfit she bought him—it is definitely more to her taste than his.

"I'm going out. . . ."

"Where?" Johnny asks. He is looking at himself again, tilting his head left and then right. Foozler struts, enjoying his new look, realizing it has been some time since he had any up-to-date clothes.

Joan has tugged her severely modified shorts back on. They are only a hint of their former self. The two half moons of her bottom hang deliciously out back. In front, she has to trim away the strands of pubic hair that puff out from behind what little fabric remains there. She pulls the zipper up half way, and tucks the open ends back down in, revealing a good bit of her belly as well as her belly button.

"Have you gone crazy?" Johnny asks, turning around in surprise.

Joan has dug a white T-shirt out of a drawer and is snipping at that. She removes her blouse and bra and slips what is left of the shirt over her head. The thing must have been too small for her years ago. Her nipples bulge clear and opulent through the stretched thin cotton. She has trimmed the shirt so short that the bottoms of her breasts hang out below it, echoing the globes of flesh displayed on her backside. Looking at herself in the mirror,

Joan frowns. She takes the scissors and cuts a deep "v" at the neck. A valley appears on her chest.

"Jeez! Who the hell are you trying to be? . . . goddamn Daisy May."

Joan laughs and fluffs up her breasts: "That shows how old you are . . . you actually remember Lil' Abner. . . ."

"Sure I remember Lil' Abner . . . and when I was a little kid I used to get a hard-on just looking at Daisy May in the funny papers. Which I am sure a lot of guys around here are going to get if you go out in the street dressed the way you are. . . ."

"That's the plan, stupid. I'll go out the back and lounge around in the yard . . . maybe bend over and sniff a few flowers and all that. I am sure to get the landlords attention . . . and that of any cops who may be watching the place. Which, by the way, if you take a peek out the window you will see a plain black Ford parked half way down the block . . . it's been there since I came home."

Looking aslant out the window Johnny can see the car, and also that the landlord has gone back to his watering.

"I won't fuck the landlord for you . . . but I can give him a good show. And while he and the cops are checking out this not-bad-for-an-older-woman's body displayed in the backyard . . . you will be sneaking out the front door. If you turn left at the corner there's a Catholic Church three blocks down, toward the river . . . Saint Joseph's. Go there and wait until I come for you . . . which may not be until after dark. But I will come."

"A church?. . . I haven't been in a church in decades. Don't they lock up churches these days . . . when nothing's going on?"

"Saint Joseph's is a very old church . . . a kind of tourist attraction. They actually leave it open all the time. That's why you shouldn't be noticed . . . there are always a lot of people there, coming and going."

"Maybe I'll even say a few prayers. . . ."

Joan kisses Johnny lightly on the mouth, her tongue parting his lips. She takes his hands in hers and puts them on her breasts, giving each a gentle squeeze: "I'll see you in church," she says, turning to go.

"Not dressed like that, I hope," Foozler whispers after her as he watches her bouncing bottom descend the stairs.

Johnny shuts the apartment door and steps to the window. Peering down he sees that Joan is already in the backyard and has caught the landlord's interest. Posturing in her abbreviated outfit—which on a teenaged girl these days would simply pass for summer clothes, Johnny thinks—Joan was clearly erotic. She told him he should go down as soon as he saw her in the backyard, so Johnny heads for the front stairs.

He has been crouching in the front vestibule for ten minutes. Johnny fears the plan is not working. Joan's appearance in the backyard has caused the police car to pull up closer for a better look, affording the cops inside a full view of the front door. This was something she had not planned on. Foozler can't see the backyard, so has no way of knowing if she is still there. Perhaps she assumed he has left, and gone back upstairs. He can see the police car. He can't stay in the vestibule much longer—one of the other tenants is bound to come home. However, Johnny can't slip back upstairs as he has let the door lock behind him. In the hot confines of this small space the sweat is running down his forehead. He takes off his black, Greek fisherman's hat and mops his brow. Johnny looks at the hat. Why did she get me a Greek fisherman's hat? he wonders. I mean I'm not supposed to be noticed, but who in hell wears a Greek fisherman's hat in Charlesboro?

The musty silence is broken by the rude clatter of small wheels coming nearer on the hard sidewalk. Three black boys roll past the house on skateboards. The police car fires up its engine, makes a brisk u-turn, and heads off after the three baggy-panted, and backwards baseball capped youths. Seizing the opportunity, Johnny shoves his fisherman's hat under his shirt and bolts out the front door.

THIRTY-SIX

JOHNNY'S DESTINATION SAINT Joseph's Roman Catholic Church towers before him, a massive gray stone structure, surrounded on all sides but one by modest houses of another era, buildings nowhere near the elegance of the mansions of three blocks away. A small and ancient cemetery, with its tombstones and tall trees, crowds right up to the painted gray, wood frame rectory which appears to have been added on in more recent times. Foozler decides to wait in the cemetery for a few moments, where he can see the front and side doors, before he commits himself to going in.

All around him Nature, indifferent to Johnny's fate, is preparing to don her bright spring colors. Trees display their branches covered with tiny young leaves; birds sing amid the fresh foliage; bees hum along the opening magnolia buds; everything is breathing a new life and joy. Hidden in the grass surrounding the soundless graves a cricket carries on its unflagging song; the mindless destruction of living things and all the sorrows of the world counting for nothing in its tidy world. The flight of a butterfly through the iron fence, blown on the sharp scent of the wind, is enough to convince Johnny that there is still order in the universe, and raise his spirits so high that the indisputable proof of his immortality forcefully enters his soul and fills it wholly.

He is growing tired of the sciamachy of the past two days, running from all these imaginary enemies. Is he really in danger? Or is this all a creation of his and Joan's over active imaginations? He wants to see cops, or at least someone who looks suspicious, waiting for him outside the church, or maybe inside. Then he would run. So far he has been running from nothing. After all, Johnny thinks, he was in the police station. They couldn't be that stupid. If he was really wanted for something wouldn't they have kept him there? Or is it that he really is just a pawn in some grand conspiracy. Do they know he really hadn't planned to do anything, but are waiting to catch him alone in some dark alley where they can do him in, and then blame him for whatever it was he is supposed to have done?

A stream of sweat is running down his forehead. The Greek fisherman's hat is too hot. Johnny looks for a place where he can throw it away, some high weeds or bushes, but the cemetery is too neatly kept. Had Joan got this hat for him on purpose? Foozler wonders, a sign that he could be recognized by. No, he's being too paranoid. Nevertheless, he carefully tucks the conspicuous head cover behind a wreath of plastic flowers decorating a granite headstone lettered Calvin Beaufort. The name is strangely familiar, although the dates are long ago. He thinks about it for awhile, and then it comes back to him. Beaufort is the name of a town nearby. The final town of any size he would hit before he turned off the main highway onto the road that leads to Parris Island, where his son is stationed—and Solo died. He wants to visit his son, and his wife, and the grandchild he has never even seen.

Johnny lets his eyes wander around the other monuments leaning helter-skelter in the shadows, straining to make out what he could of the letters and numbers etched into the worn surfaces. The white limestone markers show up better in the late afternoon light than the granite or marble ones. But the limestone has eroded more over time. In this, the oldest section of the cemetery, the names and dates are barely readable.

The heavy wooden side door of the church swings open, surrendering an elderly man and woman, the same two people he saw going in the front door when he arrived almost twenty minutes ago. No one else has been in or out. Joan told him this was a busy place, that he would not be noticed, but this does not seem to be the case today. Johnny stands next to a rather large monument, pretending to be trying to read the unreadable names. He will have to go somewhere soon, he reasons, aware that his remaining in the cemetery much longer will make him appear conspicuous. The elderly couple speaks softly as they pass by Johnny and his monument, as if they do not want their conversation to intrude on his reverie. However, their sound carries clearly in the empty air.

"Sure is fine weather we're all having for late winter . . . I tell you it's a gift. . . ." the man says.

"That is indeed true. And it would be a pleasure to be out . . . if one didn't have to worry about some crazy assassin running loose in the city," the woman responds.

"Well, I hear that they are about to catch him," the man goes on. "The police know where he's hiding out . . . just waiting for him to make a move, so's no one will get hurt. . . ."

"Well I hope they catch him soon enough . . . the death penalty is too good for the likes of him. . . ."

Johnny sticks his head from behind the monument to hear better as the man says: "The death penalty? Aren't you-all being a little harsh . . . I mean he hasn't really done in anybody yet, not that they know of . . . only made a rather bungled attempt at killing Senator Billy Bob. . . ."

Half way down the block now, their conversation barely audible to Foozler, the woman adds: "Well, creatures like that don't deserve to be alive, imagine making your living being paid to kill somebody you don't even know. My God . . . the man must be insane or something. . . ."

Being paid to kill someone that you don't even know; isn't that what's being in the military is all about, Johnny thinks to himself, considering the woman's statement.

Inside the church now, John Foozler catches the scent of incense. Flickering candles glow in red glass tubes. Foozler has chosen a place midway between the back and the side door. He blesses himself before sliding into the hard wooden pew. He kneels down. Johnny doesn't know why. He only remembers that he always had to kneel for a little while when he came in before he was allowed to sit back. He thinks he should pray, but can't recall any prayers, at least not all of the words. But then he never prayed very much when he was young anyway. Foozler reasons that he will probably be less noticeable with his head bowed.

Not used to the kneeling his limbs soon become sore. In fact his whole body aches from the beating he took in The White Whale, a condition he has forgotten in his flight. He sits back, but then slides forward to a crouching position, somewhat half way between kneeling and sitting, his knees not actually on the kneeler, the posture his father always assumed during his rare appearances in church. His mother always kneeled upright, with all the other really religious persons. When he was younger she would scowl at him until he followed her example. However, as he grew older he was allowed to slouch back like his father—his mother just content that her men were in church at all.

In the tall, cooler space inside the church, Johnny somehow feels less confined than outside. The fading colors of the stained glass window announce the departure of the late afternoon sun. The sound of an airplane passing low overhead briefly invades the eccentric silence. Time, which had been moving so rapidly since that moment he first stepped onto the parade ground leading his calf, has begun to lag.

Tugged by some invisible hands, or perhaps a mechanical device, the bells in the belfry begin to toll. Johnny counts each peal, one after another, sounds he does not know the meaning of. The last ringing draws a sigh from his breast, giving him a singularly unpleasant feeling, the diminishing vibrations of the resounding brass trembling in his head. He wonders if their peal might be signaling the end of his journey, the details of the past few days having become as remote to him as the travels of Ulysses. Or perhaps the bells have tolled the start of a new phase of his life. He feels as if he is poised between two voids, balanced on the edge of a knife blade. Time now seems inconceivable to him, almost as if it doesn't actually exist.

A robed figure enters silently from a small door on the left, pauses, genuflects, steps up to the altar and adjusts something, and then exits through a portal on the right. People are beginning to arrive, taking places randomly in the pews.

A flash of light, coruscating through the leaded image of Saint Joseph above him, flickers in Johnny's eyes, causing him to look upward. He had not paid much attention during his catechism, but had been especially impressed by the story of Saint Joseph. He remembers that the husband of Mary, though a humble carpenter, was supposedly descended from the great kings of the tribes of Judah; and that God had entrusted him with the education of his divine son; and that Joseph had traveled far and wide to protect his wife and son from harm and persecution. And then no further mention of Joseph is made in the Gospel, the sole source of information concerning his life after his son's twelfth year.

Therefore, we have no knowledge of Joseph's death. It is assumed he must have died before Jesus for as Saint Francis de Sales, the patron saint of novelists, theorized much later, it would have been unthinkable that when Jesus was on the cross he would have entrusted his mother to Saint John if Joseph had still been around to take care of her.

Foozler also recalls that Saint Joseph is the patron saint of a happy death. He doesn't know why but the notion moves him and under his breath he whispers: "Saint Joseph, please grant me a happy and painless death."

Sitting back in his pew, Johnny relinquishes his thoughts to more pleasant meditation. Other people are entering the church, apparently anticipating some kind of ceremony. No one is paying any attention to him. He is content to wait. Joan will be coming shortly, that he is positive of—when she is sure everything is all right. Thus settled in, the hours slide rapidly over John Foozler, disappearing into eternity, while he does not even notice their melancholy passage.

THIRTY-SEVEN

THE FINAL CONFROTATION with the suspected assassin was widely covered in the newspapers. Much is made of the fact that John Foozler was found with a gun in his possession. Considerable praise is heaped on Charlesboro's hero police officer Kenneth Beaugard, "who bravely took on the potential killer even though he was off duty at the time he encountered the armed man on the run." Senator Plantigrade publicly thanks all who were involved in the search as well as those who so faithfully protected him and his wife "while the bad guy was on the loose." He uses his speech as an opportunity to point out that his assassination attempt was probably a plot by the Mafia to rub him out because he wouldn't play along with them, proof that he was not under their control, "despite what them damn Yankee news reporters tried to say."

* * *

Some weeks later Joan Tray receives this letter:

> Charlesboro College
> Charlesboro, South Carolina
> Office of the Dean

Miss Joan Tray, adjunct instructor
Art Department
33 Liberty Hall, campus

Dear Miss Tray:

    At yesterday's meeting of the Faculty Review Board your work here at the college was taken into consideration. While the board took into account your excellent student evaluations, and your service to the art department, which your chairman informed us was outstanding; it has voted that you should not be reappointed for the coming year.

Charlesboro is a very old college, with a long tradition to maintain. Your conduct during the recent affair with the terrorist John Foozler, and the publicity surrounding it, has made it clear to us that you do not cling to the basic values our fine college is based upon. Therefore, it is with deep regret that I must abide by the boards decision and terminate your employment here as of the end of the current school year.

You have our best wishes for success in your future endeavors, whatever they may be.

Sincerely,

Pearson D. Oldbushe, Ph.D
Dean of the College

THIRTY-EIGHT

SOME MONTHS LATER Joan Tray writes this letter to her mother:

Dear Mom,
 I am sorry we have been out of touch for so long. I have been meaning to call you on Sundays like I used to, but if you tried to call me you probably know my phone is turned off because I haven't paid the bill. This is why I am finally writing, stamps being cheaper than telephone calls. This is a hard letter for me to write, as it will be for you to read, and I don't just mean my handwriting. Well first the bad news, which I should have told you some time ago. I have lost my job at the college. They didn't renew my appointment last year. So, when we were still talking on the phone, and you were asking me about how things were going, and I was saying everything was fine, well it was all a lie. But then so much of what I have told you over these past years was a lie. Some day, if you really want to know, we can sit down and I will tell you what my life really has been like.
 You know how much I always wanted to be an artist when I was younger, and how I always though that if you were an artist you were one for all of your life. Well I guess it's not true Mom, because I haven't been doing art for some time now, and I don't miss it, and no one misses me. I can't say I didn't have a moment, but I'm not famous the way you keep telling people. In fact, when I lost my job here I sent out thirty-three queries and didn't get a single interview.
 And so I have been working at odd jobs, mostly as a checkout clerk at Wal-Mart, and at a coffee shop in the evenings. But the coffee shop had to close last month. It had been there for years, but the neighborhood it was in had become gentrified, and

the new people claimed that the shop attracted a bad crowd, artists, poets, writers, and such, and they got up a petition and had the zoning ordinance changed, and so the coffee shop had to close down. The owner just gave up. She wasn't making enough money to move to another section of town.

Well now the good news, at least I think it's good news, although you might not think so. You know how I never wanted a baby, although you were always telling me that I should settle down and get married and have kids, but I always wanted to have a career as an artist. Lately I'd been thinking that maybe I should have a baby before I'm too old. Well Mom, I have had a baby, a little boy. He's beautiful, and very healthy, and I love him so much.

You are probably asking right now who the father is. He was a nice man, rather strange, although I only knew him for a short time, two days to be exact. But then he had to go away, for reasons I still do not understand, and so he's not here anymore. But I have named my son John, after him. You know I am not religious, at least not like you, but I am sure his father and I will meet up again some time in the future.

I have found out my baby's father had a son by his wife who is dead. I have finally gotten in touch with that son, who is in the Marine Corps, and has a son of his own. He is stationed not far from here, so I am taking my baby to see him. After that I am planning to come up to see you. I am going to have to ask you if my baby and I can stay with you for a while, until I can find another job. I am sorry to ask, as I know you are not doing too well yourself, but my money is almost gone. I have sold my furniture and everything else of value I had. I have a few drawings and things to pack which I will send to you as I need to be out of my apartment by the end of the month. I will be traveling by bus, so it will take a while to get up there. I will call you from John's son's house, whose name is also John, when I am ready to leave there.

Thank you very much Mom, I'm sorry I have been such a burden to you all these years, and becoming a burden again, but I am sure you will like the baby.

Love you,
Joannie

THIRTY-NINE

JOAN TRAY THINKS about what is it she should be thinking about as she rides along in a bus that will take her and her baby to another bus, that will take them to yet another bus that will take them to a place where they can get a taxi—if they are lucky—that will take them to where they really want to go, but aren't sure that they will even be welcomed when they eventually get there. Joan wonders why automobiles have come to rule the world. Why must she have a car to get anywhere, even if she would rather not own one, or can't afford the expense? Not just any car; as the TV ads used to crow: *You are what you drive.* But Joan doesn't drive anything. Does that mean she doesn't exist? Like when she had to give up her telephone. "What is your phone number?" someone would ask her, usually a bank clerk who didn't want to cash Joan Tray's check, or to give her a loan. Her answer; "I don't have a phone," usually brought an incredulous stare, with the person looking right through Joan as if she wasn't there.

Joan uses public transportation, a token service for token people; the penalty one must pay for being poor, or stupid, or poor and stupid, or retarded, or a pervert, or a poet, or a clown—or an artist. Her destination, Parris Island, is for poor people too; no one ever joins the Marine Corps to become rich.

Rapidly lurching along the steaming black tarmac, the bus somehow manages to spew its oily exhaust back into her slightly open window. Outside the mostly vacant landscape looks funereal and remote. Discreetly removing one of her now ponderous breasts from her blouse and bra, Joan inserts the nipple into her hungry child's mouth. An older white woman, sitting across the aisle from Joan, wearing a hat and gloves that must have passed through many a rummage sale, and fanning herself with a local newspaper, glares disapprovingly, the expression on her face meant to convey the idea that the woman she is staring at is doing something wrong, something unnatural and obscene. Her own three children, now grown and surely with children of their own, were no doubt nursed in an embarrassed secrecy, and soon given a rubber nipple on the end of a bottle to suck on.

The woman sees that Joan is alone. She has no husband the woman thinks, or perhaps her man is in the Marine Corps. He has probably deserted her—left her with this little bastard creature as a memento of their night of filthy pleasure. Now she is are going to confront him. Yet the nursing woman looks too old for this to be her first child, the elderly woman observes.

Joan wants to return the woman's stare, to say: Yes, I have no husband. I never have had a man I cared enough for to marry, at least when I was younger. Then I had my art, now I have nothing. No, I have this baby, and it's my baby. The man who fathered it is dead—shot down for no reason, not even a mistake—or at least the police won't admit to it. The authorities say that they have clear evidence he was a hired assassin from New York, part of a terrorist conspiracy to kill a senator, and then to blow up the Charlesboro Naval Base. She knows for a fact that Johnny Foozler had never seen Billy Bob Plantigrade until that day. And the stories that have been concocted—a gun that appeared from nowhere, letters he is supposed to have written to her telling when he was arriving in Charlesboro, three alleged accomplices that have fled to Yeman.

The bus rattles on; Joan recalls that night.

* * *

She had told Johnny they would meet in the church three blocks from her apartment. As she knew that her building was being watched by the police, Joan had to wait until after dark to slip away by crawling across the backyard and then climbing through some hedges. When she finally got to the church, Johnny wasn't there, or at least Joan didn't see him. Then she discovered Johnny asleep in one of the confessionals. Joan told him they were going to a carnival that was being held in a field on the edge of town. She had no other plan. Having no automobile, Joan couldn't drive Johnny anywhere, and the TV said the police were watching the airport, bus terminal, and train station. As the carnival was leaving town the next morning, she thought perhaps Johnny could get a job with them helping to disassemble things, and that then they would take him away with them. Johnny thought her plan was a good one. What else could he say?

It had been a nice warm night almost hot. They didn't speak very much as they walked along keeping to the darker side of the streets. It was as if neither one of them could figure out what was really going on—kind of like being in a bad dream that they were both fighting to come out of.

When they arrived at the carnival they tried to mingle with the crowd. Nevertheless, Joan and Johnny had the distinct feeling that they were being watched. There seemed to be considerably more policeman on the grounds than she remembered from her visit there three nights earlier. Johnny felt a tension in the air, a sense that something was about to happen. They tried to tell each other it was only their imaginations. What else could they do? They lined up to go on rides and played games, feeling that as long as they were surrounded by bright lights and other people they were safe, and that the police, or whoever, were waiting to catch them alone before they would do anything.

Then they turned around a corner of some tents and Kenny was standing there. He confronted them right on the midway. It was as if he couldn't wait for what the others were planning to do. Or maybe he just couldn't stand to see his old girlfriend having fun with another man. Yes, Joan thinks, we did have fun in that short time Johnny and I were together before it happened—the most fun she could ever recall having had at a carnival. They went on all the rides, and ate cotton candy, kicking at the sawdust as they walked along. Johnny had even won a teddy-bear for her by throwing baseballs at stuffed Indian heads.

Without any warning, Ken Beaugard had just appeared in front of them yelling loudly, and calling her all kinds of names—like whore and slut. Johnny had no idea who this man was, as Kenny wore plainclothes and had not produced a badge, nor announced that he was a police officer. Johnny thought Ken was just another drunk, the kind you find at carnivals, and threw a punch at him. Taken off guard, Ken staggered and fell down, but when he came back up he had his gun out. Foozler saw the gun,

Foozler Runs

and turned and ran. It wasn't the smartest thing to do, and she isn't sure why he did it. He just ran.

Kenny didn't yell that he was a police officer or anything official like that, but started after Johnny who had ducked behind the tents. Several other uniformed officers appeared from different directions and joined the chase. And then Joan heard a shot from in the direction Johnny had disappeared, followed by two more. At that moment, she was grabbed from behind by two police officers, one of them a woman. Joan was handcuffed and read her rights. Then she was dragged into a dark space behind the tents where several other officers were shining their flashlights on Johnny who lay on the ground covered with blood.

Kenny came running up to Joan. He was shaking, and holding a gun, a rather small-looking gun, half wrapped in a handkerchief. He asked her if she had ever seen the gun before, and she said she had not, which was the truth. Kenny told her that he had taken the gun from Johnny, who was still alive and writhing on the ground in a pool of his own blood. He was trying to say something, but an officer was holding Johnny's mouth shut while two others stood on his arms. Joan knew the gun wasn't Johnny's as she had helped him get undressed to take a shower when he first arrived at her apartment, and then taken his clothes downstairs to wash. There was no gun in his clothes, and he couldn't very well have concealed one on his naked body.

A lot of people were milling around, trying to get a good look at her and Johnny. The police weren't doing much of a job of crowd control. She heard angry voices saying thinks like: "You-all should have just killed that goddamn terrorist," and, "He don't look like no A-rab to me. . . ."

After what seemed to Joan like a really long time—too long, an ambulance finally made its way through the crowd. The medics slid Johnny into the back. He didn't seem to be conscious, and his face, reflecting the flashing lights, looked sad, so very sad, like he had given up. Then they put Joan in a police cruiser and drove off with the ambulance. The woman police officer, who was in back with Joan, began asking her questions like, how long had she known Johnny, and did she know that he had a gun on him. The next thing Joan knew they were at the hospital, in some dingy, over-lit, faded yellow room, where the police kept asking her the same questions the woman officer had asked over and over again. She sensed they were trying to trick her into mixing up her answers for some reason.

After a period of time Joan could not reckon, they took her into the emergency room where the doctors were working on Johnny. They asked her to identify him, calling him "the suspect."

"Can you tell us the suspect's name?" one of the officers said.

"John Foozler," Joan replied. "At least that's what he told me. . . ."

"Foozler's not a real name," another policeman, who must have been a golfer, interjected. "It means someone who's hit a bad shot in golf. . . ."

"It also means to bungle," Joan added—having become aware that this was something John Foozler was quite adept at doing.

She sensed Johnny was dying. He lay there with tubes and wires stuffed into his every orifice. His right hand, outstretched to take an IV tube, was handcuffed to the bed railing, as if they were expecting him to get up and try to run away. Johnny saw her when she came in—his eyes told her he did. Foozler had that look as if he had been waiting for her. But all he could do was slowly move his fingers on that handcuffed hand as if he were waving goodbye.

The police made Joan stand at the foot of the bed. She wanted to bless herself and say a prayer—she didn't know why she was not very religious—but Joan's hands were shackled behind her. The doctor and nurse appeared detached, just looking after another shooting victim, yet carefully observing their patient's every detail. Although Joan was in pain herself from the rough way she had been handled, and in a near state of shock, she stood there reverently, not wanting to interfere. John Foozler, a man she had only met yesterday, with a death rattle in his throat, and an oxygen cannula in his nose, was measuring out his last breaths. She will forever remember the two sounds of his noisy breathing; one slow and hesitating, produced by the air he breathed in, one hurried, when the air was expelled from his lungs. It was as if the former rock drummer was beating out the rhythm of his own death.

The doctor and nurses talked in low voices, reluctant to disturb the dying man. The coming and going attendants and police officers also spoke in hushed voices, perhaps more out of habit than of respect.

Then Johnny suddenly sat up—this action upsetting the bedside stand, and pulling the tubes from his nose and mouth.

"Why is everyone being so quiet?" Johnny gasped his voice a harsh, ironic rasp. "I'm not lining up a birdie putt . . . I'm dying. And if I am going on my last journey . . . I would rather be accompanied by loud, clear voices that remind me of life . . . maybe even singing . . . I was a rock star once, with my band, The Artful Foozler. . . ." Johnny moved his hands together as if to beat a drum. His right hand jerked back, the handcuff holding it to the rail. Just as suddenly as he had gotten up, Johnny Foozler fell back on his bed. A smile came over his face, as if astonished at finding himself there lifeless.

* * *

Joan has been trying to put together Johnny's life story, his real story. The two had talked a great deal the one night that they spent together. At the time Joan found it hard to believe all of what he was telling her. She does not want Johnny Foozler to be remembered only as an alleged terrorist who appeared at a military parade with a calf on a rope and supposedly attempted to kill a state senator. He was not just a one-liner, a single story man.

As a youth Johnny Foozler was a champion golfer, with great potential. Perhaps his father had pushed him too hard, so he gave up golf to become a talented drummer in a never-quite-made-it rock band. Foozler was confused, and although he tried to act tough, he was a thoughtful and gentle man, perhaps even a good father. She knew that he was a good lover. Joan had discovered that Johnny had a son in the Marine Corps, and a daughter-in-law, and a grandson. She is on her way to meet them now—and to show them her baby.

Why does that old woman keep looking at me like that? Joan thinks. I did the right thing, didn't I? Joan had the baby. Even though it has no father she is going to keep it. She never even gave the slightest thought to having an abortion. In this part of the country they burn down Planned Parenthood clinics anyway, don't they?

The bus is slowing down. The old woman in the white hat and gloves is getting ready to get off. As she stands she gives Joan a cold stare, a self-righteous look cultivated through years of feeling superior to other people. The woman stops and speaks to Joan. Her ancient voice sounds as if she is chewing on a pecan as she talks: "You-all must be from somewheres up north . . . down hare white women just don't sit on public transportation with a child sucking on their ninny . . . we-all got better breeding than that. . . ." Her piece said she continues down the aisle with a step as light as if she was on here way to her high school prom, dismounting with a pleasant, "And you-all be good now. . . ." to the black driver who replies: "You-all have a nice day, Ms. Steadberry."

The old woman's town is a nice town, Joan thinks; if this is where she actually lives. Tall shade trees droop with moss. The streets are clean and wide, lined with rows of nicely painted houses, each with its neatly manicured lawn. Joan Tray cannot imagine anything ever going wrong in this town. She also cannot imagine herself ever living here.

The noise of the bus pulling away from the curb drowns out the song of the cicadas shrilling in the trees. Joan's baby cries. It is still hungry. She unfastens a button and lets her other breast slide free. After a few blocks the bus turns and guns its way back out onto the highway. Freed of the dark umbrella of trees, Joan's window accepts the sunlight, casting a luminous glow on the tiny creature in her arms. She looks down at her child. A soft smile comes across Joan Tray's face.

* * *

ABOUT THE AUTHOR

STEPHEN (STEVE) POLESKIE was born in Pringle, PA in 1938. The son of a high school teacher, Poleskie graduated from Wilkes College in 1959 with a degree in Economics. A self-taught artist, Poleskie had his first one-person show at the Everhart Museum, Scranton, PA in 1958, while he was still in college. These large works were mainly abstract expressionistic in style.

After graduation Poleskie was employed briefly as an insurance agent and commercial artist, before moving to Miami where he worked in a screen-printing shop. After three months there he left for the Bahamas and Cuba.

His next job was as an art teacher at Gettysburg High School where David Eisenhower was one of his students. During this time he exhibited at the Duo Gallery in New York, and the Pennsylvania Academy of Fine Arts in Philadelphia.

Leaving Gettysburg, Poleskie traveled to Mexico and California, returning via Canada, before taking a studio on East 10th Street in New York City. There he enrolled in art classes at the New School and studied for a term with Raphael Soyer. The two became friends, and Soyer painted several paintings of his former student. At the time, Poleskie was doing figurative work. When he had his first one-person show in NYC, at Morris Gallery, Soyer bought a painting. Morris also sold a large Poleskie painting to the playwright Lanford Wilson.

Living on 10th Street, which then was the art center of New York, Poleskie became friends with many of the artists and critics of the day including, Elaine and Willem deKooning, Larry Rivers, Frank O'Hara, and Louise Nevelson.

In 1963 Poleskie opened a screen-printing studio in a storefront on East 11th Street. This became Chiron Press, the first exclusively fine art screen-printing shop in New York. The business was soon moved to larger quarters at 76 Jefferson Street. During the six years he ran the operation the names of the artists who had prints made at Chiron Press reads like a who's who of the artists of the 1960s and includes such figures as Robert Rauschenberg, Roy Lichtenstein, Andy Warhol, James Rosenquist, Alex Katz, Robert Motherwell, and Helen Frankenthaler. One of the printers at Chiron Press was the then young artist Brice Marden. In 1972 the Museum of Modern Art held an exhibition called "76 Jefferson Street," that included most of the prints made at Chiron Press, including a series of posters that they printed for The Paris Review.

Poleskie's own prints from this time, rather minimal landscapes, the figures of the earlier works had walked out of the picture, were exhibited widely in one person shows including at the Corcoran in Washington, D. C., the Hermitage in Russia, and the State Museum in Poland, and were purchased by numerous museums such as the Metropolitan Museum, the Museum of Modern Art, and the Whitney Museum in New York, the Walker Art Center in Minneapolis, and the National Collection in Washington, D. C.

In 1968, wanting more time to devote to his own art, Poleskie sold Chiron Press and accepted a teaching position at Cornell University in Ithaca, NY. It was here that he learned to fly, and later developed his Aerial Theater, a unique art form for which he is best known.

In his Aerial Theater, Poleskie flew an aerobatic bi-plane, trailing smoke, through a series of maneuvers to create a four-dimensional event in the sky. Musicians and dancers on the ground, and sometime parachutists, often accompanied these pieces. This work was very popular in Europe, especially Italy, where Poleskie lived on and off for over three years, and was also a resident at the American Academy in Rome. Italian art critic Enrico Crispolti called Aerial Theater the logical extension of Futurism, and the French art critic Pierre Restany, writing in *D'ars* dubbed it "Planetary Art" on the scale with Christo's installations.

Poleskie's biplane and drawings for various performances were exhibited at the Louis K. Meisel Gallery in New York in 1978. Poleskie also flew his biplane in numerous aerobatic competitions. He won the Canadian Open Aerobatic Championship in 1977.

In 1998, having reached the age of sixty, and feeling his body could no longer take the excessive G forces imposed on it by the aerobatic maneuvers, Poleskie ceased flying altogether, and sold his airplanes. Two years later he retired from Cornell University, where he holds the rank of emeritus professor.

Works on paper from his Aerial Theater period are in many public collections including the Victoria and Albert Museum, and the Tate Gallery in London; and the Castlevecchio in Verona, and the Caproni Museum in Trento.

Over a fifty year period Poleskie's work has been exhibited widely. Included among the cities he has had his work shown, or done performances, are New York, Boston, Cambridge, Washington D. C., Philadelphia, Syracuse, Scranton, Wilkes-Barre, Reading, Los Angeles, San Francisco, Berkeley, Sonoma, Toledo, Providence, Richmond, Williamsburg, San Antonio, Detroit, and Miami, in the USA; London, Southampton, Loughborough, and the Isle of Wight in the UK; Rome, Milan, Bologna, Brescia, Como, Trento, Turin, Verona, and Palermo in Italy; Munich, Stuttgart, and Kassel, in Germany; Linz in Austria; Ljubljana, Rijeka, Zagreb, and Belgrade, in the former Yugoslavia; Moscow and Saint Petersburg in Russia; Warsaw, Gdansk, and Lodz, in Poland; Tbilisi in the Republic of Georgia; Vilnius in Lithuania; Freetown in Sierra Leone; Stockholm in Sweden; Rio de Janeiro in Brazil; Tegucigalpa and San Pedro Sula in Honduras; Barcelona, Madrid, and Cadaque in Spain; Locarno in Switzerland; Varna in Bulgaria, Hong Kong in China, and Tokyo and Kyoto in Japan.

Since 1993 Poleskie has been devoting himself mainly to writing fiction and has published six novels. His writing also has been published in numerous journals in the USA, as well as in: Australia, Germany, India, Italy, and Mexico.

Additional information on Poleskie can be found on his web site: www.StephenPoleskie.com.